Emily Noble's Disgrace

MARY PAULSON-ELLIS lives in Edinburgh. Her critically acclaimed debut, *The Other Mrs Walker*, was a *Times* bestseller and Waterstones Scottish Book of the Year. Her second, *The Inheritance of Solomon Farthing*, was long-listed for the McIlvanney Prize for best Scottish crime novel and a Historical Writers' Association Gold Crown. She has an MLitt in Creative Writing from Glasgow University and was awarded the inaugural Curtis Brown Prize for Fiction and the Maverick Award from the Tom McGrath Trust. Her non-fiction and short stories have featured in *The Guardian* and on BBC Radio 4. In 2019 Val McDermid named her one of the most compelling LGBTQ+ writers working today. *Emily Noble's Disgrace* is her third novel.

Also by Mary Paulson-Ellis

THE OTHER MRS WALKER
THE INHERITANCE OF SOLOMON FARTHING

MARY PAULSON-ELLIS

Emily Noble's Disgrace

PICADOR

First published 2021 by Mantle

This paperback edition first published 2022 by Picador
an imprint of Pan Macmillan
The Smithson, 6 Briset Street, London EC1M 5NR
EU representative: Macmillan Publishers Ireland Ltd, 1st Floor,
The Liffey Trust Centre, 117–126 Sheriff Street Upper,
Dublin 1, D01 YC43
Associated companies throughout the world
www.panmacmillan.com

ISBN 978-1-5290-3619-0

A CIP catalogue record for this book is available from the British Library.

Typeset in Stempel Garamond LT by
Palimpsest Book Production Ltd, Falkirk, Stirlingshire
Printed and bound by CPI Group (UK) Ltd, Croydon, CR0 4YY

MIX
Paper | Supporting
responsible forestry
FSC® C116313

Visit www.panmacmillan.com to read more about all our books
and to buy them. You will also find features, author interviews and
news of any author events, and you can sign up for e-newsletters
so that you're always first to hear about our new releases.

For Catherine, Christopher and Peter,
with love

Who killed Cock Robin?
I, said the Sparrow,
With my bow and arrow,
I killed Cock Robin.

Who saw him die?
I, said the Fly,
With my little eye,
I saw him die.

Traditional

PROLOGUE

The bones fell from the ceiling as though from the sky. A tibia. A fibula. The notches of a spine. Scattering about her feet like spillikins just waiting for the game to begin. Dust and grit and flakes of ancient paint circled above her, glinting in the air as though she was standing in a universe, somewhere amongst the darkness and the never-ending stars.

Then the dust began to settle; a thin caul of grey to add to all the rest. It settled on her arms, clinging to her skin. It settled on her clothes, caught in the weave. It settled on her hair, turning it the colour of an old woman's. It settled on the tips of her shoes.

The bones were small things, not much longer than the span of her hand, a scattering of something old, something long-since dead and buried, risen to the surface now. She stared at the little nubs, the hollow flutes, at the patch of floor turned into a graveyard about her feet. Then she crouched, reached a hand to touch, knew at once that these were the remains of a child.

PART ONE

Essie Pound

One

Portobello, Edinburgh's seaside, 2019.

We enter by the backyard, a small space surrounded by a fence rotting from the ground up. Inside, the concrete area is piled with junk. I can see old chair frames, scraps of desiccated carpet underlay, a thousand bin bags appearing from amongst a thick stand of willowherb. The willowherb is pretty, flowers still blooming, though even I know the season is almost ended now.

Daphne goes ahead, disappearing for a moment amongst a craze of thistledown. We follow – a narrow trail hacked out by the police a day or so before. The tall stems have been bent and pushed aside where the police tramped their way in and tramped their way out. I touch my hand to the nearest blossom, pink juice on my thumb. Who called them, that's what I want to know, when the owner of the property had already waited two years for somebody to come.

The back porch, when we get to it, is a rickety thing, open to the elements, paint peeling, glass muzzy with cobwebs. Hundreds of seashells have been piled along a narrow shelf. I count the kinds:

snail
razor
limpet

Surfaces chalky after so much exposure to the sun and

the rain. On the ground beneath I spy a pair of rubber boots, split and faded. Also a snake of silk spotted with mildew, a strange sort of green. I watch as Daphne slides a key from her pocket, tackles the padlock newly fitted to the back door. When it swings open, I wonder why the police have bothered. The entrance is almost blocked by a huge cliff of rubbish, layer upon layer of one old lady's leftovers long since abandoned to rot.

We play *Scissors, Paper, Stone* to decide who should go in first. I come last, of course. Monika wraps her hand around my fist, grins in triumph. Pawel laughs as he glances from my toes to my hair. I know what he is thinking. I am fat. The entrance way is narrow. Not to mention whatever might be lurking beyond. But I don't really mind. Unlike the others, for whom this is just a job, I am drawn to the darker side of what we might find.

First in. Robed up. Tiger Balm beneath the nostrils. Cover your face with your mask and try to breathe through your mouth. That's what I've been taught. It's only eight forty-five a.m. but already my skin is sticky as I zip my suit from crotch to chin, pull my hood over damp strands of hair. My heavy limbs chafe against the coverall's flimsy weave. Monika dabs balm on my top lip. I prefer to go in without it, face free to *Breathe, Essie. Breathe*. But Daphne gave the order.

'Might be a bad one.'

And what Daphne wants, Daphne gets. It's the reason we're the best cleaning outfit in the city, sorting the soft underbelly of Edinburgh's overlooked so that everybody else can continue on their gleaming, oblivious way.

Pawel props the back door open for me. We stare at

the cliff of rubbish rising from floor to ceiling and ceiling to floor. Then at the culvert carved out by its side. I take a deep breath, smell Tiger Balm and salt. Also the fragrant scent of willowherb. Then I step over the threshold, into the unknown.

Two

The case is unexceptional, that is what I know. A house full of stuff left behind by a dead woman. Eighty-one (or thereabouts), abandoned at the last. No next of kin, not even any neighbours to pass the time of day. Laid down to sleep one night, *click switch*, lights out, never turned them on again. Nothing left but a large stone property with generous Edinburgh rooms and a view over the sea. Once a family home. Then a private hotel. After that a boarding house that leaked what little heat there was and let in all the wind.

Found in her bed.

That's what Daphne said when she briefed us at the office. Two years. That's how long they reckoned it had been. Two years where the breeze and the brine and the absence of any sort of central heating preserved everything about the deceased.

Like a mummy.

That's what Daphne told us as she reversed the van into a space on a side street, eight twenty-five a.m., Monika and Pawel sharing the seat in front while I crammed in behind. At least there wouldn't be any putrefaction to deal with, that's what I was thinking as I decamped, scrambling from the side door of the van with my caddy full of chemicals to spray it all away.

I've been there before, of course, wading through the

remains of a thousand bluebottles to get to the heart of the scene. A thousand little crawling, buzzing things searching out their perfect nest, laying one day, dying the next, scattering the floor like miniature kamikazes:

crunch

crunch

crunch

But this case is different. Not a body swollen with heat and damp, rather a slow decay, skin shrinking and retreating over old bones as the sea winds blew in and blew out. Our new client was the colour of peat by the time they found her – feet black. Hands black. Skin like the tanned hide of a cow – before someone finally thought to knock on her door.

Now here we are, walking in without even that courtesy, the cleaners of Edinburgh's extremities armed and ready to sweep it all out.

Trespassing.

That's what Granny Pound would have called it. Like the bluebottles. Crawling over the last known abode of a woman who spent her life opening her house to others, only to discover that when the moment came, nobody came for her.

Three

I squeeze into the narrow passage the old lady hollowed from the mound of her own rubbish. It is dark, the small amount of light spilling from the back entrance already obscured. By me. By the size of me. And the debris that we've found. It's almost like being swallowed, like Jonah inside his whale.

The corridor is oppressive, a man-made alleyway crammed and congested with junk. Beneath my feet there are magazines, once glossy, now torn and faded, carpeting the floor. I glance down, find myself edging forwards in my shoe covers over women's eyes and teeth, their sleek shiny hair. I have been inside a hoarder's house before, but never one as full to the brim as this. My body presses against the mound of rubbish, wedged for a moment as though caught in a strait jacket. The house holds its breath. Then I limber an arm free, turn sideways, squeeze further into the gloom. To look at me it might not seem possible, but I can get in anywhere as long as I try. One foot, then the next. One shoulder, then the next. Away from the willowherb. Away from the seashells. Away from that September breeze, the taste of salt on its tongue.

In front of me, at about eye level, I discover a seam of plastic. An old dish rack. The lip of a dustpan. Also a pair of tiny feet. A doll, perhaps, buried in the debris, those sharp little toes. I wonder about pulling the doll from its grave, sorting its hair. But the rest of its body is hidden by a microwave oven emerging from the rubbish like a portal to another world. I raise a finger to touch the microwave's black glass, glimpse a grown woman staring back, hair covered, mouth covered, nothing to see but her eyes.

I move on and a door appears on my right, frame patterned with a thousand dirty fingerprints. I place the tips of my gloved fingers over them, fitting my hand to a dead woman's as though to say hello. The floor in this room is on a different level from the passageway, two feet up or so, a shifting mass of empty bottles and ancient food cartons, piles and piles of discarded tins. Another narrow path has been dug into this sea of rubbish, like a trench leading to the front. Or in this case to a sink brimful of abandoned crockery and a cooker painted black with the burned-on fat of a thousand meals. Also there, in the centre, a small Formica island in primrose yellow, chair tucked neat beneath.

I stand for a moment, my gloved hand on the doorframe. I know dangerous territory when I see it. Then I pull the mask from my face, breathe in, breathe out again, make the call.

'All clear!'

I listen as Pawel relays the information to Daphne, already on the phone to another job no doubt, earrings flashing in the early morning sun. Despite there being no guarantees in our line of work, there's no shortage of it in this city. Edinburgh's full of the neglected and worse – people abandoned to the vicissitudes of life, everything around them decaying just as they begin to decay, too.

Four

I am standing in a trench. Outside, Pawel prepares to wield his blade. Inside, there is the shift and morph of a thousand empty bottles and cans. Beneath my suit flesh rubs on flesh, skin itchy. I feel nervous in kitchens, always have done. I don't know why, but I do.

The light in the room is dim. I try the switch, *click flick*, but of course the electricity is off. At the far end of the trench, above the sink, I can see a window covered by a net curtain. I navigate towards it, careful not to touch anything in case the whole lot begins to slide. The curtain is drenched in dust, behind that the glass cracked across its pane. Thieves and chancers, that's what Granny Pound would say. Or one more of the old lady's mishaps that never did get sorted. Amongst all the rest.

Dust plumes in the air as I drag aside the net, adding a new layer to the general mess. Mugs dip-dyed with tannin. Forks crusted between the prongs. I feel the quick pulse of blood in my wrist as I search. But there are no knives that I can see. Only a half-eaten packet of Jacob's cream crackers and a draining board piled with ice-cream tubs stacked in graceful curves. *Raspberry ripple*. An old lady's favourite. And mine, too.

Also something propped against the filthy window pane. A calendar, pages blackened at the edges. I reach across, lift the calendar from its resting place. Daphne will be pleased. Calendars are useful things. An aid to exact date of death, to add to date of birth. I am expecting August 2017 or thereabouts, the year the old lady turned off her bedside lamp, *click switch*, lay down, never got up again. According to Daphne, that is. But the calendar doesn't say 2017. It says 1996.

I blink at the numbers. In 1996, I was five years old, a small skinny girl with hair in rats' tails, swimsuit and a pair of blue jelly sandals. Lost now along with all the rest. What happened here in 1996? That is what I'm thinking. The last year the old lady ever counted. Nothing, perhaps, the world just stopped. Or she decided not to count anymore.

I tuck the calendar into my caddy, move back along the trench towards the opposite wall where a wooden dresser rises from the debris.

Personal stuff first, nothing else for now.

That was Daphne's instruction.

Address book. TV licence. The paperwork of life. There is a brooding sort of atmosphere in the kitchen, as though the house is taking the measure of me, as I take the measure of it.

The dresser is laden with all sorts – tangled cassette tapes and unopened envelopes, KitKat wrappers and a radio with a bent antenna. I try the radio, but it is dead just like its owner, not receiving anymore. A set of teacups hangs from a row of hooks, delicate things with a pattern of orange flowers just visible beneath a film of soot. I lift one, discover a centipede resting on its back, one hundred legs raised. I tip the centipede onto a pile of old receipt books, watch it trickle away, find something grinning at me from amongst the muddle. A pair of false teeth, grey about the gums. I lift the teeth out, hold them on my palm. They are like the bottom half of a skull, the rest of the person missing. I put them into my caddy next to the calendar. The teeth won't help us learn anything new about our client, but they might make her look better once she's laid out in her coffin. These things matter at the end.

After that I sift through some of the envelopes. They are all junk, as far as I can tell. *To the Occupier. To the Occupier.* A lifetime of unpaid bills. I put the paperwork aside, poke my fingers into every nook and cranny. Most of this job is spraying and shovelling, wiping away mould with a thick slick of bleach. But sometimes it is also detective work, opening jewellery boxes and tipping books upside down to let the crucial piece of evidence fall free. Right now I am hoping for photographs with a name and date on the back. Letters with greetings from a relative that might give some clue as to the next of kin. But there's nothing more here than decay and the dusty ephemera of an everyday sort of life. Just the ordinary things.

I retreat along the trench towards the Formica table, imagine the old lady manoeuvring like a ghost amongst her rubbish so she could eat her supper each night in this small cocoon. She must have been tiny to survive in this warren, that is what I'm thinking. Or perhaps it was just that she shrunk herself to continue to exist in this labyrinth of filth. It always seems impossible when viewed from the outside that anyone could live like this. But I've been doing the job long enough to know that if a person wants to find a way, they certainly will.

The table is clear, but beneath it is a large biscuit tin,

barrel shaped, rust grown like a rash across its surfaces. I rub at the lid, discover a family looking back. A mother. A father. A girl. A boy. I lift the tin onto the primrose Formica, hear the sudden rattle. A lady's ring, perhaps, row of opals winking like cats' eyes? I think of Granny Pound:

An eye for an eye

Ease the lid off, dip my hand in, scrabble for treasure. I know I ought not, but what is life for?

Five

I get home at six thirty p.m. filthy with an old lady's leftovers, the taste of the boarding house still lingering on my tongue. We have spent all day *hacking*, *lifting*, *shovelling*, dismantling the mountain in the corridor. I can feel the calluses forming on my thumbs.

The flat where I live is on the third floor of a tenement not far from the bottom of the Walk, but the wrong side of Easter Road. I have always lived on the wrong side. It is where I belong. The main door to the street is often left on the snib, an invitation to anyone from the pub on the corner to wander in and use the close for their personal toilet. Despite the stink of urine, this is where I call home.

I climb the tenement stair to the third floor slowly. The evening is warm; a mugginess threatens rain. I'm sweating by the time I achieve our landing, can feel that uncomfortable damp under my shirt, the moisture gathering beneath my breasts. At least I no longer have to suffer the claustrophobia of my coverall suit – the mask, the hood, those gloves that make my wrists itch – all stripped off at the scene like a snake shedding its skin. But still, I am fat. A vast, ungainly girl.

In the kitchen I drink from the tap, gasping as the water bubbles in my throat. I can feel something pressing on the nape of my neck. The past, perhaps. The weight of everything our latest client has left behind. When I finish,

I open a cupboard and take the first thing that comes to hand. A Battenberg, all pink and yellow squares. The wrapper is flimsy. I slice it with my nail. I don't bother with a plate. My fingers make soft dents in the marzipan icing as I lift the cake to my mouth.

In the shower, I bow my head, let hot water batter my scalp. I stare at the solid mass of my thighs, rivulets running across pale flesh, think of the old lady. Black hands. Black feet. Reach for the soap. The soap comes from our last-but-one job, a woman who ate too many pills, left vomit all over the living-room carpet. Which meant scrubbing till my knuckles were raw and a whole can of deodoriser, *spritz, spritz, spritz*. The soap was inside the woman's bathroom cabinet, next to a half-used packet of contra-ceptive pills I knew she wouldn't be needing either, so I took one for myself. Sometimes I think my whole life has been furnished by dead people, to make up for never having anything of my own.

After my shower, I sit at the kitchen table with damp hair, dabbing pink and yellow crumbs from the surface with one wet fingertip, surveying my spoils. A lipstick with the imprint of a mouth still on its waxy tip. A green plastic lighter. The empty box from a bar of soap. Also a gold locket on a cheap chain. The locket glints in the overhead light as I touch each thing in turn. After that I remove the empty soap carton, put something new in its place. Treasure taken from a biscuit tin belonging to a boarding house in Portobello. Not a ladies' ring, opals glimmering like cats' eyes. But a tiny notch of bone.

Six

Day two and inside the boarding house we have barely dug out more than a few metres down the back corridor. A small triumph, hard fought. We tackled it with the bladed instruments, Pawel hacking at the grey mass with his pickaxe, me and Monika shovelling it out with the spades. We tossed it chunk by chunk into the skip Daphne hired the day before once she realized the size of the task. And still the rubbish looms as Daphne slides her key into the padlock, pulls the back door open, steps aside to let our guest see.

I watch from the safety of the willowherb as Margaret Penny of the Office for Lost People picks her way through the debris to assess her latest client's leftovers. She's wearing a pair of red shoes, straps buttoned across her ankles. I stare at them, then at my own, clumsy in their shoe coverings. A breeze whispers through the thistledown and Margaret Penny shivers as though a ghost has walked across her grave. She lifts the collar of her coat. Still, I see the black eye glinting. Margaret Penny is wearing a fox stole, that is what I know. All its little paws.

Daphne taps one painted fingernail on the surface of her phone as we await the official assessment. Daphne is immaculate, pleats like knife blades in her trousers. The opposite of me. When the assessment comes it is succinct:

'You'll need more time.'

Margaret Penny is well known in Edinburgh for the efficiency with which she dispatches the affairs of the deceased, but even I know that clearing the boarding house will take a week at least. Maybe two. Daphne opens her work book with its calendar pasted onto the inside cover, begins to check the other jobs we have lined up that might need to be shifted. Rentals that have been trashed. A drug den with needles scattered across the floor.

'I think we can arrange it.' Daphne is the queen of the schedule. 'We can put back the rental, split the crews to cover the rest.'

They operate well together, Margaret Penny and Daphne, as though they might actually be a team. But Daphne isn't an employee of the Office for Lost People. She's independent. Likes to keep an open mind to whatever opportunity might come her way.

I watch as Margaret Penny studies the little porch:

snail

razor

limpet

Tiny broken pieces scattered about her feet. Look again for the long coil of silk with its spatter of mildew. But it has vanished, along with the rubber boots.

Margaret Penny turns from the back door, brushing at her coat as though to rid herself of some bad memory as Daphne assigns the jobs.

'You start on the storeroom, Essie. Pawel and Monika, you continue clearing the passage. If we're lucky, we'll make it to the hall today.'

I am grateful. I don't much like sharp objects. The shovel. The pickaxe – black handled, red tipped – Pawel swinging with relish at the tightly packed detritus of a life while I stand well back amongst the weeds. Monika doesn't mind, she enjoys the cut and thrust, whereas I always turn away from the glitter of a blade.

Now as I robe up, gloves over wrists, hood over hair, I see Daphne hand some stuff to Margaret Penny.

'All we could find, I'm afraid.'

The personal things.

A calendar from 1996. A postcard Monika discovered propped on the shelf in the porch.

Will see you on the 12th. Save the room. Miss M.

Also a set of false teeth.

'Thanks.' I watch as Margaret Penny tucks the calendar and the postcard into a brown loose-leaf folder, in much the same way she tucked the paws of her fox stole beneath her lapels. She drops the teeth into her pocket. 'Let me know if you find anything else.'

A small bone, perhaps, hidden inside a cleaner's fist. Nothing more than the joint from a drumstick. Or a child's knuckle. Heat blooms beneath my coverall suit at the thought that we are digging in what might already be a grave. As though she can read my thoughts, Daphne glances up from her checklist, asks Margaret Penny about the old lady who was carried out feet first.

'What was her name again?'

'Dawson,' Margaret Penny says. 'Isabella.'

'And do we know anything about her?'

'Not much.' Margaret Penny doesn't even need to study her file. 'Single lady, never married. Lived here with her mother when it was run as a boarding house.'

'No children?' Daphne says.

'Not that we know of.'

But who knows everything about a person? That is what I'm thinking as I tie on my mask. Especially once they're deceased.

Seven

'Specialist.'

That was how Monika explained it to me when I first started with The Company almost a year ago. Clear up after folk who don't have anyone else to take them on.

'I like the variety,' she told me as she held out the suit, the mask, the gloves that first time. 'Never know what might be coming down the road.'

Which makes sense, because occasionally we have to sort the mess left behind after a road-traffic accident where someone didn't skip away from what was coming quite soon enough.

'So it's Daphne's business, then?' I asked as we suited up for my first encounter, Daphne standing by, phone clamped to her ear. Monika laughed at that.

'No, Daphne runs the crew on the ground. McDermid and Sharp are the brains behind the outfit.'

The ones who started it all.

I asked Sasha about McDermid and Sharp when I got home that first evening, two women who made their reputations navigating the hidden geographies of Edinburgh armed with not much more than a bucket and a mop. Turns out they started a different sort of cleaning company from the run-of-the-mill operations headed by the Polish residents of the city. McDermid and Sharp clear up after the kind of people the locals try to pretend do not exist.

Trauma, that's their specialism. Not to mention all the rest. Searching out hidden bloodstains. Abandoned properties left to rot. Hoarders who can't help themselves. Also the long-since deceased.

The territory of the dead.

That's what Sasha calls it. Or the territory of the unloved and overlooked, that is what I think. A place I might have ended up myself one day if Daphne hadn't saved me. Daphne has a thing for orphans. Sasha, too, of course.

Turns out, for once in my life, I landed on my feet. The Company is one of the most lucrative in the city. Not for the actual work it does – that's hard graft, £12.50 an hour, extra for brain matter. But for the access it gives. Just as likely to find a hoarder who's a millionaire, as an old lady dead in her bed with nothing more than two pound coins to rub together at the end. All the hangers-on in the city follow where McDermid and Sharp lead. The estate agents and the Heir Hunters. The dealers in second-hand goods. Every one of them is looking to see where a profit might be made from whatever the neglected and abandoned have left behind. But first it has to be cleaned and not many people in Edinburgh want to volunteer for that.

Your mess is our mess

That is The Company's motto. I take it literally. I have good role models. McDermid and Sharp are self-made, started with a mop and bucket, no one to touch them now.

Eight

The storeroom is a dark narrow space that opens from the back corridor. We found it yesterday when Pawel's pickaxe took off the door handle, discovered what looks like a bunker prepared for disaster. Which is what the boarding house has become, I suppose.

'Bloody hell,' said Pawel as we crammed in to see. 'What was she stockpiling for?'

Twenty years of not going out, that's what I was thinking as we stared at shelves crammed with supplies. Corned beef and cream crackers. Custard powder and tinned carrots. Old people's meals. Though even I wouldn't want to ingest any of them. They look as though they haven't been touched since 1996.

I begin on the left and work my way round *sliding, lifting, binning*, sweating under my suit as droppings scatter at my feet like black rice thrown at a wedding. Mice, probably. Maybe rats. I have brought bleach and several types of spray. Also industrial-size sacks, extra thick plastic. By teatime the whole thing will stink of disinfectant, the scent of a good day's work.

Halfway in I discover more tins, paper labels faded almost to nothing. But still I can tell what is in them. *Hot dogs. Green Giant sweetcorn. Alphabetti Spaghetti.* The meals of my childhood. I slide a can from the shelf, give it a shake, hear the familiar slosh inside.

'Making lunch already?'

Monika squeezes past the doorway with her shovel over her shoulder ready for her next assault. I flush beneath my mask, thrust the tin into one of my industrial-size sacks. Monika and Pawel often make jokes about my eating, though they never see me do it. I like to keep that hidden, too.

I move on to a shelf stacked high with jars of strawberry jam and dusty packets of oatmeal, bicarbonate of soda. Also a pot balanced on one of the shelves as though waiting to be replaced on the kitchen stove. Isabella Dawson's last meal, perhaps. I reach for the pot, peer inside. There is the sudden stench of a carcass boiling dry, tiny flies swarming before my eyes like bluebottles hatching in their thousands, filling the place with their busy angry noise. My throat constricts as though I might not be able to *Breathe, Essie. Breathe.* I try to steady myself against the remains of the old lady's stockpile, look again. But I am not mistaken. There is a graveyard in the bottom of the pot, the curve of a skeleton, tiny bones bleached.

Nine

Just like Isabella Dawson, I grew up by the sea. Me and Granny Pound and all the rest, washing in and washing out. Not here on Edinburgh's coast, but further out. Past the Pans. Past the old power station. Almost at the Bents. I lived near a beach that nobody but us wanted to visit. Grey sand and not much of it, that grass which pricks at the soles of your feet. We never went to Edinburgh, just looked at it sometimes in the distance, the city on the hill.

I grew up with the smell of coal dust in my nostrils, salt and sauce on Friday-night chips for tea. I had one hundred and three brothers and sisters, though not at the same time. Some came for one night only. Others for weeks. Two or three for years. Granny Pound took in all comers, a bit like Isabella Dawson. She had a thing about orphans, too.

Granny Pound's pantry was always full to bursting, just like Isabella Dawson's. Vats of cheap baked beans. Turkey burgers and potato waffles stuffing the freezer. Huge bags of frozen peas.

Got to feed you up.

That was what she used to say when I arrived. 1996 and like a wild thing, nothing but bone and scruff. It never did any good, the meat tarts and raspberry ripple. Only started to stick once she was gone. Now I'm as big as Granny Pound used to be. I like that we have one thing in common after all these years.

But unlike Isabella Dawson's boarding house, Granny Pound's home was small. Three bedrooms. One for her. Two for us, double sets of bunk beds in each, all ages crammed in top-to-toe. Never a space to keep anything of our own. Downstairs there was an outhouse with a washing machine and a dryer. A kitchen sink heaped with discarded teabags. A living room with a coal-effect electric fire and an armchair. Granny Pound would sit in the armchair of an evening, biro and *TV Times* in hand, ringing the programmes she planned to watch once we'd gone to bed. I used to lie at her feet on the carpet, drawing with my crayons. There were lots of comings and goings.

No wonder Granny Pound died when she did, before any of us were ready. She must have been worn out, though she never showed it. Got fed up putting the washing machine on five times a day and insisting on homework. Sometimes I wonder why she did it. Then I remember what she used to say:

Who else would have you?

Plus she taught me how to clean.

If you can clean, you can work anywhere.

That was what she used to tell me. There's always somebody who wants someone else to clear their mess away.

Ten

That night I wake gasping, sheets saturated, heart flaying my insides. It isn't a surprise. Next to me Sasha breathes out, a soft exhale, as though nothing has happened. I close my eyes, wait as my heart begins to slow, feel again the knot in my chest tightening like a tourniquet, the solid press of the darkness. I've been dreaming about bones steaming in a pot, about blood pooling on the floor. About a door with no handle, pressing my eye to the keyhole, its imprint on my skin. Then the sudden glitter . . .

The orange sulphur of the street lamps filters through the curtain as I slide from beneath the bedcovers, heavy legs searching for cool night air. I make it to the door before Sasha turns, rolls towards the wall.

In the kitchen, I run the tap until my fingers almost freeze, dip my head to drink. Downstairs in the flat below a child is crying. I lift my head to listen, lips wet. It's the crying that has woken me. And the dream, of course.

Next to the sink there's a wine glass, leftover contents a dark pool. The child's crying is louder now, angry and jagged. I drink, a sour mouthful, before I hear it. The sound I wait for every night. A woman singing, some sort of lullaby. Everything's all right now.

Three forty-eight a.m. and I stand at the living-room window, the flat beneath silent, nothing but my reflection and the soft *skit skat* of raindrops gathering on the pane. The pavement below darkens, a damp spreading stain. Outside the street lamps still give off their strange orange glow. I can feel a draught seeping from between the sashes, like at the house in Portobello, sea air creeping into all its nooks and crannies, rubbish piled floor to ceiling and ceiling to floor. How did Isabella Dawson end up like that? I can't help wondering. Then again, I know the real question isn't how a person ended as she did, house filled to the brim with stuff she couldn't let go of. But why more people don't go that way.

I stare through the glass to the windows of the tenement opposite, watch the girl on her bed peering into her laptop. The girl is about my age, or thereabouts. Late twenties, maybe. But thin, almost skeletal. The size I am inside. The pool of her computer screen lends her face a greenish tinge. I stand and watch until she closes it. Then I drop the curtain, shut out the neighbours. And myself, too.

In the kitchen, I count my treasures. A lipstick. A green plastic lighter. Also the locket, two tiny birds engraved on the front, beak to beak, kissing. I took the locket from the house of a girl who died with a needle stuck in her arm, hair like summer hay spread all about. At least that was what Daphne said. By the time I arrived, it was bed sheets stained with something unidentifiable in great concentric rings, the reek of decomposition. I was going to gift the locket to Sasha, then I looked inside.

I open it now, thumb clumsy on the tiny catch. They gaze out at me, with their cheerful smiles. A mother. A father. I touch each one, smile in reply. Then close them back in with a *snick*, hold the locket in my fist for a moment before laying it down and lifting something else.

The photograph is creased, folded in the middle then back again over and over. Someone cut it in half, long ago. Another piece missing. It shows a girl standing on a beach wearing a red swimsuit with a little white skirt. The girl's body is all angles, hair in rats' tails. On her feet are a pair of jelly sandals. The colour in the photograph has faded, as though what it depicts belongs only in the past. I know better. This photograph is the one bit of me left from before.

'What are you doing?'

Sasha leans in the doorway like some sort of night creature who doesn't belong to this world, limbs bare, hair falling about her shoulders. I curl my hand over the photograph.

'Nothing.'

'Did you have the dream again?'

And the sweat is suddenly there, on my fingertips. I don't reply. Sasha's earrings glint in the dark – three little skulls.

'Never mind.'

I wait till I hear the click of the bedroom door closing. Then I fold the photograph along its familiar crease and slide it back into the dark.

Eleven

My night creature works at the Office for Lost People. That was how we met. I was standing in a corridor at the council headquarters waiting to get in, bucket at my feet, can of bleach spray in my hand. She was standing in her office, putting on her coat. I had on a blue overall, like something a woman twice my age would wear. She wore something that looked as though it came from a dead animal, albeit artificial, three silver skulls studding one earlobe. I knew at once we would get on.

Sasha, she said. And held out her hand. I didn't reciprocate. I was wearing my gloves.

There are three of them in the Office for Lost People: Janie Gribble, Margaret Penny and my girl. Plus a list of all the dead people in the city who don't have anyone else to take them on. Sasha's job is to try and find a family for each of the deceased, if she possibly can.

'To pay for the funeral?'

That was what I asked when she told me what she did for a living. As Granny Pound used to say, someone always has to pay, even when you're dead. But Sasha protested.

'Not just for the money.'

'Like an angel of mercy, then.'

'Sort of,' she laughed. 'If you want to think of it like that.'

Even before we kissed, vodka-stained lips and hearts

fluttering like wing beats, I liked the idea that Sasha might be an angel of mercy. I haven't had many blessings in my life. But she is certainly one.

We went for a drink that same evening, in a bar not far from where Sasha works. She had to wait for me to finish *squirting, wiping, hoovering*, skin on my hands rough from hospital-grade detergent. I was amazed she was still there when I appeared in the doorway of the basement bar, blocking out the light with my bulk. She grinned when she saw me, slid off her stool still draped in her dead-animal coat, waved me over.

'I got you a cocktail.'

Vodka and pomegranate, sugar crusted round the rim. I took a sip, licked crystals from my lips.

'How did you know I liked cocktails?'

Her eyes glittered as she laughed.

We drank till they threw us out. Then we went dancing, a dark cave in one of Edinburgh's underbellies, a frenzy of lights and music pounding in my ears. What I remember most is the flash and glimmer of her skull earrings. Also her hair, wrapping itself around her face and neck as she spun on the dance floor. Afterwards she invited me up to her third-floor flat the wrong side of Easter Road. I climbed to the landing with sweat like a river between my shoulder blades. Not because of the stair.

She kissed me in the hall, pushed me against the back of the door, the sweet tail end of vodka and pomegranate. I'd kissed plenty of girls before, but they usually tasted of cigarettes, of cold concrete underpasses. I stank of disinfectant and sugar, but she didn't let me shower. When we finished, the pale slab of my thighs naked in the orange glow from the street lights, all her hair was spread about on the pillow. She slept as I touched its ends. I have been here ever since.

Sasha was the one who got me the job with Daphne and The Company – the Edinburgh Way of getting things done.

'There's some work going, if you're interested,' she said when we'd been together about a month. 'It's not everyone's cup of tea, but they need someone reliable. Someone who won't bail on them after a few weeks.'

'What is it?'

'Cleaning. But specialist . . .'

Blood splatter

Faeces

Acids leaking from the body

'I thought it might suit you.'

Just like the cocktail.

So now I am one of Daphne's orphans, like the washing machines and television sets she has to find new homes for once they've been removed from the homes of the deceased. Sasha understood that somehow, even though we'd only just met, I needed a home. And I needed a family. Now I've got both.

Twelve

Day three and she catches me before I leave for work. The reason I have a home. The reason I have a job. The reason I have any kind of life at all. Sasha stands in the door to the kitchen, the scent of sleep rising from her while I shovel Frosties into my mouth. She is still in her pyjamas. I'm already dressed. Silver glitters from her ears and her knuckles. Sasha sleeps in her treasure, whereas I prefer to keep mine hidden if I can.

'What's that?' she says, pulling out a chair to sit at the kitchen table.

She doesn't mean the Frosties. She means the doll rescued from within a seam of rubbish, those sharp little toes.

'Just something I found.'

My mouth is full of milk and sugar. Sasha folds her arms, silver rings like knuckle dusters.

'It's from the house, isn't it.'

She doesn't even bother to make it a proper question. I know what she's thinking. But can you steal from a dead person? I look at the doll lying on the table, its plastic breasts, its bud for a mouth, hair in disarray. Despite her tiny waist, the doll reminds me of myself.

I tease a Frostie from where it's got stuck under my lip. 'Don't suppose you know anything about her?'

Not the doll, the old lady. Isabella Dawson, owner of

all the rubbish I've been wading through for a couple of days now. Sasha gives me that look again.

'You know I'm not supposed to discuss work, Essie.'

I grin back, my teeth smeared with cereal. 'It's my work, too.'

Cleaning the stuff no one else wants to be bothered with. Although, fair enough, Sasha's sorting actual people, whereas I'm sorting their leftovers. Still, it's the same thing, isn't it, in the end. One gets thrown into a bin bag and incinerated; the other gets zipped into a body bag and incinerated. The only difference is that one is done with due ceremony and the other with none.

'Fuck's sake.' Sasha gathers that great yank of hair in both hands, pushes it over her shoulder to keep it out of the mess I've made of the kitchen table. I love Sasha's hair. It's like a mermaid's flowing down.

'She's nothing special,' Sasha says, swiping at a droplet of milk with her fingertip. 'Just another dead old lady.'

I stare at the milk, the tiny pool, like a teardrop on the tabletop. 'Have you found any family yet?'

'Have you found anything for us that isn't just rubbish?'

A will, perhaps. An address book. The personal things.

'Nope, just the usual.'

I don't mention the knucklebone hidden in my lockbox. Sasha never likes to give ground. But neither do I. Sasha yawns as though the boarding house and its contents are nothing special.

'You'll have to wait and see what I can dig up, then, won't you,' she says.

Though I've been through enough dead people's left-overs to understand that sometimes the things our clients accumulate over a lifetime say more about who they were than any story a distant relative might tell. Still, one is rubbish and the other is human and McDermid and Sharp insist on the difference. I get up from the table, shrug on my coat. I'm almost out the door when she says it.

'By the way, I meant to ask . . .' She pulls a bowl towards her, a spoon. 'The parents of one of our clients mentioned a piece of jewellery that seems to have gone missing. A gold locket.'

Cheap chain. Two birds kissing. A mother and a father. My coat is suddenly tight about my arms, as though I might not be able to *Breathe, Essie. Breathe.*

'Which client?'

'That girl. The drug death.'

Hair like summer hay, needle in the crook of her arm.

'You didn't see it, did you?' Sasha asks. 'When you were cleaning.'

'No.' I look away. 'You know what it's like with addicts. Not much left by the time we get in.'

Sasha nods, reaches for her granola. 'Well, if you hear anything.'

I stare at the doll where it lies by Sasha's elbow. Suddenly, I want to cover its naked body, stop it getting cold. I reach my hand, place it over the doll. Sasha reaches with her hand, places it over mine. Keeping me safe is what Sasha tries to do. Still, I can't help worrying that the doll is going to suffocate. I curl my fingers round the hard little body, slide it away.

'She definitely didn't have any children, then?' I say. 'Isabella Dawson.'

'None that we can find.'

Thirteen

That morning, I do not take the bus to the seaside, Portobello and Isabella Dawson's boarding house. I visit Dr Anju instead. Dr Anju is my saviour. Or perhaps I am hers. Or maybe it is Daphne who is saviour to us both. In my pocket I have a doll with hair in disarray.

'Come on in, then.'

Dr Anju holds the door of her Edinburgh bungalow wide. It is my day for visiting – an angel of mercy with cleaning spray and a broom.

Inside, the bungalow is as it always is – on the verge of chaos – books and papers piled everywhere, a whole ocean of them washing about our feet. Dr Anju's hoarding isn't on the scale of Isabella Dawson's, but that's only because she's done a deal with her nephew. He pays The Company to come and help her once a month. She agrees to let us in.

I first met Dr Anju a few weeks into my new job. Daphne doing her matchmaking:

Second Wednesday of each month, keep the tide at bay, maintain one Clear Zone in which you can both sit and have a cup of coffee.

Something told her we would get on.

Dr Anju generally sticks to her side of the bargain. The kitchen is piled with enough food for the Apocalypse, but the conservatory is an oasis. I look through the glass towards the leylandii and the birdfeeder. The grass is well overdue a go with the strimmer, but still I can feel it, the letting go of that tourniquet in my chest.

Before I begin with my spray can and my polish, Dr Anju appears with her usual offering – a plastic tub full of roti and a jar of Dundee marmalade. Dr Anju's nephew brings the roti in bulk, just in case. Doesn't want his aunt to become an Edinburgh statistic, one of those old ladies who starved themselves to death because no one paid enough attention. The bread is moist, refreshed by a blast from Dr Anju's microwave. I take one round. Also a large dollop of the Dundee, thick crystalline strands of orange peel dripping from the spoon. Second breakfast, that is what Dr Anju calls it. I never say no. Dr Anju is tiny, face like a pickled walnut. I am sweaty and huge. Still, we both like to eat.

My giantess. That was what Dr Anju called me the first time we met, as I loomed over her in the front porch of her bungalow with my caddy at my feet. *Have you always been a large girl?*

It's only recently that I've begun to wonder if, in fact, Dr Anju was asking something different: have you always been small inside?

Now, over roti and marmalade, Dr Anju insists on the latest news. This is her quid pro quo for keeping the Clear Zone free of debris – the Edinburgh Way of spreading things around.

'I hear you've been in Portobello.'

Even though she never seems to leave the bungalow, Dr Anju is very well informed.

'Yes,' I nod, wad of roti in my cheek, 'an old boarding house on the promenade.'

'Much in it?'

I give her the list. Custard powder. Unopened bills. False teeth. I don't mention the bone found in a biscuit tin beneath the primrose Formica table.

'Nothing useful, then.' Dr Anju reaches for another spoonful of marmalade. 'House will be worth a bit, though.'

She has a keen eye for the price of things, especially property. An Edinburgh pastime. I shrug, wipe sticky fingers on my knees. I am not an Edinburgh native. I was brought up on the periphery. Edinburgh was only somewhere to come because there wasn't anywhere else.

'Mr Farthing will be all over it, no doubt.'

Dr Anju is well acquainted with the territory of the dead. McDermid and Sharp of The Company. Margaret Penny from the Office for Lost People. Also Solomon Farthing, the Heir Hunter who takes a particular interest in property left by people who've died without a will. Dr Anju used to be on the indigent funeral rota, that is what she told me. Professional mourners from every faith and none in the city waving goodbye to those unfortunates who have nobody else to see them to their grave.

'Not that we got many of my kind,' she said. 'Too many busybodies amongst the Hindus to let one of ours alone to rot.'

Now she rubs her hands on her fleece, leaving floury smears. 'I heard your new client had been dead two years before they found her.'

Black hands. Black feet. Skin like the tanned hide of a cow.

'Something like that.'

Whatever Dr Anju knows already, I don't want to say too much. It is company policy not to blab about our clients, let alone the mess they leave behind. McDermid and Sharp insist on it. *Discretion*. The Company's USP. Dr Anju laughs, screws the lid back on the marmalade jar.

'I'm lucky to have you, Essie Pound. The world's most discreet cleaner.' She winks at me over the plastic tub. 'Her name was Isabella Dawson, if I'm not mistaken.'

I choke on the remains of my roti. 'How did you find that out?'

'Ways and means.'

Edinburgh ways, she means.

'Did you know her?' I ask.

'We're not all related, you know.' Hoarders, she means. 'But I might have had a slight acquaintance.'

'What was she like?'

'Unfortunate.' Dr Anju licks marmalade from her thumb. 'Never got out from underneath her mother. Old Mrs Dawson ruled the roost. By the time she died, Portobello was already on the downslide. No more holiday guests coming in for the season. Isabella had to resort to students and DSS to pay the bills in the end. Old Mrs Dawson would have rolled in her grave.'

I chew the last of my bread, swallow it down, think of a doll sandwiched in the rubbish. A knucklebone in a biscuit tin.

'She didn't take in children, did she?'

Like Granny Pound and me and the one hundred and three, washing up on the shores of Edinburgh's periphery. But Dr Anju is adamant.

'Oh, no.' She presses the plastic lid onto the tub of roti.

'Adults only in that house. Then she retired, of course, shut up shop for good. Took to hoarding stuff instead.'

I think of a storeroom packed to the rafters with supplies. Then of a calendar blackened about its edges.

'When was that?'

'1996.'

'1996?'

Dr Anju gives a grim little turn of her mouth. 'The final death of Portobello. Haven't you heard?'

Fourteen

The boarding house is quiet when I arrive after a morning vacuuming various pathways through Dr Anju's muddle. I approach via the promenade. Today Portobello is not looking its best. Overcast. Wind blowing the sand in great flurries. A spattering of rain.

Far away, by the edge of the water, there is some sort of commotion. A dog dancing in the shallows. A man shouting. A police officer is trying to drag something from the surf. The dog attempts to grab at the object, before the officer pulls it away. I would like to have a dog, I think. Something fearless to run with into the wind. For a moment I watch as the police officer drags the object further up the sand, crouches to look. I frown. There is something about her, the curve of her back. I blink into the breeze, squint at a sudden glare of sunlight, warmth on my skin. Then the shout:

Em!

In front of me someone running. When I look again, the police officer is standing, turned towards the promenade, as though she might be coming for me. I retreat up the side street, slip through the back gate of Isabella Dawson's boarding house. The police and I have never got on.

Inside the boarding house the passage from the back door to the front is finally clear. I run my finger along the greasy wallpaper, discover a repeating pattern of blue and red sailing boats surfing a tide of nicotine. Where the passage ends I emerge into a space with a high ceiling stained by years of damp, corners swathed in cobwebs. We have made it to the hall at last.

I shuffle into the centre of the space, place my caddy and my mop as though marking territory. I am here now. The floor is a mess, shoe covers sticking with each step. I survey the curl of plaster ivy running around the rim of the ceiling. The flock paper covered in a wash of dirty emulsion. A crackle of ancient gloss painted from skirting to dado rail. Students and DSS, wasn't that what Dr Anju said? Anything to pay the bills. Isabella Dawson's front hall reminds me of the places I stayed in after Granny Pound died. Sixteen and nowhere to live but hostels and emergency B & Bs. Institutions where what mattered was being able to wipe clean every surface. I rub at the muck on the floor with my foot, glimpse an intricate pattern of terracotta and blue.

In front of the main entrance there is a great pile of furniture barricading the door. Dining chairs and side tables. Odd cabinets and what looks like some kind of desk. More orphans needing a new home. I think of Isabella Dawson and her biscuit tin. Of a child trapped somewhere in her boarding house trying to get out. 1996, the death of Portobello. Around me the house shifts.

Almost hidden behind the jumble of chairs and other furniture, I discover an empty plant pot, all about it the remains of a hundred cigarettes ground into the tiles. I peer into the pot, heart in my throat at the thought of finding another carcass. But it is only cigarette butts, a great tide of them, washing up amongst a pile of dead leaves. I stir at the debris with the handle of my duster, just in case. Whatever plant used to live in this pot must have been eating ash for years, that is what I'm thinking. Probably died long before the lady upstairs.

To the left of the plant pot is a solitary hat stand set a bit away from the rest. A Mackintosh hangs from it, as though someone took it off yesterday when they came in from their walk. I lift the coat from the stand, try it on for size. But the Mackintosh is too small. Or I am too large. I can barely get both arms into the sleeves. I tug it off again with some trouble, hang it back on the stand. Already I am sweating and I have only just begun. I dip a hand into one of the pockets, draw it out quick as I touch something soft. A mouse, perhaps, not yet decayed, still a flash of silver in its grey coat. I don't remove it. Despite doing this job I am not a fan of rodents, prefer to leave those to Monika who goes at them with relish and the flat of her shovel, *bam bam bam*. Instead, I try the other pocket, touch something cool and solid. A metal key. I do take that.

I begin cleaning with my overhead duster, sweep wreaths of cobwebs from the high corners, let them trickle down the walls. There is something graceful about cobwebs, the way they adorn a property once everything else has left. They fall in swathes from the ivy cornice, drift onto the furniture beneath. I follow with a sponge attachment smearing a path through the dirty emulsion. The sponge comes away black every time, me dousing and wringing it in my bucket of water over and over, until the water is black, too. By the time I've done one wall, my coverall suit has gone grey from neck to ankle. I know there is fresh water in the scullery we discovered off the kitchen, a cold tap attached to the mains. But I do not want to go back in there. Not since my dream of blood pooling on the floor.

Instead, I shuffle to the back of the hall, heavy bucket sloshing about my feet, open the door to a water closet tucked beneath the stairs. A small space with a sink in crazed ceramic and a toilet with a wide wooden seat. I brush aside the threads of dust which hang across the closet entrance, manoeuvre inside. The closet is small. I am large. The bucket knocks against my shins, water slopping onto my shoe covers as I attempt to lift it over the toilet. The pan is dry, a thick run of rust disappearing down the U-bend. I tip the dirty liquid in, wait for it to dissipate. But the water just sits there gazing at me. A filthy black pool.

Suddenly my heart is hammering, darkness pressing in. I reach with my arms to steady myself, touch the walls, find them nearer than I thought. I attempt to turn in the tiny space, panic rising in my throat. The tourniquet in my chest twists. There is the sound of someone breathing. I feel with my hands across the powdery surface of the wall, find myself grasping at something, the rustle of nylon. A child's anorak. Red, like the swimsuit in my photograph. Like blood on a kitchen floor. I stare at the coat, at the keyhole with its tiny shaft of light, eye pressed in. Then the sudden glitter as the blade . . .

The door to the water closet opens, the light so bright I squint and shrink away. There is a woman standing there clad in a coverall suit, all eyes, nothing else. I press back against the broad edge of the sink, hear the voice in my ear.

Who's there?

It's me. It's me.

Then someone else speaking. Monika, mask about her neck.

'What are you doing, Essie? Daphne needs your help.'

Fifteen

Just like Isabella Dawson, my whole life is hidden. From me. And from everyone else, too. But not because I've buried it in someone else's rubbish. More because I don't have anything or anyone to remind me of what it might have been. I asked Granny Pound about it once.

'Where did I come from?'

She just laughed and gave me a hug with those big flabby arms. 'From here, of course. The seaside.'

But she never told me if I was a monster. Or just an abandoned child.

Sometimes I think of my past like a great void inside me, a huge space that's never held anything of importance. Other times I think the void is so full I might explode. Then it will spew out of me like the boarding house is spewing out now that we've opened the door. One grey shovel of junk after another. One dead orphan after another. All just waiting for someone to come and pick over the bones. I wonder what they would find. The hundred and three, perhaps, with their bickering and their scrapping. Granny Pound with her biro and her *TV Times*. The washing machine with its constant hum and spin, all about it pile upon pile of dirty laundry waiting to be cleaned. Also grey sand. Grass that pricks the soft soles of your feet. Vomit splatter on the back paving stones from too much raspberry ripple. Not to mention four bunk beds to a room and the smell of one hundred and three other children deep in the weave of the sheets.

Sasha asked me once, 'What was it like when you were growing up?'

I gave the usual answer. 'Fine.'

She knew that I was lying. 'It must have been strange, all those other kids coming and going.'

Granny Pound's flock. I didn't reply. I don't like to be reminded that I was not the only one. Still Sasha persisted.

'Do you see any of them now?'

'Why would I?'

Sasha doesn't understand. She comes from a family where there is one mother and one father and one brother and that's that. Her questions are never over, though. The most recent she asked was:

'Why were you with her anyway?'

What she really means to ask is, *What did you do?*

Sixteen

That afternoon the boarding house is a heavy presence. I feel its hand on my neck as we carry orphans from the hall to the yard. One dining chair after another. One cabinet after another. One pot stand. One fire screen. Even a ladies' desk, a neat bureau. I open the lid of the desk, discover six little drawers inside. But they are empty, no row of opals glimmering at me like cats' eyes. Unlucky for some.

We lay Isabella Dawson's furniture in rows amongst the trampled willowherb, ready for the dealers to come pick over her spoils. Which to keep. Which to sell. Which to throw away. It reminds me of Granny Pound and the one hundred and three coming and going. Except, nobody ever came for me. Still, I know it's for a good cause. Re-homing is one of Daphne's specialities, the reason she is always on the phone. A favour here. Another there. The Edinburgh Way of getting things done. Between them, Daphne and McDermid and Sharp have furnished most of Edinburgh's needy; three wise ladies bearing gifts.

The backyard is like a bombsite now. A trail of debris litters the path from the back door to the skip. A jar of jam smashed on the pavement. A white explosion of flour where I dropped a bag of it in the gutter. The shed has been emptied of its suppurating bin bags, but the side return is still choked with rubbish, faint whiff of human waste rising from the moss.

At least inside we don't have to worry about the smell, that is what I'm thinking as I carry out another chair to add to the rest. That sweet stink of putrefaction which lodges at the back of the throat for days. Ammonia from cat urine. Those are the scents I usually carry home with me after a long day's work. But inside Isabella Dawson's boarding house the smell is almost pleasant, the sea air blowing through her accumulated remains until it became an ancient dig, everything preserved.

Still, there is something not right. That is what I'm thinking as I settle the chair amongst the trampled willow-herb, give the seat a quick wipe with my cloth. Despite all our cleaning. Despite all our efforts with the shovel and the pickaxe, the bucket and the spray. It is rotten. The whole yard is rotten. Perhaps the house, too.

Pawel and Monika pause in our lifting and carrying to argue over a coffee table with a cracked foot. Whether to keep or whether to skip? I wander back into the hall. The front door is almost clear now, revealed in all its glory. A grand mahogany thing, smoked glass with bevelled edges, huge brass doorknob. But the wood surround is black, swollen with years of rain and wind, doorknob misted with tarnish. The glass panel is cracked across the middle like the window in the kitchen, as though someone hit it once with a stick. Someone trying to get in. Or someone trying to get out. I stand close, peer through the smoky glass towards the garden. But it is obscured, a viridescent blur as though in a dreamscape.

I slip a key from my pocket, try it in the lock. But the key is too small, the lock too large. So I try it in the other doors instead. One each side of the front entrance. But the key doesn't work in these either. Isabella Dawson's house likes to keep hold of its secrets. As I like to keep hold of mine.

The scent of cigarette smoke drifts along the passageway with its wall of little boats. Monika and Pawel having a break, no doubt, since Daphne departed to sort the dealers. I crouch by the door to the right, press my eye to the keyhole. The room is shrouded in gloom, heavy curtains drawn across the windows. But I can see it. China of all shapes and sizes. A life's work laid across a dining table big enough to seat twelve, maybe more. Dinner services and toast racks, egg cups and sugar bowls. There's even a clutch of cake stands. French Fancies, I think. Sandwiches with their crusts off. I always wanted a birthday spread like that, but Granny Pound never had the time. Instead, it was fizzy juice and a Mr Kipling from the Spar. If we were lucky, a packet of iced gems.

Across the hall, I put my eye to another keyhole, imprint on my skin. Inside I spy a parlour, newspaper covering the window this time, sofas and chairs turned top-to-tail, stuffing spilling out. On the far wall a piano rises from the clutter. Dr Anju says that Old Mrs Dawson used to play the piano while the guests ate dinner in the dining room. I try to imagine melodies floating across the hall to merge with the scrape and clatter of knives on china, the chink of a teaspoon circling in a cup. What must it have been like to live here? That is what I'm thinking. A house full of comings and goings like the house I lived in once. But that is a dream of another life, nothing but a memory. Grey sand and Granny Pound sitting in front of the coal-effect fire circling programmes in the *TV Times*, while I lie at her feet drawing with my crayons. One thick slash of yellow for the beach. One thick slash of blue for the sea. A girl in a red swimsuit. The girl is smiling. Above her the sun shines.

I turn my gaze towards the water closet at the back of the hall, think of the child's anorak hanging in the dark, a knucklebone discovered in a biscuit tin. 1996, that was what Dr Anju said. The death of Portobello. A girl who went to the play park along the promenade, never came home again, disappeared into thin air. The girl was five years old, the same age as me. Dr Anju showed me a picture. V-neck jumper and hair in bunches. 1996. The year Isabella Dawson closed her door and barricaded the entrance. The year a girl got lost, like I am lost, too.

I hold my breath, wait for the house to tell me something. But there is nothing except the soft contours of a piano melody playing, the murmur of the waves.

Seventeen

Day four and inside Isabella Dawson's boarding house the smell of the sea drifts towards us from across the promenade. The locksmith has opened the doors to all the rooms off the hall. Her dining room, its table laden with china. Her parlour with its piano. Her front door with its smoky bevelled glass and huge brass knob. Now the light pours in.

Together we stand on the doorstep. Daphne with her diary. Monika, Pawel and me in our coveralls. Margaret Penny with a fox about her neck. We gaze into a jungle of brambles and couch grass, hydrangeas gone mad. Also a grove of ancient raspberry canes, thorny and spindle-like, the sort of forest it might require a prince to slash through if there wasn't The Company to sort it instead. This is Isabella Dawson's secret garden, that is what I'm thinking. The perfect place to hide a child.

The garden is surrounded on all sides by a wall so high no one can look in from the outside and no one from the inside can look out. At the far end is a door embedded in the wall. Beyond the door is the promenade. There's an amusement arcade along the promenade, that is what I know. Also a play park, swings and a roundabout.

'What's that?'

Pawel points at something rising from the undergrowth. Some sort of washing machine, its torso speckled with corrosion, two black holes in the top.

'Twin tub,' says Margaret Penny. 'My mother used to have one.'

'What's it doing in the garden?'

But none of us know the answer to that.

'She'll have sent out the laundry when she ran it as a boarding house,' says Daphne. 'Easier than doing it all by hand.'

Probably hired in a skivvy, that's what I know. Or washed out her undies in the water closet once she decided to barricade herself in. No need to bother with the rest, no one to complain about the smell. It's one way of living. But really, who knows anything, that is what I'm realizing. Isabella Dawson might have swum in the sea every morning, for all we know, salt in her lungs.

Margaret Penny fiddles with the fox about her neck. She is nervous this morning, I can tell, huffing at the sight of the garden. Or perhaps at the spectre of more rubbish needing to be moved.

'Might take an extra day or two,' she says.

'No problem,' says Daphne. 'We can manage.'

Pawel with his pickaxe, Monika with her spade. Maybe even the industrial strimmer with its cloud of petrol fumes. Though we all know Daphne will need another skip, if only for the twin tub. But Margaret Penny is happy enough, eager to move on. She settles her fox beneath her coat, turns and heads towards the back door which has become the main entrance now.

'All right,' she calls as she disappears. 'I'll leave you to it.'

Daphne follows, to sort the new skip no doubt, instructions trailing behind. 'Pawel. Monika. You begin with the parlour. Essie, you start packing the china. Should be able to clear the front rooms today.'

But before I begin, I cannot resist.

I make my way down the rough stone steps and into the garden proper, feel the ground soften beneath my feet. I tread carefully through overgrown shrubbery and nettles almost as high as my waist, goosegrass that clings to my coveralls with its tiny spines. It has rained in the night. It reminds me of Granny Pound's grave, that loamy smell of freshly damp grass. There is the faintest of paths visible amongst the snarl of weeds. I follow it deeper into the morass. On my right there is the twin tub. On my left what looks like a mattress left out too long in the rain. Also what could once have been a cold frame, for summer salad or autumn squash growing ripe in the short Scottish season. Just a pile of broken glass now, crawling with woodlice.

I reach the bottom of the garden and the door set into the wall. It is clear from the moss growing up the wood on this side that the door has not been open in years. I slip the key from my pocket, try it in the lock. But it does not fit here either. I cast about me, pondering all the ways in which this house seems to snag and obstruct, look for evidence of digging amongst the undergrowth, any disturbance that might indicate another key was once buried here. Across the tangle of the garden, from out of the mouth of the house, a voice comes calling.

'Essie Pound, how's it going with that china?'

Daphne, keeping an eye.

I grasp the handle of the door for one last try, put my shoulder to it, my not inconsiderable bulk. The frame is rotten, just like everything else. It disintegrates almost as soon as I try. I tug the door free, step through.

The promenade is a long stretch. Edinburgh on its hill to the left. Joppa high-rises to the right. In front I suddenly feel it again. Warm tarmac on bare feet, sand up my calves. Someone calling to me:

Essie!

As I run into the wind.

Not all my memories are dark ones. Only those I cannot see.

I pull down my mask. The smell of the salt is like the hit of Tiger Balm, straight to the back of the skull. I suck it into my lungs. Then all the rest. Takeaway coffee and bike oil, the sticky scent of ice cream, wet dog passing as it trots by its owner's heels. I lean to strip off my shoe covers, unlace my trainers, peel away my socks. Then I walk along, feet naked. It is strange to be out in the world unclothed when I am so used to being covered, every single inch. I peel off a glove too, run my fingers over the rough stone of Isabella Dawson's garden wall till I get to the corner, peer round.

The skip is parked some way along the side street, and behind it, The Company's van. Monika and Pawel appear, dumping what look like decaying sofa cushions from the parlour, before flitting inside again. I must be getting back, I think. Start sorting all that china. I return my gaze to the sea, strands of hair escaping from my hood. One catches on my mouth and I suck it for a moment, before pulling it free. It is when I turn away that I see her again. The police officer from the commotion on the beach the day before.

I watch from the safety of the corner. She prowls around

the skip, standing on tiptoe to peer over the top. She obviously finds something of interest, places her hands on the edge, levers herself up to take a closer look. A casserole pot perhaps, chicken carcass burned to the base. I think of a knucklebone hidden in a lockbox, next to it a gold locket. Pull my mask over my mouth, my nose, as the police officer jumps from the skip and turns to look at me.

For a second we stare at each other. Two young women, one large, one skinny. The officer looks as though she has seen a ghost. All I see is trouble. Also something else. A girl disappearing down a street, nothing to see but her heels. I frown behind my mask as the police officer makes a move towards me. A shiver runs through me. Once again, I retreat. Back around the corner to collect my shoes. Back into Isabella Dawson's garden, gate closed. I weave my way through the tangle in reverse, feet bare on damp grass, rush of blood in my head. Back to dinner plates and soup bowls, cake stands, all three tiers. But as I hurry past overgrown shrubs and huge clumps of nettles, I am searching, like the officer outside is searching. For disturbed areas of ground. For piles of suspicious branches. For the dip in the leaf mould that indicates a shallow grave.

Eighteen

Inside the safety of Isabella Dawson's dining room, her life's work laid out on the table, I pull aside the heavy velvet curtains to let in the light. Moths have eaten away the curtain trims. They disintegrate beneath my fingertips, tiny feathers of fabric floating to the floor. It's as though the boarding house is crumbling before my eyes now that the doors have been unlocked, fresh air allowed in.

I circle the table, touching here and there. Salt and pepper crocks. Gravy boats. Also stacks and stacks of plates. Most of them are good china, bone and porcelain, some decorated, some plain, a fine set of willow pattern. But all of it is sticky, a patina of grime around every rim. Isabella Dawson's china needs a good scalding, that is what I'm thinking. Dunk it in the old earthenware sink in the back kitchen, sleeves rolled above elbows, skin livid as we *scrub, scrub, scrub*.

'Well, well.' A man in his sixties appears in the doorway. 'What have we here.'

He is wearing a tweed jacket, socks the colour of the willowherb that used to flower in the yard. It is Solomon Farthing, the Heir Hunter, come to see what treasure he might find. He lifts the flap on a box of crockery, looks disappointed.

'Plebeian ware,' he announces, holding up a dish. Thick, white, sturdy china from which to eat and drink. 'Unbreakable.'

Except when it isn't. I pick out a plate that has been cracked in half then glued back together. I can't help thinking how much washing and drying it would take to keep this lot clean. Years of Isabella Dawson's life standing by the sink. Or perhaps she hired in help. Skivvies. That's another name for them. I lay the broken plate on the edge of the table amongst the rest. I'm a skivvy. It's just that we're not called that anymore.

I watch as Solomon Farthing checks over Isabella Dawson's spoils, drawn to the best of them like a wasp to sugar. He makes notes in a little book as he goes.

'Worth something?'

Margaret Penny leans on the doorframe, fox still about her neck, brown folder under her arm. Isabella Dawson's file. I wonder what might be in the file, the stories it could tell. Solomon Farthing lifts a gravy boat, puts it down again.

'Maybe,' he says. 'The house certainly is, even in its current state. How long has it been since it operated as a boarding house anyway?'

'Over twenty years,' Margaret Penny replies. 'Not since 1996.'

'1996?'

I see them glance at each other. There is a flutter in my wrist as I think of the death of Portobello. A tiny knucklebone hidden in a tin. What else might Isabella Dawson's house reveal once we get to the bottom of her accumulated rubbish? Margaret Penny tucks a fox paw behind her lapel as though she's thinking of that, too, doesn't like where it might lead.

'Reckon you'll find someone to take it on?' she says to the Heir Hunter. 'The house, I mean. Everything in it.'

'Where there's a will, there's a way.'

We all know the joke. Sasha explained it to me. Solomon Farthing wouldn't be here if Isabella Dawson had left a will. There'd be no commission in it for him.

The two of them gravitate towards the forest of glassware covering the top of an antique buffet that takes up the whole of the back wall. The buffet is hideous, a huge Gothic thing in dark-stained oak. But practical. Big enough to take all the china. Also a good place to hide a child. Margaret Penny readjusts the fox beneath her coat as Mr Farthing fingers a set of diminutive sherry glasses; the fox fixes the Heir Hunter with its dark eye. Solomon Farthing and Margaret Penny are a double act now, that's what Daphne says. Where one appears, the other follows. They help each other with the stubborn cases. He finds an heir, she sorts the rest. But that doesn't mean she trusts him not to take stuff for himself.

They move on to the wide mantelpiece with its cluster of ornate candlesticks in tarnished silver, almost as black now as Isabella Dawson's hands. I follow behind, counting the sherry glasses just to make sure. Mr Farthing used to be light-fingered, that's what I've been told. But the sherry set is complete, as far as I can tell, nothing but a slight disturbance in the dust that has settled across the glassware like a veil of ancient lace. Beneath the dust I count at least thirty champagne coupes laid out as though for a party that never happened. Perhaps that explains why there is no obvious heir. Isabella Dawson was a smaller version of Miss Havisham, disappointed on her wedding day, never cleared up after. Left that to whoever would come next. Turns out it was me.

From the room opposite there is the sudden sound of

a piano playing, a disjointed melody marked by muffled keys and flats where there ought to be sharps. It is melancholy, a lament for everything that has been lost. We all stop to listen. Then it morphs into *Chopsticks*, Monika and Pawel laughing as they take turns to bash the keys. Mr Farthing and Margaret Penny drift into the hall. I am left alone with Isabella Dawson's china. I put a finger to a willow-pattern plate, the tiny figure standing on a bridge in her kimono. Then I look inside the Gothic buffet, just in case. There is no sign of a child on any of the many shelves. Nor in the cubby holes. Not even a skeleton. Just more china. A soup canteen, this time, in the shape of a chicken with a ladle to match.

Nineteen

I first came to live with Granny Pound in 1996. At least, that was what she told me. I don't remember. It's as though my brain has decided to wipe out anything that happened before.

Bedraggled.

That was how she described me. Granny Pound never minced her words, not once in all the years I knew her. She told it like it was, and then some. Her way of toughening us up.

When I first arrived at Granny Pound's, I used to scream in the night.

Like a banshee.

Keeping everyone awake. Part of me thinks that can't be true. I've always preferred to observe rather than speak. It's what makes me good at my job, the ability to spy out any last trace of dirt, not to mention blood. Also, normally, I sleep like the dead. *Click switch*, lights out, nothing to bring me round till the alarm clock's piercing call. It's only recently I've started to wake at three in the morning, pale orange light from the street lamp, thin wail of a baby calling to me through the floorboards. Though it began before the baby arrived, of course. Not long after I started work with The Company. Daphne and the crew, my new family. Plus a caddy full of bleach and bloodstains on the floor.

Sasha is getting tired of it now.

'Don't you think you should see someone?' she said the third or fourth time it happened. Her answer for everything.

But I've been 'seeing' people my whole life. Social workers. GPs. Mental health professionals. Amongst all the rest. And this is where they've got me. Right back at the beginning, waking in the night with a scream hanging from my lips. Like a banshee, I think, that's what I will become if I let that scream go.

I asked Granny Pound once who I belonged to. *Me*, she said. *Don't let anyone else tell you otherwise.* She even lent me her name. *Essie Pound.* Still I kept asking. Then she gave me the photograph.

It is 1996 and I am five years old, standing on a beach wearing a red swimsuit and jelly sandals. In the photograph I am nothing but angles and bone, unlike now when I've become so fat I'm like a plum gone too long in the sun. The swimsuit I am wearing has a white, pleated skirt, four large buttons on the front which are white too. I have no memory of wearing a swimsuit such as this. But the photograph does not lie, unlike some of the other things I have inside my head. And besides, I do remember warm tarmac, sand on my calves, salt on hot skin.

Twenty

At teatime, after I have packed away Isabella Dawson's life's work, I visit Dr Anju again. It isn't my day, but sometimes needs must. She opens the door to a waft of detergent from where I spent the afternoon washing china.

'Essie Pound,' she says. 'As I live and breathe.' As though I haven't seen her for a month. Dr Anju has an excellent sense of humour to go with her tiny frame. It's only me who is morbid and obese. I present her with a handful of all the willowherb I could salvage from the yard.

'So pretty.' Dr Anju's face glows as though I've offered her a fifty-pound bouquet. 'To what do I owe this honour?'

'I wanted to ask about Isabella Dawson.'

'Isabella Dawson?' Dr Anju fixes me with her cool gaze. 'You'd better come inside.'

She leads me to the conservatory where I can see that some of the stockpile from the kitchen has already begun to gravitate. Dr Anju knows it, too. She offers me a Blue Riband from a multi-pack of multi-packs by way of apology. Or maybe more of a bribe. Either way I take it, like she knew I would. She disappears into the kitchen, reappears with an old catering-size mayonnaise jar stuffed with the willowherb, balances it on a pile of books.

'So, Essie. What do you want to know about Isabella Dawson?'

'1996,' I say. 'The death of Portobello.'

Dr Anju eyes me like a bird eyes a worm. 'You think Isabella Dawson had something to do with that poor girl?'

Hair in bunches. Red V-neck jumper.

'Maybe . . .'

It seems ridiculous when I say it out loud. But the doll. The coat hanging in the water closet. The knucklebone, of course.

'Why would Isabella Dawson take a girl?'

'To keep her safe . . .'

Dr Anju raises her eyebrows. 'What, like *Flowers in the Attic*?'

The attic, I think. Does the boarding house have an attic? I must remember to check. I take a bite of my Blue Riband. I can't help noticing that Dr Anju's oversize fleece is grubby about the zip area, her silver hair a tangle that hasn't been combed in a week. She looks rather like a child herself. She places a hand on my arm. It looks a bit like a chicken's foot.

'What's this really about, Essie?'

I feel the damp grow beneath my shirt at what she's really asking.

'I just thought you might have information on her. A file, perhaps?'

Dr Anju laughs then, a delighted jingle of a thing. 'Well, if it's files you're after, Essie Pound, you've come to the right place.'

Dr Anju says everyone has a file somewhere. And I believe her. What is life without paperwork? That is what I've learned from working with The Company. Birth certificate. Death certificate. Insurance policy. Will. These are what outlive us, if only because somebody else has to deal with them once we are gone.

Isabella Dawson has a file, I already know that. But it's so slim it's almost anorexic, no indication that there might be anything suspicious, let alone untoward. I stole a look at it when I was meant to be clearing the china, Margaret Penny and Solomon Farthing conversing over the orphans in the backyard. There wasn't much to it. A sudden death report by the police. Confirmation from the Fiscal that her demise was non-suspicious. A letter from *Ultimus Haeres* authorizing Edinburgh's Bereavement Services to work on their behalf in an attempt to find an heir. Also a contract between the council and The Company, two confident scrawls at the bottom: McDermid and Sharp. I studied the contract carefully, to see what their take is compared to mine. The only way to get ahead in this city.

The rest of the information was what I already knew. Unmarried. No children. Lived in the boarding house since she was born. A family business, three generations of greeting people at the door and seeing them off again year after year. It seemed clear from the file that Isabella Dawson was a skivvy just like me for all of those years, washing and drying the plebeian china. I felt a sudden affinity with her, even though she's dead. Black hands. Black feet. A life spent clearing up after other people, no one to clear up after her.

But there was nothing to indicate who Isabella Dawson loved. Or what her favourite dress was. Why she left behind a child's red anorak hanging on the back of her water-closet door. Nor whether she might have stolen a girl, harboured her and kept her hidden, starved her until she transformed into a skeleton like the chicken bones in her casserole dish. Like the knuckle discovered inside a biscuit tin. Then again, there was nothing in the file to say that she did not. It was all just so much paperwork. The bureaucracy of death, but not the stuff of life.

Dr Anju's life's work is her cupboard full of files. They live in a glory hole under her stairs, the one place in her converted bungalow I am not supposed to go. The door is secured with a combination padlock. I've spent ages trying to work out the code.

'Not that,' Dr Anju instructed the first time I came, waving at the cupboard with a dismissive gesture as she showed me around. 'Files. Confidential.'

I consulted Daphne after, of course, about whether to persist. But this time she surprised me.

'Everyone deserves at least one space into which no other person can pry, Essie,' she said. 'As long as whatever it contains is kept at bay.'

Daphne has an instinct for these things.

All in good time.

That could be her motto. The difference between a job getting done today and undone tomorrow; or completed a month down the line and staying that way forever.

'But what's in it?' I asked Dr Anju, once we'd got to know each other.

'My life's work,' she said. And smiled.

Now we stand together in her hall, ankle deep in paperwork. There won't be a problem finding the personal things once Dr Anju goes on her way, that is what I'm thinking. Birth certificate. Bus pass. Gift card from a relative. Dr Anju has it spread across her carpets. I try not to trample anything important as she works on the combination padlock, greedy eyes registering the numbers as she turns the dial. *1 9 6 9*. It was obvious really. I could have guessed it if I'd tried.

Dr Anju came to Edinburgh in 1969 to get married. Then she decided against it. At least that is what she told me.

'The glittering spires went to my head, Essie. Or maybe it was the summer of love. I found other things to do.'

She winked when she said it, made me blush. Her idea of a joke. Like many people who can't quite arrange their own stuff, Dr Anju has a lively mind. Too lively, perhaps. When she isn't hoarding unnecessary items, she hoards qualifications. As far as I've gathered, Dr Anju let go of marriage to qualify in psychology and sociology. Psychotherapy and analysis.

'What's analysis?' I asked when we first discussed it over marmalade and roti.

'Dream stuff. Well, my sort . . .'

'I have bad dreams.'

'Oh yes?' She turned to me then. 'Tell me more.'

But I am afraid of my dreams, of what they might reveal.

Now Dr Anju releases the padlock mechanism, steps back to let me see. Just as I thought, the glory hole is full, jammed from carpet to architrave with a wall of paper. Some files bulging. Some slim. Others in between. Unlike in Isabella Dawson's house, everything here is carefully labelled, names and dates running from top to bottom and back again like something carved on a war memorial:

We Shall Never Forget

I understand then why Dr Anju calls it her life's work. She is someone who will never forget either, if only because she has it all written down.

The files begin in the 1970s and go on from there, petering out in the 2000s once she retired. There is no obvious categorization as far as I can see.

'Who do they belong to?' I ask.

'To me, of course.'

I can tell by Dr Anju's smile that she really does regard them as the children she never had herself.

'But what about the – patients?' I say. 'Shouldn't they have them back?'

'Oh no. They wouldn't want the trouble.'

'I'd want it if it was mine.'

Dr Anju turns to look at me then. *An eye for an eye.*

'Have you asked for your file, Essie?'

Another life's work, sitting on the shelf in a social worker's office, as thick as my thigh by now with everything that's in it. But sometimes getting something isn't as simple as asking, that's what I've discovered. Even when it belongs to you. When I don't reply, Dr Anju's face takes on a sly expression as though she knows exactly what I've been thinking.

'That girl of yours could help, couldn't she? With securing it.'

Black hair spread like a mermaid's upon the pillow, two birds kissing. But stealing for yourself is one thing. Getting your girlfriend to steal for you is another thing entirely.

'I don't know,' I say. 'Maybe.'

'What do you think might be in it?'

Darkness, perhaps. A tourniquet in my chest. I shrug again. What could be worse than what I've imagined? Dr Anju pats at my arm, reaches across and pulls something from her stack. Suddenly my heart is thudding fit to burst at the thought that Dr Anju is about to reveal what she makes of me, rather than Isabella Dawson. My hands begin to tremble.

'Breathe, Essie. Breathe,' Dr Anju says. 'It's not what you think.'

Dr Anju is right, of course. The file has nothing to do with me whatsoever. Or Isabella Dawson. Well, not in the way I imagined. It isn't even a file. There is nothing official-looking. No social worker number. No name or address. Nothing that resembles a report. Instead, it is a journal with a cloth spine, inside one page after another covered in an anonymous scrawl. The writing runs across each page, faint and blue, as though it is a ghost of the original.

'Carbon paper,' says Dr Anju, reading my thoughts again. 'So that whatever has been written can leave an imprint.'

Which is a bit like how I feel about myself. The imprint, I mean. The original was lost long ago, that is what I know. I turn the pages of the journal, one, then the next. None of the words make any sense.

'What is it?' I ask.

'A dream diary. An excavation of sorts.'

'An excavation of what?'

'We all have something inside we can't let out, Essie,' Dr Anju says. 'Don't you think?'

My voice, when it finally comes, is suddenly small, like the girl in the photograph grinning for the camera.

'What if we do . . .' I say. 'Want it out, I mean?'

Dr Anju smiles, eyes crinkled at the edges as though finally we have come to the point. She indicates the sheaf of pages in my hands. 'Attend to your dreams, Essie. That is the answer. Attend to your dreams.'

Twenty-One

That night I have the dream again. Three a.m. and a baby crying. The tightening of the tourniquet. The darkness pressing in. I am in Isabella Dawson's storeroom with its tins of hotdogs and Alphabetti Spaghetti, looking into the kitchen across the way. The kettle is boiling, Granny Pound flips a teabag into the earthenware sink. Milk dribbles across the surface of the counter where it has got spilled. I watch as it drips onto the floor, a pink pool spreading and spreading across the lino. A plate has been smashed into two on the tiles, cereal bowls tipped over on the table. Sasha is there, with a knife in her hand, chopping and chopping. I watch from the black mouth of the cupboard as she glitters. Her rings. The skulls piercing her ears. The blade. I can feel the imprint of the keyhole on the skin about my eye. The harsh roar of someone else's breathing in my ears. I am holding the doll, its tiny plastic body suffocating in my hand. Then there is Dr Anju, her tangle of silver hair, holding out a jar of Dundee marmalade, saying, 'Wake up, Essie. Wake up.'

So I do.

In our kitchen I drink from the tap, the cold water an elixir in my throat. Across the hall, in the bedroom, Sasha exhales, turns towards the wall. I lay my spoils on the table. A lipstick with the imprint of a dead girl's mouth on its tip. A green plastic lighter. A bone taken from a biscuit tin with a family on the lid. Also a locket on a cheap chain, two birds kissing, beak to beak.

I touch the locket, think of the mother and father inside. Sasha leaves early tomorrow to go to Hamilton. She has to visit U.H. *Ultimus Haeres*. The last heir. U.H. are the recipients of all the estates that get lost or abandoned once someone dies without a will. Where does the money go if nobody is found to take it? I asked Sasha once. To the Crown, she replied. The Queen. I wonder about posting the locket to U.H. so they can add it to the rest of the treasure, no one the wiser. But the Queen has enough money to buy a thousand necklaces. A million. She has plenty of jewellery already, that is what I know.

Instead, I undo the clasp on the chain, slide the locket off. I don't even take a final look inside before slipping it into the pocket of Sasha's coat. Let her decide, that is what I'm thinking. Queen? Or someone else who deserves the locket more.

In its place, I thread Isabella Dawson's knucklebone onto the chain, fasten it about my neck, feel it settle into the hollow at the base of my throat. The knucklebone is as light as a whisper, as though it isn't really there. There is something comforting about it, as though it belongs. But I know that somewhere, just like the locket, it has its own family to go back to. A mother. A father. A boy. A girl.

Twenty-Two

'Your mother's dead.' That's what Granny Pound told me once. 'So don't bother asking.'

About her hair. About her laugh. About her clothes, her teeth, her smile. I was just another orphan. Like the chairs laid out in the backyard of Isabella Dawson's boarding house waiting for the dealers to come and decide which to take and which to discard.

I was drawing pictures, that's what I remember. Blue for the sky. A slash of yellow for the sand. Also me wearing a swimsuit coloured red, big smile on my face, holding hands with a lady who had a big smile on her face, too.

'Who's this, then?' Granny Pound said as she paused from marking up her *TV Times*. Even then I knew she wanted the woman to be her.

'That's Mummy,' I said.

'Your mummy's dead.'

She never even paused before she said it, Granny Pound peering at me over her large glasses, tea mug in her hand. There was writing on the mug:

WORLD'S BEST MUM

A birthday present from me and whichever of the one hundred and three were around at the time. I tore a tiny corner off my drawing, placed it on my tongue. All my drawings were nibbled at the edges then, as though to mark them. Some kind of trace.

'What did she die of?' I asked.

'In an accident.'

'What accident?'

'The kind you don't come back from.'

Crushing, perhaps. Falling from a high building. Drowning or decapitation. I've imagined every one.

I chewed on what was left of my mother while Granny Pound drank her tea and read the *TV Times*, putting a ring about the programmes she planned to watch once we were in bed. Granny Pound loved to watch TV: *Emmerdale* and *Coronation Street*. All the soaps. When I was older, we used to watch them together. But Granny Pound is dead now, like Isabella Dawson, everything she ever used to have about her long since tidied away.

I wonder sometimes as I clear out other people's houses, what happened to the drawings. Me with my big smile. My mother with her big smile. The two of us standing holding hands. Sometimes I added flowers, a little row of them along the bottom of the paper. From what I remember, the flowers looked as though they were smiling too.

I used to think Granny Pound knew everything about my mother, that one day she would tell me. About her hair. About her laugh. About her clothes, her teeth, her smile. But after Granny Pound died, I looked for the drawings, in and out of her kitchen drawers, her bedroom wardrobe, the display cabinet in the living room that we weren't supposed to touch. But I never found them, not even one.

After Granny Pound's funeral, I was about to turn sixteen, so they sent me to a room in a hostel. When I arrived, the room was empty, nothing but a bed and a wardrobe that didn't match. Probably more of Daphne's orphans. They showed me in and I sat on the bed and they closed the door and I thought, *Who am I now?*

Twenty-Three

Day five and I arrive back in Portobello at lunchtime, a cool light refracting off the Firth. But I am not at Isabella Dawson's boarding house. I am heading for another property, a block or so away.

Daphne and the rest of the crew have been diverted to a road traffic accident on the bypass. I got the call this morning, just after Sasha left for U.H. Monika will be picking up glass by the shovelful by now. Pawel busy with his hose. I have been instructed to start clearing the side return, but there is somewhere I must visit first.

When I get to my destination I expect to find the street quiet, nothing but a man walking his dog. But as I get close, I see there is a scrum right outside the house I plan to visit. Journalists, that is what I realize. Photographers, too. All huddled on the pavement. Also passers-by.

Rubberneckers.

That's what Granny Pound would have called them.

Come away now.

But I am not a rubbernecker. I have something which belongs to the woman inside. Repatriation, that is what I am thinking of: returning a daughter to where she belongs.

The house isn't special, set back from the beach by a street or two, pebbledash and a neat front garden, path to the gate. I've passed it every day since we started working at the boarding house, never even realized. V-neck jumper.

Hair in bunches. This is where she lived. Curtains have been pulled across the main front window, salmon coloured with a sort of frill at the edges, so none of us can see in. I wonder what the house is like inside, whether it has changed much from when the girl walked out one day to play on the swings, never reappeared. I hover at the back of the crowd, grass stains on my coat from a morning spent at the cemetery visiting Granny Pound. Amongst other things. The absence of something, that is what I'm thinking about. How sometimes knowing nothing is so much worse than learning the truth.

As I try to decide whether to stay, or come back another day, a commotion starts up. The cluster of journalists and bystanders begins to part as though Moses has thrust his staff into their midst. It was Granny Pound who taught me about Moses. She thought I'd be interested in the baby from the bullrushes. That and an eye for an eye, of course.

The crowd parts and being a giantess proves useful for once as I see two police officers proceeding through the scrum. I begin to sweat beneath my coat. There is a male officer using his arm to keep back the crowd. But also a young woman, the same officer who was searching the skip at the boarding house yesterday afternoon. As I spot her, goosepimples rise like a tiny mountain range across my skin. Is she following me? Or am I following her?

Before I have time to move away, the journalists begin with their shouts:

Is it her?

Have you found her?

Pushing and jostling in an attempt to get close. I get a brief glimpse of the police officer's face as she brushes past. She is scowling. She is thin. She's sort of like the girl I watch in the tenement opposite our flat when I wake in the night, face a green pool. I wonder what it is this police officer is going to impart to the mother inside. That at last the wait is over, her daughter's coming home. But how does she know?

The blood in my wrist beats a wild pulse as I clasp the bone on its chain tight in my fist. I wonder about sliding into the house in this police officer's wake, offering to make tea and biscuits while she imparts her news. I've discovered that being my size makes for invisibility at times, nobody bothering to look at me properly after that initial glance. Apart from Sasha, of course. Right from the beginning she looked me straight in the eye. But what would I say once I got inside? Once I stood face to face with a mother who has lost her child, just like my mother lost me? Your daughter is hiding in Isabella Dawson's boarding house, she's been there all along?

The police officers reach the front gate, the scrum pushing forwards as though to pin them in. I stand still, wait to see what might happen. As she turns to shut the gate the police officer pauses for a moment, glances over the crowd and looks straight at me. We stare at each other and I feel stripped bare, not just my feet this time, but every single inch of flesh and bone. Then she turns away and I step back as though I am nothing but a rubbernecker after all.

As I hurry along the road towards the boarding house, I find myself re-tracing the steps of a dead girl: down the street to the play park, along the promenade, round the corner to a secret garden, the perfect place to lure a child.

Everyone here wants a piece of this girl, one way or another, that is what I'm thinking. Whereas I already have one. But how to repatriate a daughter when all you have to offer is a tiny knucklebone.

Twenty-Four

The thing is, I am a thief. That is the reality. A locket. A lighter. Even the imprint of a dead girl's mouth. Not just recently, in and out of dead people's belongings. I have been stealing for all of my life.

I used to thieve coins from Granny Pound's purse. Ten and twenty pences, slid from its fat insides when she wasn't looking. I would take them to the chip shop and its bubblegum machine, one twist of the knob and a handful of sweeties in bright yellows and greens. I liked the way the colours stained my palm, inviting me to lick it. Also how I could chew the gum one day, then stick a wad of it onto the underside of the bunk-bed frame, chew it again the next. I've always been good at saving things.

Granny Pound caught me, of course. She knew everything that was going on in her house, even when she couldn't possibly have seen it. But she didn't insist on her money back. Instead she said:

Get yourself busy with this.

And took me to the utility shed out the back, with its washing machine and heaps of dirty laundry. Anything I found in the pockets I could keep, that was the deal. As long as I sorted it all. Into darks. Into coloureds. Into whites. I never looked back. Toffos and Hubba Bubba. Five-pence pieces. Single Pokémon cards bent at the edges. Crisp packets with salty crumbs lining the seams. I enjoyed licking those, too. Then later, fifty pences and pound coins. Single gold earrings. Once even a tooth. It's amazing what you can find if you look. Children carry everything in their pockets. What else do they have?

I kept the tooth with my other favourites in a lacquered trinket pot which Granny Pound gave me once for my birthday. She let me store the pot inside her glass-fronted display cabinet in the living room, a place where no one else was allowed to go. Once a month I took the pot out and counted its contents. Granny Pound would watch from her seat in the armchair, big plastic glasses balanced on her nose so she could read the *TV Times* and keep an eye on me at the same time.

It's important to have something of your own.

That was what she used to say.

After Granny Pound died, when I knew the house was going to be sold, I broke back in. Over the fence. Through the utility room. Into the living room and straight to where the display cabinet used to live. But it was gone. Everything in it gone, too. All Granny Pound's little china bits and bobs.

Dr Anju says it isn't a surprise. Everyone steals, one thing or another. She has stolen other people's lives and stored them in her glory hole, if her cupboard full of files is anything to go by. Granny Pound stole the truth about my mother, assuming she ever knew it, kept it to herself. Whoever cleared her house after she died stole my childhood. The tooth. The gold earring. A fifty-pence piece. The Company is stealing whoever Isabella Dawson used to be by junking and fumigating, clearing her stuff away. But I am the worst. I have stolen all that remains of a child from out of the boarding house. Kept it a secret, too.

Twenty-Five

We see everything. That was what I realized one week after I began with The Company. Faeces smeared across the bathroom tiles. Blood spread like a lagoon beneath the underlay. All the mess a person leaves behind. We arrive with all the paraphernalia we need to deal with the things people cannot sort themselves. Great vats of cleaning fluid. Brushes for scrubbing. Vacuums in three sizes ready to suck out the stink and cloy.

Don't ask.

That was what Monika said the first time, me standing in the doorway with my mop and bucket as though it was just another ordinary job, a bit of Flash here, the run of the vacuum there, a quick wipe with a cloth and pull the door to. Instead, it was the shape of a body marked out on a mattress, fluids seeped from every orifice to leave an outline where a person had once been. A girl, that's what Daphne said. Last seen curled on a bed with a needle piercing the soft cup of her elbow, hair the colour of summer hay. She left a pint of milk on the side in her kitchen, the lid still off. That is what I remember the most.

They hadn't found her for a week, maybe two, that was what Daphne said. Two weeks of glorious weather, July, and any grassy space crammed with bodies gone pink in odd patches. Two weeks of barbecues every evening, the whole city scented with smoke from those small foil trays. Two weeks of no curtains pulled across the girl's windows, the sun edging across her mattress and back again day after day.

I remember the sweat, my whole body damp beneath the unfamiliar suit, reeking like the corpse I was being paid to clean up after. Like the milk left standing on the counter. Monika offered to take the bedroom.

Seeing as it's your first.

No need for *Scissors, Paper, Stone* then. But despite the heat, the stink of it, the stench the girl had left behind, I didn't really mind. I entered covered from tip to toe – mask, gloves, hood – and tried to do her proud. I bundled away her sheets with their concentric rings in orange and brown. I removed all the drug paraphernalia so her parents wouldn't have to see. I peeled back the carpet and the underlay where it had been stained. I sprayed everything with industrial bleach. In the bathroom I emptied her cabinet, codeine to return to the pharmacist because the packet was new, lipstick into my caddy to take home because it was old. It wasn't until I was almost done that I found the locket, tucked inside an old powder compact that looked as though it belonged to someone who was long dead, too. I shook it out into my palm, saw the two birds kissing, couldn't resist. It reminded me of the utility room, of going through the pockets of the one hundred and three.

Afterwards, as I stripped off my mask, my gloves, my shoe covers, slipped the locket into a pocket of my own, I realized that I like to clean. Every single inch. I like to sweep and mop and fumigate. To wipe it up and spray it down. Clear it all away.

Twenty-Six

I slip through the back door of the boarding house to discover a home that is beginning to breathe again, all its ground-floor arteries freed from a lifetime of clog. Yesterday Pawel drove everything that wouldn't fit in the skip to the dump at Seafield. They call it a recycling centre now, Seafield. But even I know they won't be recycling anything much of Isabella Dawson. It must have taken years for her to get the ground floor into the state in which we found it. But we've only needed four days to clear everything away. All we have to tackle now is the upstairs. First floor. Second. Maybe even an attic. That might take some time.

I walk along the passage with its blue and red boats. Everywhere about me is the stillness of a house that's only been inhabited by the dead for two years now. A place heavy with absence, like a building abandoned due to illness or disaster. The hot sweep of scarlet fever. The bloody splatter of TB. I touch one gloved finger to the wall as I pass, leave a print in the dust. Some kind of trace.

The Turkish pattern stair carpet has worn bare on every tread. I skirt the thick drifts of sediment rolling on each step, make my way up. On the landing a painted china dog stands guard, even though every person he's ever known left long ago. The dog has a chip on its nose, an old injury.

He looks sad, as though he realizes his destination is Seafield unless one of the dealers decides to rescue him, find someone who will pay. I wonder about taking the dog for myself, bringing him home to guard the third-floor landing. Then I remember Sasha, the way she looked at the doll lying on our kitchen table. I survey the doors before me on the first floor. Five rooms and a back corridor, all waiting to be cleared. I am dressed for work. Gloves. Mask. Coverall. Also a caddy full of cleaning products hanging from my hand. But that is not why I am here. I am looking for the further remains of a child.

The first room I enter is a bathroom, narrow and high ceilinged, lino curled at the edges as though eventually it will roll in on itself. The room has a chill to it that reminds me of something, thin curtains and windows clouded with condensation, feet thudding across the landing. The cast-iron bath is awash with dead insects, an arid killing ground. I turn the tap. Nothing comes out other than a rasping sound. But somewhere I can hear it, water running and running until it spills over to flood the floor.

The sink is rimed with three or four milky tidelines as though the sea has ebbed and flowed through the drain leaving only its salt behind. Above it is a medicine cabinet layered with ancient paint. I open the cabinet to find a crepe bandage in a neat roll and a tube of TCP crusted about the screw cap. It reminds me of Granny Pound and her ministrations. A plaster on the knee. A spoonful of cough mixture. Dab of a kiss, all better now. There is also a small glass jar, label obscured by grease and time. I unscrew the lid, discover fingermarks in the salve. I peel off my glove, dip my fingers in. A heady scent releases into the air, lilies of the valley. I rub the cream into my knuckles, imagine Isabella Dawson doing the same.

Next along the corridor are three bedrooms fitted with Chubb locks, for students and DSS, emergency B & B. None of them are secured. I enter each with a strange sense of trepidation, as though I might swing the doors and find myself on the other side. A girl standing in the middle of the floor wearing nothing but a red swimsuit with a white, pleated skirt. But the rooms are ordinary and plain. Rose-patterned wallpaper in one, scuffed and scratched. A bedframe in another, piled high with what look like old curtains. Heaps of clothes as though gathered for a jumble sale. None of the rooms have much by way of furniture. Probably gravitated to the pile that blocked the front door, never made it upstairs again.

At the end of the landing is a sort of crossroads. A corridor on my right leads towards the back of the house, walls painted over with old gloss. There is another door at the far end, shut tight. Another floor above, perhaps. Maybe even an attic hidden beneath the roof. But first, opposite me, at the front, is a room from which an old lady was carried out, feet first, only a few days before. If what Daphne says is correct. As I approach Isabella Dawson's bedroom, I'm aware of blood jumping in my wrist, sweat like oil on my fingertips inside my gloves at the thought of what treasure I might find. Unlike the other doors, this one stands half open as though it has been waiting for me to arrive. I hesitate, catch the sudden patter of footsteps overhead, like a child running from room to room on the floor above. Then I hear it, the whisper of an ocean, and push the door open to see what I can see.

Twenty-Seven

Unlike Isabella Dawson, Granny Pound never left a mess behind when she died. She just sat down in her chair one evening to watch *Coronation Street* and never got up again.

Heart attack.

That was what the paramedics said. Nothing to be done. It was me who found her. Cold and stiff like the lino in Isabella Dawson's first-floor bathroom, *TV Times* still in her grip. I came down early in the morning for breakfast and thought she had slept in her chair all night. Until I touched her hand. Sasha's hands are always warm, but Granny Pound's felt as though she'd spent a lifetime in her freezer. I knew at once what it meant. Granny Pound had risen, like she'd always said she would. But I made sure to open the window anyway, just in case. Didn't want her to be stuck somewhere she wouldn't want to stay.

Sometimes I wonder if my mother has risen, climbed out of wherever she was laid and shot into the sky. Granny Pound used to say that it depended on what you'd done when you were alive, whether you got to rise or not. But Dr Anju says that is nonsense. Like her, I don't believe in God, but I believe in Granny Pound. Either way, there's something about being saved that never leaves you, that is what I've learned. Granny Pound saved me, like Jesus saved her. But I have no idea if anyone saved my mother, before they let her fall.

I checked Granny Pound's pulse several times before the paramedics arrived. Just in case. But there was no doubting what had happened, so I sat on the rug by her feet, held on to her hand. I was trying to make up for the fact that none of us were with her when finally she passed. But later I wondered if perhaps that was what she had wanted, to be on her own. Away from the hustle and bustle of the one hundred and three. Not everyone wants to depart with a crowd around their bed, that is what I've learned by working for The Company. Some people are happy to slip away when everyone they love is in the other room.

Granny Pound was buried. She had it planned out long before she left us, used to pay in every week. She would have enjoyed her funeral. There was a lot of singing, a lot of exhortation. Lamenting too, of course. What I remember most is standing with my toes almost over the lip of the pit crying like there would be no tomorrow, even though tomorrow always comes. At least there was a grave to stand over. I have no idea where they buried my mother. Or whether they burned her instead. I wonder sometimes, as I visit Granny Pound in the cemetery, whether it makes a difference to the chance of resurrection. Buried or burned. On the other hand, it could be like Dr Anju says. Once you're dead you're dead.

Isabella Dawson was on her own, as far as we know. Lay down in her bed two years ago or so, didn't get up again. Unless she had a child with her, of course, hidden somewhere in her bedroom, to make up for the one she never had herself. I'm hoping that if I search hard enough I will find the rest of that girl so that she can be laid to rest, too. Some teeth, perhaps. The joints of her toes. That way I can return her to her mother, like Moses returned to his mother, in a roundabout sort of way. It won't be what the girl's mother has been hoping for all these years – a parcel of bones rather than a living, breathing child. But it will be something. And as Granny Pound used to say:

Something's better than nothing.

Besides, if a girl who's been lost for more than twenty years can rise again, perhaps I can, too.

Twenty-Eight

The carpet in Isabella Dawson's bedroom is grey, a thin tread worn almost to nothing. A faint path weaves its way from the door to the bed, from the bed to the window, then back. I know what it is. A dead woman's last journey, before she lay down.

I follow the path to the window with its cheap cotton curtains in a faded floral pattern, useless for keeping out the cold. There are fingermarks on the sash where Isabella Dawson must have stood to gaze over the sea. I look out across a front garden grown wild, the warm tarmac of the promenade, wind whipping along the beach. Then at the sea, rolling in and rolling out, nothing left on the sand but a thin line of froth. Like the milk I used to drink for breakfast, that is what I am thinking, cool in my throat. A needle of cold air penetrates the flimsy fabric of my coverall suit at my thigh. The window is open, nothing more than a sliver. Still, Daphne will not be happy, anyone might have got in. But I am smiling beneath my mask as I push the sash down. Even though she was on her own when it happened, Isabella Dawson had the chance to rise, too.

I turn my back on the view to survey the room, its clutter and mess. It is scattered with paperback books come unglued at the spines. Soft mounds of abandoned clothes. A chair (what remains of it), upholstery worn to threads.

Everywhere there is evidence of moths eating and mould growing, of damp that's got in and stayed. The room smells faintly of carbolic, as though Isabella Dawson scrubbed herself with it every night before she went to bed. Beneath that, a subtle whiff of something else. Face powder, maybe. The fragile scent of a child. Or a corpse left lying for two years and counting, bluebottles long since laid and hatched.

The covers on the bed are heavy, almost black, turned aside as though someone has just got up to go to the bathroom with its cold lino, will return at any second demanding:

What are you doing in my room?

Looking, I think. Looking.

At the shallow indent in the mattress. At the stains on the pillow. At an empty glass from which the water has evaporated. I follow the path to the bedside, touch a finger to the tumbler, ghost of a mouth still lingering on the rim.

Next to the bed a pair of brown lace-ups have been discarded on the floor. They are stiff with age and salt, tongues curled, like Isabella Dawson waiting here for somebody to come. Still, I measure my foot to them, just in case. I scan the room for bibles or crucifixes, prayer cards slipped between the pages of a book. Anything that might help Sasha and the Office for Lost People decide which method of disposal will need to employed. Burying. Or burning. Also, evidence of remorse. But there is nothing to suggest Isabella Dawson had any sort of regrets. Or even a faith. Other than hoarding, of course. A very particular kind of religion, if what Dr Anju says is correct.

The chest of drawers next to the bed is a solid piece of furniture, the bloom on the wood dimmed now, unpolished for years. I take a cloth from my caddy, spray on some Pledge. Then I give each of the wooden handles a quick rub so that I can say I was working when, in fact, I'm doing something else. The top of the chest of drawers has been used as a dressing table, face powder speckling the surface, a hairbrush abandoned with most of its bristles missing. Also a few dead bluebottles, crooked legs pointing up.

I slide open one of the top drawers, find nylon tights balled and sticking to each other, flannel nightgowns and a muddle of underwear. As I empty everything out, tossing it on the floor to add to the general mess, I discover that each of the drawers has been lined with off-cuts of wallpaper from elsewhere in the house. I recognize the blue and red boats from the back corridor. The heavy flock from the hall. A rose pattern from one of the bedrooms on this landing. Also something that I haven't come across yet – pale blue background dotted with small knots of strawberries in a repeating pattern. It is pretty. The kind of thing a child might choose for their room.

The bottom drawer is heavy, tilting as I tug it open. Inside is layer upon layer of tissue paper scented with cloves. I rummage amongst the paper, pull something out. Another ladies' undergarment, pale green and slippery. I hold it to the light, see the shape of a woman's body unfurl, slender breasts and hips, suspenders dangling. It is a corselet, lace along the trim. I hold it against my body, smooth it against my coverall suit. The corselet is the kind of thing I would like to wear if I was small enough. But it seems an odd thing for Isabella Dawson to own, given the rest. Wool vests and bed socks, American Tan tights.

But who knows what goes on beneath a person's clothes, that is what I know. I trace a finger along the corselet's stitching, all its narrow seams. I am hoping for treasure. A tiny spike of rib, perhaps. A metatarsal. But there are no bones sewn in here to keep a body upright. Not whale. Not even human. Nothing other than elastic that is as taut as it must have been when the corselet was new. Reluctantly, I fold the undergarment, to add to the rest of the pile destined for Seafield. It's then that I sense it – somebody else inside the house.

Twenty-Nine

You only need to have cleaned a few dead people's houses to know the difference between an empty space and one that is inhabited by someone who still knows how to breathe. I am highly attuned to imperceptible shifts in atmosphere. It is a skill I've had ever since I was a child. Also finding a place to hide.

Come now, Granny Pound used to say when I shrank into whatever hole I could find at the knowledge that somewhere in the house a fight was about to break out. Her pantry with its tins of baked beans. The slender gap in the utility room between the dryer and the washing machine. Rolling in the dust under the bunk beds. She would search me out, unwind me from the living-room curtains where I'd secreted myself in the nap.

No need to hide, worse things might happen.

Except even then I knew that they probably already had.

That is why I'm so good at this job. The mask. The gloves. The coverall suit. Hiding is what I've spent my whole life doing. It's kept me safe so far.

This time I do it in Isabella Dawson's wardrobe, two doors and an interior stuffed with blouses stained at the collar, crumpled summer dresses and wool skirts. I stumble on a mishmash of discarded shoes as I open both doors, step inside. My attempt is clumsy. The hinges creak, the wardrobe lurches. But once I am in, I am in. There is never any going back.

In the dark, doors pulled closed behind me, I try to get my bearings. I have a legitimate reason to be in the boarding house, but after fingering Isabella Dawson's remains in pursuit of her secrets, I can't shake the feeling that I am the one who is trespassing, rather than the person manoeuvring downstairs. I touch the inside of the wooden doors, feel the rise of the grain beneath my fingertips. There is the sudden stink of camphor in my nostrils as I get entangled in a dress covered in a pattern of yellow roses, the sort of thing a woman might wear to play the piano while her guests eat high tea off willow-pattern plates. Beneath my coverall suit my skin begins to itch, foetid air closing in. I remind myself to *Breathe, Essie. Breathe*, try not to gag behind my mask.

The space is narrower than I imagined. Or I am bigger. It is hard to tell which. All about me is the soft shift and rustle of a dead woman's clothes. It's a bit like standing in a coffin, that is what I'm thinking. Like Granny Pound, laid out on her coloured-satin ruff. I crouch to try and keep myself small, breathing camphor, wait for my eyes to adjust to the gloom. As they do, I realize there is writing on the inside of the door:

Miss M stinks

Like a child has been here, left her mark.

I lift a cramped finger to touch the pen mark, think of the postcard Monika found in the porch the first day we arrived. *Will see you on the 12th. Save the room.* Did she mean this one? Or is there somewhere else in the boarding house that I haven't been yet? A room with pale blue wallpaper crisscrossed with a pattern of strawberries. The kind of room a child might want. I think of the door at the end of the back corridor, where it might lead. That is when I hear it. Footsteps on the landing. Someone coming my way.

I try to hold my breath. But there is a roaring in my head, so loud I'm certain somebody must hear. I am suddenly as cold as Granny Pound's hand, as though I am the one who's spent a lifetime in the freezer. If I stare through the slit where the wardrobe doors meet, I know I will see it. The dark mouth of the room opposite. The blood on the floor. Then the sudden glitter as the blade . . .

I close my eyes. Someone is breathing right outside my hiding place. I try to think of milk cool in my throat, warm sand on my calves. Somebody is calling to me:

Essie!

As I run towards the water.

Then I open them again.

She is standing in the middle of Isabella Dawson's bedroom. A woman wearing a mask, like I am wearing a mask. A woman wearing gloves, like I am wearing gloves. Nothing to see but her eyes. I stare at her and she stares at me. This is the dream, I think. This is the dream.

Thirty

The thing is, I do not exist. I found out this morning. Sasha on her way to U.H. Daphne and the crew to a road traffic accident on the bypass. Me heading into town with a bone about my neck. Light slanted across grey stone, the sky was the colour of the palest bird's egg, flags fluttered in the breeze. Mornings in Edinburgh are the most beautiful time of day. Except when they are not.

I made the appointment after Dr Anju presented me with her files. Sasha smoothed the way. A favour, that was what she called it. The Edinburgh Way of getting things done. I walked from our flat. Up the Walk. Down the back of the railway station. Under the bridge where the pigeons roost and the pavement is splattered with droppings that require a specialist like me to remove. It was several months since I had been that far into the heart of the city and it felt strange, as though I didn't really belong. Then again, nobody real lives in the centre of Edinburgh anymore. It's been given over to the tourists who wash up and down the High Street taking in the spires and the castle, before washing away. What the visitors don't realize, is how close they are to the mortuary, to the Sheriff's Court, to all the bad things that can happen when you're looking the wrong way. It should have been my natural habitat. But people like me never live anywhere near the middle of things. We live on the periphery, in our own little centrifuge of chaos. Not anywhere the tourists might want to go.

The council offices glinted in the sunlight as I approached. The promise of treasure within, perhaps. Or nothing more than an eye for an eye to warn me off. The security guard didn't bother to check my credentials. I took the lift to the relevant floor, rubbed my fingerprint from the button before I stepped out. It is an instinct I was born with – covering my tracks. But I didn't turn right towards the Office for Lost People. Instead I went left.

The social worker kept me waiting. I sat on my hands on the chair outside her office, heavy legs jiggling till I was all over sweat. Around me was the familiar rattle and hum of the place I used to clean before I specialized in dead bodies. All those carpet tiles I once vacuumed back and forth, back and forth. By the time the social worker called my name, my heel had practically hammered a hole into the one beneath my seat.

'Hazel,' said the social worker as she ushered me inside. 'Hazel Abebe.'

I have been in lots of social workers' offices over the years, too many to count. But never this one. I had avoided it since I moved to Edinburgh from the periphery. Like the Egyptians tried to avoid the plagues called in by Moses. Frogs. Locusts. Fire. Not forgetting blood, of course. But just as there was no escape for the Egyptians, there could be no escape for me.

Hazel settled herself on the far side of her desk, leaving me marooned with my back to the door. I took the chair opposite and it sank almost to the floor with my weight. I waited for Hazel to begin with the usual:

What has brought you here today, Essie?

Thought of what I might reply.

The sea. The sun. The decay. The fact that the bones of my past lie all around if only I care to look. Or because my life is a sort of patchwork, a sort of jigsaw puzzle, without the picture on the box.

But Hazel didn't ask that, because she already knew. Instead, she leaned back in her chair, the full tilt of it, surveyed the desk in front. The desk was covered in files. Lever arch files and box files. Files in coloured cardboard wallets and wrap-around brown folders like the one Margaret Penny of the Office for Lost People carries tucked beneath her arm. The whole spread of it reminded me of Dr Anju and the cupboard beneath her stairs.

Hazel saw me looking. 'So you've come to see me today to discuss your file, Essie.'

Except, I never asked her to call me that. Like all the rest, she just did. I nodded, then clarified.

'To take it away.'

Hazel touched a hand to her neck.

'The thing is, Essie . . .'

Hazel's neck was a beautiful thing, her nails manicured and sleek. I thought of my own, nibbled to the quick. Then of Isabella Dawson. Black hands. Black feet. Rotting somewhere in her coffin, waiting for the funeral to begin. I resisted the urge to chew at my fingernails, waited to see what Hazel might say next. To my disappointment, she repeated herself.

'The thing is, Essie . . .'

The thing is, Hazel was nervous. I could see that in the way she fiddled with the coloured beads about her neck.

In the way she wouldn't look me in the face, though I was staring straight at her. Instead, the beads went *clack clack* and her eyes kept flicking to a brown folder that had taken centre stage on her desk. The file was fat. Much fatter than I expected. Almost as fat as me. I felt the pulse quicken in my wrist. All the other files on Hazel's desk had been moved to make space for this one, as though it might be contagious. It was my file. There was no doubt about that.

I waited for Hazel to slide my file across her desk, greedy eyes eating the contents already. I like to eat. And eat. And eat. Don't even regurgitate afterwards like all the other women I've ever known. But Hazel did not. Instead, she put one hand on the top of the file, as though to hold it down.

'The thing is, Essie,' she said, a sudden spring forward in her chair. 'There are things in your file that you might find upsetting. That we have to clear with other people first.'

'Sorry?'

'Things we need to discuss in advance, that require another meeting.'

I felt sweat gather between my thighs, the slipperiness of hot skin.

'What meeting?' I said. 'This is the meeting.'

'The thing is . . .'

The thing is, Hazel was not going to give me my file, that was what I knew. Even though I was asking politely. Even though it was sitting on the table in front of us. Even though it contained my life, not hers. She was going to turn out just like everyone else I had ever asked, liked to keep my secrets to themselves.

I had warned Sasha before:

They won't give it to me.

She had insisted:

It's your file, isn't it? You have the right.

But I know already, life is never as simple as that.

Hazel began to talk again and I looked at her mouth opening and closing as she explained something about the contents of my file. I thought about opening and closing my mouth too.

Saying, *Give it to me.*

Saying, *It's mine, not yours.*

Saying, *Fuck off, you bitch.*

But I didn't, because that was what I used to do before Granny Pound taught me to keep my mouth shut.

I stared at the file in front of us, burning it with my eyes as though I might be able to see right through to what lay beneath. Chew it up. Swallow it whole, like Jonah inside his whale. I was hidden somewhere between those brown covers, that was what I was thinking. Everything I had ever been, just waiting to spew. Then I realized Hazel had stopped speaking, was sliding the file across the desk towards me.

Blood beat in my temples at the thought of everything that could be revealed. Granny Pound sitting in her armchair circling the *TV Times*. A child lying at her feet nibbling the edges of a drawing. A mother's laugh. Her hair. Her smile. Her decapitation. Blood on the floor of a kitchen. The glitter of a blade. Once I opened the file I would see it all:

An eye for an eye

Everything that had been written. Everything that had

been said. Also a girl wearing a red swimsuit, running on the sand. Perhaps it might be best to leave her there, I thought. My former self, hidden in the dark. Then I heard Granny Pound saying it, as she unwound me from the living-room curtains:

Come on now, Essie. Come on.

So I did.

The file began with my name, ESSIE. A good start. But straight away I could see that something wasn't right. For the rest had been eliminated, my surname hidden beneath a thick line of black. I frowned, scanned the rest of the details on the first page looking for other names, addresses. The personal things. But they had been eliminated too, nothing but a page of writing crossed out at every turn.

Hazel sat in her chair across the other side of the desk, beads silent, face impassive, as I stared at the paper in front of me. My hands were trembling as I pinched the corner of the first page, turned it to look at the next. But it didn't make any difference. The contents of my life were nothing but a sea of black between two brown covers. My file had been redacted. And me, too.

Thirty-One

My mother doesn't exist other than inside my head. I learned that long ago, should have known that it would never change. The sort of accident no one comes back from, that was what Granny Pound said. I've imagined everything over the years. Burning. Crushing. Decapitation. And still she comes up smiling like the flowers along the bottom of a page. The funny thing is, I never think about my father, that he must have been out there somewhere all this time, too.

The cemetery at Seafield was quiet by the time I made my way from the council offices in town, to the periphery where I belong. I headed towards Portobello on the bus, nothing left to do but clear the side return of Isabella Dawson's boarding house. But as the cemetery approached, I got off. Granny Pound lives in Seafield. Not recycled, just buried in the earth.

When I arrived the cemetery was empty apart from a dog walker sauntering through. A small terrier tugged on its lead, sniffing at where a dead person's feet must be, the remains of their heart. I lurked amongst the graves waiting for the dog and its owner to move on. We are old friends now, me and the more elderly residents of this cemetery. Been visiting for almost fifteen years.

Granny Pound always knew she would leave me before I was ready. She tried to prepare me, but who can be ready for that? Now I have grown up, become large and cumbersome, while Granny Pound has started to sink. Into the grass. Into the leaves. As though she really has escaped, risen into the sky, left nothing but her shape behind. I came to stand at the place where the only woman who ever looked out for me lies in her repose. I thought of her beneath my feet, stretched in her coffin on that satin ruff. Her leg bones. Her arms. The curve of her skull. What was left of her other than whatever I remembered? That was what I was thinking. But I already knew the answer. And it would never be enough.

The day had turned cool after a lovely morning. Autumn was coming to Edinburgh, the world was on the turn. I lay across all that remained of Granny Pound, my back to the earth, my face to the sky. In my pocket was a plastic doll with her hair in disarray. A bone about my neck. I touched the little knuckle, sharp edge pricking at my throat. I must return her to her mother, that was what I thought. As I would like to have been returned, too.

For a moment I put myself back there – in Granny Pound's living room, lying on her rug. The coal-effect fire rotated in a steady whirr of red and black. I pushed a crayon into paper. She circled her programmes with her biro. There was a muggy damp in the air from the boiling of the kettle. Granny Pound loved me, that was what I knew. The only real mother I ever had. But she is gone now.

The thing is, I have been annihilated. Like the people I clean up after, all they ever were thrown onto a junk heap at Seafield as though into a grave. Like Granny Pound, sunk now into the earth. Like a girl who disappeared from a play park, never did return home. I'd opened my file expecting to find all the answers, discovered that everything Granny Pound had told me was correct. I am nothing more than thick lines of black running through every piece of information that might prove useful. The name they once called me. My original address. What they called my father. My mother. Or anyone else who knew me before I was five years old. All I have left from before is a photograph of a girl on a beach wearing a red swimsuit with a white, pleated skirt, jelly sandals and sand in her hair. And the dream, of course.

Thirty-Two

It begins like this. In the dark . . . In a cupboard in the hall . . . In a bedroom wound inside the curtains . . . No. It begins in a bathroom, sink with milky tidelines and a cast-iron bath. Water runs from the taps as though it will never end. A thousand insects float on the surface – dead moths and flies with crooked legs. A centipede drifts in a lazy circle. Downstairs angry voices rise, a baby calls and doesn't stop. Someone is whispering to me:

Run, Essie. Run.

Cool air on hot legs, warm tarmac and salt on the skin. But instead I push myself to the back of the wardrobe. Into the dust beneath a bed. The hidey-hole under the stairs.

In the hiding place it is dark, no light but whatever filters through the keyhole. I press my eye to the hole, feel its imprint on my skin. There is the hall with its scratchy carpet and crayon marks on the walls. Beyond that the black mouth to the kitchen where something spreads and spreads across the floor. I can hear a baby crying, nobody to make it stop. All around me is the darkness, and the sound of someone breathing, a shallow rush of air. The breathing is so quick it's like a creature that's been running, or playing hopscotch on the beach. I put my hands over my ears and the sound gets louder, like the sea in a shell:

snail

razor

limpet

Roaring and rising, waiting to swamp me. Until I realize – the breathing is me. I try to close my mouth as I've been told, pinch my lips together like the little gold kiss on the top of Mummy's purse. I press my hand against my mouth, damp on my palm, like the boys are damp when they come out from their bath.

But I cannot stop the push of it in my throat, the burn building in my chest. In the kitchen, somebody is calling:

Essie. Where are you, Essie?

But I know if I make a noise, they will find me and the game will be over, a hand on my neck. I stand still, like a statue, try to keep myself small like I've been taught. Outside a shape looms in the kitchen. Inside the dark is like the curtain I wrap myself in, turning and turning until my body is entwined, everything outside muffled, inside the stink of camphor in my nostrils. I lift a hand before my face but I cannot see it. Somewhere a thread of cold air leaks in. I try to stay quiet, like a mouse curled inside a pocket. But I cannot stop my breathing. In and out and in and out. Until I realize, the breathing is not just inside, but outside, too. Somebody standing just beyond the door.

The knot in my chest tightens like a tourniquet. My heart flays my insides. Across the hall in the kitchen there is the sudden glitter of a blade . . . I close my eyes, pray like I've been taught:

An eye for an eye

Open them again to see a woman staring back. She is wearing a mask, her hair covered by a hood, nothing to see but her eyes. Her whole body is covered in something white, too, as though she must be a ghost. I watch as she peers towards the hidey-hole, as though she knows there is something trapped behind the door. She reaches with her hand, says:

Who's there?

Then there is another voice:

Essie?

Daphne, my saviour.

I close my eyes, let out a breath. When I open them again the other woman is gone and I am staring into Isabella Dawson's empty bedroom, nothing to see but a window. And beyond that the beach. The sea.

Thirty-Three

I wake to discover I am still inside Isabella Dawson's wardrobe, huddled like a baby amongst the muddle of shoes on the floor. I emerge to find the day almost over, nothing left but a glorious streak of orange stretching above the Firth. The boarding house is silent, nobody inside but me. Also a lost girl's knucklebone nestled at my throat.

I step onto Isabella Dawson's bedroom carpet, follow the path to the door. On the landing I stare over the banister into the hall below. It is empty, a cathedral of space compared to when I first entered, swallowed by the dark like Jonah inside the whale. Now the ground floor of the house is clear from end to end, the last of the sunlight filtering through the smoked-glass panel towards the passageway with its blue and red boats. I am still wearing my camouflage – my coverall suit, my mask, my hood, my gloves. But it is as though I have been regurgitated, made it to the beach at last.

Downstairs, Isabella Dawson's kitchen is an empty square, nothing left but an earthenware sink. Still, I can see it as I stand with my hand on the doorframe. Cereal bowls tipped over on the table. A dish smashed into the sink. In one corner, my mother. In the other corner, my father. The blood upon the floor. Something happened to me in a kitchen, a long, long time ago.

In the hall, I imagine myself as a small child on the far side of the water-closet door. It is dark. So dark I can almost touch it. I am hiding, that is what I know. Inside the closet, my breathing is loud, but I am trying to stay quiet, so that nobody will hear.

Upstairs, back on the first-floor landing, I stand at the crossroads. I can see the dog still guarding the top of the stairs. There is the sound of water running, over and over, as it trickles from the bath. Someone is waiting for me in the bathroom, but I must not go in there. I must find the rest of the girl instead.

I touch the bone at my neck, think of Isabella Dawson and what she might have hidden. Of how we have eradicated her by tossing everything she owned onto a rubbish heap. Of how she tried to eradicate herself beneath the huge mound, when all the time her rubbish was shouting, I am still here. There is something in the house that hasn't been thrown away yet, though. I can smell it. Something rotten seeping through the ceiling from the floor above.

The door at the end of the back corridor is shut tight. But it isn't locked. I don't need to use my key. The door opens onto a staircase that leads to the second floor of the house. The steps are bare, not even a carpet worn to almost nothing, gateway to a space in Isabella Dawson's boarding house that doesn't need clearing because it was emptied a long time before, perhaps. The stairs creak as I climb, as though no one has used them for years. At the top I discover a small landing, drab walls, distemper rather than emulsion, cobwebs falling from the corners. Off the landing is a bathroom with a china bowl on a stand. A thick crack runs from the lip of the bowl to the base, a dried flannel hanging from its edge. The bathroom is cold, a chill to it that is familiar. Much colder than the rest of the house.

The only other room on this floor is a single bedroom. I step through the door to the crack of a floorboard sharp in the stillness. The hairs on my arms rise beneath my suit, skin chafing against the weave, as though I know someone is waiting here to greet me. Above me, the ceiling is bowed, as though it might fall at any moment; the wallpaper painted over and stained to match the underlying odour of stale nicotine. But something tells me. I *scratch scratch scratch* with my glove at a patch by the light switch. It doesn't take long for them to appear. Clumps of strawberries against a pale blue background. The kind of thing a child might choose.

The orphan left here is a narrow bed frame, coiled springs naked without their mattress. It reminds me of a hospital bed, or something from a sanatorium. The kind of place little girls used to be sent when they were convalescing. Or older ones when they wouldn't behave. Another form of eradication, something I know all about.

In one corner of the room, there is a narrow door that looks as though it must be a linen press. Next to it a mirror propped against the wall, spotting about its edges. Unlike the bedrooms downstairs, the floorboards here are exposed, full of knots and scars. Cigarette burns dot the surface. I follow the constellation to the window, find myself staring over the side return. It is still choked with rubbish, an old washing line snaking over the moss. The scent of damp rises towards me, the faint odour of a waste pipe that has got blocked somewhere along the way and never been cleared. I look out over the chimney pots and backyards of Portobello, in the opposite direction from the sea. There is nothing here, that is what I'm thinking. It's then that I turn, see the house.

Thirty-Four

I am not a well girl. They have told me this. And I know that they were right once. But I am well now.

This is what I remember:

Nights spent whirling and laughing, drinking shot after shot mixed with anything sweet I could get my hands on to make the darkness go away.

Climbing out of one window after another when they tried to lock me in.

Cleaning offices with a hangover, the slow push pull of a vacuum over the same strip of carpet tiles.

Threatening to jump.

They sent me to a hospital once, somewhere I spent all day watching TV. I'd have watched it all night, if they'd let me. It reminded me of Granny Pound. I remember chalky tablets at bedtime and gelatine-coated ones in the mornings that stuck in the throat. Some blue. Some white. Like the buttons on a swimsuit. I guzzled the tablets, whatever I was offered, swallowed them down with an eager swill of water like Jonah slipping into the whale. I liked the haze, the fact that I couldn't remember what day it was, what year. It's only recently, since I met Sasha, since I met Daphne, since I met Dr Anju, that I've begun to try and keep track.

There was one time, between my daily appointment with the tablets, when the television blinked off and wouldn't come back. I tried it every way. Plugging and unplugging. Thumping and shaking. Even a kick. But it wouldn't re-start, whatever I did. I went to find someone to fix it, but the nurses' station was empty, the corridor bare. I kept walking till I came across a room that was open, turned the handle, went in. That was where I saw them. A mother. A father. A girl. And a boy.

They were jumbled in a box, as though they were waiting for someone to come along and play. I stared at the little family – their hair made of wool, their clothes that came on and off, their soft malleable limbs. The table they were lying on was low, like a child might sit at. On the table was a house.

I crouched before the house and stared in as though I was a child myself. There was a kitchen with a stove. And a living room with a sofa. A bathroom with a sink. I picked up the boy and put him in the bathroom. I picked up the mother and put her by the stove. I picked up the father and put him at the kitchen table. I picked up the girl and—

'What are you doing?'

I dropped the girl and she fell to the floor. I put my foot over her.

'Nothing.'

The woman had a look on her face like, *I'll tell on you.* She stood with her arm stiff, holding the door open, inviting me to leave. I didn't argue. I went out with my face averted so she wouldn't see me close. She closed the door after me and I walked back along the corridor to find the television working again, so I settled into my usual chair. It was only later, in my bed, that I un-rolled the girl from the hem of my T-shirt. All the time I stayed in that hospital I kept the girl beneath my pillow so I could talk to her at night. But somehow, just like me, she got lost along the way.

Thirty-Five

This house has been cut to child size, too. It has three storeys like the boarding house – ground floor, first floor, attic – a house within a house. I squat and stare in like I stare into my neighbours' flats across the street at night: the eye at the door.

The house is divided into four squares, in between them a staircase, above that an attic. On the ground floor, to the right, is a room with a small sofa and a tall clock leaning against the wall. To the left is a kitchen with a table in the centre, on it a plastic ham with a tiny carving knife alongside. There are three chairs and a stove with little saucepans balanced on the hotplate. One of the pans has been tipped over. It reminds me of my dream.

Upstairs are two bedrooms, one with matching single beds covered in stiff little cloths. Another with a double bed and a window with tiny curtains pulled closed. I stare at the double bed as though to pull aside the scrap of patterned cotton, reveal who is sleeping there. But something stops me. Between the bedrooms, carved from the landing, is a tiny bathroom with a matching three-piece suite – small white toilet, small white sink, small white bath. Then there is the empty attic above.

There are no inhabitants of this house that I can see. I bend my head to look further, peering into the bedrooms with their small squares of leftover carpet, thinking of the girl that I lost, her straggle of wool hair. Where would I place her? I think. I can see that each of the rooms has been decorated with off-cuts of wallpaper. There are the boats and the flock and the roses, but this time in a different order. The boats are in one of the bedrooms. The flock in the kitchen. The roses in the parlour. And the strawberries are in the attic, where a child might play.

I gaze into the attic of the doll's house, then up at the bowed ceiling. After that towards the narrow door in the corner of the room. I take the plastic doll from my pocket, smooth her hair, bend her legs at the knees, sit her at the table in the kitchen next to the ham and the miniature carving knife. Then I slide out my photograph of a child on a beach, leave that in the house, too.

Thirty-Six

My mind sometimes gets in the way of everything else. If I could only switch it off, I would be fine. But I've spent my whole life attempting that and it hasn't worked so far.

After they let me out of the hospital I tried working with families for a while – a mother, a father, a boy, a girl. I cleaned their bathrooms and tidied after their children so as always to have someone around. But sometimes they liked to talk, to make conversation, asking me questions like:

Where was I from?

What did I do before this?

Did I have any family?

I think they were just trying to make conversation. But I didn't have any of the answers they needed. So I became a liar instead. There's only so much lying you can do, before it catches up.

So then I started cleaning offices, everyone left for the day and the constant push, pull over the carpet tiles to keep my mind occupied. But it got so I did it without thinking about what I was doing, meaning I could think about everything else instead. Over and over in my head like the push, pull of the vacuum. The father. The mother. The girl. The boy.

The dead are so much easier to work with, that is what I've learned. They can't trouble me with questions or complaints as I sort through their muck. Suicides and drug deaths, that is my life now. People found lying in their beds, or sitting in front of their television sets, whatever programme they were watching playing into the void. My world is accidents just waiting to happen. Car crashes. Sometimes even murder. With a hammer. Or tights around the neck. Or a knife that glitters . . . All of these have happened in Edinburgh. A very safe city, tourists washing in and washing out.

Whatever it is, I come along after the event, when all that's left is fingerprint dust scattered across the doorframe, a half-pint of milk grown sour on the side. I crunch my way across the bluebottles, set about my task. Top down, cornice to skirting, skirting to cornice, annihilating everything that has gone before so I don't have to think about it. Where I come from. What happened to my family. What I might have done. Instead, it is dusting. And mopping. And fumigating. Clearing it all away.

It's worked so far.

But now, just like Granny Pound, something is rising. Outside I might be a giant, looming over whomever I stand next to, stinking of stale sweat and hair that hasn't been washed for a week. But inside I am a butterfly cocooned in its fragile chrysalis. A grub just waiting to unfurl.

Thirty-Seven

I open the door to the attic using the key I liberated from the pocket of a Mackintosh abandoned in the hall. It fits perfectly, turns first time. Before I pull the door clear to see what is in front of me, I glance back to see what I am leaving behind. Cigarette burns. A stained and fractured ceiling. The view of the side return. Also a miniature house, new inhabitants waiting for someone else to come and play.

Beyond the door is another set of stairs, narrow, steep walls on either side. At the top, a grey rectangle. I feel for the bone at my throat, hold it like some sort of talisman, take the first step. I climb with difficulty. The steps are small. I am large. But I am determined. Once I am in, I am in.

The attic is the one place I have not yet been in Isabella Dawson's boarding house. I imagine it to be empty, like me, nothing but shadow. Or perhaps it will be cavernous and still. I wonder if standing inside will be like standing in my living room at three in the morning listening to a baby crying, knowing its mother will come. When I get there I will wait for the sound of a mother's footsteps. After that, the lullaby.

The entrance to the attic is dark. So dark I can almost touch it. So dark it might swallow me whole, like Jonah inside his whale. On the threshold, at the top of the narrow stairs is a black mouth. In front of that, a small girl wearing a red swimsuit with a pleated skirt. The girl is smiling at me. In her hand she holds a knife.

PART TWO

Emily Noble

One

Portobello. Edinburgh's seaside, 2019.

PC Emily Noble sat in the driver's seat of the squad car, engine still running, staring through the windscreen towards the faraway sea. Sand blew across the beach in snaking waves, scattering the place with tiny silver grains. Emily squinted through a sudden glare of sunlight, the sting of hair whipping across her eyes. Two boys splashed towards the shallows, feet bare, shoes neatly placed. Behind her a voice called:

Em!

Ahead two small shapes already at the water's edge.

Em!

Emily switched off the ignition, listened to the engine settle beneath her with its little *tick tick tick*. It was September, a cold harbinger of autumn, nothing but damp days and worse to come. Through the windscreen she could see the white horses out in the Forth, small angry waves whipping up and whipping up, wind blowing the crests so that foam drifted away across the grey. It was choppy today, no time for tourists, only the ever-bracing populace of Portobello ready for whatever the weather threw at them. She reached for her hat on the passenger seat, checked her notebook was in the top pocket of her stab vest, ponytail fastened. Then she opened the door, released herself into the wind.

*

The call had come through to the station at Gayfield at around eleven. Emily Noble had been the only one to look up. No mug of tea to hide behind. No takeaway coffee. No food of any sort. Not even any paperwork to keep her occupied. Nothing but the shadow of DCI Franklin across the vast empty space of her desk.

'PC Noble.'

'Ma'am.'

The DCI had told her not to use that term, but Emily Noble could not help herself. She'd spent three years as her bag woman; DCI Franklin would always be 'ma'am' to her.

'Busy?'

It wasn't really a question. Both women looked at the abnormal emptiness of Emily Noble's desk.

'Just getting ready to write some reports, ma'am.'

A lost dog. A missing cat. An argument with a neighbour. Such were the crimes PC Noble was relegated to now.

'Well, leave that for the moment. I need you to follow up on something for me.'

'Ma'am.'

DCI Franklin tutted as though she had been insulted. She was wearing her woollen coat with the orange lining. Like burnt cinder. Like the leaves of a beech tree once all the green was gone. Emily Noble knew there was no better sign that autumn had come to Edinburgh than the coat DCI Franklin chose to wear.

'Probably nothing,' the DCI said, fingertips resting on the edge of Emily's desk as though to check for dust. 'A report of a disturbance. Something to do with a dog.'

'A dog?' The voice came from two desks over. 'In a car, was it?'

DC Blackwood getting her dig in, just because she could. Emily could feel the heat rising on her neck. There was a snigger from across the far side of the room, not in her favour. The DCI ignored it all.

'Only if you're free, of course.'

Emily flushed again. She was always free. That was the problem.

'Yes, ma'am. Where do you need me to go?'

The DCI smiled then, as though she'd known Emily would agree all along.

'Portobello. A bit off our patch, but the local chief asked me for assistance.'

Portobello. Edinburgh's seaside. Ice cream and picnics on the beach. Sand in every crevice. Emily felt it then, that sudden panic in her throat.

At the edge of the sea a dog was playing. It ran in and out of the shallows, water whipping from its fur. A collie, thought Emily as she set out across the beach. They had such slender legs, collies, twisting one way then the next. Emily envied the dog, its unbridled passion for the sand and the froth. The dog is free, she thought as her heavy boots sank into the soft surface. Not wading through life like me.

The tide was out this morning, the grey sea far away, the wet ripples of sand studded with worm casts and stray shells, long snakes of seaweed abandoned here and there like the laces from a boot. Emily breathed in the familiar briny air, glimpsed the glitter of a wave as it caught the light.

'Hey!' The shout came from some distance. 'Leave that alone.'

A man gesticulating at two boys in black jackets, backpacks sagging from their shoulders. The boys were kicking at something that rolled and dragged with the surf. At their feet the collie barked and darted in, then away, attempting to grab at whatever they were playing with.

The man shouted again.

'Leave it!'

Began to run, lumbering towards the boys. This was it, then, Emily thought, heading that way, too. Trouble with a dog.

At the sound of the man's voice, the boys turned from their prize, saw him, saw her, began to run, stumbling up the beach towards the promenade, from which they made their escape. Like two black starlings, Emily thought, as she watched the boys flit towards the Joppa end. She let them go, continued towards the man and the water, its small angry waves. The dog kept up its dance, tossing something with its mouth now that he had it to himself. A bin bag, Emily thought as she got near. Black plastic, in a sorry state.

The man shouted again.

'Eli, heel.'

Grabbing for the collie as it darted forwards, then away, worrying the prize. The dog took one more turn around the shredded bin bag before it obeyed, running towards its master and lying low, belly to the sand, panting as the man clipped on the lead.

'You took your bloody time.'

The man was breathing heavy too, like the dog. He sucked in a gulp of gritty air as Emily reached him.

'Are you the one who called, sir?'

'Yes, ages ago. Couldn't stay with it, though. Had to drop my daughter at school.' The man dug his hands into his waist as though to quell a stitch. 'Bloody kids. Never imagined they might get it. Thought the sea would take it, if anything.'

'What's that, sir?'

'I only moved it a little. Didn't want to touch.'

'Touch what, sir?'

The man gestured towards the black bin bag rocking gently in the ripples of the incoming surf. The bag had been tied once, a rough knot, come loose now. Emily Noble crouched over the plastic, wet sand pooling beneath her heels as she drew a pair of gloves from her pocket, wriggled them on. She teased the rest of the knot free, lifted the lip of the bag to see, glimpsed some kind of faded orange cloth, beneath that a thick wrap of newspaper. A rubbish bag, she thought. Something dumped or stolen. A dog that should have been buried in a garden, perhaps. A dead cat. Emily sighed, rubbed at her forehead with the back of her glove, grit on her skin. Then she peeled back a corner of the fabric, the paper underneath, understood why the man had called, perhaps the local chief too. Here it was, a massacre on the shoreline, tossed hither and thither amongst the foam by a dog with one white eye.

Two

'What on earth were you thinking!'

The door to the DCI's office was locked from the inside. The black bin bag was laid on the desk, PC Emily Noble on one side of the divide, DCI Franklin on the other. Outside the day had turned grey, a haar rolling in. Indoors, Emily could still feel its chill.

'A basic mistake.' DCI Franklin's arms were folded across her chest in a tight sort of fury. 'Should have left the evidence where it was, if it is what you think.'

Bones, Emily thought. Maybe a cat. Maybe a dog. Maybe a tibia or a fibula. Perhaps even a skull. She saw herself again standing on the beach at Portobello as the tide played about her ankles, no one to help but a man and his dog. Then the back seat of the squad car, that large damp patch edged with a salty line spreading across the fabric as though it would never stop. She'd known the moment she drove away from Portobello with her treasure safe on the back seat that she'd made an error. The car would stink of seaweed for weeks – a reminder to all the officers based in this station that once again PC Emily Noble had proved that in an attempt to do the job right, she could only ever get it wrong.

'The tide would have got it,' she said. Not a good excuse but the only one she had.

'You could have moved it further up the beach, called from there.'

DCI Franklin was annoyed. But Emily Noble was stubborn, looked straight at her superior.

'I did call. Twice.'

'And?'

Emily slid her eyes away. 'I got cut off.'

Standing on the beach, surf lapping at her feet, waiting and waiting for her call to be transferred. Emily could imagine the laughter down the line when the message came through to the office.

A dog, she says. A dead one.

'I didn't want to make a fuss. Just in case.'

Last time Emily made a fuss it had not gone well. She knew that, and so did the DCI. Still, DCI Franklin let her arms fall to her sides in exasperation.

'This is a potential dead body we're talking about, PC Noble. We're meant to make a fuss.'

Coverall suits and masks. A perimeter fence. Edinburgh's seaside cordoned off from the amusement arcade to the Swim Centre, blue and white police tape flapping in the wind.

'Sorry.'

Emily said it, but she didn't mean it. She knew the bones were already compromised long before she brought them to the safety of Gayfield Police Station. Tossed about the low tide mark by a couple of lads playing on the shoreline when they should have been at school. Not to mention the attentions of a collie with salt water dripping from its coat. Besides, Emily had known what she was looking at before she made the call. An opportunity, lying on the wet Portobello sand – for redemption, or something like it – not one she would let go.

A trickle of salt water meandered across the veneer of DCI Franklin's desk, *drip drip drip* onto the stained carpet tiles at Emily's feet. Gayfield Police Station needed a make-over – a thorough scrub. Rather like the makeover Emily was attempting to engineer for herself now.

'I gathered up what I could,' she said. 'Tried to preserve the evidence in the absence of Scene of Crime. Removed it from harm's way.'

'Christ's sake.' DCI Franklin put two hands to the edge of the desk, leaned forwards, her coat falling open to reveal its fiery display. 'If it is what you say it is, you'd better get your story straight.'

A mistake. A misapprehension. A misidentification. PC Emily Noble moved the tip of her boot away from the steady salt water drip.

'Yes, ma'am.'

She was good at stories, all the different shades of grey.

'So you've looked inside, then.' DCI Franklin pinioned Emily with her gaze. 'Bones, you say?'

'Ma'am.'

'Not a dog, is it?'

The DCI looked away from Emily as she said it. But Emily felt skewered all the same.

'No, ma'am. I don't think so.'

The DCI hesitated for a moment, as though she wasn't sure whether to insist her young PC return the black sack from whence it had come, cast it to the grey waves, start over. But DCI Franklin knew, and PC Emily Noble knew, too, that however much one might wish to erase the past, there was never any going back.

'All right, then. Let's see what you've got.'

The DCI produced a pen from the breast pocket of her coat, lifted aside the lip of the plastic sack to peer in. Sand trickled onto the tabletop. The DCI frowned at the mess of orange fabric.

'What's this?'

'Some sort of clothing, ma'am,' said Emily. 'Nightwear, if I had to guess.'

DCI Franklin glanced at Emily. 'I think we'd better leave the guessing to the experts, don't you?'

Emily coloured, two spots on her cheeks. DCI Franklin slid her pen further between the folds, eased aside some of the newspaper. Emily realized she was holding her breath. A dog, perhaps. A cat. Or a child's skeleton, all higgledy-piggledy, wrapped in newspaper and a piece of old clothing. That was what Emily Noble was certain she had glimpsed.

There was an odd noise from across the table, a sort of mewing, DCI Franklin making a sound in her throat as though she was a child in distress herself. The chief's face was pale as she withdrew her pen, slid a phone from the other pocket of her coat, aimed the camera at the contents of the bag. She took a photo, tapped a rapid message, sent them both into the ether with a *swoosh*. There was silence between them for a moment, the DCI smoothing down the front of her coat.

'What matters is the age,' she said, not looking at Emily but at the bin liner on the desk. 'Want to get a steer on that before we call the cavalry.'

The Major Incident Team from Gartcosh, that was what the DCI meant, riding in to take charge. Though Emily understood it in a different way:

Finders Keepers

Until DCI Franklin knew otherwise, she was determined to retain what was hers. They both waited, nothing but the slow tick of the clock on the wall and a bag of bones on the table between them. Then the sudden *ping* of the phone startling them both. DCI Franklin couldn't prevent a smile growing as she read whatever had been said in the text.

'Our friends in the north are interested.'

The forensic anthropology lab in Dundee. For the first time that day Emily felt a spot of warmth inside her skinny chest. So she had been right. Not a dog, then. Or even a cat. DCI Franklin knew it, too.

'We'll need someone to transport it,' she said, using her pen again to flip the edge of the bin bag closed. 'The mortuary could arrange it, but they might have something to say about the circumstances in which it was recovered.'

This, Emily knew, was her chance.

'I can sort it, ma'am. No problem.'

Whisk the compromised evidence away before too many more questions were asked. About protocol and cross-contamination. About a young PC who should have known better. DCI Franklin studied Emily from across the bag of bones as though weighing the pros and cons. As Emily had hoped, her chief fell on the side of the devil.

'All right, then. It's in your hands.'

'Ma'am.'

'But not a word of this to anyone, PC Noble. Not till we know whether it's worth pursuing. I know I can trust you on that.'

It was Emily's turn to smile now.

Down in the garage, signing out the car she had only just returned, Emily understood. If there was a mess to be made, she would take the blame. If it was serious, DCI Franklin got the case. DCI Franklin had chosen well. Emily Noble was known for being the most discreet officer in the station. Or perhaps the one who had the most to lose.

Three

The Centre for Anatomy and Human Identification at the University of Dundee was a clinical sort of place, covered gurneys and pristine surfaces, everywhere a quiet sort of hum. It was a bit like the mortuary in Edinburgh, all of life hidden inside the forty-eight fridges, bodies just waiting to be sliced and diced until their secrets had been thoroughly exorcized. But in Dundee Emily knew that any human traces could also be dealt with on a skeletal scale – a nub here, a fracture there, the finest shard from a dead person's remains. What mattered in this mortuary were the age and particularity of bones, a specialist unit unconcerned with the normal ways of death.

She arrived around mid-afternoon, driving north from Edinburgh with her precious cargo on the back seat once again, deposited inside a proper evidence bag now. Each mile away from the capital she found her limbs relaxing, her shoulders and her neck. Emily hadn't realized how toxic her situation at Gayfield had become; sent to Coventry by every other person there because of her disgrace. She'd had no one to talk to for a couple of months now, other than the DCI. And DCI Franklin did not do small talk, so it was practically the same thing.

The entrance to the Centre was unassuming, but Emily knew that inside somewhere were the bodies. Or bits of them, at least. She was buzzed through by the receptionist, evidence bag tight in her fist, to be met by an anatomy technician who stepped through to greet her.

'Anwar,' he said, holding out his hand. Emily glanced at the thin glove she was being presented with, didn't reciprocate. Anwar grinned. 'Sorry. I always forget.'

Anwar led Emily into the complex where indiscriminate bones could be investigated – age, type and antiquity – along with everything else. They passed by the offices first, then into the mortuary suite. In the Dissecting Room, a phalanx of cadavers were laid out on gurneys positioned in a neat grid, each covered with a blue cloth. The room was well-lit and gleaming, all much shinier than Edinburgh's dark pit just off the Cowgate. It was hard to remember that here, under each cover, lay a body donated by its owner so that a student might learn how not to make mistakes.

In contrast, the teaching facility was a functional environment full of microscopes and glass slides, long benches with exhibits in Perspex containers. Surgical lights illuminated each work station, hovering above computers on which the practitioners could study enlargements of whatever lay within. What would she see if she took a look? thought Emily. The whole of life hidden in a tiny splash of someone's marrow? Or just an inconclusive mass of cells?

Next they came to the mortuary itself. Anwar showed Emily the embalming room with its Thiel tanks, inside bodies gradually disintegrating into some kind of plasticity. The facility in Dundee was the only one in the country where a cadaver could be prepared in such a way that its joints would still move, its colour retained, no smell to speak of. Almost as though the person wasn't actually dead.

Beyond the tanks, on the far side of the space, was a cliff of stainless steel, drawers like filing cabinets patterning the wall.

'Where the bodies are stored,' said Anwar, waving his hand. 'Cattle tagged on ears and feet, then vacuumed packed ready for the students to dissect them.'

It was a practical business, Emily thought, death in Dundee. Perhaps if her nascent career in the police turned out to be stunted, she could retrain, seek truth and justice in a Thiel tank or down the lens of a microscope instead. Anwar led her towards a locked room, the place where police cases were dealt with, two dissection tables awaiting their bodies, video cameras and specimen containers, lots of PPE. Anwar beeped his pass at the entrance.

'We'll take it from here,' he said.

'Right.'

Emily found herself reluctant to let go of her treasure. Anwar smiled as though he understood.

'Don't worry. We'll look after it.'

There was a kind quality to the way the technician handled the bag, as though it really might contain a living child.

Once inside the facility, Anwar deposited the evidence onto one of the tables as Emily watched through the half-open door. Not for the first time Emily wondered where the bin liner had come from before it ended in the Firth of Forth.

Anwar unrolled the top of the evidence bag, slid the rubbish sack from inside. Then he took some sort of long, thin metal implement and lifted the lip of the plastic to see what he could see. Was this the beginning of the investigation, Emily wondered, or was the technician just sneaking a look like she had? The desire to know – wasn't that what made them good at their jobs?

There was a sound behind her. At once Anwar laid down his metal tool and stepped away from the table. The new arrival was small and stocky, around her head a halo of bright hair. She was wearing a coat, rather like DCI Franklin, though here the coat was white. An angel, thought Emily. Of a certain type.

'Not messing with our new arrival, are you, Anwar?'

'Professor Watt,' Anwar said with what looked to Emily like a small bow.

'Let's see it, then.'

Anwar moved aside and the professor stepped through the door and up to the dissection table, an inquisitorial light in her eyes. When she saw the bin bag, her face set in a frown instead.

'Why on earth is it in this condition?'

Unsecured, that was what Emily knew Professor Watt meant. Not properly contained by Scene of Crime before the scientists got to work. She thought to make an intervention, attempt to explain how a bin liner stuffed full of evidence had arrived on the doorstop of the anthropological forensic team, rather than the team arriving to collect it themselves. But Anwar was murmuring something in the professor's ear as though to placate her.

A favour.

That was how he had described it to Emily when she first arrived. His chief owed her chief and this was a good opportunity for the debt to be paid. Still, the professor had another word for it.

'Incompetence,' she sniffed. 'Might have destroyed evidence.'

She glanced towards where Emily was standing just outside the door. Emily felt that familiar prick beneath her uniform, the sensation of being too hot and too cold at the same time, knowing she might have done something wrong. But Anwar was smiling.

'Shall I get coffee?' he asked the professor. 'Before you begin.'

Professor Watt nodded. 'Might as well start with something right.'

'Fear not,' Anwar whispered as he exited the room, indicated Emily should follow him. 'The seawater will have done its worst long before you got involved.'

In the canteen he bought Emily a coffee to keep her warm on the drive home. As he handed it over he said:

'1996.'

'What?'

Emily had no idea what Anwar was referring to, only that he seemed mightily pleased with himself. He smiled as she took the cardboard cup.

'That's how old they might be. The bones you brought us.'

Emily was puzzled. 'How do you know?'

Anwar laughed. 'The alchemy of science.'

Though wasn't that a contradiction? Anwar laughed again when he saw her frown.

'Only joking,' he said. 'There was newspaper inside the bin bag, date printed on the edge.'

Not alchemy, then, or even science. Just observation. But the technician wasn't finished with his assessment yet.

'Came from Portobello, right?' he said.

'Yes,' Emily replied and Anwar leaned back against the milk and sugar station with a satisfied nod, as though this was as he expected. There was excitement in his eyes as he said it:

'This case could be huge.'

Four

Emily arrived home that evening to a letter lying on the floor of her empty hall. There was nothing on the envelope but her name. No stamp. No postmark. Which meant it had been hand delivered this time. Which meant one of her neighbours had let whoever wrote it in by the main door.

Emily left the letter lying on the mat as she shut the flat's front door behind her, locked it three times – dead bolt, chain, mortice – took a quick look through the spyhole just to be sure. She stowed the keys in her bag so as not to leave them on the hall table visible to anyone who might wish to break in. She would have liked to render the letter in the hall invisible, too, pretend it did not exist. But she knew she could not.

Dinner was a packet of Ritz crackers, didn't even bother with cheese. She ate the crackers sitting at the fold-out table in her living-room window bay. She had a fine view of all the neighbours across the street from here, right into their flats. TVs and pot plants. Bright lights and tables set for dinner. Whereas her flat was dark, nothing but dry crackers and a small anglepoise lamp rescued from within one of the boxes jumbled along the wall. The boxes had been there since Emily first moved in, eighteen months ago, after her grandparents died. One, then the next. She'd meant to unpack, but somehow it had felt like playing at something she was not.

The unopened letter lay alongside the solitary box of crackers. Emily lifted it towards the window as though to check its contents. She didn't bother to unseal it. The letter would be the same as all the others. Apart from being hand delivered this time, of course. She took another cracker from the box, licked salt from the surface, placed it on her tongue. Life was all about communion, wasn't it? Especially with the dead. Then she turned to her laptop, typed with one hand:

1996 Portobello

Leaned in to see.

The first letter had arrived a few months before. Emily had found it when she was on her way to work, a small thing almost hidden amongst that morning's scatter of junk mail. Inconsequential. And yet, who wrote letters anymore? Who put actual pen to actual paper and laid out the words? Emily had known the moment she saw the handwritten envelope that it would not be good news.

She'd stuffed the letter into her pocket without opening it, grabbed a cereal bar from her otherwise empty kitchen cupboards and made her way down the stair to the outdoors. How had they got her address? she'd thought as she rode the bus to work. Then again, how did anyone get a person's address these days? By looking it up, of course. By typing it into Google. Besides, Emily hadn't exactly gone far from where she started. She hadn't changed her name or done anything that might disguise who she was. She had been waiting for this moment ever since she was nine years old.

She'd opened the letter once she got into the office at

Gayfield, as though that might make its contents safer. It had been a short note, on a single folded sheet. The person who wrote it obviously understood that less was always more. The letter enquired after Emily, then mentioned her mother. Emily read it, then folded the paper and slid it back into the envelope, put that into her pocket. When she got home that evening she put the envelope in the drawer next to the one with the knives. She'd gone to sleep that night trying to pretend it did not exist.

Then another one came.

It was dark outside by the time Emily finished with her scrolling, flipped the laptop screen down. The image disappeared. A girl, barely more than five years old, V-neck sweater and her hair in bunches, vanished from a play park near the Portobello promenade in 1996, never returned. Emily sat back in her chair, realized how dark her living room had become in contrast to the warm glow emanating from the windows opposite. This was what Anwar had meant by huge – a national story that had never been solved. No wonder the DCI had wanted to keep the discovery of the bones to herself until she was sure. It could be the making of them, Emily thought. A serious feather in the DCI's cap. And hers too. Or another disaster. Either way, there was something about the case that had Emily's fingerprints all over. Not just because she had been the one to drag the bones from the surf. But because it was Portobello. Because it was 1996.

Emily licked a final slick of salt from her lips, crushed the empty Ritz packet. Then she took the letter and the flattened box into the kitchen, tossed one in the bin, pulled open the drawer for the other. There were six letters in the drawer now, one for each of the months that had passed. None of them had been opened apart from the first. Emily ran her fingertips across the surface of the paper. Then she touched the folder beneath – a police file liberated from the system when nobody was watching. She let her fingers rest on the file for a moment before sliding the drawer closed, moving to the next. The knives were laid in a row, their solid black handles. She lifted one, pressed the point into her palm. She imagined it pushing through flesh, through cartilage and bone.

The past was rising, didn't like to be kept down.

Five

The next day, Emily returned to Portobello an hour before her shift was due to begin. It was a beautiful Edinburgh morning, September sky as clear as a prayer. But still Emily shivered as she stepped from the bus, began her walk along the promenade. Spread before her was the beach in all its naked glory, beyond that the Firth. Sunlight glittered on the surface of the water, as she imagined lost bones winding here and there with the tide.

The last time Emily set foot in Portobello she'd been a child herself. Nine years old, a skinny little thing, like she was now, still, spent her days flitting between Mrs Wren's shop on the High Street and the amusement arcade on the front, lights flashing on the machines. Portobello had been a faded place then, a down-at-heel resort scattered with nothing other than sand. But for Emily it had been a refuge, sun on her hair, wind on her skin, nothing to do all day but spend hours on the beach or the promenade when she should have been at school. Then a girl went to play on the swings one afternoon, never returned.

The death of Portobello.

That was how the newspapers described it. The beginning of the end. But Emily knew the decay had started long before that. In a rented house some distance from the beach, three meagre bedrooms and a kitchen with a dirty vinyl floor. Emily remembered everything about that house. The nylon carpet on the stairs that burned her feet. Condensation on the inside of the bedroom windows. Mould growing on the walls. *A fucking dump.* That was what her father called it. Damp polyester sheets and babies always crying, the ever-present threat of an argument that might get out of hand. No wonder Emily had never returned.

She slowed now as she reached the section of the beach where she had recovered the bin bag, turned to look at the properties fronting the promenade. The houses on this stretch were nothing like the one she grew up in, that run-down terrace with cement for a yard. Instead, they were great monoliths of the Victorian era, turrets and big windows, gardens hidden behind high stone walls. These houses were a reminder of what Portobello used to be – Scotland's premier holiday destination, with a pier and an observatory, halls for dancing and a fun fair. Not forgetting the ice-rink, of course. They would have been worth a fortune then, holiday homes for the rich, or guesthouses for the never-ending stream of tourists scattering their money around. White elephants by 1996, subdivided into flats for DSS or emergency B & B. Now Emily realized they must be worth a fortune again with their gardens that opened onto the promenade and amazing views. The perfect place from which to spy someone discarding a bag of bones into the sea.

Emily took a step back to check out the nearest house's blank facade. Despite its prime position, this property had not weathered well, flashing missing from the gables, tiles from the roof. The only obvious way in or out was a faded wooden door set into a wall, paint ravaged by the wind and the sand. Emily stepped across the promenade to rattle at the handle, but it was locked, moss creeping from whatever lay within. Nobody had opened this door in years, that was what Emily realized. And certainly not to discard any bones.

She crouched as best she could and put an eye to the keyhole. Behind the gate she glimpsed a large garden, once a haven for roses, now covered in a riot of rubbish and grass. Emily could see at least one dining chair nestled amongst a mound of nettles and what looked like a kind of washing machine, two gaping holes on top. Also a thousand bin bags rising from the weeds.

She considered whether to scale the wall, clamber over to see what else she might find amongst the mess. Maybe a dog. Maybe a cat. Maybe a missing girl from 1996. But the wall was high and Emily was not. *A wee slice of a thing, barely any meat on you.* Wasn't that what DS Lawrie had said as he pulled her towards him across the back seat of his pool car? Detective Sergeant Lawrie liked women with not much to them, was well known for it within the station, always grinding himself against them as though to crush their bodies into his own. Emily had carpet burns on her knees for a week after their liaison, raw streaks that lasted much longer than it took her to realize there wouldn't be any more. DS Lawrie had pursued her and taken her and once for him had turned out to be enough. Emily had let him because she'd wanted it more than anything – to feel something as he milled her into the back seat. It was only afterwards she understood their encounter for the disaster that it turned out to be. *Like a dog*, that was the rumour which circulated after everything came down. How DS Lawrie had taken PC Emily Noble. And how she had begged him for more.

Emily tried to shake the memory rising in her head, concentrated on the task in front. DCI Franklin may not have sanctioned it exactly, pursuing the origins of the bag of bones before they knew exactly what they were dealing with. But she hadn't said no and to Emily Noble that was as good as saying yes. She touched the rough stone of the wall, decided against attracting further disgrace by breaking and entering in favour of finding another entrance with which to facilitate access. She checked left, then right, made for a nearby side street that ran perpendicular to the promenade along one flank of the house. She was rewarded at once. Some way further up the street there was what appeared to be a back gate into the property. And next to that, a skip. Even from a distance Emily could see that the skip was filled to the brim with rubbish, a huge, slithering pile of bin bags like the one Emily had ferried to Dundee only the day before.

Parked behind the skip was a van emblazoned with a familiar logo. The Company. Edinburgh's premier cleaning outfit, specialists in trauma and extremity, plus all the rest. Emily was familiar with The Company and its founders McDermid and Sharp, two women who cleared up after the city's neglected and abandoned because nobody else would. She approached with caution. The last time she had crossed paths with The Company it had started with a call from a neighbour complaining about the smell and ended in accusation and suspension, rumours about a dog. Also, the remains of an innocent girl who died with a needle in her arm, hair like summer straw spread all about.

This time Emily discovered the remains about her feet. A bag of flour smashed like a bomb on the curb. The sticky remnants of what appeared to be jam. Also a coil of dirty silk, trailing in the gutter. The sash from a dressing gown, perhaps, a strange sort of green. She grasped the metal sides of the skip, levered herself up to see what else she could spot. Inside was a repository of everything a person thought they couldn't live without; and everything they could not take with them once they were gone. The entire contents of the house, that was what it looked like. Broken chairs. Mouldering curtains. A microwave oven with a cracked door. There was precious little smell. Rather like the cadavers in Dundee, this body of evidence had been treated in such a way that it, too, did not give off the scent of its owner, so much as the scent of the sea.

Emily dropped from the side of the skip and fumbled for her phone so that she could take a picture. Of the bin bags. Of the environs, the proximity to the beach. Context was everything, that was what she'd learned, when it came to building a case. When she lowered the phone she discovered a ghost watching her from down near the promenade. A figure dressed in white from top to toe, mask across her face. Emily blinked at the memory of another house in Portobello, another person clad in white from head to foot emerging from a doorway hand in hand with a child. But when she looked again, the apparition was gone.

The sound of a piano being played drifted from the back gate of the house, some sort of lament. Emily was about to follow it, discover what treasure lay within, when her phone burst into song, too. A message from DCI Franklin.

Office, 1 hr. News from Dundee.

Just time for a couple more things first.

Six

Detective Sergeant Nowack was based at Portobello Police Station, but he used to work out of Gayfield, a member of the now defunct Police Enquiry Team sorting all of those indigent dead. Dr Death, that was what some of the officers called him. DS Nowack didn't seem to mind.

'Somebody has to do the right thing by them.'

That was what he told Emily when she dropped by to ask about the house on the promenade with a skip full of bin bags outside and a perfect view of the beach.

'Isabella Dawson,' DS Nowack said at once without even looking at his computer. 'Found dead in her bed a week ago. Been there two years, it seems. Not a pretty sight.'

Emily thought of the first scene she had attended where they'd had to force the door. A girl, twenty-three years old and dead with a needle in her arm, been lying in the sun for two weeks and counting before anyone came. There had been a half-pint of milk abandoned on the kitchen counter, stinking almost as much as the girl must have stunk, gone sour in the sun. It was the milk that Emily remembered the most, stepping into the girl's kitchen as though she was stepping back in time – another abandoned pint, empty this time, the last dregs dripping onto a dirty floor. Also the grip of something in her chest as she pushed open the bedroom door, at the thought of what might be waiting on the other side. Two boys curled about each other like sea creatures in a shell, perhaps. Or a girl Emily had spent a lifetime hoping to recover, long lost to her now.

Instead, it had been yellow hair spread across a pillow, toes bloated from the heat. Also something Emily had not expected. A miniature bag made of stripy cloth clutched in the dead girl's hand. Emily had checked the bag, of course. She'd not been a detective in training for nothing, passed her exams a few weeks later, highest marks in the division, been waiting for the heads up from DCI Franklin to join her team as a proper detective ever since. She'd thought the cloth bag might contain powder or pills, whatever substance the girl had injected into her arm. But it had contained something else instead. Six tiny figures fashioned from lengths of wire, their heads made from paper, their clothes made from scraps. Worry dolls, slipped from beneath a dead girl's pillow to keep her company at the end. A mother. A father. Two boys. Two girls.

Emily had retained the worry dolls – personal things first, leave the rest to the cleaners – evidence-bagged them and handed them to the senior officer in charge when he arrived. DS Lawrie, standing over the corpse with the Fiscal, regarding the dead girl as though she was nothing more than a shop-front mannequin, a piece of rubbish to be thrown away. It was only a week or so later, after the DS took Emily for a drink to celebrate her exam success, after he pulled her towards him across the back seat of his car, after he placed his hand on her neck and she felt the sick excitement of something forbidden, that Emily realized what she had been looking at the whole time he ground into her from behind. There, under the passenger seat of DS Lawrie's car, tucked away as though it was meant to be hidden. The same triangular bag in stripy fabric she had prised from the dead girl's fingers, next to it a wrap of brown crystalline powder. Waiting for the next victim, perhaps.

Walk away.

That was what Emily told herself after DS Lawrie drove off and she checked her neck in the bathroom mirror for that familiar crescent of bruises. Let the devil have his day. But Emily had walked away once before, and it had ended in disaster. She would not repeat the same mistake.

Still, every time Emily thought about what might have been, she felt sick. She should have been a detective of several months' standing by now. Searching out the guilty. Protecting the innocent. Preserving the integrity of the scene. Instead, she was nothing but an extra pair of hands to help with legwork while DC Blackwood and her like got on with the glamorous side. Blood spatter and hard questions in the custody suite, chasing up the leads. Emily Noble had been branded, that was what it amounted to. A clipe. A dog. Maybe even a liar. That was her reputation now. Ever since she'd told DCI Franklin what she saw and opened DS Lawrie's can of worms. He'd known the victim, that was what it amounted to. Had previous contact of some kind, perhaps even a relationship. The moment she heard the rumours, Emily understood the detective sergeant's tactics. Attack, the best form of defence. And DS Lawrie still had his day in court to fall back on. Whereas Emily was left with nothing but missing cats and dogs.

Also an old lady in Portobello, dead in her bed for two years and counting. Plus all her rubbish, of course. A hoarder, that was what DS Nowack said. House piled high with junk. Another lost cause. But Emily was hoping that Isabella Dawson and everything she'd left behind might be so much more than that.

A second chance.

Wasn't that all anyone ever wanted? A second chance at life.

'Who found her?' she asked now as DS Nowack retrieved the sudden-death report from his computer.

'Couple of local constables,' he replied. 'Got the call from a neighbour. Some sort of disturbance at the property, went in to look.'

'What was the disturbance?'

'Lads, I think, trying their luck. Scarpered with whatever they could put their hands to as soon as we turned up.'

Two boys in black jackets, bags hanging from their shoulders, kicking something they had stolen into the froth. Emily wondered for a moment what Isabella Dawson's rubbish might be hiding, who she had once shared the house with before she shut the door.

'I don't suppose you dug up anything about her? Family, perhaps.'

But DS Nowack shook his head. 'No relatives that we could find. Ran the property as a boarding house until she retired.'

He swivelled in his chair, handed Emily the report.

'What you want is the Heir Hunter,' he said. 'Solomon Farthing. Ultimus Haeres have asked him to dig into the case to see who the house should go to now that we've done our bit. He should be able to put some more flesh on the bones.'

After she departed Portobello Police Station, Emily decided she still had time to try and put a bit more flesh on Isabella Dawson's bones before answering the summons from the DCI. It wouldn't hurt to have something to take to the chief when she returned, anything to keep her on side for whatever might be coming once DS Lawrie's case was heard. Disgrace, that was what Emily Noble was facing, standing up for a dead addict over a superior officer. Best to get her ammunition prepared.

She set off at a brisk walk back to the promenade and a bit of house to house, knocking on the doors of Isabella Dawson's neighbours right and left, just in case.

'Didn't even know she was living there,' the first neighbour said. 'Thought it was abandoned. Quite a shock when they told us she'd been inside all along.'

'Total dump,' said another. 'Eyesore. Let the whole area down.'

Rats and cat shit. Weeds and junk. That was what Isabella Dawson's neighbours complained of, one man describing it as a playground for anyone who wanted to chance their luck.

'Used to try and break in when I was a lad,' he said. 'For a bit of a laugh. People would tell stories about there being treasure inside. Nothing but an old lady and a house stuffed with crap.'

Nobody mentioned anything about a family. And certainly not a child. *Fool's errand.* That's what Emily was thinking as she rang the bell of the house that overlooked Isabella Dawson's backyard, a last go before she returned to Gayfield and the news from Dundee. The door was opened by another elderly lady, purple crimp to her hair and a determined stare.

'Yes?'

'PC Noble.'

Emily introduced herself and the woman peered at her for a moment before reciprocating.

'Mrs Wren.'

At once Emily felt it. Sticky hands and a pocket of hot coins. The waxy cloy on her tongue from too many Fruit Salads. Mrs Wren, the shopkeeper from the High Street. The last person Emily spoke to that day, before it all came down. She faltered, the old lady's eyes eating her up the way they used to eat up all the children whom she accused of stealing from her shop.

'I'm enquiring about Isabella Dawson,' Emily began. 'Lived in the ex-boarding house on the promenade.'

Mrs Wren's eyes grew shrewd. 'Oh aye. I remember Isabella Dawson, if that's what you're after. All sorts, she took in.'

Students and DSS, renters and people who'd just got married. Not to mention all the folk who came on holiday before.

'Used to go like a fair, that boarding house,' Mrs Wren said. 'Couldn't keep people away then. Must have made a fortune, Isabella and her mother. Sad how it turned out.'

The closure of the Marine Gardens. The draining of the Lido. The bulldozing of the skate rink. Though that wasn't what Mrs Wren was referring to. She was talking about Isabella Dawson and the closure of her boarding house. And not in the tone of a friend.

'Shut the door, didn't she, wouldn't let anyone in. Though that wasn't a bad thing, considering who she'd had staying just before.'

'When was that?'

Mrs Wren waved her hand. 'Twenty years ago, or so. Around that time the wee lassie went missing.'

V-neck jumper. Hair in bunches. Went to the play park, never returned.

'1996?'

'Aye, that's it. Terrible. I told your lot at the time. That's what happens if you let them play on their own.'

Children running free along the promenade. Knocking on people's doors for the fun of it. Figures of eight on the beach, two boys crouched by the water's edge, behind her someone calling:

Em!

As she ran towards the sea. Emily couldn't remember their mother or father ever going with them to the beach, just shouting from the kitchen to be back in time for their tea. She put a hand to her neck, feeling for that familiar crescent of bruises, smelled a waft of cheap beer and Benson and Hedges. But Mrs Wren wasn't finished yet.

'Couldn't pay folks to holiday here after that.' Mrs Wren put a finger to her hair, its purple tint. 'Not that they would have wanted to stay with Isabella anyway. She'd let it all go by then – the house, I mean. The smell was something awful, if the wind blew the wrong way. Her mother would have been birling in her grave to see what happened to the place.' Mrs Wren wrinkled her nose. 'Hard type, old Mrs

Dawson. Had a way of cutting you in the street. Hypocrite, that's what she was, everyone knew.'

'Isabella had trouble, didn't she?' Emily said. 'After she closed the door. People trying to break in.'

'Kids . . .' Mrs Wren dismissed Emily's question with an impatient gesture. 'Nothing more than that. Just having a lark like children do. And let me tell you, I know kids. Been dealing with them my whole life.'

Fruit Salads and liquorice laces, the rap on the back of the hand if you dared to reach for them yourself. Emily thought of the bones folded into a bin bag.

'You never saw either of them with a child, did you? Isabella and her mother, I mean.'

'A child?' Mrs Wren was still for a moment, like an animal suddenly alert to danger. When she spoke again her voice was more guarded than it had been. 'Isabella never had any children of her own, dear. That was all done and dusted by the time she grew up.'

'What was?'

'Oh, nothing, dear. Nothing.' Mrs Wren's face turned then from something lit by gossip, to a darker cast, more circumspect. 'She wouldn't be told, Isabella. I tried to warn her. Be careful who you let the rooms to, never know what they might do. Took in the worst kind of person and look where it got her.'

Dead in her bed with nobody to give her a second glance. That was where, Emily thought as she took her leave of Mrs Wren, made her way back into town to Gayfield and the summons from DCI Franklin. Like a girl with a needle in her arm, nobody to advocate on her behalf but a police officer who was sent to Coventry as a result. It was nothing new. Emily had a way of attaching herself to lost causes, had been doing it since she was nine years old.

At Gayfield Police Station the froideur remained. Sly looks and whispers behind hands, the bump of a shoulder in the corridor. Not to mention that quiet *yip yip* in the canteen queue which Emily knew was meant to sound like a dog. DS Lawrie's case was being heard this week, too late for Emily to walk away now.

DCI Franklin was in her office attempting to get through to someone on the phone. 'Where have you been?' she said. 'There's news from Dundee.'

Portobello, thought Emily. Digging. Digging. But not on the sand this time.

'Doing a bit of follow up,' she said.

'Oh yes?'

The DCI put down her phone as though inviting Emily to continue. Emily had done a lot of follow up for DCI Franklin over the past few months. Taping off scenes, going house to house, guarding whatever needed to be guarded. But now she proceeded with caution, didn't want the DCI to think she'd been talking out of turn.

'Something and nothing,' she said. 'Just a thought.'

A house with a view of the sea. A pile of bin bags in a skip. Two boys in black jackets flitting like starlings along the promenade. Emily looked across the desk at her chief, found DCI Franklin regarding her from the other side.

'Something and nothing?' Emily didn't reply and DCI Franklin nodded as though she approved. 'Well, PC Noble. Let's keep it like that, shall we, until we know otherwise.'

'Ma'am.'

'Speaking of which . . .' DCI Franklin reached for her phone. 'CAHID left a message. They have news, but they didn't say what. I've tried calling, can't get a reply. If it is what I think it is, you'll have to go and get the news first hand. Chapter and verse. No room for mistakes here.'

Seven

Two hours later and Emily was back in Dundee, the
evidence laid out before her for everyone to see. Not a sea
creature that belonged at the bottom of the ocean, the
crushed remains of tiny shells lingering in its folds. But a
child resting on one of the mortuary's polished surfaces.
Its skeleton, at least.

Anwar had allowed Emily into the mortuary room this
time, didn't even argue when she slid through the door
behind him wearing a pair of borrowed gloves. DCI
Franklin had sent word ahead. The favour that she was
owed must be repaid. And it must be repaid today.

Together they stood and surveyed the treasure. PC
Emily Noble. Anwar the anatomy technician. And Professor Watt with her halo of curls. Before them were three
exhibits spread across two dissection tables. Orange fabric.
A newspaper. An array of bones. Professor Watt began
from the outside in.

The cloth wrapped about the bones had unfolded itself
to reveal that Emily had been right all along. It was a
dressing gown, or what was left of one, at least. Kimono
style with wide arms and a long body, a beautiful drape
across the sterile table, dipping towards the floor.

'Silk,' said Professor Watt. 'Good quality too, once
upon a time.'

The gown must have been something to behold when

it was new, Emily thought. A fantastic sweep of fabric in which to take breakfast or step into after a bath. It had once been a gorgeous dark orange, judging by the area beneath the collar that Professor Watt turned back for Emily to see. Deep as the setting sun of a summer evening, a glorious streak. But the cloth was faded now, rotten and shredded, would fall apart if held to the light. All across it were the thready remains of embroidery, leaves and some kind of flower.

'Roses, perhaps,' said Anwar. 'Japanese style.'

Emily noted the delicacy of the stitching, the intricacy of the design. There was something else too, at the point where the waist should be. Two loops of fine thread sewn at top and bottom, one each side.

'For a sash, I imagine,' said Professor Watt. 'Given that it's a dressing gown.'

Emily looked closer at the remains of the fabric – at the flowers, the contrast their colours made with the faded silk. She had seen it before, she thought, this combination. A coil of cloth trailing in the gutter outside a boarding house in Portobello, an odd sort of green.

'Do we know anything about it?' she asked. 'Age, for example.'

The professor nodded as though Emily had asked the right question. 'Quite old, we think. Maybe 1920s, judging by the style and label. We'd have to send it to the lab in Glasgow for more tests to be sure.'

'1920s?' That was not what Emily had been expecting. 'But what about the newspaper?'

She moved along the table to where several sheets of newsprint had been retrieved from the inside of the bin bag. Double-page spreads, tabloid style, unfolded to reveal blocks of black text and pixelated photographs. Some of the sheets had been water damaged, but others were still intact.

'We were lucky,' said Professor Watt. 'Not been in the water long. Gives us a steer.'

She pointed to one of the double-page spreads. A sports report on what once must have been a back page, Hearts v Hibs. On the other side, the name of the newspaper on the masthead. *Edinburgh Evening News*. Beneath that a headline that Emily had seen before. Sitting in her window bay scrolling through her laptop as the dark crept in:

MISSING

Alongside that the photograph. Emily didn't even have to look at where Professor Watt was indicating to know the date or what it said. 1996. The year a girl disappeared from a play park in Portobello and Isabella Dawson closed the door of her boarding house, never opened it again.

Emily moved to the final exhibit displayed on the second table in the room, bones liberated from their flimsy plastic coffin and positioned as though to make a whole once more. She tried to name what she saw laid out before her. A tibia. A fibula. The tiny curve of skull. The latter stared at her from two dark hollows where its eyes should be. Was this the little girl from Portobello? Emily wondered. Returned to the land of the living after more than twenty years at sea?

'It's not complete,' Professor Watt said. 'Unsurprising, really, given the condition in which the bones were found.'

Emily could already see that the child before her only had one whole leg. The skeleton's feet were missing too, the small array of bones that would have once made up its toes. Probably surfing the Firth of Forth, Emily thought, floating on the surface of the water as they drifted further and further into the deep. But still, it was unmistakable. The skeleton was a human being. Not a dog. Not even a cat. But a child bundled inside a newspaper from 1996 as though it was nothing more than a chicken carcass boiled down for stock.

Professor Watt continued with her lecture, using some sort of metal scalpel to indicate the learning points, here, then there. Emily kept her hands behind her back so as not to interfere. She was drawn to blades, especially sharp ones. Had spent many hours in police training learning how to disarm attackers so that she might take their knives for herself.

'Do you know if it's a girl or a boy?' she asked.

'This is what we would normally use to determine sex.'

Professor Watt pointed her scalpel at the small plate of the child's pelvis. Emily stared at it, imagined her own pelvis jutting from beneath her skin. She was thin. Too thin, Emily knew that. But she also couldn't stop.

This child's pelvis was tiny, like a flower, two petals turned to the huge surgical lamp fixed above the dissection table as though to the sun. Was it a girl? Emily wondered. Or was it a boy? She twitched her shoulders, felt that familiar bud of panic deep in the centre of her body at the thought of a boy. Above the pelvis she stared at the display of the child's ribs, spindle-like things, curved and delicate, as though at any moment they might take flight and disappear. There were several missing, a miniature cage destroyed, whatever lay inside long since set free. For a moment, Emily struggled to breathe, her lungs constricting at the thought of two boys crouching at the water's edge, the dark gloss of their eyelashes on pale skin as they lay next to each other in a bed. Then the professor said something and Anwar turned towards Emily.

'Did you get that?'

'Sorry?'

The skeleton was too young for the sex to be determined either way. The treasure was neither boy nor girl. Confusion buzzed inside Emily's head as Professor Watt explained.

'Impossible to tell with a child under five or thereabouts. Even using the skull.'

Teeth, Emily thought. Wasn't that where the answer lay? Fillings and dental work. Cavities and decay. She thought of the teeth she had found inside her grandparents' bureau after they died. Three little ivory chips wrapped in a piece of tissue and zipped inside a plastic bag. A hollow tooth. Another with the speck of dried blood. One filled with decay. They were in her flat now, hidden somewhere inside one of the boxes she had meant to unpack – a small cannibalization to remind Emily of everything she had lost. But this child's teeth were nothing but crowns waiting to grow through.

Emily studied the remnants of the child. Its tiny ribs. The absent foot. All the life sucked out of it by the sea. She had to admit the skeleton did look a bit like cat bones. Or even a chicken. Not what she had expected at all.

She tried to think of the bones differently, to match them to the reports of the girl who had disappeared. Not a V-neck jumper and hair in bunches, but a summer dress, wasn't that what the girl had actually been wearing at the time? Cotton smocking and hair tied with a green ribbon.

Emily knew that this was not how anyone would remember the girl if she asked around. They would recall the school photograph that appeared in all the press. Red V-neck, hair in tidy bunches. Also a gap between the girl's front teeth where one had fallen out. Did the girl's mother still have that tooth? Emily wondered. But she already knew the answer to that.

Emily reached one finger as though to touch the skeleton, remembered another girl who disappeared from Portobello in 1996. Swimsuit and soft limbs. Hair a tangle of sand. Last seen peering at Emily through the letterbox in the front door, calling to her:

Em!

As she ran away, her pocket full of sticky coins. Then she noticed what was happening at the far end of the room, Anwar and the professor standing by the door, peeling off their gloves.

'What's going on?' she said. 'You're not finished, are you?'

'For tonight.' The professor nodded. 'We won't learn anything new now.'

Anwar began to click off the lights, leaving the skeleton behind in the gloom. But Emily found she didn't want to let the child out of her sight. Not when she had been the one to pick it bone by bone from the shoreline, carry it to safety inside that bin bag, to some sort of illumination, whatever that might be.

'But do you know how old it is?'

'We can't be certain,' Professor Watt turned towards her, 'the bones aren't fresh, so not very recent. But they also haven't been in the sea for long. I'd hazard a guess they've been kept somewhere, protected from the elements, damp and warmth and so forth. But other than that, there's really very little to go on, except the dressing gown and the newspaper fragments, of course.'

'So they could date from 1996?' Emily said. 'I need to know if they do, people will be asking.'

Professor Watt regarded Emily then, full on for the first time.

'Oh,' she said, 'I thought you realized. This can't be your missing girl. Our new friend here is a baby. Barely even grown.'

Eight

That evening Emily returned home to find one of the people who might be asking at her own front door. Amber Ogilvie, chief amongst the current *Edinburgh Evening News*'s wolf pack. A young woman on the rise. The word on the bones must be out, Emily thought as she approached. Someone at Gayfield had leaked.

'Don't bother storming the ramparts,' she said as she climbed the stair towards where Ogilvie lounged on the landing. 'It won't be worth your while.'

Emily knew that Amber Ogilvie was paid for clickbait and not much else, wasn't going to give her the satisfaction of a scoop one way or another, even if the skeleton she'd found on the Portobello shoreline wasn't who they'd thought.

'PC Noble.' The journalist held out her hand as Emily got near.

The woman had black fingernails, Emily noticed. A bit like Isabella Dawson's if DS Nowack's report was correct. Also the girl who died with a needle in her arm by the time Emily arranged for the door to be forced. But Amber Ogilvie's nails were the result of a particularly glossy varnish. Whereas the girl's had been down to decomposition. Another wasted life.

'What do you want?'

Emily didn't bother to take Ogilvie's hand. She knew

what the journalist was. A vulture. Nothing more, nothing less.

'Wondered if I could have a quick word, PC Noble.'

Emily didn't like the way Ogilvie kept repeating her name and rank, as though she was trying to make a jab at Emily's expense. She knew that her most recent disgrace was common knowledge amongst Edinburgh's fourth estate, just waiting for DS Lawrie's hearing to conclude before spilling the details all over the front page.

'What about?' she said.

Don't give them anything, that was what DCI Franklin had taught Emily. And certainly not until you knew exactly why they had come. Journalists could be useful sometimes, but they always had their own agenda. Emily knew there had to be a reason why Amber Ogilvie was here and she suspected it had something to do with a bin bag recovered from the Portobello surf. As though to confirm her suspicions, the journalist continued.

'Portobello,' she said. '1996.'

Red V-neck jumper, hair in bunches, gap between the teeth. Wherever it had come from, Ogilvie's source was good. DC Blackwood with her taunting eyes, perhaps, last seen drinking shots of Pernod with a certain DS Lawrie in a George Street bar. Either way, Emily knew to keep her mouth shut.

'No comment.'

She put her key in the lock, slid into the hall and reached for the dead bolt, the chain, the mortice. But Ogilvie was too quick, put a foot across the step to prevent the door closing.

'I wonder what you make of the recent news? Given what happened then.'

Emily felt the sudden bloom of sweat between her shoulders at the thought of devastation in a kitchen, the sticky glitter of a blade. She stared at the chunk of trainer wedged between the public and the private space.

'I wouldn't do that, if I were you.'

Attempted to shove the door closed. But Amber Ogilvie rested her hand on the jamb as though daring Emily to slam her fingers in it.

'Just looking for a comment.'

'I'll ask you politely first. Please leave.'

'And then what? You'll call the police.'

Amber Ogilvie raised an amused eyebrow, another sleek curve. Emily felt scruffy all of a sudden, nothing but bare skin buffeted by the sands of Portobello and a scraggy ponytail.

'Leave me alone,' she said. 'You know I won't say anything.'

'And yet you're so good at telling tales.'

Emily shoved the door harder then, no concern for fingers or toes. Ogilvie whipped her hand away, stepped back and Emily closed the door at last. Deadlock. Mortice. Chain. Leaned against the inside breathing hard. She waited for the sound of the journalist's footsteps retreating down the communal stair, felt the shadow of a hand on her neck. But then came the *tap tap tap* of that black fingernail and Emily realized Amber Ogilvie was not finished yet.

'I know it must be hard for you . . .'

The young woman's voice was low, sort of *hush hush*, like a journalist who knows she may be onto something. At once a flutter of fear started in Emily's stomach.

'I've got nothing to say about it.'

'About what, Emily?'

'1996. The girl.'

The moment she said it Emily knew she'd been lured into a trap. Like the trap set for her by DS Lawrie, sprung before she realized it was even there. She wished at once she could take her comment back. Deny, deny, deny. But she knew that would be pointless, have the opposite effect. The DCI would be furious, that was what Emily knew, the press all over the discovery before they knew the truth of the bones themselves.

But Amber Ogilvie didn't bite, not as Emily expected. Instead there was silence from outside the door, as though the journalist was recalculating, had come upon something she did not expect. When she did speak, the journalist's voice was cautious, a testing of new waters.

'What girl, Emily? Who do you mean?'

The first sign that Emily might have got it wrong. Behind the door she shook her head, as though attempting to clear it.

'I've got nothing to say.'

'No, sorry . . .' Amber Ogilvie hesitated, as though unsure of herself now. 'This isn't about a girl. This is about your mother.'

Another knife to the heart.

It was dark inside the flat by the time Amber Ogilvie beat her retreat, got bored of waiting for Emily to appear. Emily slumped on the bathroom floor, propped against the toilet bowl, listening to the journalist leaving as everything around her grew obscure. By the time she heard the slam of the communal door to the street there was nothing left in the flat but shape and shadow, nothing left of her but shape and shadow, too. Emily wiped her mouth on a piece of toilet paper. She had eaten a single Rich Tea biscuit while she waited for Ogilvie to leave, round and round from the outside in till it was gone. Then she'd run to the toilet, stuck her fingers into the back of her throat, retched the Rich Tea back. Her hair smelled of vomit, but it hadn't made any difference. The sound was still inside.

Emily listened to it now. A sort of keening. A sort of crying reaching out to her over all the time that had passed. Nine years old again and standing on another doorstep, Portobello and the sun almost down, fumbling her way inside to a place of strange and shifting objects, unfamiliar, as though she had never lived in the house before. To walls marked with crayon. A stair carpet that skinned your knees if you tripped. To a bathroom covered in a mess of damp towels, water cold in the bath. To a bedroom where two boys slept beneath one cover, curling into each other like shells from the beach. To a dark hall, no sound but her breathing. Then the kitchen, vinyl sticky beneath her feet. In the corner someone was crying. Like the boys used to cry when they were sent to bed without supper, hot stains on their cheeks, sobbing like he sobbed after he had done it. A hand on the neck.

'No.' That was what Emily remembered saying. 'No.'

But the moment she stepped through the kitchen doorway, she knew that it was too late.

Emily got up now from the toilet floor and went through to her bare living room, stood in the window bay and looked into the flats across the street. She watched as families of all shapes and sizes got on with their evening routines. Fathers loading the dishwasher. Mothers talking on the phone. A teenager plugged into his music. A toddler sleeping beneath stars stuck to the ceiling, while his sister hid beneath her bed. Then she went through to the kitchen, slid the file from the drawer.

She laid them on the table. Photographs, spread about, a scene of devastation. A smashed plate. An empty pint of milk. Two cereal bowls tipped over. Blood so bright it appeared artificial, lit by the flash of a crime-scene investigator's camera. The black handle of a knife. It was theatre, really, that was what Emily thought. A scene just waiting for the moving parts to arrive. Sun filtering through a bedroom curtain. A girl running in figure of eights on a beach. A child peering through a letterbox, nothing to see but her eyes. Also a mother, ready in the wings to take centre stage.

Emily got up from the table, opened the drawer with the knives. She let her hands wander – over the solid handles, the steel with its dull glow. She lifted a knife from the drawer, put the blade to her wrist. The skin was thin here, silver lines scored like bracelets into her flesh. Inside her the yearning rose from her belly to her throat. For the shock of the slice, the heat of the blood welling from her veins. Then she put the knife down, closed the drawer, opened the one next to it instead.

Emily laid every letter she'd received on the table, unopened except for the first. She began with that and worked her way through. The last letter was the only one that was different from the rest. Not a sheet of decent writing paper, watermark and the confident exhortations of a fountain pen. But a solitary scrap of something torn from a notebook, a single fold. Emily's name had been scribbled on the front in a hand different from the others. She still felt the shock of it, even after more than twenty years. Emily took a breath, felt her palms sticky, as though clutching hot coins in her pocket. Then she unfolded the paper to see. There was only one sentence.

I forgive you, it said.

Nine

The next morning, Emily woke to disaster in her kitchen, the contents of a forbidden file spread all about. She averted her eyes as she gathered the photographs together, slid them between anonymous covers and into the drawer again. All except a small rectangle, sliced along one side. A girl with a tousle of hair, standing on a beach as she squinted at the camera, legs all over sand and a blue and pink bikini. Emily took that photograph through to the bedroom, slid it into the pocket of her uniform. One way to keep it safe.

The file in the kitchen drawer was one of the first things Emily had done wrong when she became a detective in training. Used a fellow officer's login to access a case from more than twenty years before. There hadn't been much in it that she didn't remember, burned onto her retinas like that flash from a crime-scene investigator's camera. But it was one thing to live it and another to see it written down in black and white.

She ate her breakfast standing in her living-room window bay instead, watching the familial activity across the street. As she nibbled hazelnuts from the top of a cereal bar she thought of the skeleton in Dundee waiting to be returned to whomever it belonged. Its single foot. Its tiny cage of ribs. It might not be the missing girl from 1996, but it was somebody's child. In a bedroom opposite a small girl returned her stare, five years old or thereabouts, still wearing her pyjamas. Emily lifted a hand and the girl raised hers in reply.

Emily arrived at Gayfield ready to fill in the DCI on all the details from Dundee. She was hoping for a special incident room, a wall with photographs of a skeleton, a rotting dressing gown, black bin bag and sheets of newspaper from 1996. Perhaps even a man and his dog waiting in an interview suite, one white eye peering at Emily from across the dirty floor. But when she appeared at the office door with a half-nibbled breakfast bar in her hand, there was nothing. No photographs of yesterday's forensics. No maps of the Portobello shoreline. Nothing but a used takeaway cup abandoned in the middle of her otherwise naked desk.

She headed along the corridor towards DCI Franklin's office, met DC Blackwood coming the opposite way. DC Blackwood's face was impassive, but there was a gleam in her eye as though she had heard something Emily had not. Emily's stomach began with its churn. News travelled fast at Gayfield, that was what she knew. Especially if it was bad. But the DC passed by without a word, not even the hint of a bark.

DCI Franklin was not to be found anywhere in the police station.

'Road traffic accident on the bypass,' said the PC at the desk when Emily enquired. 'One dead. Chief's at the mortuary, if you want to catch her.'

Emily hurried there on foot. Past the Playhouse, through the back of Waverley, then out the other side and across the Mile to link with the end of the Cowgate, that narrow chasm of a street. The Edinburgh City Mortuary was busy this morning, several private ambulances parked outside. Emily ducked beneath the roller shutter and into the receiving bay, joined the trolleys transporting the deceased. Last time she'd been here it was to escort a girl with yellow hair, toes gone mottled in the sun. She remembered how the girl had looked as the funeral directors lifted her body from the mattress, nothing left behind but stains, zipped her into another black bag. Peaceful, as though nothing could touch her. Perhaps the worry dolls had done their job, Emily had thought, as she slipped them into a plastic evidence bag ready to hand over to the officer in charge.

She found her own chief in the Transfer Area standing by as the mortuary technician wrote up the latest arrival.

4 September: Male, Road Traffic Accident

DCI Franklin had an evidence bag in her hand, too, inside a mobile phone, screen smashed like an exploding star. Another driver who thought he could text and change gear at the same time. Emily waited for the DCI to finish, eyes wandering towards the forty-eight fridges, their stainless-steel doors. Isabella Dawson was inside one of these. Black hands. Black feet. Waiting for someone to claim her. Or for the Office for Lost People to fill that void. Edinburgh was full of people who busied themselves sorting the abandoned when nobody else could be found. A parallel existence, that was how Emily thought of it. Rather like the way she lived herself.

'PC Noble.' DCI Franklin was wearing her coat with the fiery lining again, a flash of cinder revealed in the blink of the overhead lights. It reminded Emily of the dressing gown in Dundee. 'Shall we grab a coffee?'

The chief ducked beneath the roller shutter, indicating Emily should follow, was met on the other side by one of the mortuary's regular pathologists, arrived for a day of slicing and dicing, every bodily secret revealed.

'DCI Franklin,' said the pathologist. 'Glad to see you finally made it to our patch. Better late than never.'

'Dr Atkinson.'

Emily could tell at once that there was something between the two women. A skeleton pulled from the shoreline at Portobello, perhaps, should have come to this mortuary first before being spirited to the one in the north. As though to confirm, the pathologist stood square in front of the DCI, made no move to get out of the way. The DCI wrapped her coat about her, hiding the flash of the lining.

'Didn't want to bother you with what could have been a triviality,' she said. 'Something or nothing.'

'Was it a dog, then?' Dr Atkinson asked as though she already knew the answer. 'Or perhaps a cat?'

'We're waiting on the final report.'

Though DCI Franklin already knew it was a baby. Emily had phoned her the night before to report.

'Well, whatever you discover, we'll chalk it up to inexperience, shall we?'

The pathologist's eyes slid beyond the DCI to Emily instead. DCI Franklin nodded and Dr Atkinson stepped aside to let them pass. Emily understood. The DCI would protect her up to a point, but there was only so much chaos she was prepared to take on before she cut Emily loose.

*

'It's too young.'

That was what the chief said as she handed Emily a coffee in a cardboard cup from the takeaway on St Mary's Street. Liked to get straight to the point. Emily had hoped they might sit inside, drink from a china mug, perhaps, chew over the details of the case. But that was not the DCI's style.

'I don't understand,' Emily said.

'It's quite simple, PC Noble.' DCI Franklin was already walking, back towards the train station and the Calton Road tunnel, the quickest route to Gayfield, ready to get on with her day. 'The bones belong to a newborn, almost impossible to trace.'

'But . . .' Emily scurried to follow, hot coffee spilling onto her thumb. 'It's a child. A baby. It must have come from somewhere.'

Yet even as she said it, Emily knew what the DCI believed the skeleton to be.

A fool's errand.

That was what this case amounted to now. An attempt to identify a newborn who had been thrown away like any other piece of rubbish, nothing to go on but a silk dressing gown that was already almost a hundred years old, and a copy of the *Edinburgh Evening News* featuring a case that had merited all the attention in the world but still hadn't been solved. It happened in Edinburgh sometimes, despite the wealth and promise going around. Babies discarded for reasons that could only ever be guessed at. In a park. In a bin. Once even on a golf course. Another form of annihilation, to go with all the rest.

Ahead of Emily, the DCI stopped walking, turned to face her.

'I'm sorry, PC Noble. I'd like to progress things, but it's not an urgent case.'

There was something about the chief's eyes then that made Emily think she really was sorry. A glitter to them, as though DCI Franklin might cry over a baby that someone had discarded, a child that no one would ever know or honour now.

'But what will happen to it?' Emily said. 'The baby.'

DCI Franklin sighed then as though she was very tired. As though she might have argued for something, only to lose. 'They'll ask Glasgow to consider a DNA test, to see if it gets a hit on any of the databases. We'll decide how or whether to investigate further after that.'

Emily knew how long that would take. Weeks. Maybe months. No hurry when the baby was long dead, no relatives to answer to, no one waiting to find out how and why. She felt like crying herself, then, angry little tears gathering in the corner of her eyes, threatening to leak onto her cold cheeks. What was real work if it wasn't digging for the truth? That was what she was thinking. However long ago the crime took place.

'The case isn't finished,' she said. 'There are leads.'

She was thinking of a boarding house overlooking the promenade at Portobello, skip filled with bin bags, green sash trailing in the gutter. Surely that was worth a second look. Also of a small girl standing at a window, hand raised as though in farewell. A sister, perhaps. The kind you share a bedroom with. The kind you sit at the table with to eat breakfast.

DCI Franklin frowned at Emily. 'What leads? You didn't tell me—'

The chief's phone rang, a shrill interruption. The DCI shoved her coffee cup towards Emily, fished the phone from her pocket.

'Yes?'

Emily couldn't help noticing how the DCI's grip tightened as she listened, how she stared at Emily the whole time someone spoke into her ear. When the call ended there was no sign of tears in DCI Franklin's eyes any longer. She wasn't shouting when she spoke, but there was ice in her tone.

'That was a journalist on the phone, PC Noble. Asking questions about what we might have found at Portobello. Now how on earth does she know about that?'

Amber Ogilvie, glossy nails fingering Emily's doorjamb. She dissembled.

'I don't know, ma'am.'

'So you're not someone who tells tales, then.'

It wasn't a question. Emily felt her neck grow hot at the accusation. Or perhaps at the fact that it contained at least an element of the truth.

'Maybe it came from another source.'

The man from the beach, his collie watching Emily with its one white eye. Anwar or Professor Watt, probing at a skeleton with their metal implements. Or DC Blackwood, perhaps, passing in the corridor with that impassive look. Revenge, that was something Emily Noble was familiar with. But DCI Franklin just glared at Emily as though she'd given her young PC a thousand opportunities to show her worth, only to get burned herself.

'For Christ's sake, Noble, I told you to keep it quiet. I'm trying to give you a second chance here, unlike everyone else at Gayfield. You might want to take it.'

'Yes, ma'am.'

For a moment there was silence between them. Then the DCI moved on – to damage limitation.

'We'll have to warn the mother,' she said, reaching for her phone again. 'They'll be all over her unless we get there first.'

Emily understood. Once the word got out, even if it was the wrong word, the vultures would be swarming around a house in Portobello waiting to see if a girl who disappeared over twenty years before was about to make it home. She watched as the DCI dialled a number, then cut it off, stared at her instead.

'You could do it.'

'Ma'am?'

'It's your case, after all.' DCI Franklin slid the phone back into her pocket as though she'd made a decision. 'Go back to Portobello and tell the mother what we've found. Then follow up on your lead, whatever it is, kill two birds with one stone. I'll see what I can do at my end. No promises. But for now, Emily Noble, you get to live another day.'

Ten

PC Emily Noble returned to the scene of the crime well after all the rest. It wasn't hard to find them, she just had to follow the noise. Two streets up from the promenade and there they were. The vultures, just as DCI Franklin had said. Journalists and photographers. Locals who just happened to be passing. Rubberneckers all. Emily could hear the journalists arguing over the best spot on the pavement from several metres away, taking turns to ring the doorbell of the house, littering the kerb with their takeaway cups. She was tempted to charge them with trespass, or if not that, then anti-social behaviour. Had to remind herself that she was not there on ordinary police constable business any longer. She was there as a detective, a probationary one at least.

She approached from the city side, the vultures oblivious to her presence until it was too late. As she stepped off the pavement and onto the road, she found herself treading on a discarded copy of a newspaper. *Edinburgh Evening News*, early edition. She recognized the picture at once. V-neck jumper. Hair in bunches. That gap-toothed smile. Underneath a shouting headline:

HAVE THEY FOUND HER?

Bastards, thought Emily. And worse.

'PC Noble?'

Another officer pushed past the crowd towards her. DS

Nowack from the local nick, come to assist. He touched Emily's elbow as though to steer her in the right direction, put out his other arm to part the crowd.

'We'll go in together, shall we?'

She didn't resist.

Emily passed amongst the vultures as authoritatively as she could. It was tricky. She was only small, a toothpick of a thing, whereas the assorted hordes knew how to push. But the vultures divided from the outside in when they approached, the very presence of the officers acting as some sort of plough. Emily felt a certain satisfaction at how the rabble peeled off to allow them through. There was power in the uniform yet and PC Emily Noble was leading the way.

Once they landed safely at the front gate to the property, her hand on the latch, Emily glanced across the rabble, found one of the rubberneckers staring back. A young woman, tall and ungainly, hair in a mess. There was something familiar about the woman's stance, the way she studied Emily as though she might know her. But when Emily turned to look again, as she stood at the front door waiting to be admitted, she discovered that the girl had disappeared.

Inside the house, the first thing Emily noticed was the photograph. Not the one that was ubiquitous, but another image of the missing child. Summer frock decorated in smocking. A green ribbon in her hair. Emily faltered when she saw it, almost crumpled, until she felt DC Nowack's steady hand upon her arm.

The woman waiting to greet Emily in the living room

looked like her missing daughter. Or rather, the missing daughter looked like her.

'Kirsteen,' she said, as though Emily might not know. 'Kirsteen Morrison.'

Though Emily knew she used to be known as something else. The woman was divorced, the missing girl's father long since vanished to live elsewhere. Not everybody could stay in the same house in which a disaster had taken place. Emily understood all about that.

'Emily Noble.'

Emily didn't say 'PC'. If she'd been this woman, she would have wanted to know why they hadn't sent the Assistant Chief Constable. Or maybe even the Chief Constable. This woman's daughter had been lying hidden somewhere for more than twenty years, but nobody seemed that bothered anymore that she'd never risen to the surface. Or that there was no longer any effort to dig for her bones.

'Please, sit down.'

Kirsteen indicated an overstuffed sofa upholstered in a sort of salmon-pink. Emily felt as though she was dirtying it the moment she perched on its edge. The house was the complete opposite of what she had grown up with. Ornaments on the mantelpiece and pretty wallpaper instead of broken toys scattered amongst the cigarette ash. DS Nowack remained standing. He stationed himself by the door to the living room so that he could keep an eye on the rabble through the glass panel at the front, didn't attempt to usurp Emily by stating his superior rank. DS Nowack must not have heard the stories from Gayfield, Emily thought. Or perhaps he had, had made up his own mind about what had gone on.

'I'm sorry about all this' – Emily gestured towards the living-room window with its Venetian blinds folded against the vultures beyond the gate – 'we don't know how they got hold of the story.'

Always good to start with an apology, even if it was a lie. Kirsteen sat opposite with her hands in her lap, the personification of calm.

'I'm used to it,' she said.

'Would you like a tea or coffee?'

A second person appeared from the kitchen and Emily forced herself to look. A young woman, twenty-five, or thereabouts. The sister. She looked like the missing girl, too.

'Yes, that would be lovely.'

Never refuse a drink, another tip Emily had learned from DCI Franklin. The young woman disappeared to the kitchen at the back of the house and Emily breathed out. There was silence for a moment. What must it be like to have your vanished daughter looking at you every day through another child's eyes? Emily wondered. Then again, this woman had a photograph of her missing girl over the fire, to greet her every morning and say sleep-tight to every night. Unlike Emily, she had not spent a lifetime trying to forget.

Kirsteen cleared her throat, as though it was Emily who needed fortifying, rather than the other way round.

'You have something to tell me.'

It wasn't a question so much as a statement. Emily felt Kirsteen Morrison's steady gaze assessing her. She appeared calm, almost serene, like the dead girl with the needle in her arm, as though nothing could touch her anymore. But there was something else. Emily frowned, puzzled for a second, then realized what it was with a curdle in her gut.

Hope.

That's what she was looking at, the tiny bud inside.

Emily leaned forwards on the sofa, elbows pressing into her knees, two sharp points. She wondered how to say it. We made an unexpected discovery . . . We believed it might be relevant . . . We needed to do more tests . . . We thought it could be something, it turned out to be nothing . . . Except what was there to do but tell the truth?

'I'm sorry,' she said, looking Kirsteen Morrison right in the eye. 'It isn't your girl.'

It was the woman's eyes which did the talking then, their sudden filmy blur. Emily felt hers blur in reply, tried to keep her grip. But as soon as she blinked, prepared herself to deal with this mother's distress, she realized that the haze in Kirsteen Morrison's eyes was gone, replaced with something else Emily recognized. Relief. Emily understood at once. If the skeleton washed up on the beach was not this woman's daughter, that meant her girl might still be alive.

Emily emerged from the missing girl's house thirty minutes later, after two cups of coffee and several biscuits, headed down the front path towards the horde. DS Nowack was still by her side, ready to ensure safe passage. As they approached the gate, the journalists surged forward, shouting their questions:

Is it her? Have you found her?

For a brief moment Emily glimpsed Amber Ogilvie thrown in with the rest, black fingernails scrabbling with the best of them. She felt a certain grim satisfaction in knowing that the journalist's inadvertent scoop was about to take an unwelcome turn. Emily glanced back towards the house, saw two eyes watching her from between the slats of the Venetian blind. The sister. Turned away to unlatch the gate.

She was about to step into the fray when it happened – a rash of pings and notifications, lots of checking of phones. DCI Franklin had authorized the press release now that Emily had completed her task. Official confirmation that the bones on the shoreline did not belong to a five-year-old girl from Portobello who went to play on the swings and never came home, but to a newborn instead. Neither one thing or the other. Not a girl or a boy.

Emily could almost taste the bitterness in her mouth as she walked through a now-deflated crowd. No vultures pursuing her for follow up. No demands to know what the police plan of action would be. As far as they were concerned, the baby skeleton already belonged to history, even though it had only just come to light. Nothing but a side-note to be written up for the inside pages, then left to moulder until somebody came along to kick the traces, see what might arise. It might as well be her, Emily thought as she left the crowd behind. She should have done it years ago. Dug into everything that happened then, all the people who went missing, dragged them into the light. But Emily had been afraid of what might be revealed, the monster hiding in the dark.

She said her goodbyes to DS Nowack at the end of the street.

'Back to Gayfield, is it?' he said.

Emily was certain she could see it lurking in his face. Sympathy. She looked away to hide the flush on her cheeks, noticed the debris strewn about. Paper coffee cups and takeaway wrappers, cigarettes ground to ash on the road. It reminded her of the boarding house and another trail of debris left behind by somebody who had already been consigned to history if The Company had done their job. A bomb of flour on the kerb. A smash of jam. A streak of dirty silk in the gutter.

'Not yet,' she said to DS Nowack, not wanting to involve him in what would almost certainly turn out a fool's errand. 'Other fish to fry.'

She gave him a brief wave as she turned towards the promenade, re-traced a missing girl's footsteps towards a different sort of prize.

Eleven

Outside the back gate of the boarding house, Emily discovered another skip had arrived. This time it was bursting with garden rubbish. Also some smashed china plates. Balanced on top was what looked like an old twin tub, two dark voids staring at Emily like the eyes in the infant's skull at Dundee. Emily searched the ground. The jam was still visible, a sticky patch like a bloodstain, not quite dried. But the explosion of flour was faded now, dispersed by the boots of the cleaners coming and going. This was what happened to evidence, Emily thought, if no one bothered to secure it. It dissipated, drifted away like bones in the surf, till nobody knew the truth anymore, let alone the facts. She searched for five minutes, in the skip and out of it. But however hard she looked, Emily could not find the coil of cloth that had been lying in the gutter the day before, its strange kind of green.

Inside the backyard of the boarding house everything smelled of decay. Earth turned to mould. Concrete soaked with oil. Thick drifts of willowherb trampled and flat. Also lines and lines of chairs and other types of furniture, cluttering the space.

The side return was covered in a rash of colonizing moss. A washing line snaked on the ground, clothes pegs still attached, small ghosts in pink and blue. Emily felt one press into the soft ground beneath her foot as she edged closer to the side of the house, cleaved to its shadow. She put her hand to the stone as though she might feel it breathing. What would she find inside? she wondered. Treasure? Or something much worse. The faint odour of human waste rose from the ground. The whole yard was rotten. Perhaps the house, too.

In the porch Emily discovered a stack of protective supplies left behind by the cleaners. Masks. Gloves. Shoe covers. Some coverall suits. She hesitated, then lifted a mask, hooked it over mouth and nose, pulled covers over her boots. Preserve the scene, that was what she'd been taught, even if it came back to bite. Along with save life and protect the innocent, of course.

Inside, the smell was less unpleasant than Emily had expected. A dry almost desiccated scent inflected with industrial-strength disinfectant. She stepped along an empty passage that ran from the back door to the front, put a hand to touch the wallpaper, small boats in blue and red. The atmosphere in the passage was still, a sort of absence to it, as though waiting for Emily to fill it with something. She called, 'Hello?'

But there was no reply.

The kitchen had been cleared to nothing. No plates smashed in the sink. No blood on the lino. No sticky glitter of a blade. Emily stood in the doorway looking at surfaces wiped clean with bleach, an empty earthenware sink, a gap where a cooker must once have stood. Against one wall was the shadow of what appeared to have been a dresser, an ashy line marking the vacant space. The Company deserved their reputation. Less than a week since she had been carried out and already any sign of Isabella

Dawson had been wiped clean, from the ground floor, at least.

In the grand but shabby hall Emily found the main door to the property, an edifice of faded mahogany and smoked glass. It had been secured with a new lock to prevent any further incursions. Boys, Emily thought, searching for treasure just like she was doing now. She cast about for any evidence of a dressing-gown sash, found nothing but a piano key abandoned on the floor in one room and a single plate with a crack across its face in another. She stood for a moment at the large oval dining table, tried imagining what the boarding house must once have been. A bustle of guests arriving and leaving, brown suitcases and hats, eggs for breakfast, cold ham for high tea. In the hall she eased open a door under the stairs, discovered a water closet with a stained toilet pan and a wide ceramic sink. The closet was the perfect place for a child to hide, Emily thought; could watch through the keyhole as everyone came and went. She thought of the file she kept in the kitchen drawer at her flat, what had been found in another cupboard under the stairs, put a hand to the powdery plaster to steady herself.

She is not here, she said to herself. She is not here.

But inside her head Emily could hear it. The solitary drip of water into a bath. The sound of someone breathing. And that keening, over and over, drawing her towards a room with blood upon its floor.

Upstairs the landing had not been cleared yet, still retained traces of what the boarding house must have been like before The Company were called. Dust rose from the remnants of a Turkish carpet to mingle with the perfume of heavy, brown furniture left to rot. At the top of the stairs Emily discovered a china dog with a chip on his nose. She touched the dog's head as she passed, left a print in the dust, felt a sudden panic that she had ruined the integrity of the scene. Then she told herself not to be ridiculous. The cleaners would already have disturbed whatever integrity there might have been with their spray cans and their mops.

Emily made her way along the landing, pushing at each of the doors. A room with a faded pattern of roses on the wall. Another containing a bed piled with what looked like old curtains. The last but one with a huge mound of clothes scattered everywhere, saturated with the stink of unwashed cotton and wool. Also a bathroom with a suite in faded turquoise. Emily hesitated before stepping into the bathroom, heard again the *drip drip drip* of water from a tap, saw a boat circling on the surface of the bath-water, damp towels on the floor. She realized she was holding her breath, let it go. Inside, the bath was empty, nothing but a scatter of dead insects, legs curled.

There was something about the upstairs that felt different from the ground floor, Emily thought as she withdrew from the bathroom. Unwelcoming. A threat around every corner. Blood beat beneath the skin of her wrists as she remembered the first floor of another house. Three meagre bedrooms with their flimsy plywood doors, inside damp polyester sheets and children's toys scattered. A Barbie doll with a rough tangle of hair. Those Lego pieces bought second-hand from the charity shop on the High Street. She remembered how the shadows had fallen across the nylon carpet as she crept up the stairs, stood before each door with her heart in her throat knowing something wasn't right. Her parents' room with its stink of Benson and Hedges. The empty bathroom, water gone cold in the bath. The bedroom she shared with her sister, yesterday's clothes still piled on the floor. Then the room where the boys slept, how she'd closed her eyes before she entered because she'd known, somehow, that after she pushed open the door nothing would ever be the same. Emily had read the file. She had looked at the photographs. She had re-lived it a million times. But still she didn't understand how things could go from the everyday to disaster, in the time it took for someone to run to the shop for milk.

Emily stood outside the final room on the first floor of the boarding house and told herself to breathe. She thought of her own flat with its blank walls waiting to be painted, any colour she wanted. The people in the houses opposite going about their normal lives. She could have that life, if she wanted it. Could reach to grasp it rather than let the past pull her back. Emily put her hand to the door of the final room, the patina of wood grain beneath her fingertips. It was then that she heard it, some sort of disturbance. Another person in the house. Isabella Dawson's ghost, perhaps. Or more boys come to take a look. But when Emily pushed open the door, stepped inside to see, what she found was a view of a garden. A promenade. The beach in all its naked glory. Beyond that the sea.

Isabella Dawson's last resting place was littered with stuff. Paperback books and discarded clothes. Abandoned ice-cream tubs and a bed with the covers thrown back as though Isabella Dawson had stepped straight out of them, would return at any moment to resume her night's sleep. Curiosity drew Emily towards the bed. She had seen a few bodies, but never one that had been left to decompose for two years before anyone dealt with it. The covers on the bed were deep dyed, nasty stains on the pillow. Emily stumbled upon a pair of brown lace-up shoes, tongues stiff. The Company had not tackled this room yet, that was clear. It was still as it must have been when Isabella Dawson lay down to sleep one night, never woke again.

Next to the bed was a chest of drawers speckled with dead flies. There was the faintest hint of Pledge still scenting the air as though Isabella Dawson had been doing the polishing before she succumbed. Emily pulled open one of the top drawers, found it stuffed with tights, underwear that smelled as though it hadn't been washed for years. She tried the rest of the drawers, too, but however much she rummaged, she could not find any sort of sash for a dressing gown. Or even an ankle bone to add to the rest.

She abandoned her search of the chest of drawers, trod a narrow path on the carpet to the window. There it all was – the whole spectrum of the beach, the sea, the sky, beneath that a grand vista of the garden Emily had only glimpsed through a keyhole before. The garden must once have been a haven for roses and lupins, the kind of place Emily would have loved to play in when she was young. But now it was covered in a riot of weeds, yellow patches where some things had been removed. But the cleaners weren't quite finished, Emily realized, counting at least one three-legged dining chair and what looked like a sofa cushion nestled amongst a mound of nettles. Why would an old lady put a sofa in the garden? That was what Emily was thinking when she shivered suddenly as though somebody had walked across her grave.

She turned, looked across the empty room towards the bedroom door where it stood half open, the landing beyond. But nobody was there. Emily moved into the centre of the room, waited, tried to capture what she had felt a moment before. The house was very still, as though holding its breath. Emily studied the cluttered floor with its worn tread of carpet, the window with its cheap cotton curtains, the bed. Then her gaze landed on the wardrobe, the thin slit of its eye.

The wardrobe was a large thing, perfect for hiding in, especially if you were a child. Emily heard her own breathing, harsh from beneath her mask, as she stepped closer, drawn to the wardrobe as though by some invisible thread. She reached a hand towards the door, imagined the remains of a baby's skeleton scattered on the floor inside. Or a child crouching in the dark, eye to the slit to see what she might see. The past was close here, pressing against Emily like a child in a bed curling in to steal her warmth. In her chest her heart began with its figures of eight, running, running. Then she heard the call:

Essie!

Filtering to her over twenty long years. Emily stopped, dropped her hand, stepped away from the wardrobe and turned towards the bedroom door instead. The call came again, different this time. A voice rising up the stairs. It came from somewhere in the hall:

'Hello. Is somebody there?'

Twelve

They were gathered in the hall. Two people dressed from top to toe in coverall suits. A third carrying a clipboard under her arm. For a brief moment Emily thought they were scene-of-crime operatives, sent by DCI Franklin to help her search. Then she realized it must be the cleaning crew, returned from disaster on the bypass to continue their clear-out of Isabella Dawson's boarding house. She made her way to the top of the stairs, stood by the dog.

'Who are you?'

The woman with the clipboard was accusatory, as though Emily had no business treading all over The Company's territory without having been given her permission first. Emily was relieved that she had put on the shoe covers, the mask. If she was going to get caught snooping, at least she would have left no trace. She began her descent, feeling like an awkward queen making her entrance, whereas the three members of The Company stared at her as though they were the royalty and Emily the kitchen maid caught above stairs.

'State your business.'

The woman with the clipboard accosted Emily before she'd even stepped onto the fractured terracotta tiles. But what was her business? Emily thought as she hovered on the bottom stair. Searching for the truth about a baby washed up on the Portobello shoreline? Or a strange sojourn into her own past? Either way, Emily had a feeling deep in her gut, like a real detective, that something in this house was not right.

'PC Emily Noble.'

She didn't hold out her hand towards the owner of the clipboard. What was it DCI Franklin had taught her once? Meet like with like. The woman didn't even bother prevaricating, got straight to the point.

'Is there a problem?'

'No. Well – I'm here on official business. DCI Franklin's case.'

'What case?'

'Missing person,' Emily said in a determined tone. 'Follow-up inquiry.'

'Missing person?'

The woman frowned, ran a manicured hand down the front of her blouse. Beside her, the two cleaners appeared to be grinning beneath their masks. One of them was leaning on what looked like a hoover, industrial size compared to the neat proportions of the Henry which Emily pulled around after her when she had the occasional day off. It only took her twenty minutes or so to clean away the non-existent dust from the corners of her empty rooms, as though that might make a difference to the emptiness of her life.

Now the woman reached for her phone as though to confirm Emily's credentials. But before she had even scrolled through to the number, the cavalry arrived.

'What's going on?'

Margaret Penny of the Office for Lost People appeared from out of the passage. Here to check on her latest client's remains, Emily thought. Despite the woman with the clipboard's stern demeanour, Emily knew that Margaret Penny was ultimately responsible for Isabella Dawson and her rubbish. Unless she had arrived to check on Emily Noble, of course.

'PC Noble.'

Emily did offer her hand this time, by way of formal introduction. She had met Margaret Penny before, several times, while doing bag-carrying duties for DCI Franklin. But she wasn't sure if Margaret Penny would remember her. Too busy making sure the DCI's enquiries didn't stop the timely dispatch of the neglected and abandoned, or at least those who had died with no one else to take them on.

The senior case officer from the Office for Lost People gave a brisk nod when Emily announced her name, as though she knew all about PC Noble. Which, knowing Edinburgh, she probably did.

'To what do we owe this honour?'

Margaret Penny was resplendent in her usual red coat. Also a pair of what looked to Emily like inappropriate shoes for this type of job, heels and a strap across the ankle. Then again, Emily knew it was not Margaret Penny who did the actual cleaning. Nor the woman with the clipboard, judging by the pristine creases in her trousers. Like knife blades, Emily thought. And she knew something about that. She had no doubt these two women got their hands dirty, but not in a literal fashion. No problem washing off Edinburgh's muck at the end of the night.

'A missing-person inquiry,' Emily said. 'Just following up some leads.'

Margaret Penny looked Emily in the eye. Emily caught

a glimpse of a fox, its bent ear. The fox winked at Emily. Or perhaps that was just a trick of the light.

'The girl from 1996? I thought that case was sorted.'

Unlike the cleaners, Margaret Penny was up to date. V-neck jumper. Hair in bunches. Still missing after all these years. But Emily stood her ground. The girl from 1996 might be lost to her, but she had a newborn to defend.

'This is something different. We have some further inquiries to make, about your recent client.'

As though to confirm that she was the real power here, Margaret Penny stood her ground, too. 'What, Isabella Dawson? This isn't a criminal case, as far as I'm aware. It's already been cleared by the Fiscal.'

Scotland's crown office, ultimately responsible for declaring whether someone's demise was suspicious or not.

'No, but I do need to take a look at—'

Margaret Penny dismissed Emily with a regal wave. 'Your case has nothing to do with Isabella Dawson, I'm sure. Or my cleaners would have found something.'

'I wouldn't be too certain of that.'

The man who appeared behind them in the hall was in his sixties, tweed jacket and socks the colour of the willow-herb trampled in the yard. Emily recognized him at once. Solomon Farthing the Heir Hunter, last seen begging at the feet of Greyfriar's Bobby a few years before. Isabella Dawson must be rich in something more than rubbish, Emily thought, for her to merit this kind of attention. If not in neighbours who cared enough to check while she lay dead next door to them for two whole years.

'Solomon Farthing.'

The Heir Hunter came straight over to Emily and held

out his hand. Emily took it with the hint of a smile. She knew all about Solomon Farthing, a man who liked to curry favour, that was what DCI Franklin said. Could be useful, especially if there was something in it for him.

'PC Noble.'

'Yes.' Solomon Farthing winked at her, like Margaret Penny's fox. 'You drove me to a reckoning once. At the Sheriff's Court.'

The rumpled hair in the rear-view mirror. Those muddy knees. 2016 and the imminent vote. How time had moved on since then, Emily thought. And in other ways, not at all. Solomon Farthing had been destitute, that was what Emily remembered. Saved by a favour, just as DCI Franklin had said. Things must have come right for the Heir Hunter if he was working with the Office for Lost People, found a way to pay off his debts.

Margaret Penny twitched as though she felt the need to reassert her authority. 'What brings you back here? Have you found someone?'

'Found who?' Emily said.

But she knew, as soon as the words were out of her mouth. Isabella Dawson's boarding house might look like a pile of rubbish now, upstairs at least. But once it was cleared it would be a very valuable property, for the view alone, not to mention all the rest. Something worth finding an heir for, in return for commission, just as DS Nowack had said. What was it the DCI had told Emily? Solomon Farthing had a knack for finding those who had been lost. DCI Franklin had made use of his services, if the rumours were correct, something lurking in the chief's past that she wanted to keep hidden, too.

Solomon Farthing did not demur and Margaret Penny's eyes glittered then, like her dead fox. 'You've dug someone up, haven't you. An heir to take it all on.'

The new arrival was cautious. 'Not an heir as such . . .' He turned to Emily again. 'But it could be relevant to your case, I think.'

How does he know about my case? Emily thought. An anonymous baby washed up on the Portobello shoreline. Not a boy. Or a girl. Then again, this was Edinburgh. Everybody knew everybody else's business. Particularly if there was property involved.

'What about my case?'

The Heir Hunter grinned.

'Isabella Dawson had a baby once.'

They sat outside to hear the news. Margaret Penny of the Office for Lost People next to Solomon Farthing the Heir Hunter. Daphne from The Company next to PC Emily Noble. All sitting on what remained of Isabella Dawson's dining chairs laid out in her backyard. Inside the house, Emily could hear the two cleaners from The Company ripping a threadbare Turkish carpet from Isabella Dawson's stairs. Life had a funny way of bringing people together, she thought. Even if that was because one of them had died.

Margaret Penny was as delighted as Emily at Solomon Farthing's news, couldn't contain the gleam in her, or her fox's, eye. Emily understood the reason. Solomon Farthing's digging might mean that Margaret Penny had someone to take on Isabella Dawson. Plus everything she had left behind. The bin bags. The rubbish. Not to mention the house. Someone who could decide what coffin the old lady might prefer, who should read her eulogy. Also where the council could send any outstanding bills. But still, Margaret Penny wanted to check the facts first. Like a good detective, Emily thought.

'We were told there were no children.' Margaret Penny fixed Solomon Farthing with her stare. 'U.H. were certain.'

Ultimus Haeres. The Last Heir. Or at least as far as Solomon Farthing was concerned.

'False trail,' he replied. 'Happened all the time then, the falsification of paperwork. A common feature where illegitimacy was involved.'

'What exactly are we talking about here?'

Emily wanted the facts, too, like Margaret Penny, not a history lesson. Solomon Farthing drew a piece of paper from his inside pocket, a magician springing a rabbit from a hat.

'The child was registered by Isabella Dawson's mother. She used Isabella's middle name when giving the details of the baby's mother, but the rest adds up.'

A birth certificate with neat signatures in the proper boxes. Name, date, place and witness, all laid out in black on white. Mrs Lillian Dawson signing for her daughter Isabella, with only a minor sleight of hand.

'Why would she do that?' said Daphne. 'Cover things up.'

But Emily knew the answer to that:

Disgrace.

Solomon Farthing handed the birth certificate around so that everyone could have a proper look. Emily tried to ignore the quiver in her fingers as she studied the text, searched for the sex. A baby boy, that was what the certificate stated. By the name of Ted. 6 lb 13 oz, born at one fifty-two a.m. Like a boy crouching at the edge of the sea with his toes in the surf. A boy sleeping curled around his brother. A boy with lips tinged violet, as though he had been swimming in the sea too long, couldn't make it back. She thought of the skeleton laid on the work station in Dundee. Its missing toes. Its single leg.

'Where was he born?' she asked.

'In the boarding house,' said the Heir Hunter. 'According to this.'

Which room? Emily thought then. The one at the front with its view of the beach? Or the one at the back with its faded roses on the wall? It was strange to think of the boarding house as ever having been home to a child. There was something so hollow about it, despite everything it contained.

Margaret Penny surveyed the paperwork, nodded in satisfaction and thrust it back into the Heir Hunter's hands. She had more pressing concerns than where Isabella Dawson's child had been born. Her only interest was in calling upon his wallet.

'Where is he now?' she said. 'We must get in touch.'

But just as Emily had suspected, Solomon Farthing was shaking his head.

'No joy on that, I'm afraid. No trace of him in the records after the birth was registered, not that I can find anyway.'

'What does that mean?' Margaret Penny demanded.

'Could be alive somewhere under a different name. Or dead, of course.'

'Dead?'

Ribs like a tiny cage. Two holes for eyes. Solomon Farthing turned to Emily then.

'If my information's correct, I think you might be able to help with that.'

Thirteen

Emily Noble returned to Gayfield Police Station bearing treasure in her hand. Not a leg bone belonging to a newborn. Or even a coil of silk in a strange sort of green. But a piece of paper, black type on white, the cursive script of a registrar. A name and a date. She was holding a copy of a birth certificate proving that once, long ago, Isabella Dawson had a baby of her own. Evidence, that was what she wanted to call it, though Emily knew that it could be construed as circumstantial at best. It was raining by the time she got into the centre of town. Not hard, more a drizzle, but enough to ensure that she was damp all over by the time she arrived. But even that could not diminish the fizz inside. Emily was as close as she might ever be to saving a skeleton from oblivion, one lost child returned to the fold at least.

Her cheerfulness did not last long. The glances and the whispers began as soon as she stepped foot over the threshold of the station. In reception, the desk sergeant's eyes followed Emily from behind his Perspex screen, like some sort of family portrait that never spoke but saw everything. And judged it, too. The sergeant had his arms folded across his chest, his normal pose for booking in the most recalcitrant suspects. It did not bode well. As Emily flicked her pass at the keypad to gain access to the back office, two civilian staff came through from the other direction, glancing at her, then away, whispering together as they moved towards the interview room. Up the stairs, it was a DS, hissing at Emily as she passed in the corridor.

'Bloody clipe. Your turn to get what's coming now.'

These were almost the first words anyone had spoken to her for weeks, other than DCI Franklin, of course. Emily flushed, stared at her boots till the woman passed, realized that she was looking at a long trail of seawater dribbled along the carpet tiles, dried now and salty, marking where she had ascended with her other treasure only two days before. That had been a potential disaster, too, turned into possibility, a way out of her disgrace. But despite the prize in her hand, Emily wasn't sure she could manage the same trick twice.

The office was disappointingly empty, no detectives to receive the news that a constable had shown them how to do their job. Emily breathed heavily as she abandoned her stab vest and its defensive paraphernalia on her desk. Pepper spray. Handcuffs. Baton. She felt naked without it. There was something about being protected, even against one's own side.

DCI Franklin's office was muggy when Emily entered after knocking several times. Three cups of coffee in various stages of decomposition were lined on the top of the filing cabinet by the door. But the chief was absent, no sign of her coat with the cinder lining. Emily stood forlorn, wondering whether to leave a note, or call the DCI, perhaps. There was something about the good news that felt it couldn't wait.

'I heard you were back.'

DC Blackwood lounged in the office doorway, leaning against the jamb. She was smiling, as though to emphasize the fact that she had always known everything Emily Noble touched would somehow turn to dust.

'What do you want?'

'I have news from the chief. She asked me to pass on a message.'

DC Blackwood held a piece of paper between her finger and thumb, as though it might contaminate her if she grasped it any tighter.

'What message?' said Emily.

'See for yourself.'

Emily waited for DC Blackwood to pass the note to her. But she didn't, forcing Emily to step forwards and take it from her. As Emily reached to pluck the paper from out of DC Blackwood's fingers, the detective held on to it for a moment.

'Better luck next time,' she said. 'Maybe stick to dogs.'

The bones were old news, that was what the DCI's message amounted to. Over fifty, according to the mortuary in Dundee. Maybe much older. A grey area, the Chief had written. Meaning the skeleton was being assigned to the Historical Cases Unit. Another sort of grave. Dismay ran through Emily like ice in a frozen river. Historical Cases were the team behind the door at the far end of the furthest corridor in Gayfield. The team which no one bothered with most of the time because they didn't have any real police work to do. Cold cases, those were what they worked on. The name said it all.

Emily studied the DCI's note again in the hope of another outcome, thought of the lost children who had sought refuge in the Cold Case filing cabinet, still waiting for their deaths or disappearances to be resolved. Then she thought of the mothers they had left behind, the fathers, the brothers and the sisters, people who loved them and might still be around. They would want to know that everything had been done to resurrect their lost ones, Emily was certain about that. Before they laid down, too.

She glanced at the birth certificate in her hand. If the skeleton found on the Portobello shoreline really was Isabella Dawson's son, he had been born in 1953, which would have made him sixty-six this year if he had survived. Or his bones, of course. In line with Dundee's time frame, but not yet archaeological as far as the police were concerned. A small glimpse of light. Emily considered the missing sash from a dressing gown lying in a gutter, a pile of bin bags in a skip. It might be circumstantial evidence at best, instinct at worst, but if it was true and the bones really did belong to Isabella Dawson's dead child, then perhaps she could liberate the file from the Historical Cases Unit, try and close it herself.

She left DCI Franklin's office and headed towards the far reaches of Gayfield Police Station, down a corridor which culminated in a dead end. She knocked once and a voice answered.

'Come in.'

So she did.

They were expecting her. DCI Franklin had warned Cold Cases that Emily Noble could come. Needless to say, her remonstrations didn't do any good.

'The birth certificate doesn't prove anything,' said the DI who was in charge. 'It's purely circumstantial. We'll put it on file, wait for it to rise to the top. But don't hold your breath. In the absence of any hard evidence we can't prioritize this case.'

'What will happen to it then?'

'If you want to be helpful, Emily, you can collect the bones from Dundee, deliver them to the funeral parlour at the bottom of Leith Walk.'

Last home of the indigent. Last home of those who had no one else to take them on. Emily was well acquainted with the funeral parlour at the bottom of Leith Walk, all its lost souls stored in the basement fridges waiting for their council coffins to be brought down. She had shepherded several bodies in that direction over the last couple of years. Stood by as a locksmith forced the door, the Fiscals bent over a body to confirm non-suspicious, the private ambulances pulled to the kerb with their neatly folded body bags. She'd watched as they carried the bodies out feet first, while the cleaners in their coverall suits filed in with their mops. The cleaners' job was to wipe everything and spray everything, to clean it all away.

Like when Emily was young, driven from a three-bedroom terrace house in Portobello to another part of the city, told to leave everything behind. Emily had accepted it then, done what everyone said, tried to forget about what had been abandoned behind the door. But Emily would not walk away this time. There must be something she could do to keep the bones alive.

'What about the DNA test?' she said. 'We could do a match, check to see if they're related.'

Emily knew how to be persistent, whatever trouble it might get her into. The DI pressed a finger to her temple as though to curb some throbbing inside.

'Forensic tests cost money. Take time. We don't have the resources.'

Emily understood. Ever since they had formed Police Scotland seven years before there had only ever been talk of *cuts, cuts, cuts*. Then there had been the Vote and now maybe No Deal, which might only mean more cuts. And who knew what could happen after that. 2020, the door to a whole new decade of disaster. This country really was going to shit, thought Emily. A land where some people had the money to do whatever they wanted, while others ended as flotsam and jetsam on the shoreline, nobody with the time or inclination to even find out their name.

'But the family. Don't they deserve to know?'

The DI was getting impatient now. 'If your theory is correct, then there aren't any family. They're all dead. Best to let it go now, Emily. Fetch the bones from Dundee and hand them over.'

To the Office for Lost People. Meaning Margaret Penny with her fox stole and her inappropriate shoes ordering up the most basic measures. A miniature coffin. A single crematorium officer to carry it in. Not even any hymns as the tiny box rolled towards the flames.

It roared in Emily's head then, like the roar inside a shell collected from Portobello beach. Anger. At how the truth could be hidden. At how the sins of the past might never come to light. This could be murder, she thought. Or something just as bad. Abandonment. A child left on its own to moulder until it was all bone and no flesh, tiny organs nibbled to nothing by the fish. Either way, it was annihilation, however long ago.

*

When Emily returned to the Gayfield reception once again, DC Blackwood appeared, too. As though she had been waiting for her. As though she had known that Emily would come this way. Emily attempted to ignore the DC as she flashed her pass for access to the outside world. To air. To rain. To escape from the people who only wanted to pull her down. But just like the rest of them, DC Blackwood was not done yet.

'The decision on DS Lawrie came through,' the detective called as Emily pushed at the door. 'Thought you might be interested.'

Emily flushed, flashed her pass again. But the door wouldn't budge. She glanced over to the desk sergeant, but he refused to catch her eye, or to press the button that would facilitate her exit. DC Blackwood took advantage, as they must have planned. She came to stand behind Emily, so close Emily could feel the DC's breath on her neck.

'Looks like he's going to get reinstated,' DC Blackwood said. 'Back where he belongs. Then he can let the dogs out, see where they lead.'

Emily smelled peppermint, the faintest whiff of Pernod. A celebration, perhaps? She rattled the door again and at last it clicked open. She pushed through into the fresh air, desperate for rain wet on her face, only to find DC Blackwood's foot preventing the door from closing, her hands pushing something into Emily's.

'He left a present for you. Said you'd want to keep it.'

Not a note this time, the fate of a baby's skeleton contained in its fold. But a small triangle of cloth sewn into a miniature bag, tied at the top with a coloured piece of string. Emily didn't need to open the bag to know what was inside. Six dolls fashioned from tiny lengths of wire, their heads made from paper, their clothes made from scraps. Worry dolls, slipped from beneath a dead girl's pillow. A mother. A father. Two girls. Two boys.

Fourteen

That afternoon a light rain fell over Edinburgh. It covered the city in a soft blanket of haze, from the folly on the hill, to the Golden Boy standing atop Old College holding the torch of knowledge in his hand. Cold leeched into the sandstone. Autumn was coming, the seasons on the turn.

PC Emily Noble sat on a bench in Gayfield Square, a dead girl's last gift in her lap. Two boys. Two girls. A mother. A father. She rolled the father between finger and thumb, picking at the paper that made up his head until it came loose. Then she unravelled him. His black hair and painted mouth. The blue thread that wound his arms. Also his legs.

She discarded the doll's remains in the grass about her feet, till he was nothing but a stick of wire. Then she pressed the sharp end against the back of her hand, punctured the skin. A bead of blood welled up. She sucked at it, blood warm on her lip, jabbed again. It was written through her, Emily thought, like lettering through a stick of seaside rock. The instinct for destruction. She'd been taught it since the day she was born.

The last time Emily had seen her father he was in a coffin, a man like the worry doll, stripped of everything that once made him. Cheap cans of lager and T-shirts grown baggy at the hem. A rasp for a laugh as he flicked sand at her on the beach, Emily running, screaming, with a laugh of her own. It had been her final day in Portobello, nine years old and standing in a pew at the back of a church in the High Street, while her father lay in a box at the front. There had been singing in the church, in a language Emily could not understand, a soaring, haunting thing that mingled with the incense, curling to the rafters and making her cough. Everyone around her had been sobbing like they would never stop. But Emily's eyes were dry. She'd known, even then, that she would never cry for him.

Her mother had been hysterical, standing in the front pew between two police officers screaming and wailing, reaching her hands towards the coffin as though she might be able to claw Emily's father from the box. That always had been their problem; they were never able to leave each other alone. Her mother had been wearing a sweatshirt Emily had never seen before, shapeless and faded. It had been strange to see her dressed like that, when Emily knew her mother preferred jeans and cami tops with spaghetti straps, which her father had preferred, too. Her mother's wrists had been shackled, like Emily was shackled, her grandmother keeping her hand on Emily's wrist throughout the service as though she was a prison guard and Emily the prisoner, nowhere left to go.

What Emily remembered most was digging her finger-nails into the pew in front until she marked the wood. Five little crescents, like the marks her father used to leave on her mother's neck. Also the two other coffins, balanced on their trestles, the ones her mother ignored but which Emily could not take her eyes from. White and small, as though they were toys rather than boxes cut to child size. Inside, two boys.

For years, Emily used to think that moment was the last time the family were all together. Her father in a box. Her brothers in a box. Emily at the back. Her mother screaming at the front. It was only later that she realized she had left her sister out. A girl last seen being escorted from a terraced house by a woman wearing shoe covers and a mask, gloves and a coverall suit, emerging from the front door hand in hand with a ghost.

Her sister had still been wearing her pyjamas, that was what Emily remembered the most. Though it was dark by then, the sun long since set over the sea. They had found her in the cupboard under the stairs, that was what the report in the file said. Curled around like a foetus, so quiet they missed her the first time. It had been several hours of comings and goings before the alarm was raised, a scene-of-crime operative wearing a mask and gloves and all the other paraphernalia opening the door of the cupboard to find a child inside. Emily had returned to the house by then to find blue lights colouring the street, a sort of mayhem, had been locked in the back seat of a squad car to keep her safe. She had been crying when they led her sister away, as though she would never stop. Never did get to see her again.

Emily left the church in Portobello that day with her grandparents on her father's side. They drove her from Edinburgh's seaside to a place she'd not been before. A new home on the far side of the city, with trees and grass and cherry blossom in the spring. Edinburgh had more than one face and, aged only nine, Emily understood that just like the city she was about to put on a new one. But as they drove away, past the beach, past the amusement arcade, past the dump at Seafield, Emily had known that it would run through her always.

Disaster.

Written in blood rather than sugar. No way to get it clean.

Emily stared at the remnants of the worry doll scattered at her feet. Then at the remains of a family resting in her lap. She picked out four of the dolls, two boys, two girls, slid them into the triangle of cloth, put that into her pocket so they at least could stay warm. She was about to lift the mother when she looked up, found a woman standing before her wearing some sort of robe.

'Hello, Emily,' the woman said. 'I am Sister Josephine.'

Sr Josephine lived in Portobello, at a convent that was also a halfway house. She took in women who had been in prison, needed somewhere to stay once they were released.

A refuge.

That was how she had described it in the letters that she sent to Emily. We all need refuge, that was what Emily had thought.

She didn't say anything now as Sr Josephine sat next to her on the bench. Nuns had a way of inviting themselves into your life; that was what Emily had discovered. Whether you wanted them there or not. Sr Josephine was wearing sandals without socks, despite the weather having taken a turn. How did she keep her feet warm in winter? Emily wondered. Perhaps it was an act of penance, to keep them bare all year, even in a place like Scotland. Or maybe it was just that Sr Josephine enjoyed walking on the Portobello sand. Either way, Sr Josephine did not seem perturbed by the cold. She leaned back to rest against the bench with a look on her face that suggested all of life had just come to her.

'I'm sorry to have waylaid you while you are working,' the nun said. 'But you didn't reply to any of my letters. Even the last.'

Emily had a vision then of Sr Josephine waiting on the street outside her flat, a night or so ago, holding on to a handwritten envelope till a neighbour held open the communal door. It didn't surprise her now that Sr Josephine had managed to gain entry. Nuns could get in anywhere, they only had to ask.

'I've been busy,' she said.

'Yes, lots of missing dogs and cats, I believe.'

Emily scowled. That was the other thing about nuns, they were very well informed. She wondered for a moment if Sr Josephine was angling for information on a skeleton washed up on the Portobello shoreline, as well as all the rest. Another candidate for salvation, if ever there was one. But the nun soon dispelled that notion.

'It's about your mother,' she said.

Emily's internal sigh was small and bleak. It was always about her mother. Never the other way round.

'She's looking for somewhere to stay,' said Sr Josephine. 'Once she's released. We thought you might be able to help.'

Emily's mother lived in an open prison on the outskirts of Edinburgh, at least that was what Sr Josephine had said. Even though she was a police officer, Emily had never ventured into that nether-world – a place where the guilty were taken once they were preparing to re-enter society.

Or something like that. Flowerbeds and art activities, that was what Emily had heard, as though her legwork on behalf of the innocent had ended, consigning the guilty to a venue more suited to a garden party or a village fete.

Who had ordered it? That was what Emily wanted to know. Without telling her. Without telling anyone. Who had signed their name to an instruction that said her mother could wander amongst the begonias and go for day-release without explaining to anyone what she had done?

'I'm not interested.'

Emily's tone was hard, like a stick of seaside rock, easy to break teeth over. But Sr Josephine wasn't the sort of person to take a re-buff, she had lived and worked in Edinburgh for too long.

'She's been coming to us for day-release. Doing very well . . .'

'To Portobello?'

Emily couldn't hide the shock in her voice. The nun put a hand onto Emily's knee, a brief touch.

'She's there right now, if you'd like to see her.'

'Why! Why would I want to do that?'

Inside Emily the panic bloomed. But Sr Josephine just smiled, a simple gesture.

'It might help you lay your burdens down.'

Fifteen

The Portobello convent was a funny sort of place, a two-storey building set back from the street, accessed via a narrow slit between a row of private dwellings as though it had been designed to hide whoever went in, and whoever came out. They took the bus to get there, Sr Josephine and Emily Noble, sitting in silence as it trundled to the seaside. At every stop on the way, Emily thought she would jump off.

They disembarked at the stop outside the local police station, DS Nowack inside compiling his sudden death reports. Then Sr Josephine led the way along the High Street to the corner where Mrs Wren used to run her shop, turned down Bath Street in the direction of the promenade. Emily followed, as though drawn on a string. They were close to Isabella Dawson's boarding house, she thought as they neared the promenade. Another person who needed salvation, rather like her. In the gap between the buildings, she could see the sun sinking towards the horizon. Evening would be here soon.

Sr Josephine's brown habit swung about her bare ankles as she disappeared between two houses, beneath an arched metal sign. Emily glanced at the sign as she passed under it:

Lambs of God

That was what it said. Sr Josephine's order. Underneath there was what appeared to be a qualifying statement:

Willing to the Slaughter

Emily could hear it then, the alarm bell ringing in her head. Was this what she was destined for? Another room filled with blood?

The alleyway opened into a rectangular area with a small car park on one side. Back access, Emily thought with an odd sensation of relief. An escape route, should it be required. The convent building itself was nothing special, square and squat, overshadowed by the houses in front and to the side. There were dark streaks on the stonework from a broken gutter, weeds rampant amongst the gravel. An order that believed in abstinence and poverty, Emily thought. Or just one that catered to the fallen, people who had done the worst thing possible, but still got out to wander amongst the rest.

By the time she reached the convent step, Emily discovered that Sr Josephine was nowhere to be seen, had disappeared in much the same way she had appeared – with no warning, no suggestion of where she had come from and where she might have gone. Emily searched for a doorbell, found two. One was marked, *Lambs*, the other, *Spiritualists*. She was surprised. She knew that both denominations believed in life after death, but not the form that it took.

Through the windows on the ground floor Emily could see that the interior of the convent matched the demeanour of the outside. Sash cords were broken, the walls bare. She glimpsed what appeared to be a drawing room lit by nothing more than a single bulb. It reminded her of the terraced house in which her whole family had last been together. Two boys upstairs. Two girls downstairs. A mother and father lying on the kitchen floor. Then she thought of her own flat, its unpainted walls and empty kitchen cupboards. Perhaps she should become a nun. That would be one way to avoid the reckoning she felt certain was coming to her now.

'You looking for the sisters?'

Behind Emily a man materialized on the gravel, holding a pair of secateurs. His hair was matted, skin beaten by the weather, but his voice was like honey and cream.

'Yes,' said Emily. 'I was following one, but she seems to have disappeared.'

'Knock there,' said the man, indicating steps to a door in a basement area that Emily hadn't noticed. 'Soup kitchen. They let anyone in.'

Emily traipsed down the steps to a dank galley, wondering if she could be classed as anyone, or if a police officer at the door was the last thing the nuns here wanted to see, given who they harboured. Then again, she had been invited, whatever that entailed. As though to cement that fact the door opened before Emily could raise her hand to knock – a nun in a brown habit, sandals and bare toes.

'Emily,' Sr Josephine said. 'I wondered where you'd gone.'

Inside, the convent was as shabby as the building's facade implied. As Sr Josephine led Emily through the soup kitchen to the back stairs, Emily couldn't help thinking that the convent was a bit like Isabella Dawson's boarding house. A large property catering to strangers, whose glory days were long in the past. As befitted a woman who had spent her life communing with the divine, Sr Josephine read every one of Emily's thoughts.

'It's not fancy,' she said over her shoulder. 'But it is home. We all need a home, don't we?'

Emily thought of another house in Portobello, three meagre bedrooms and a bloodstained kitchen. Then of the burdens piled upon its floor.

They reached the threadbare living room that Emily had glimpsed through the window and Sr Josephine indicated that Emily should sit, while she made a drink. The sofa was dotted with cigarette burns like stigmata. It was the complete opposite of the one Emily had sat on only that morning, in another Portobello home hoping for salvation, missing girl watching from the wall. Sr Josephine reappeared with two steaming mugs of coffee, carried in on a plastic tray. Emily took the mug that was offered, but already her hands were beginning with that quiver, her eyes darting in search of anything with a blade. In her pocket, separated from the rest, a tiny mother's wiry body pressed into Emily's thigh.

Sr Josephine settled into the chair opposite, kicked off one sandal, then the next.

'You met John, then,' she said.

'The man outside?' Emily replied.

'Yes, one of our regulars. He's been coming to Portobello for years. More than twenty.'

'Does he live here?'

'Itinerant. We've offered him a bed, but he prefers to stay on the road.'

Emily took a sip of her coffee. What must it be like, she thought, to make a life that doesn't keep you in one place long enough to have your own pillow? Her mother might know something about that.

'He used to stay at Isabella Dawson's boarding house.'

Sr Josephine's remark was casual, but Emily almost chipped her tooth on the lip of her mug as she jerked to attention. Hot coffee sloshed onto her hand, a sort of balm. She put the mug down, wiped her fingers on her trousers.

'You knew Isabella Dawson?' She shouldn't have been surprised.

'We used to do a bit of shopping for her,' said Sr Josephine. 'Once she stopped going out. Left it by the back gate, milk and so forth. Poor soul, no one else to look in. We hadn't realized she was gone till the police told us she'd been found.'

Emily thought about a pint of milk sitting on Isabella Dawson's back doorstep. Another abandoned on the side in a kitchen, gone sour in the sun. Hot coins and a reminder scribbled in a hand she had seen only recently, on another piece of paper. It always came back to milk in the end.

Outside the window Emily watched as John tidied the straggle of a shrub. Beneath her uniform she could feel the cold sweat crawling. At the thought of edging shears, or the slice of a spade, the efficient *snip* of secateurs. A lot of damage could be done with a pair of secateurs, and not just to the stems of a hydrangea. Emily tried to stop the image of a blade on bone rising, put her hand into her pocket to feel for the dolls.

As though aware of Emily's agitation Sr Josephine reached a hand across and laid it on her knee. Despite herself, Emily felt the warmth of the nun's fingers and for a brief moment her heart slowed, her breathing deepened. Then Sr Josephine said it.

'Would you like to see her now?'

Emily's knee began to *chitter*, her heel to drum a tattoo on the floor. She didn't reply, but she was aware of Sr Josephine rising to exit the room. Above her head there was the sound of footsteps crossing a floor. Emily tried to think of why she had come. A sister playing on a beach, calling to Emily as the sun shone down. A mother might know where to find her, that was what Emily hoped. But inside her head, with nothing to stop it, the past unspooled like a film playing in reverse, until it got to the opening scene.

Outside, the rush of sea air in Emily's lungs was like the shock of a baptismal bath. She stood on the promenade, dusk creeping in, gripped at the metal railings and leaned over to retch into the sand. A sudden gust whipped Emily's ponytail across her face, left sand on her lips. When she stood again she could see them in the distance, two small boys crouched at the water's edge, toes in the surf. Behind her someone was calling:

Em!

But she must not look back, that was what Emily had spent a lifetime telling herself. She would not look back. Otherwise it would lead to disaster. Except now it seemed disaster was upon her, whether she liked it or not. She bent again to retch, nothing to see but bile, felt the spike of something in her pocket. A solitary worry doll, wrapped in a scrap of cloth to make a skirt.

Emily had run from the convent without even realizing what she was doing. Out of the living room and into a small reception hall, pulling and banging at the front door – dead bolt, chain, mortice – until she found herself sprawled on the gravel, lying amongst the weeds. When she opened her eyes, the man was standing over her with his secateurs, a strange smile on his face.

'Are you all right?'

Emily stared at John in the grey light, then at the stubby metal shears. She wanted more than anything to grab the secateurs, run inside again, put blade to skin. She knew, and her mother knew, that Emily would do it. Sr Josephine, too.

Instead, Emily scrambled to her feet, knees scored by chips of stone, prepared to exit. Down the alleyway beneath a curved metal sign. Or through the back, perhaps, another escape. But as she turned and turned again, searching for the way out, she could not help looking back. At a building stained by afternoon rain. At a man holding a blade. At a woman standing on the step, bare feet and sandals, next to her a sort of apparition. A ghost at the door.

Emily closed her eyes, thought of two boys sleeping, one tucked into the other. Of a girl entwined in a curtain. Of damp polyester sheets and the sun beating down. When she opened them again it was to grey hair, badly cut and an unfashionable pair of glasses. A body that should have gone thick with middle age, but which was thin like Emily was thin, all angle and bone. Her mother was standing before her, the first time Emily had set eyes on her for more than twenty years. A mother and a daughter gazing at each other over an ocean of time. Emily knew that the only possible topic of conversation between them was a bathroom with damp towels scattered, blood on a kitchen floor.

I forgive you.

Should have been the other way round.

Sixteen

That evening, Emily ran along the promenade at Portobello as though she was a child again, nine years old and darting in the gloaming, banging on doors in the hope that somebody would come. This night she dodged cyclists on their commute home, locals walking their dogs as the sun disappeared over the lip of the horizon, a soft light falling where the afternoon's rain had dampened the tarmac. That night, Portobello had been deserted, darkness falling as neighbour locked door against neighbour, somewhere in Portobello another girl wandering, summer frock with cotton smocking, green ribbon in her hair.

Now, Emily ran and ran, didn't stop until she got to a door in the wall that she recognized, paint ravaged by wind and sand, moss crawling from beneath. The gate to Isabella Dawson's garden. Refuge of a sort. Emily pushed at the rotten door, found it open this time. She stepped through into a wonderland of scrub. Thick clumps of nettles grown wild. Feral hydrangeas. Everywhere the scent of loam. She trod a faint path through the tall grass till she came to the main front door, pressed her face to the glass. Inside the hall was empty, shadows casting across the terracotta tiles. Emily could hear Isabella Dawson's boarding house calling to her as the sun went down.

She entered via the side return, squeezing past the rubbish to get to the back porch with its floor of broken shells. This time she didn't bother to put on a coverall suit, or anything else – the mask, the hood, the gloves. It was far too late for that. How strange life was sometimes, Emily thought as she slid into the dark passage. The way it shifted and warped, came round to the start.

She came to the kitchen first, hesitated in the doorway to glance into the room. Shadows played across the empty floor. She didn't step inside.

In the hall she averted her eyes from the water closet, the thought of who might be watching from inside. Instead, she made straight for the stairs, bare now, the remains of the Turkish carpet rolled up and discarded in the skip. Something was drawing her upwards, towards a room with a view over the sea and a wardrobe, someone hidden behind its doors.

The dog was no longer guarding the first-floor landing. Emily sensed a fleeting note of loss as she passed the place where he used to sit. The house was different in the dark, a place of secrets to be tidied away, like Emily had attempted to tidy everything away. But secrets had a way of revealing themselves, that was what she had learned. Just as what happened in the past could never be left in the past, would always live another day.

Emily trod the bare boards of the first-floor landing till she reached the bedroom at the far end. She stood outside the door for a moment, heart leaping in her chest. But the minute she stepped into the room, moonlight casting its otherworldly light across the remains of the carpet, she knew she was too late. The wardrobe doors hung open, a yawning mouth, nothing inside but a muddle of shoes and a crumpled tea dress. Amongst other things.

Emily stepped over the debris covering the floor to stand in front of the window instead. She gazed towards the promenade she had just run along, beyond that the sea. Everything was coloured in shades of grey. The water. The tarmac. The beach was deserted, not a soul walking out. But still, Emily could see her. A girl running figures of eight upon the sand.

Back on the first-floor landing, Emily stood at the cross-roads. Downstairs the boarding house was still and silent. But upstairs she could hear footsteps, somewhere above her head. She turned along the dark corridor that led towards the back of the house. The door at the end was ajar. Emily put her hand to the knob, pushed the door open, discovered another set of stairs. They were narrower this time, leading to a second floor of the house. For the servants, perhaps, girls who were trained to keep them-selves hidden. Or a child's bedroom kept away from all the rest. Emily could feel the quick flicker of her pulse beneath the bracelets on her wrist as she put her foot on the first step, the second. This was the film inside her head, she thought, the file and all its contents, unspooling to the start.

It began with a beautiful day, that was what Emily remem-bered. Waking to sunlight filtering through the curtains, the whole room aglow. It was easy when it was like that, to forget all the rest.

The baby had been crying. Like it always cried. That was what she remembered next. She slid her legs from beneath the sheets, skin itchy from the polyester, pulled on her swimsuit and her shorts. It was hot in the house, a dirty heat that clung to her like the smell of her parents' cigarettes. Her sister's side of the room was a mess, toys scattered, clothes abandoned in a heap on the floor by the bed. Emily folded her nightie, laid it beneath her pillow, smoothed the cover with her hand.

In the kitchen, the baby sat in his highchair, tears dried on his cheeks. A small boy and a messy-haired girl were sitting in their pyjamas, munching their way through two bowls of Shreddies. There was a puddle of milk spilled on the table. Their mother's T-shirt was dirty, no bra underneath. Emily remembered staring at the damp patch that bloomed across the fabric. The only other milk in the house.

On the far side of the room her father was propped against the kitchen units next to the kettle, waiting for it to boil. He was useless in the mornings if he hadn't had his Nescafé. The remains of his usual spoonful were scattered on the counter. Emily had tasted the Nescafé granules once, licking them from the surface, then spitting to try and get the taste off her tongue. Coffee made the world go round, that was what their mother used to say.

Can't face life without it.

Emily wondered whether that was still true now.

It began because of an absent pint of milk and went on from there, already hot by nine a.m., not enough air for them all to breathe. Their mother hauled the baby onto one arm, scuffing Essie on the head for licking Shreddies from the table, took away Jonno's bowl. Emily watched, blinking, staying silent as her father began with his usual complaint.

Who used the milk? There's no fucking milk.

The stink of him, stale lager and Benson and Hedges,

stuffing a slice of white into his mouth as he turned towards Emily at the door. It was the milk, that was what Emily thought afterwards. If only she had fetched it. But she knew now that it wouldn't have made a difference. Like the sour half-pint abandoned on the side in the flat where a girl died with a needle in her arm. That girl had milk. They'd had no milk. But in the end it hadn't made a difference either way.

She came back because it got cold on the beach. Nine years old and the afternoon spooling towards its end. She had spent all day playing outdoors, wandering up and down the promenade and hanging around by the amusements, hoping someone might let her in to push the buttons on the machines. She drifted to the play park, had a go on the swings, in front of her nothing but sky, behind her hair streaming. It had been warm when she left the house, but by the time she returned it was goosebumps on her arms and a hungry hole in her stomach, nothing to eat all day but Fruit Salads and liquorice laces from Mrs Wren's. The house was grey when she got home.

She went upstairs first, just as she was going upstairs now. She never knew why. Afterwards they asked her and she didn't know what to say. It hadn't been normal. But then there was nothing normal about that day, apart from how it began. She tried their room first, her and her sister's, no longer bathed in fresh light, but darker, the sun moved round to the far side of the house. Despite having been out all day the room was just as she had left it that morning. Her bed neat, nightie folded beneath her pillow. Her sister's side was its usual mess of tangled sheets and covers, the pillow squint. There was no sign of her sister's pyjamas, the hand-me-downs with the flower trim, normally tossed on the floor along with the rest. There was no sign that her sister had got dressed that day at all.

In the bathroom there were damp towels on the floor. The bath was half full of water, a plastic boat floating on the surface as though her brothers had been playing. Emily remembered staring into the water, the drip of the tap the only sound. The house was so quiet, as though it had been abandoned, the rest of the family having left without her to go and live elsewhere. Then she went to the back of the house, to the bedroom where her brothers slept, found them waiting for her there. They were lying together in Jonno's bed, one curled about the other, skin still damp from the bath. They had been waiting for her, to come and kiss them goodnight. It was only later that Emily realized she should have known by the silence that something wasn't right.

The landing was dark by the time she heard it. A creature, calling to Emily from somewhere downstairs. She slipped on the steps, felt the raw burn of the carpet on her skin. In the hall she stood waiting, nothing but the sound of her own breath, loud and panicked, before it came again. A keening, seeping from the kitchen, its open door. Shapes shifted in the shadows. The floor was sticky with something Emily didn't recognize. There was the spin of a blade's dull glow. Also that voice, whispering to her over and over:

Essie . . . Where is Essie?

Before Emily ran. Down the street. Along the promenade. Banging on the doors. Forgot all about her little sister hidden in the cupboard, what she might have seen, too.

*

The stairs to the second floor of Isabella Dawson's boarding house ended in a landing barely bigger than a blanket laid upon the floor. Emily stood in the middle and pushed at the door to the right, the slow swing revealing a narrow bathroom with cobwebs hanging from the ceiling, a dried-up face cloth abandoned on the floor.

The only other room off the landing contained a single metal bed frame and a mirror propped against the wall. Emily glimpsed herself in the mirror as she opened the door, rabbit heart leaping at the sight of a girl she didn't recognize for a moment, nine years old and waiting. She put a hand to her pocket, felt for the little bag to check. Two boys. Two girls. Then in the other. But the mother was gone, dropped somewhere along the promenade, or in amongst the undergrowth of Isabella Dawson's garden, sifting into the soil.

Emily stood in the doorway for a moment breathing stale air. Old cigarette burns dotted the floorboards, a trail leading towards a window that must look out over the side return. There was the faintest smell of human waste rising from somewhere, beneath that another odour, potent and heady. Lilies of the valley. All around Emily, the boarding house exhaled.

To the right of the redundant light switch was a scratch in the paintwork, pale blue wallpaper and the faintest pattern of strawberries beneath. This was a child's room, Emily thought. A good place to hide, like her sister used to hide. Wrapping herself in the living-room curtains, or inside her parents' wardrobe, pushing back amongst their clothes. It was only as Emily stepped further into the room that she saw it. A doll's house sitting on the floor behind the door. Four rooms and an attic, a house within a house.

Emily crouched to see, peered inside. At a sofa and a grandfather's clock. At two beds with stiff covers. At a bathroom suite in white, toilet, sink, bath. At a plastic doll with nylon hair sitting at a kitchen table, in her hand a miniature carving knife. There was a roar in Emily's head then, like the sea inside a shell when you hold it to your ear. She felt faint, the whooze of not ever eating enough, of watching blood bright as a flag spread across a floor. She put a hand to the house, as though to an anchor, found herself looking at something else, propped inside the attic. A photograph. A girl standing on a beach, wearing a red swimsuit with a white, pleated skirt. The girl was all elbows and angles, collarbone sharp beneath her skin, hair a mess of rats' tails and sand. On her feet were a pair of jelly sandals. Even though the photograph was faded, Emily could still remember how the sandals glittered in the sun. She reached into the attic, fingers trembling, lifted the photograph out. Then she held it close, looked her younger self in the eye.

It was the dust she noticed first, a thin drift floating to land on her sleeve. She touched at it, fingertips coming away filmed with a sort of powder. Like talcum after a bath. Then on her hair. Emily looked towards the ceiling, blinked as more dust landed on her face, a tiny stream of it sifting from a crack like sand running through an hourglass, nothing to stop it. Somewhere beyond where Emily could see, a creature shifted and the sift became a slow cascade, a dark fissure opening in the dirty plaster. Emily stared at the crack growing in the ceiling. Then the bones fell.

PART THREE

The Boarding House

One

Portobello, Edinburgh's seaside, 2017.

The day had been warm, a last throw of summer before the haar rolled through. Locals strolled along the promenade, dogs and children weaving between people of all ages taking the air. The day had been busy, ice-cream sales and takeaway coffee, teenagers and toddlers playing in the surf. Now, as evening crept in, it was crepes and beer on the promenade, laughter filtering along. Portobello was thriving, a popular place to visit and live.

That night, a summer storm gathered on the horizon. Isabella Dawson woke to lightning flickering across the sky. The path on her carpet was suddenly illuminated, from bed, to window, to wardrobe and back. The wardrobe loomed, doors ajar, a whiff of carbolic drifting into the room. Somewhere beyond the sea edge thunder rumbled. It would be Isabella Dawson's last night, though she didn't know it. One more evening amongst the living, then nothing but the dead.

Thieves. That was what had woken her, Isabella thought as she clutched the feather eiderdown at her chin. Boys who broke the glass in her kitchen window. Who slid in the back gate so that they could steal. The willow-pattern plates. Her microwave. Those brown lace-up shoes. Isabella was certain she could hear the boys now, rustling outside her bedroom door, the dog on the landing silent like it had always been silent. She gripped the purple cover, stained black with the grease from her fingertips. She was waiting for her mother to shut the doors and bar the windows, keep everyone safe. But her mother wasn't here anymore. She was in the attic, along with all the rest.

Isabella lifted the heavy covers from the bed, slid her feet from the mattress and placed them on the floor. It was cold, the carpet rough on her skin. Through the back she was sure that she could hear her mother coughing. Above her head, the children played.

At the window Isabella pulled aside the curtain to see. Dark clouds had gathered on the horizon. The sea was high, the wooden groynes submerged. Outside, on the shore, a girl ran in a figure-of-eight upon the sand. She must warn the girl, Isabella Dawson thought. It was not safe for her to be out tonight. She reached for the window sash to lift it. But the window was heavy, nothing but a cold thread of air stealing in. Isabella looked down, realized the brass finger-lifts had gone black with the tarnish. Mother would not be pleased. Isabella must polish them in the morning, once the light came. She searched for the curtain, to pull it across the glass once again, cover over the finger-lifts till she could return with the Brasso, found herself gripping at a flimsy fabric, cheap cotton. Isabella frowned. How had these curtains got here? What had happened to the ones they used to have, heavy velvet to cut out the draughts? All gone, she thought, with the constant comings and goings. Her whole life had been nothing but coming and going. Only one of those left to do now.

Outside, the wind gathered pace, salt spattering the window pane, sea surging up the sand. It wouldn't be long,

Isabella thought, before it reached the promenade, climbed the great stone wall and stole over the top. Then it would flood the grass, the steps, seep beneath her mahogany front door. Like the flood in 1953, took the face off those houses up north, never gave them back. When Isabella was young her mother told her the sea had reached the front door of the boarding house once, lashed at the smoked glass, begged to be let in. They'd had to line everything with sandbags, fit shutters to stop pebbles breaking the pane. Like in the war, Isabella thought, heavy velvet to black everything out. 1941 and the throb of planes hidden in the clouds as they made for Clydebank. Isabella and her mother had huddled in the shelter then, with Mr and Mrs Wren. The *click click click* of the knitting needles, that was what Isabella remembered the most. Mrs Wren and her mother knitting socks and never stopping with their chat. Also the way she could not get the stink of mould from her skirt for a week.

Isabella peered through the dark glass again at the black line of the sea. She must warn the girl, she thought. Get her off the beach before it was too late, hurry her to the shelter. Or under the kitchen table, if the shelter was too far. But the girl had vanished, disappeared from the sand, headed to the play park instead. Isabella gripped at the sill, her body swaying as though she was standing up to her waist in the waves. The girl must not go to the play park, she might never return. Isabella tried to lift the window again, call out. But it was so heavy and her arms were so frail. She touched her neck, looking for the string with her notepad, the tiny pencil, wondered about writing something to remind herself to warn the girl next time.

But the notepad was gone, and what would she write anyway? Isabella had done what she could all those years ago. She couldn't do it again.

Isabella dragged the cheap curtain along its runner, shut out the storm. She would go to the shelter herself, that was what she thought. She turned from the window, trod her path to the wardrobe. The floor was covered in tumbles of clothes and books with their covers bent. Mother would not be happy. Isabella would have to tidy before morning came. But first she must find something warm to wear in the shelter. A dressing gown, perhaps.

The wardrobe was bursting, shoes in a muddle on the floor. Perhaps her brown lace-ups were here after all. Isabella bent to search, lifting one, then another. The musty scent of camphor and old wood rose up, moths hibernating amongst the dresses and the other clothes. So this was where they had been all this time, Isabella thought, handling that wool skirt, her mother's tea dress scattered with yellow roses. Isabella fingered the seams of the dress, remembered her mother sitting at the piano playing for the guests. Then she let it go, slid the dressing gown from its hanger.

The dressing gown rippled in the grey light as Isabella lifted it from the wardrobe into the room. It was still a luminous thing despite the years that had passed. Deep orange. Embroidery scattered all across. Roses, perhaps, like her mother's tea dress, delicate petals shining in the gloom of the bedroom, bright despite a lifetime having passed. The dressing gown was waiting for Miss Macdougall to return, that was what Isabella knew. But she was going to take it for herself.

She slid her right arm into one sleeve, grappled for the

other, trembled at the chill of real silk slithering across her skin. It had been so long since Isabella had felt that, the promise of something. The sleeves of the dressing gown draped almost to the floor, touching their tips to the carpet as she lowered her arms. The gown was larger than she remembered. Or she had got smaller. She couldn't be sure. Either way, the fabric was old now, a thousand tiny tears shivering across the silk where Isabella raised an arm to look. She could smell the mothballs in its folds. Isabella stared at her feet, searching for that puddle of orange cloth, like the sun when it dipped below the Portobello horizon, that sudden deep blaze. But the dressing gown was faded now, the sun almost gone. Isabella gathered the delicate fabric between finger and thumb, lifted it from her toes as though she was a lady ready for the ball. The sash trailed behind her as she trod her path to the door, a snake of silk on the bare bones of the carpet, a strange sort of green.

She was already at the top of the stairs on the landing when she remembered, heart fluttering at the thought that she might have left it behind. The child. She had forgotten the child. She must get it to safety too.

Isabella returned to the bedroom, rain lashing at the glass behind the curtain. The child was in the chest, the deep bottom drawer. She crouched on her bare feet, grasped both handles, attempted to tug the drawer free. It was a heavy thing, like the window. Like a coffin before it is lowered into the earth. But Isabella Dawson had been strong once, lifting kettles from the stove, heavy irons wrapped in tea towels, hauling the sheets from one drum to the other of the twin tub. She would not give up.

The drawer came free with a sudden tug, tilting on its runners, all its contents on display. Isabella dipped her hands into layer upon layer of fine tissue, the scent of cloves releasing into the air. She rummaged amongst the paper till she touched the metal. Huntley & Palmers, a tin big enough for a season's worth of biscuits, lifted it from the drawer. There was dust on the lid of the tin. Isabella brushed at it with the sleeve of the dressing gown, a smear of dirt across the orange silk, and they stared back. A family taking tea in a parlour. A father. A mother. A girl. A boy.

Inside the tin the corselet was just as Isabella had left it, folded and neat. Pale green, lace trim, the slipperiness of washable satin that felt as though it might be silk, too. Isabella's heart flittered like a bird in a cage as she ran her fingers over the stitching, the sheen of the fabric. The corselet would fit her now, that was what she was thinking, her belly and her hips gone skinny with age. She thought about putting it on, over the dressing gown. Then she lifted one corner of the pale green fabric, folded it back to see.

In the hall, behind the front door, the beast loomed, rising from floor to ceiling and back again, a great grey pile. That would keep them out, Isabella thought as she skirted the plant pot full of ash, dressing gown trailing, biscuit tin clutched in her arms. She didn't look at the beast as she trod her cramped path towards the kitchen and the shelter of the table. She had never looked it in the eye, perhaps that was the problem. While all this time, Isabella realized now, the beast had been looking at her.

The parlour door was locked. Isabella bent to the keyhole just to check. The piano was still there, though her mother was missing. But someone had opened up the dining room, ready to steal her best china, her sherry glasses with the thistles, her silver candlesticks. Isabella stood with her hand on the door knob staring at the table laden with all those plates waiting for the guests to return. From the beach. From the Lido. She must remind her mother about the chicken for dinner, white meat for sand-wiches and the rest in the pot for soup. Isabella closed the dining-room door, turned the key in the lock and withdrew it from the hole, held it tight in her fist. Where to put the key to keep it safe, she thought, so that no one might get in? She retraced her steps to the plant pot, dug into the ash, dropped the key in.

At the back of the hall Isabella discovered that Miss Macdougall had left her Mackintosh behind again, draped over the banister. The most forgetful woman in the world, Miss Macdougall, would forget her own head if it wasn't attached to her body. Isabella carried the coat to the hat stand, placed it on the hook. Then she blinked at the furniture piled at the door, behind that the garden, behind that the sea. She put a hand to her face, touched her nose, her hair. She must get the child to safety, before the storm rolled in.

Isabella shuffled as best she could down the ever-narrowing passage towards the kitchen, dressing gown tangling about her feet. Somebody had forgotten to put out the rubbish again. It was piling high, pressing on Isabella from all sides. She would have to get someone to help her move it. One of the students, perhaps. Or John with his voice like honey. Mr Gifford when he got back from the solicitors' office in town. She didn't like the way Mr Gifford stubbed his cigarettes out on the tiles in the hall. But if Isabella asked him, she knew he would agree. Being a woman was useful in that way.

The kitchen was full of rubbish too, a great sea of bottles and tins. Where had they come from? Isabella wondered. Who had eaten it all? Across the room she made out the shape of the gas stove, old casserole pot on the burner, the dresser where she kept her grandmother's teacups hanging in a row. Everything was in shadow. Isabella heard the sudden smatter of rain on the cracked window pane, felt the beast watching, understood that she was in the end of times now.

Across the passage the storeroom was in darkness too. Isabella stood just inside the door peering into the gloom, trying to decide what to make the guests for dinner. Hotdogs, perhaps. She must get on with it, or Mother would be angry. She fumbled along the shelf, reaching for whatever was there. A packet of flour. A jar of strawberry jam. She emerged with a box of cream crackers in her hand, made her way back across the passageway, drifted to the stove. She placed the cream crackers on the draining board by the sink. Then she reached for the casserole pot.

The chicken bones had burned to the bottom of the pan, small bleached things staring up at Isabella. She gazed at their frail beauty. A disaster, that's what it was. Something to be got rid of before Mother found out. She must toss them out with the rest of the rubbish, Isabella thought. Hide the pot. She carried it back along the narrow trench to the kitchen door, across the passage to the storeroom, slid it onto a shelf. Then she pulled the storeroom door closed behind her, turned the key in that lock, too.

In the kitchen she discovered her mother's old Huntley & Palmers biscuit tin abandoned on the table, lid lifted off. Inside was a bundle of newspaper. Isabella laughed. Perfect for the chicken bones! She lifted the newspaper out, peeled away one layer, then another, frowned when she discovered the bones had already got inside, were waiting for the rubbish. She brushed at them with her fingers. A tiny rib. The knobble of a joint. Beneath the bones was the girl. Isabella smiled at the girl, touched a finger to her face, that gap where her teeth should be. It was a long time since Isabella had seen the girl. It was so good to know that she was still here.

Isabella gazed at the girl, then at the small graveyard in the cradle of the newspaper. She must keep them warm, that was what she thought, if she was going to take them to the shelter. She shook the bones back into the centre of the paper, folded it as she had been taught. One sheet at a time, over and over until the parcel was secure, like a chicken carcass and all its juices wrapped tight. Then she let the dressing gown slide from her shoulders, spread that across the tabletop, too.

The dressing gown lay with its sleeves draping over the corner of the table like some sort of crucifix. Isabella laid the bundle of newspaper on the dressing gown, began again with the wrap. One side, then the next. One sleeve, then the next, swaddling the thing in soft orange folds. The silk slipped through her fingers, fragile now, like her skin was fragile after so many years washing up the plates. She must rub them with the cream, Isabella thought. Lilies of the valley. Miss Macdougall wouldn't mind. But even that was too late, because beneath her skin Isabella could see her bones now, all knuckles. She must throw out the chicken, she thought. Before her mother found out that it had been burned.

At the end of the culvert in her passage, Isabella stood with her ear to the back door. She was listening for boys, for creatures hiding amongst her willowherb. But all she could hear was the moan of the wind amongst her pretty shells. So she drew back the bolt, turned the key.

In the porch everything was grey. Rain spattered on the pitched roof, an angry sound. Isabella reached her hand to feel her way, touched a slither of something chalky, limpets brought up from the beach. She could just make out a whole shelf of them running around the rim of the porch, underneath a pair of rubber boots, split and faded. Her mother's boots, Isabella thought. Too big for her now. A cold gust blew about her ankles. It was dark in the yard, no rectangle of light in Mrs Wren's house over the back fence. No street lamps casting their eerie glow. Isabella looked at the bin bag, held tight in her fist. She must get back to bed soon, or Mother would be angry. But first she must put the rubbish in the proper place.

At the far end of the yard was the bin store, a wooden shelter with a roof of felt nailed down long ago, all sorts of creatures crawling around in there. But the bin store was full. It had been full for weeks now, perhaps months. Big plastic sacks full of stuff Isabella couldn't remember owning, piled into a hill of refuse. Sometimes the seagulls came, stood on the roof of the shed pecking and tugging at the plastic mountain, things Isabella hadn't seen for weeks spilling out. Then there was the smell, filtering through the crack in her kitchen window pane, rottenness forcing its way in. Isabella would have to leave the bones at the gate where the strangers left the milk, that was what she was thinking. For the refuse men to collect in the morning once the storm had blown through. It would be safe there, till someone came along. She shuffled to the edge of the porch, shaking something from her foot where it had got caught. The sash from a dressing gown, trailing after her, a strange snake of green. Isabella stared at a crack in the concrete, the moss growing in. Then she stepped out, into a forest of willowherb and thistledown, rain slashing down.

Isabella climbed the stairs to the first floor of the boarding house in the dark, one small step at a time, shivering in her nightdress. Her legs were cold. Her ankles. She must get a good night's sleep. There would be guests in the morning, Mother would need her to help. On the landing she put a hand to the head of the dog, let her fingers wander over the chip on his nose. She was so tired now, but the dog had stayed steady, keeping them safe.

In her room Isabella pulled aside the curtain so that she could see the storm. The sky was the colour of steel, the water a grey threat, high on the sand. But there were no children on the beach now. She had made sure of that.

She crouched by her chest of drawers to tidy away the corselet, folding it back amongst the tissue paper with its faint scent of cloves. When she was finished, drawer firmly closed, Isabella remembered that she had left the biscuit tin underneath the kitchen table to keep them safe. A mother. A father. A girl. A boy. She would sort it tomorrow, that was what she thought. Deal with it then. Now she would just sit on the edge of her bed for a moment, before lifting her feet from the floor.

The covers on the bed were heavy as she drew them across, layers of old blankets and an eiderdown pressing on Isabella's body. But there was no crying drifting from the ceiling. No piano playing. Nothing but the wind and the waves. She lay on her back in her brushed-cotton nightie, barely anything left of her, head rested like a bird's on the yellow pillow, muscle all gone. She was a girl again, Isabella thought, like the girl on the beach. A thin, bony thing, racing on the sand.

She patted the bedcovers searching for the book she had been reading, the cool welcome of the page. But her fingers were frail, clutching at nothing but an eiderdown all rotted at the edges. She would have to start again tomorrow, that was what Isabella thought, begin at chapter one. She blinked at the glass of water on her bedside table, the dirty print of someone else's mouth on the rim. Where had her teeth gone? Then she reached for the lamp, *click switch*. The window clattered as the storm rose to greet her. After that, the never-ending dark.

Two

Portobello, Edinburgh's seaside, 1996.

The girl was playing on the beach again, running a figure-of-eight over and over on the sand below where the gate opened onto the promenade. Isabella Dawson watched as the girl danced, admiring the red flash of her swimsuit, the sparkle on her jelly sandals. What it would mean to be that girl, she thought, running free in the shallows, nothing in the world to worry about but grit between the toes. She put a hand to the glass of her large bedroom window, as though to touch the girl, as though to feel her feet in the froth. But Isabella Dawson had not dipped her toes in the Firth for years now, barely even lifted her skirts.

The sky was clear today, the sun already high, another fine day in Edinburgh, August and the height of the holiday season, the city thronged with tourists, no doubt. But there was nothing to see in Portobello other than a few sightseers who had probably got off the bus at the wrong stop, and a couple of locals letting their dogs shit on the sand. Portobello was a faded suburb now, shabby amusements and cheap rented housing, lots of emergency B & B. Isabella's last remaining tenant belonged to the latter, a man who stank of cut-price cider, scabs around his lips. He was a nice man, polite. But when he smiled, Isabella winced at the grey roots of his teeth. Her mother would be turning in her grave at the idea that this was what the boarding house had sunk to. Desperation, that was what it smelled like to Isabella Dawson. A bit like Portobello itself.

She watched the girl for a bit longer, before dropping the curtain and making her way along the first-floor landing to the bathroom, lino curling at the edges, letting in the dust. Just like Portobello, the bathroom was looking tired now, permanent tidelines around the sink where the enamel had worn. Isabella had scrubbed and scrubbed at the marks till her knuckles were raw, but it didn't make any difference. The sink needed replacing. The bath. The whole house needed replacing, ripped out so she could start again. New carpets and modern central heating, hot showers instead of rubber tap attachments or a plastic jug. Isabella Dawson once had a dream of restoring the boarding house to its former glory, white-ivy cornicing and polished wood, repairing the smoked glass of the front door, planting lupins in the garden. But that would take money, and where could she get that now the tourists were gone? To sell, that was her only option. But who wanted to take on a leaky boarding house in a tourist resort where there weren't any tourists? No one would be that mad.

Isabella's last tenant was sitting at the table in the kitchen when she came downstairs from rubbing cream into her hands. The faintest whiff of lilies of the valley followed her into the room. The man looked up from mopping his plate of egg with a slice of white bread.

'Good morning, Mrs Dawson,' he said, that lovely low pitch of his voice. 'How are you?'

The scabs about his mouth were not as pronounced as

they had been the day before, though Isabella noticed he had fresh scratches on his arm. What must this man's life be like?

'Good morning, John,' she said. She tried not to look at his teeth. 'I am fine. How about you?'

'Very well, Mrs Dawson. Very well. What's your plan for the day?'

Hot tea, that's what Isabella was thinking. She did at least have that.

Standing over the electric kettle as it boiled, Isabella could feel her mother's disapproval sitting on her neck. Even before her mother died, Isabella had insisted that they take in a paying guest or two, rather than relying on the dwindling trickle of holidaymakers.

All downhill from now on, if we tread that path.

That was what her mother had said between her bouts of coughing. But Isabella had gone ahead anyway and it had saved the house from being sold from under them. Besides, there had been a lot her mother didn't approve of, not just long-term tenants who provided a guarantee with their rent. Gas fires that ran off the boiler rather than a meter. Cereal for breakfast rather than eggs. Electric kettles rather than that huge aluminium thing with the Bakelite handle that had been permanently positioned on the stove for years. Not to mention the twin tub. Isabella could still remember the row about that. Her mother had wanted to continue sending the sheets out for laundering, whatever the expense.

Isabella had done her best, as she'd promised. But the boarding house had decayed as Portobello had decayed, never recovered from the mass flight to Spain in the 1970s.

Now here she was, left with a building crumbling about her ears, as she began to crumble, too.

'I'll be off now.'

Behind Isabella, John pushed back his chair, a harsh scrape on the tired lino. She would need to mop the floor, Isabella thought as the kettle switched off. Hadn't done it for two days now. Her mother would have noticed, if she'd still been here.

'Are you going?' she said. 'Not want some tea first?'

She splashed hot water into the teapot, swirled it, emptied it into the sink, threw in two teabags. It might be a few years ago now, but at least she had modernized the kettle. When her tenant didn't reply, she turned to discover he had gone.

Isabella stood inside the storeroom off the passage and surveyed her stock. There were plenty of tins on the shelf:

Hot dogs

Green Giant sweetcorn

Cheap nutritious meals for people who didn't have much. But she wanted to re-stock, just in case, never could be sure when new tenants might arrive. Isabella bought most of her supplies in bulk, used her mother's old business account that she'd never got round to closing. But there were some things she needed to get fresh. She counted the loaves of white bread and packets of Rice Krispies, made a note to buy some more bottles of barley squash. Her tenant might like to drink cheap cider all day, but that didn't mean Isabella had to serve it to him inside the house.

Isabella wrote a list of things she needed in her little book with its tiny pencil:

Bicarbonate
Eggs
Barley water

She knew she had enough in the storeroom to last a lifetime, if it came to that, maybe a bit more. But she always liked to keep on top of things, just in case. It was a hangover from the past – her mother's need to keep the pantry full to bursting. Blue bags of oatmeal. Sugar by the pound. Stacks and stacks of Huntley & Palmers biscuits in those large barrel tins. Isabella's mother had always liked to be prepared, never wanted to run out of anything that a guest might ask for. Now Isabella was the same.

She finished with her list, unhooked a large woven shopper from the back of the storeroom door, lifted her summer mac from the chair. She'd been hoping John might stay in this morning, have a talk with her over a cup of tea. He was a nice man, John, despite the slight smell about him. Nothing that couldn't be sorted by a decent wash, if she could persuade him to hand over his clothes. But he had gone out and she was left, like she was left every day, to her own devices. Long silent afternoons with nothing to do but mop the floor and polish the dining-room table, watch children run on the sand.

Isabella missed her guests, however much trouble they could sometimes be. She'd survived for years after her mother died on room and board for young professionals, new-marrieds and students, postgrads first, then under-grads with their untidy hair and late-night habits, weed smoked in the garden when they thought she didn't know. After that it had been DSS, a boom industry in the 1980s. Finally, emergency B & B. But John had been her first for a while, came knocking on the door saying a neighbour had mentioned she might have a room. Isabella was hesitant at first, because he hadn't been referred by the council. But beggars could not be choosers. That was something her mother would have understood.

She'd given John the room at the top, two flights up, away from all the rest, startled herself at how shabby it had become when she opened the door. Room Four was not well appointed, cigarette burns hidden beneath a rug and a smell rising from the side return. But at least it was clean. She showed him in and handed him a towel from the linen store on the first-floor landing.

'You have your own bathroom opposite.'

'Thank you.'

Her new tenant smiled at her, a glimpse of rottenness inside his mouth. Isabella turned away.

'Breakfast at eight thirty each morning.'

John had already paid Isabella two weeks' rent up front, in cash. The first twenty-pound notes she'd held in her hand for a while.

She had phoned the council, of course, after a month or so of no referrals, standing in the hall staring at her hair in the mirror, realizing how coarse it had become.

Overcrowding.

That was what they said. Had received some complaints. But Isabella didn't understand. She had never allowed more than the agreed number to share a room. It was only later, once she'd insisted on a visit from a housing officer, that Isabella realized what they meant. Not overcrowding of people, but of stuff. All the things that life had piled on her, now starting to pile elsewhere instead. Boxes of broken knick-knacks cluttering the hall. Obsolete furniture crowding the landing. Her mother's clothes heaped in a bedroom. She must start to clear it, that's what Isabella had thought after the housing officer left. Start afresh, like she'd meant to after her mother died. And yet somehow, just like then, she had continued as before.

Isabella went out for the shopping by the back door, stepping into the porch with its shells piled in corners, brought up from the beach by all the guests she had accommodated over the years. She almost never used the front door now, couldn't remember the last time she'd opened the heavy mahogany thing, frame swollen with the wind and the rain. Now she noticed that weeds were beginning to grow between the concrete of the yard, willowherb and thistle. She stepped across to haul the rubbish bin from the lean-to, left it just outside the back gate for collection. She was hoping that John might drag it in when he returned. John was a nice man, but no decent tenants came near the boarding house now, its slide into dilapidation complete. Isabella could hear her mother saying it.

Reputation is everything.

Once that was gone, you couldn't get it back. Her mother had been right, of course. But at the time Isabella hadn't seen any other option, if she was to keep the house. And that was something she had promised her mother she would do, above everything else.

At the far end of Portobello High Street, Isabella entered Mrs Wren's shop, *clitter clatter* of the bell ringing above her head as it had when she was a child. Mrs Wren's wasn't the cheapest place, but Isabella knew that there would be a chance to chat. She didn't like to gossip, preferred to guard her own opinions. But Isabella wasn't used to having no one in the house to talk to all day except herself.

'Hello, Mrs Dawson. What can I do for you this morning?'

Mrs Wren appeared from through the back wiping her hands on her overalls. Isabella didn't bother to correct her. Everyone called Isabella 'Mrs' now, though they knew she'd never married. Besides, her mother had been Old Mrs Dawson by the time she died, so Isabella must be Mrs Dawson now.

'Quiet today,' she said by way of greeting, searching for her shopping list in the pocket of her Mackintosh. 'Not many about.'

'Have you not heard?'

Mrs Wren's voice was queer. Isabella looked up, found Mrs Wren pressing her hands on the counter, a shake to them, something Isabella had never seen before. Mrs Wren's hands were raw across the knuckles from all the work she did. Must bring her some of that cream, Isabella thought, lilies of the valley, to smear on her palms.

'Heard what?' she said, smoothing the piece of paper.

Barley water

Eggs

Bicarbonate

'Terrible,' Mrs Wren was saying, head swinging to and fro as though in disbelief. 'From the play park, too. I'm telling you, this will be the end of Portobello.'

Though Isabella knew that had happened a long time ago.

'What are we talking about here, Mrs Wren?'

Isabella smiled, but Mrs Wren did not reciprocate, just lifted one of the newspapers stacked on the counter, moved it round for Isabella to see. It was an *Edinburgh Evening News*, early edition. On the front page was a large photograph of a girl wearing a V-neck sweater, her hair in bunches. The girl had a gap between her front teeth. A shilling, Isabella thought. That was what she used to get for a lost tooth, wondered what the currency was now.

Then she read the headline:

MISSING

In big black text.

At once Isabella felt her heart jump in her throat, saw a girl playing alone on the beach only this morning, red swimsuit and jelly sandals, running in a figure-of-eight.

'From here?' she said.

Mrs Wren nodded. 'Just a wee-bit thing. Goes out to the play park and this is what happens. She was in the shop only the other day getting her sweeties.'

Mrs Wren gazed for a moment at her array of penny confectionary right there on the counter, bubble gum and Fruit Salads, liquorice laces.

'They all come here,' she said. 'Had one only this morning loading up. I've said it before, they ought to be careful, coming out on their own like that. Never know what might happen.'

But children had been wandering the streets of Portobello on their own for years. That was what Isabella knew.

'When did this happen?' she said.

'Yesterday,' replied Mrs Wren. 'About tea time.'

Relief flooded Isabella from top to toe. She took a

breath. The girl in the red swimsuit was safe. But Mrs Wren's eye were full now as though the missing child had been one of her own.

'They've got the police out looking for her now, knocking on all the doors. Though I can't credit it's someone from here that's taken her.'

'The police?' Isabella started, a tiny shock.

'Aye. They'll come to you, no doubt, at some point. Want to look inside.' Mrs Wren looked at Isabella then, the small fix of her eye. '*You* haven't seen her, have you?'

Beneath Miss Macdougall's Mackintosh Isabella could feel the sweat begin to gather. Not everybody appreciated a house like the one that she ran in Portobello. DSS. Emergency B & B. Strangers who appeared in the resort for a few days or weeks, then left again, cut-price cider and nothing to do all day but hang around by the beach and the play park, the amusement arcade. There were some in town who thought Isabella was odd for allowing it when there was no one else in the house. And perhaps she was odd, Isabella thought now. Nearly sixty and never left home, opened her door to men like John with scabs all about their mouths and fresh scratches on their arms. Isabella saw it again then, that thin line of blood. But Portobello did not belong only to the likes of Mrs Wren. It had always contained all-comers.

'The poor mother,' she murmured. 'Must be frantic.'

'Stuck in the house,' Mrs Wren almost spat over her counter. 'Got those bastards chapping at her door.'

Isabella knew what the shopkeeper meant. The press, knocking on the mother's window, posting scruffy hand-written notes through the letterbox.

'She's not run away to a friend's, has she? The girl.'

'No.' Mrs Wren shook her head, adamant. 'They've checked all that. She's gone, Mrs Dawson. She's gone. Some bastard who doesn't belong has come down here and taken what he wanted, then left again.'

The two women stared at each other, anger lighting Mrs Wren's eyes, something else in Isabella's. It was Isabella who looked away first.

'A block of cheddar, thank you, Mrs Wren. Two pints of milk.'

The police arrived at the boarding house an hour or so later, stepping into Isabella's yard, then her porch, chapping at her back door while she stood in the kitchen with her hands in the sink. They startled her with their knock, even though she'd been expecting them, the plate she was holding slipping from her hands to smash on the floor. Two pieces. She would need to glue it, Isabella thought as she hurried to answer, or Mother would be angry. Then she let them in.

There were two of them, a younger officer and an older one, caught Isabella with her Marigolds on. She offered tea, but they refused, wouldn't sit, just got straight to the matter.

'We're looking for a missing child, Mrs Dawson. You've probably heard.'

They already knew her name, though Isabella hadn't introduced herself. She nodded and they showed her a photograph, the same as the one in the paper. V-neck jumper. Hair in bunches.

'Though she was wearing a cotton frock,' the older officer said. 'Green ribbon in her hair.'

'No, sorry,' Isabella said. 'I haven't seen her.'

Realized her hands were shaking, clasped them together. The younger officer looked at her, then around the room. Isabella followed his gaze, suddenly aware of how cluttered her kitchen had become, great stacks of ice-cream tubs, unopened bills littering the dresser.

'We understand you take in emergency tenants, Mrs Dawson.'

'Yes.' She put one of her Marigolds to her forehead. 'Though not recently.'

'But you have a guest staying at the moment.'

It wasn't a question. Mrs Wren had done the police's work for them.

'Yes . . .' Isabella's apron was damp about the front where she'd splashed it with the washing-up. She could feel the cold seeping through. 'He's been with me a few days.'

'Is he here now?'

'No. Well, he went out this morning. He'll be back later, I'm sure.'

The younger officer frowned at a tin of Alphabetti Spaghetti standing by the stove ready for John's lunch, nudged his colleague.

'May we take a look at his room, please?' the older man said.

'Well . . .' Isabella looked at her hands in their yellow gloves. 'I suppose that would be fine, given the circumstances. I'm sure John wouldn't mind.'

'John, is it?'

The officer stared at Isabella. She hesitated.

'John, yes. A lovely man. I'm sure—'

'Left this morning, you said?'

One minute mopping his morning egg with soft white bread, the next his room cleared, nothing left behind but new cigarette burns, on the sheets this time. Isabella had checked already, of course. In and out of the all the rooms. The linen closet and the store cupboard. The parlour and the water closet. The water closet had been empty, except for a red anorak hanging on the back of the door. The kind of thing a child might wear over a V-neck jumper. Blood thudded loud inside Isabella's head at the thought that the missing girl might have been in her boarding house after all. Played in and out of Isabella's rooms without her knowing. But she knew it wasn't true.

'The girl is not here,' she whispered. 'The girl is not here.'

The coat was much too old to be hers.

In the dining room Isabella had opened the doors of the buffet with its stacks of china on every shelf. The buffet would be a good place to hide. She kneeled before it, removing tea plates and finger bowls, her mother's soup canteen shaped like a chicken. Also the willow-pattern set, Miss Macdougall standing on that little bridge in her dressing gown. Where did she go? Isabella thought as she placed the set on the dining-room table along with all the rest. Disappeared one day, never came back, just like John. Didn't even send a postcard. The willow pattern was kept for special. Though Isabella was not sure she could ever remember an occasion that had been special enough.

The dining table was covered in china by the time Isabella proved to herself that the missing girl was not hiding inside the oak-stained sideboard. The mantelpiece stacked with teacups. Thirty champagne coupes laid out on the buffet top as though waiting for wedding guests to arrive. Isabella would have liked a wedding of her own, something to look back on with a smile. But life didn't always happen in the way one expected. And she'd been happy, hadn't she, in this house on the beach, everything she needed supplied.

'It's this way, is it?'

The older officer didn't wait for Isabella to show him, moved towards the kitchen door and down the passage towards the hall. Isabella followed, peeling off her Marigolds and dropping them onto the kitchen table.

'Yes, second floor. I'll show you.'

The younger officer came behind, peering into the store-room with its shelves piled with tins. The parlour with its piano. Also the dining room, china stacked hither and thither.

'Bit late for spring cleaning, isn't it?'

But it was never too late for cleaning, that was what Isabella thought.

On the first-floor landing the older officer pushed open the doors to the rooms, before allowing Isabella to show him the staircase to the second floor.

'This it?' the younger officer said as though somehow he had expected it to be bigger.

Room Four. Single bed. Cigarette burns on the floor. Also that smell. The older police officer moved across to the window, boards creaking beneath his heavy boots, looked out into the side return.

'Any idea where he went?'

Isabella shook her head. How could she keep track of

her tenants when there had been so many of them coming and going over the last few years?

'What's this?'

The younger man was pointing at something on the floor, covered by an old flannelette sheet that Isabella had recovered from the linen cupboard.

'It's nothing,' Isabella said. 'My old doll's house. It's always lived in here.'

The younger officer lifted the sheet to reveal two small chimneys and a black roof. Red brick walls. Four rooms and an attic. Despite its cover, Isabella noticed that everything in the house was covered in a patina of dust as though it had not been played with for years. But she could see now, even from the doorway, that someone had been moving the furniture around. The covers on the beds were askew. The pots on the stove tipped over. The miniature carving knife that belonged with the ham had fallen to the floor of the kitchen.

'No one plays with it, then?'

'There's never been any children living in this house,' Isabella folded her arms across her apron, 'other than me, of course.'

The officers took another look about the almost-empty room, metal bed frame with a mattress and linen piled on top. Then at the door in the corner.

'And where does this go?' said the older man.

'Nowhere,' said Isabella, eyes sliding away. 'It's just a linen cupboard.'

Outside, that evening, mist lifted from the garden as Isabella wandered through the grass in her mother's rubber boots. She moved aside a hydrangea bush here, an old raspberry cane there, peered into the empty void of the cold frame, just in case. The garden was overgrown now, the grass almost as tall as a small child. A girl could disappear in it, that was what Isabella knew. Slip through the unlocked gate from the promenade and vanish, get lost amongst the seed. Nothing left but a heap of ribs mouldering into the earth once they scythed the grass down.

She would have to warn the gardener, Isabella thought as she stepped through the undergrowth.

Watch out for the bones.

The gardener came on Tuesdays. Once a week in summer. Once a month in winter. But it must be summer, now, Isabella realized, because the grass was so tall and the hydrangeas so overgrown. Perhaps she had dismissed him, got one of the students to do it instead, for a bit off the rent. Except there weren't any students either. Isabella noticed her old twin tub stranded in the middle of a clump of nettles. She must remember to look there, she thought, because a child could easily crawl inside.

At the end wall, Isabella removed her mother's boots, pushed open the unlocked door and stood outside in her stocking feet. The tarmac of the promenade was warm beneath her soles. The tide was out, sun spreading its light across the grey strip of sea setting it a-sparkle. Isabella squinted into the glare, looking for the girl again, dancing her figure-of-eight on the sand. But the beach was empty, everyone gone, all the children safe now, shut inside their homes.

Isabella stepped back into the garden, locked the gate behind her. Then she crouched, put her hands to the earth, began to scrape at the soil.

*

In the kitchen, Isabella sat at the table with its faded primrose Formica, a glass of Robinsons barley water in front of her. The squash bottle was old, crusty around the lid area, sticky patches of grime running down the side. But squash was squash, wasn't it? Never went off. She took a sip, left a ghost of her mouth on the lip of the glass. Her fingernails were encrusted with dirt, as though she had been digging. She drank the juice down, then she lifted her mother's heavy set of keys from their hook by the kitchen door, went along the passage to the hall.

She heaved the mahogany door closed, drew the bolts across top and bottom, turned the key. Then she dragged a chair from the dining room and propped it beneath the doorknob. After that another and another, because they seemed so insubstantial suddenly, the chairs, one shove and they'd be gone. Then she went upstairs.

She ignored the rooms on the first floor, made straight for the second with its spartan bathroom and single room with cigarette burns on the floor. She crouched in front of the doll's house, straightened the covers on the bed, the pots on the stove, the miniature carving knife, all back where they belonged. Then she took her mother's keys, went through them one by one, until she found what she was looking for.

It took both hands, but the key turned in the lock first time, a door in the corner of the room that looked like a linen cupboard but was something else instead. Isabella had to tug at the handle a few times to get the door to open, but at last it gave, swung back shedding plaster dust and flakes of old paint to reveal the narrow stairs. The walls were black, soot rubbing on Isabella's cardigan as she made her way up. It would take a lot of scrubbing to get that out, she thought, damage the wool. But still she climbed on, shoulders scraping against the filthy plaster. At the top she hesitated for a moment, catching her bearings, before stepping out.

The attic was dark, the only light a shaft of grey falling from a small window far away in the roof. High above her head Isabella could just make out the great trusses holding everything up. She had not been in the attic for years, not since her mother died and made Isabella promise. Keep it all safe. Now she took one tentative step across a joist, followed by another, eyes darting here and there in the murk. She knew it was here somewhere, the thing she must find before anyone else. Hidden amongst the rubble and the cobwebs draped from the rafters. Amongst the rat droppings and thick clumps of dust, the water tank that loomed at the far end. A Huntley & Palmers biscuit tin with a family on the lid. A mother. A father. A girl. A boy.

She meant to throw it out with the rubbish – the contents of the biscuit tin. Once she'd liberated it from the attic, brought it downstairs, eased off the lid. Bones like the carcass of a chicken. A ladies' corselet. She'd even wrapped the bones, in the newspaper she'd bought that morning from Mrs Wren's shop, V-neck jumper and hair in bunches, the missing girl's face disappearing as Isabella folded one page of newsprint over another. She had been sorry to see them go, the contents of the tin. But Isabella knew that she could not take the risk. There would be prying eyes everywhere now that another child had got lost.

But after she had wrapped the bones, Isabella found she

couldn't do it. That it didn't seem right to discard them in the bin waiting by the back gate. So she placed the bundle back inside the biscuit tin and covered it with the corselet to keep it warm, a neat fold of pale green, lace trim and washable satin. Then she went upstairs and stood at her bedroom window with the tin in her arms watching as the sun began its slow fall to the horizon, long streaks of colour painting the sea. Like Miss Macdougall's dressing gown, Isabella thought, still hanging in the wardrobe after all this time. There was nothing left of Miss Macdougall now but an absent shape drifting through the corridors of the boarding house. Like the missing girl with the V-neck jumper would haunt the streets of Portobello if they didn't find her soon.

Isabella was still standing at the window when the other girl appeared once more, red swimsuit and jelly sandals, almost like a ghost herself. The girl didn't run on the sand this time, but darted along the promenade in the gloaming, banging on the doors as she passed. Isabella watched as the girl approached her own garden gate, knocked once, twice at the locked door embedded in the wall, before stepping back to stare up at the house. Isabella did not move. She was certain the girl could not see her. The room was in darkness. The landing was in darkness. The whole house was in darkness, Isabella had made sure of that.

The girl shouted something Isabella could not hear. She looked as though she might have been crying. Isabella felt the chill. But it was too late, she thought. Too late. Nothing to be done. She stepped back and pulled the curtain, the rattle of metal rings on a metal rail. The girl must go home, where it was safe. Isabella already had one child inside, no room for any more.

She laid the tin inside her chest of drawers. Wasn't that what you were supposed to do when you didn't have a proper bed for a baby? She used the bottom drawer because it was deep sided, lined with tissue paper, the sweet scent of cloves. The baby would be safe here, Isabella thought, hidden in her own room where she could keep an eye. She would deal with it tomorrow, find the right spot. Beneath a rose bush, perhaps. Maybe a hydrangea, watch the flowers change from pink to blue. Then there would be no need for fuss and bother as her mother might have said. No police to take it away. No police to take her away either. Or all the rest.

Three

Portobello, Edinburgh's seaside, 1971.

Isabella Dawson stood at the upstairs window of the boarding house and surveyed the scene. The beach was busy, a clutter of buckets and discarded tennis shoes, though it was not as crowded as it used to be. Scotland was on holiday, but the weather was poor, cool temperatures and a persistent breeze. Overhead planes flew to Majorca, long stripes of white in an otherwise pale sky.

Isabella watched as in the garden a child wearing a red anorak ferreted in one of the flowerbeds with a stick. The child appeared to be burying something, or digging something up, Isabella couldn't quite tell. She pressed her fingernails into the sill, the thick gloss of its summer coat still scenting the room with cheap, oily Dulux. Behind her the coughing began, that persistent hack. She pressed harder, knew her fingernails would leave an indent. Eight small slits. I was here.

'Belle!'

From the hall Isabella heard the slam of the front door, the sudden clatter of shoes on terracotta tiles as their newest tenant returned. Barbara Penny had been to the pawnbroker's in town, a silver apostle spoon in return for the rent. There was a pawnshop on the main street here in Portobello, just as good as any other. But Isabella knew that Barbara Penny liked to keep her business private if she could.

'You'd better go and put the tea on, or she'll make it herself.'

Lillian Dawson's voice came from the bed in the corner, weak now and rough about the edges from all the coughing. It would never do to have a guest take over the kitchen, Isabella knew that was what her mother believed, even if Barbara Penny was just a temporary guest, washed up in Portobello while she searched for a place of her own. Isabella tweaked the heavy velvet curtain to get it to hang straight, thought about what she might replace this set with once the room belonged to her. Room Two had some pretty curtains, roses, to go with the paper on the walls.

'Will you come down for some tea yourself?' she asked, glancing again at the girl digging in the soil.

'In a bit.'

'I'll set a cup for you.'

Her mother didn't reply as Isabella made for the door, straightening a hairbrush here, a cushion there, before slipping onto the landing. Lillian Dawson didn't leave the bedroom much these days, was a husk of a thing compared to what she'd once been – queen of the boarding house, spinning all the plates. Now Isabella's mother lay on her pillow in the room at the front, skin sunk to the bone as though she might be dead already, lying in her coffin. During the day Isabella worked while her mother slept, long naps as the business of the boarding house went on around her. But at night, Isabella knew that her mother did not rest, appearing like a ghost to complain about the noise from the attic, children playing overhead.

*

Downstairs, Barbara Penny was already sitting at the table when Isabella finally made it to the kitchen, had tipped off one of her shoes to rub at her stockinged heel.

'There you are,' she said. 'Shall we have tea now?'

But Isabella got to the kettle first, lifted it from the stove. The kettle was a big metal thing with a removable whistle, enough capacity to fill several teapots at the same time. It took an age to boil. Isabella topped up the kettle from the tap, set it on the stove again, lit the gas with a match. Barbara Penny opened the cutlery drawer beneath the Formica tabletop, took out a couple of teaspoons. It was a good thing Isabella's mother was too weak to get downstairs much these days. She'd be horrified at the sight of a guest making free through the back.

As she waited for the kettle to boil, Isabella leaned against the counter, watched Barbara Penny replace the shoe on her foot.

'Success?' she asked.

'He's dead,' Barbara Penny replied.

'Who, Mr Farthing?'

'Died a couple of months ago, apparently.'

Isabella stared at Barbara Penny. How could Godfrey Farthing be dead, the owner of the best pawnbroker's in town? She'd been up to him only a few months back, pawned that garnet ring belonging to her mother because times were getting as rough as her mother's cough. A gentleman, everybody knew that, had given Isabella more than the ring was worth. But now he was dead and Isabella worried she wouldn't be able to reclaim the garnet before her mother was gone, too.

'Who's running the shop?' she said.

'Nobody.' Barbara Penny snapped open her handbag and laid two pound notes on the table. 'It's shut. His son's left as well.'

'What, Solomon?'

'Yes, headed to London.'

The kettle began with its whistle and Isabella lifted it from the stove with a tea towel, poured a splash of boiling water into the round pot, swirled it about, tipped it into the sink. She glanced at the cash lying on the primrose Formica.

'You got the rent money, though.'

'Went to the one on the High Street,' said Barbara Penny, closing her handbag with a *snip* and putting it on her lap. 'Gave me a reasonable rate.'

Barbara Penny came from London originally, that was what she'd said. Had washed into the boarding house a month ago looking for somewhere cheap to stay while she built up a deposit to rent a flat of her own. She worked for a lawyers' office in town, typing, but she was always looking for ways to scrimp and save. She had a child with her, Margaret, seven years old or thereabouts, always skulking in the shadows. Barbara Penny wore a wedding ring, but Isabella wasn't convinced she had ever been married. Another reason it was a good thing her mother was more or less confined to bed now.

Isabella sprinkled tealeaves into the pot, poured on the water. She unhooked two cups from the dresser, orange flowers on the rim. Her grandmother's set, not normally used for everyday tea. But things would be different now, that was what Isabella thought as she placed the cups on their saucers, laid them on the table.

'You'll have saved enough for your own flat soon,' she said.

'Yes. Every penny counts.'

Barbara Penny laughed, but Isabella did not join in.

'We'll miss you when you're gone.'

'You might,' Barbara Penny said. 'Not sure your mother will.'

Isabella's mother hadn't wanted to take their new guest in, everybody knew that. But Isabella had insisted. How else were they to make ends meet? She'd put Barbara Penny and her daughter in Room Two, with the pretty roses on the wallpaper. Because it was near the bathroom. Because it had plenty of space. Because Isabella had been grateful to have any rent at all. They'd agreed that Barbara Penny could make her own meals and have access to the kitchen whenever she liked. *For convenience*, Barbara Penny had said. *To save you the trouble.* Though Isabella was certain it was more about saving money than anything else. Her mother wasn't happy with the idea of short-term tenants using the place like a bedsit, but Portobello was not what it used to be. Tourists no longer flocked to its amusements and its outdoor pool, but to the guaranteed sun of Spain instead.

To make space, Isabella had moved into her mother's bedroom at the front for the duration, a cot in the corner with an eiderdown and a blanket. It was what they always used to do during peak season when Isabella was young, to maximize the rooms for the guests. But summer visitors who came for a week or a month, full board, were a rare beast now. Most people were day-trippers, or weekend visitors who wanted B & B. All those dinner sets going to waste, Isabella thought, lying unused in the buffet. They would have to start taking in a new sort of guest, if they were going to survive, that was what she realized. Or perhaps they could sell, let the boarding house go.

Isabella slid through the plastic curtain into the pantry to fetch the milk. The pantry was cool, a soothing sort of space. She stood for a moment, jug in her hand, watching as her new tenant sat at the kitchen table, jacket slung on the back of her chair, looking for all the world as though she belonged to the house and the house belonged to her. Isabella would be sorry to see Barbara Penny go. They had so much to talk about. She would miss their evening chats.

'What's it to be tonight?' she said, returning with the milk and putting it on the table. 'Men or children?'

Both women laughed then as Isabella pulled out the chair to sit. She lifted the pot, prepared to pour, wondered what they might discuss. Men who had abandoned them. Or the children who had slipped from their grasp. They had barely begun when they heard the cough, a raw bark in the passage, footsteps shuffling on the flags. Isabella made to rise, but her mother batted her away as she edged into the kitchen.

'I'm still capable, you know.'

That evening the garden was still, the remains of the day lifting from the grass. Small insects and dandelion seeds circled in the cool air as Isabella stepped through the grand mahogany front door with her feet bare, pressed them to the earth. She walked along the path between the rose beds, touching a petal here, a leaf there. Everything else might be on a downward trend, but the garden was still thriving. Her haven, Isabella thought, a place to get away.

Above her, the sky was clear, nothing but two vapour trails from planes that had long since disappeared. Isabella would have liked to go to Spain, if only there were not so many things to look after. The house. The guests. Also her mother, coughing away in the bedroom upstairs, pretending it was nothing more than a bout of summer flu. They both knew it was much more serious than that. Cancer, eating her mother from the inside out, tumour growing like a flower in her lung. She wouldn't live to see another season, that was what Isabella knew, a small bud of panic deep in her belly at the thought of what it might mean. She thought of the world beyond the boarding house, beyond Portobello. What it might contain.

Isabella approached the patch of earth where the girl had been digging, glanced over her shoulder to check. But nobody was watching from any of the windows of the boarding house, too busy eating crackers for supper at the kitchen table, or getting a child ready for her bed. The couple in Room Three were out for the evening, had gone into town. The junior solicitor, Mr Gifford, who had taken Room Four on a six-month lease was probably cramming for his latest case, one cigarette after another dwindling to a stub as he burned the midnight oil.

Isabella had put Mr Gifford on the second floor, in the narrow room at the back. Single metal-framed bed and a view over the side return. Also a permanent draught leaking from beneath the door to the attic. It wasn't the best room they had, but it was adequate for an unmarried man, especially one who was still young. Mr Gifford had returned the favour by tossing his cigarette butts into the plant pot by the front door every morning, rubbing ash into the lovely blue and terracotta tiles. Isabella spent hours cleaning that floor after him, on her knees, wiping at it with a cloth. Barbara Penny just laughed when Isabella complained. Like she laughed at Mr Gifford's jokes when he lounged against the stove waiting for his milk to boil. Isabella was always uncertain about male tenants, never sure who you might be letting in. But Barbara Penny enjoyed the attention, could teach Isabella a thing or two. Mrs Wren had quizzed Isabella about it already, while she cut and wrapped the blocks of cheddar. But Isabella refused to indulge. Gossip was something she attempted to avoid, had learned that lesson the hard way many years ago.

Now Isabella crouched by the disturbed earth, began to dig as though she was a child herself. She wasn't sure what she might find in the dirt, but she had her suspicions. A teaspoon, perhaps, stolen from the buffet in the dining room. Or the little family from the doll's house, who seemed to have disappeared. A mother and a father made from clothes pegs, two children dressed in scraps. Isabella had taken the doll's house from Room Four and put it in the parlour so that Margaret Penny might play with it if she liked. But the child had paid the thing scant attention, a desultory moving about of one item after another, room to room, before ignoring it altogether. Isabella had checked only the other day, feather duster flicking over the chimneys. The furniture was present and correct, but the little dolls were nowhere to be seen.

She wondered now, as she scraped at the earth, if she might be about to resurrect them – a family of four returned from the grave to make up for another child that had vanished and never returned. She would like to see them again, if only for a moment, the clothes-peg family. But it wasn't the dolls Isabella found dug in beneath the moss, rather something unexpected set her rocking on her heels. There, in the black earth of her garden where it did not belong, buried by a child wearing a red anorak. A single piece of bone.

* * *

That night Lillian Dawson lay in her bed as her daughter shifted and turned in her temporary cot on the far side of the room. Outside, Lillian could hear the soft murmur of the waves on the shore. Inside, Isabella rustled and muttered as though she was the one who had something to lament, rather than the other way around.

Isabella had been sullen all evening, that was the truth of it. Troubled by something she would not discuss or disclose. Lillian wanted to ask her daughter what was wrong, draw her to the bed to sit on the purple eiderdown so they could have a proper talk. They had been so close once, that was what Lillian remembered, running the boarding house together like a clock that never faltered, two cogs in one wheel. But now that old froideur had fallen between them again, the great unspoken thing.

Isabella would confide in her new friend, that was what Lillian knew. Take her worries in a different direction, her hopes and plans, too. Her daughter was giddy where Barbara Penny was concerned, Lillian realized, clipping down those stairs the moment she heard the door. It was like she was a girl again, fifteen and set for the world, rather than a woman of over thirty with responsibilities and a house to run, a future to secure. Lillian had seen them with their heads together over the teapot, whispering about the future, Isabella no doubt dreaming of getting away, like Barbara Penny was planning to get away. Isabella's head had been turned by a paying guest, that was what Lillian knew. But one who would not stay any longer than she had to, once she got what she wanted from the deal.

Across the room, Isabella turned again in her cot, arm dropping from the blanket to spill over the side. Lillian stared at her daughter's limb, luminous in the grey light. How fresh Isabella's skin was, whereas Lillian's had grown sallow, all the blood gone out of her, a ghost just waiting for the heart to fail. Isabella was a good girl, did everything for Lillian now, as well as the guests. But sometimes what Lillian wanted most was to rise from her bed like she used to as a girl, stand on the damp Portobello sand for one last time, take one more breath of the cool Portobello air. She lifted her feet from the mattress, slid them slowly from beneath the covers, placed her feet on the floor. The children were playing in the attic again, little footsteps pattering across Lillian's mind.

Lillian fumbled her way towards the bathroom, hand to hand along the flock. The wallpaper was tired now, pattern worn to dust by the hundreds of guests who had touched it over the years. They would need to replace the paper with something more modern, Lillian thought. That was something Isabella could do.

As she approached the back corridor that led to the second-floor, Lillian heard it again. Not the children with their playing, but that faint rhythmic thump. It was filtering down the narrow stairs from Room Four, had been ever since their new tenants moved in. Lillian knew what it signified. Barbara Penny and Mr Gifford, conjoined on a metal-framed bed. Lillian waited, hidden in the dark, as the noise got quicker, a disgusting *tup tup tup*. She felt the cough rising in her throat again, tried to quell it as she shuffled further along the landing to stand in the shadow beside the china dog. She laid a hand on the dog's head, a cool steady thing, had kept Lillian company all these years. Then she glanced down, noticed that the dog's nose had a chip on it, white and fresh as bone.

The next day, the last remaining holiday guests checked out. Lillian watched from the first-floor landing as they lifted their fake leather suitcases from the blue and terracotta tiles, shook Isabella's hand goodbye.

All lovely.

That was what they said. But Lillian knew they would not be back. They would be buying new outfits next year, booking an aeroplane to Spain. After the guests departed, Lillian took to her bed in the room at the front, lay beneath the eiderdown coughing and coughing till she thought she must be turned inside out. She dozed for a bit before waking again, to that familiar pain like a knife between her ribs.

The boarding house was quiet, everybody out. Barbara Penny was at work. Mr Gifford at his office in town. Isabella had gone to Mrs Wren's for the messages, perhaps. Or for a walk along the promenade. In the silence, Lillian was certain she could hear that noise again, filtering from the attic. She didn't believe in ghosts, was a practical woman, as befitted a person who'd spent her whole life working in a boarding house. But she could definitely hear it now, footsteps overhead.

The girl got in everywhere, that was the truth of it. Margaret Penny in her red anorak, sneaking into things whether she was allowed to or not. Lillian knew without question that the child was a thief. She had already found her sitting on the floor in the dining room with her hands amongst the best china, taking out one plate after another, putting them back all wrong. Another time Lillian came upon her in the kitchen, cutlery drawer open, counting out the spoons. Then there was the dog on the landing, new chip in his china paint bright on its nose. Lillian would have asked Barbara Penny and her daughter to leave by now, if she'd had the strength for it. But Isabella liked to play with the girl, patty cake and songs, once even duets at the piano, till Lillian put a stop to it.

Isabella had not spoken to her for two days after that and Lillian had lain in her bed, with that knife in her chest, wondering for the thousandth time if she had done the right thing all those years before. She had sorted the situation, that was what it amounted to. The way Old Mrs Dawson sorted situations, kept the boarding house straight. But now there was a child running free amongst the hydrangeas and Lillian knew that it reminded Isabella of everything that had been lost.

Lillian pushed aside the purple eiderdown, rose from her bed with a new sense of resolve. Margaret Penny was a thief, that was what Lillian knew. And her mother, Barbara, a false friend, tempting Lillian away from the boarding house towards an uncertain future, something

Lillian had attempted to protect her daughter from for more than fifteen years. Lillian understood the attraction. Barbara Penny was someone of Isabella's own age, who called her Belle and talked about the things they might do together – sell the boarding house, buy a flat, visit Spain. But their new tenant would only ever take what she needed for herself, leave the rest behind. Lillian had seen the packed suitcase Barbara Penny kept beneath her bed, as though she must be ready at any moment to flee. Heard the *tup tup tup*. She never gave a straight answer, Barbara Penny. Not about a husband, or the child's father, where her family came from or what they did.

A clean house.

That was what Lillian's mother-in-law used to insist on. What Lillian had insisted on, too. But she understood that it was in danger of getting grubby now, unless she acted first.

Barbara Penny's room was as empty as Lillian had expected. The bed was made, but in a rough manner, the rumpled sheets untucked at one end, the eiderdown askew. Lillian could not help but try and sort it. She might be a paying tenant, but Barbara Penny was still a guest in Lillian's house and it was Lillian who kept the keys. She shuffled to the side of the bed, pulled the covers straight. Then she manoeuvred towards the slither of gorgeous orange hanging over the bedframe that was the real reason she had come. Miss Macdougall's dressing gown.

Miss Macdougall had visited the boarding house every

year for almost thirty years when Lillian was young. She had been a fixture of the place, arriving in the middle of July and staying for three weeks, eating off the willow-pattern china and turning cards in the parlour while Lillian played the piano for the other guests. Sometimes Miss Macdougall played the piano with her, the two of them side by side on the piano stool. They had been friends, that was what Lillian had thought, taking walks along the promenade and trips on the tram into the city to shop at Jenners. Sometimes taking in a picture at one of the Portobello cinemas. Miss Macdougall used to send a post-card every year:

Will see you on the 12th. Save the room.

Stayed in Room Four beneath the eaves where Mr Gifford boarded now. She even left her clothes behind once, to save her having to pack everything each time, folding jumpers and blouses into a drawer with Lillian's help, hung her Mackintosh on the hat stand in the hall. The Mackintosh was still there now, as though Miss Macdougall might return at any minute, come laughing through the door chattering about how she had remembered to put on her galoshes, but not the rest, got caught in a rainstorm at the Joppa end. For almost thirty years she came, before the war and after, regular as the parlour clock. Then nothing, an absence Lillian still felt, rising in the night to play the piano, like she and Miss Macdougall used to play the piano, one lament after another, ghosts in the dark.

Lillian bent as best she could to retrieve Miss Mac-dougall's dressing gown from where it lay, creased and crumpled, on the floor of their paying tenant's room. The old silk was still slippery between Lillian's fingers, sash dangling. She held the gown to the light to check for rips and tears. The silk was fragile after so many years, a delicate thing, easily damaged. But the dressing gown was intact, those wide sleeves, those leaves and roses scattered across.

The dressing gown did not belong in Barbara Penny's room, that was what Lillian knew. It belonged to Isabella and nobody else. But her daughter had lent it to the paying guest, laughing as she did it, as though she didn't mind. Or perhaps Barbara Penny had engineered the loan, sitting in the kitchen one morning over breakfast saying, Look what I found, Belle. Such a gorgeous thing. You don't mind, do you? It deserves to be worn.

Lillian lifted the dressing gown to her nose. It always used to smell of lilies of the valley, Miss Macdougall's favourite scent. And Isabella's too. But now it smelled of something altogether different. Carbolic, like the soap Barbara Penny used to scrub her daughter with each night in the tub. Also the faintest hint of that oil Mr Gifford wore on his hair.

Lillian climbed the stairs to the second floor, one painful step after another, dressing gown draped over her arm, trailing in the dust. She paused now and then to suppress the urge to cough. It was always there now, the knife between her ribs, wouldn't be rid of it before she was gone. In her right fist she grasped the keys, a large bunch, one for every lock in the house. Front door and back. Parlour and dining room. Each of the bedrooms. Not forgetting the attic, of course.

The keys belonged to Lillian, as they had belonged to her mother-in-law before her, and Old Mrs Dawson's mother before that. As they would belong to Isabella before too long, the boarding house finally in her sole possession to do with what she wished. The house would provide security for her daughter's future, that was what Lillian knew. A living, as long as Isabella kept hold of it. Also a refuge, as it had proved for so many other girls over the years, a place in which to hide. Lillian would hand the keys over soon, that was what she had decided. Before it was too late. Just one more thing to do first.

Lillian reached the small landing on the second floor and stood to catch her breath. In the bathroom a flannel had been slung over the side of the china bowl, short hairs glued to the lip where Mr Gifford had shaved that morning and not cleaned after himself. Barbara Penny was welcome to Mr Gifford, Lillian thought, if that was the best she could do. But Isabella would be sorry. Her daughter liked Mr Gifford, Lillian could tell. By the way she followed after him as he went about the house. Because there was always a ready supply of his favourite cream crackers for supper, not a brand Lillian ever thought to buy. But Lillian knew that Mr Gifford would not look twice at Isabella, unless he saw her with the keys to the house, of course. Then he might pay her plenty of attention. Barbara Penny, too.

The bedroom stank of nicotine. Lillian could see the burns on the floorboards beneath the rug where Mr Gifford had stubbed out his cigarettes, tossed them from the window into the side return. She put a hand to the wall, to that wash of emulsion which had covered the strawberries, the paint faded now and scuffed, in need of a new coat. She moved herself around, small step by small step, till she reached the window, looked down into the side return. The foetid smell rose from the gully, as it always had. Lillian put a finger to the glass, left a print, thought of Miss Macdougall standing here the first time they met. How she had gazed over the chimney pots of Portobello, before she lifted the sash and breathed in, declared the glory of sea air. Miss Macdougall had always been happy with second best, right from the start. It was something Lillian had protected Isabella from, though she might not realize it, gave her a better start in life.

Lillian left the window behind, crossed the room to the bed. The spread had been pulled across the pillow in a rough attempt at neatness. Lillian drew it back, untucked the sheet and blanket, messed them a bit, like Barbara Penny's bed had been a mess, as though the person who had slept in it had only just got up. Then she bundled Miss Macdougall's dressing gown between the sheets, let a corner drape to the floor. Miss Macdougall's dressing gown was one of Isabella's most treasured possessions, something she had owned since she was just a girl. She would not expect to find it in Mr Gifford's bed, scented with Barbara Penny's soap.

Outside the room, there was the sudden scuffle of a creature on the landing. Not a mouse. Or even a ghost. But a girl, of course. Margaret Penny, still wearing her red anorak from where she had been ferreting in the garden. Lillian nudged at the door, let it swing open. They stared at each other, Lillian Dawson and Margaret Penny. Then

at the treasure the girl had found. In one hand a clothes
peg fashioned as a doll. In the other a tiny knobble of
something white.

'Give it to me.'

Lillian held her hand out to the girl, voice raw from
the cough. She knew what she looked like to the girl. A
skeleton, some sort of ghoul. The girl hesitated, eyes fixed
on the angles and planes of Lillian's gaunt face. Then she
dropped the tiny knobble of bone on the ground, skittered
down the stairs.

In Room Four, Lillian moved towards the door in the
corner that looked as though it must be a linen cupboard.
It was ajar, as she had suspected, draught leaking from
beneath. A key taken from Lillian's bunch was in the lock,
patterned with a thief's little fingers, no doubt. Lillian
grasped the handle, closed the door with a quiet *click*,
turned the key, returned it to her ring. Then she headed
back down the narrow stairs to the first-floor landing. Her
daughter would be home soon.

That afternoon, Lillian Dawson took to her bed, lay
beneath her eiderdown listening to the sea. She would not
be long for this world, that was what Lillian knew. But at
least before she went she would no longer have to listen
for children in the attic. The boarding house was safe now,
ready for Isabella to take it on herself.

Her daughter would bring Lillian tea, that was what
Lillian was waiting for. Their regular routine. She would
serve it in a proper cup and saucer, at four thirty p.m.,
before the rest returned from work, and Lillian would ask
Isabella to sit with her on the bed, so they could talk.

About what had happened then. And what might happen next. About what she should do after. Then Lillian would present Isabella with the keys to the house, the great bunch of them, one for every locked door. After that she would ask her to check for the footsteps in the attic, make her way through Room Four and up the narrow stairs to see what sort of creature had got trapped there, might need letting out.

Lillian would sit in bed, sipping tea from a willow-pattern cup, as her daughter climbed the stairs that Lillian had climbed once, too. That dark channel, un-navigated for years, opening through a hatch at the top into the great cathedral of the attic. Lillian could still see it, as Isabella would see it. The dark skeleton high above. The rough wooden rafters stretching for what looked like the entire length of the house. The tiny window set far away in the roof, the last of the afternoon sun falling in a shaft to illuminate the rubble and the dust. Isabella would wait for her eyes to adjust, as Lillian had waited, before stepping forwards, one joist, then the next.

It wouldn't take her long to find it. On one side the family from the doll's house, fashioned from Isabella's clothes pegs and laid along a spar. On the other a barrel-shaped biscuit tin, Huntley & Palmers, another family on the lid. Lillian knew that the lid of the tin would have been removed, the contents disturbed by a child with the fingers of a thief. Isabella would dip her hands in and she would find them. A piece of underwear, pale green with lace about the trim. And in amongst its folds, a miniature anatomy class. A tibia. A fibula. The notches from a spine. Isabella would see what her mother had been guarding.

And all the rest. Then she would understand why the boarding house must never go out of the family. Why that had always been the way.

Four

Portobello, Edinburgh's seaside, 1953.

It was summer. The town was busy, a new era in the air. Rationing was over, the new queen had been crowned, outside the promenade thronged with holidaymakers. And the beach, too. They covered the sand all the way from the waterline to the walkway and back again, from east to west. The ground was littered with Thermos flasks and handbags, sandwiches wrapped in tea towels to keep them fresh. The sun shone high in the Edinburgh sky, becalmed in its own blue sea. In the water young people shrieked and laughed. Portobello was bustling, a thriving seaside resort, everything anybody could want, then some more.

In the boarding house, Lillian Dawson had all the doors open, all the windows, letting in the air. The glass in the windows was clear, washed and polished every Friday with vinegar and pages from the *Scotsman*, so everybody could see. The boarding house was full this week, as it had been for every week of the season, holidaymakers populating every room. Seven days, full board, breakfast, lunch, high tea and supper. Cake and sandwiches. Eggs and toast. Ham and potatoes with tinned fruit for after, condensed milk poured on. Not to mention the endless cups of tea. Portobello was rising again after the depredations of the war and Lillian Dawson was determined to rise with it.

She loved peak season, when the whole world came to Portobello for its fun.

Lillian stood in the entrance hall, the huge mahogany door and all the brass fittings gleaming in the sun. She was in charge of the boarding house now – Old Mrs Dawson gone; her husband, Ted, gone – had swept a new broom. Fresh wallpaper in the bedrooms. A television in the parlour. A shiny new tea urn in the kitchen to go with the refreshed lino. The boarding house was spic and span, ready for all comers, the first of the new intake arriving that very afternoon, one of their longest-serving guests.

Miss Macdougall came every year. One brown suitcase. One plain Mackintosh. Sensible shoes for walking on the promenade. She sent a postcard:

Will see you on the 12th. Save the room.

Appeared in the middle of July once the trades were gone and left three weeks later. She'd been coming since Lillian was a girl, fifteen or so, the same age that her daughter, Isabella, was now.

'Isabella, where are you!'

Lillian called to her daughter as the familiar figure appeared along the promenade, making her way towards the garden gate. Miss Macdougall was unmistakable, tall and slim, a hat that belonged in the 1930s, rather than the modern era they were embarking upon now. Miss Macdougall was like something from another era, that was what Lillian thought as she watched her guest approach. A lady around whom time had stopped, while everyone else moved on. Lillian knew she had little in common with Muriel Macdougall, a woman who didn't need to work for her living and certainly not changing bed sheets and waxing the lino. But they were friends, that was what she believed, not that different in age, only a few years apart, and connected by all the summers they had spent together, playing piano in the parlour and walking on the promenade. Not to mention how they had first met, a special kind of bond.

She called again for her daughter. 'Isabella!'

Miss Macdougall stepped through the gate from the promenade and into the garden, past the roses, the potatoes thriving in the sea air, paused to admire the onion patch and the cold frame bursting with lettuces as she wove her way along the path. Miss Macdougall was carrying her usual suitcase, the one she brought with her every year, brown leather and two metal catches. It was the suitcase Lillian had helped her unpack during their very first season together, a lifetime ago now.

At last Miss Macdougall reached the house and stepped into the hall.

'Come in, Muriel,' said Lillian. 'It's so lovely to see you again.'

'It's so good to be back!'

Miss Macdougall put down her suitcase on the blue and terracotta tiles and the two women embraced, faint waft of lilies of the valley, before Lillian pulled away. Behind them, Isabella lurked in the gloom by the water closet, summer dress with a nipped waist and wide skirt, ankle socks and a cardigan to keep out the breeze. Already that morning Isabella had made the beds and swept the landing, been out to buy extra bread for high tea. Lillian's daughter was a girl drilled in everything it took to run a successful boarding house in Portobello, ready for the moment when she would take it over herself.

'Come on now,' Lillian gestured to Isabella, 'give Miss Macdougall a hand.'

'Gosh, how you've grown,' murmured Miss Macdougall as Isabella came forwards. 'Hasn't she, Lillian? Quite the young thing.'

But she was frowning at the girl as she took off her 1930s hat, patted at her hair, watching Isabella lift the suitcase and head for the stairs. Isabella always carried Miss Macdougall's suitcase to her room. And Miss Macdougall always stayed in Room Four. Now she hurried to follow Isabella, Lillian bringing up the rear. Past the china dog. Past the bedrooms on the first floor. Up the narrow staircase to the second, where they crowded on the small landing before Miss Macdougall cast a quick glance at Isabella again as she moved inside.

'That's pretty,' Muriel said, nodding at the new wallpaper. 'Did you choose it?'

Isabella nodded from where she stood in the doorway. The paper was pale blue, with a repeating pattern of strawberries. Lillian had allowed her daughter to select it. Out of season Isabella slept in this room, with its doll's house and its single bed. In season Isabella shared with her mother, a temporary cot in the room at the front with its wonderful view to the sea. Lillian knew she ought to let it to the guests, take one of the smaller rooms without a view for herself. But it wasn't that long since she had claimed the space as her own, wasn't ready to relinquish it just yet.

Miss Macdougall moved across to the window, lifted the sash.

'There's the sea air,' she said.

A finger of cold air filtered in, with it the faint smell of the drains that ran beneath the side return. Lillian felt a familiar prickle of embarrassment that she had never been able to fix the smell. But Miss Macdougall didn't seem to mind. She breathed in as though satisfied, then moved to the bed where Isabella had laid the single suitcase, opened the clasps, *click clack*.

'Shall we begin?'

Each year Miss Macdougall allowed Isabella to sit on the end of the bed in Room Four as she brought out her holiday clothes. One skirt for the everyday. One for best. Three blouses and two pairs of shoes. A couple of light jumpers and a cardigan. All the years she had been coming, Lillian had never seen Miss Macdougall wear anything different. *These old things*, Muriel would say as she touched a small darn here, or a button with a thread dangling there. Then she'd let Isabella place them in the chest of drawers or hang them in the small wardrobe with its overwhelming scent of camphor. There was a sort of ritual to it, the packing and unpacking. Isabella used to look forward to it every year.

But now, Lillian's daughter stood in an awkward slouch just inside the door as Miss Macdougall began her routine. 'Do you mind, Miss Macdougall? I have something else I must do.'

'What thing?'

Lillian's tone was sharp, but Miss Macdougall interceded before Isabella could reply. 'Of course, dear. You go and have your fun.'

Their guest sounded surprised, but she did not insist on Isabella staying. It was Lillian who stood in the way.

'Where are you going?' she said to her daughter. 'We've got the teas to prepare. Miss Macdougall's tray.'

Isabella wouldn't look at her mother, pulled her cardigan across her dress. 'To the High Street, to meet some friends.'

'What friends?'

'You don't know them.'

'Oh, let her go.' Miss Macdougall, came to the door holding a tartan skirt. 'You can help me instead, Lillian. I'd like that for a change.'

As Isabella slid away, eager footsteps tripping down two flights of stairs, there was silence between the two women. Miss Macdougall began laying out her toiletries. A hairbrush set and a bottle of toilet water. A pot of hand cream, the same brand she had been buying for years. Lillian started to hang things in the wardrobe, tidy everything away. But she couldn't help herself.

'She should have stayed to help,' Lillian said. 'Like she always does.'

'She's fifteen,' said Miss Macdougall, placing her comb next to her mirror on the top of the chest of drawers. 'Don't you remember what that was like?'

Lillian stared at the dress she had just hung in the wardrobe, crêpe du Chine. Miss Macdougall had never had children of her own, so she was more lenient than Lillian thought proper. Besides, what could Lillian say, after everything that had been done? She returned to the suitcase, took out a cardigan and folded it, then neatened the corners. When she spoke again her voice was low.

'I was working here when I was fifteen.'

'But times are different now, aren't they? For the young, I mean.' The two friends faced each other across the narrow bed, Miss Macdougall holding her nightgown, white lawn with a ribbon trim. 'What are her plans anyway? She must be done with school soon.'

'What do you mean?' Lillian frowned. 'Isabella will help me in the house, like she's always done. Take on more responsibility. I'm not getting any younger.'

'None of us are getting any younger, Lillian.'

Lillian was taken aback by the bitter edge to Muriel's riposte. The two of them continued to fold in silence. Then, as though by way of a peace offering, Miss Macdougall passed Lillian something from the case.

'Would you hang this for me? You're so careful with it.'

A dressing gown, kimono style, wide elegant sleeves, hem pooling on the floor. The colour was still glorious, that was what Lillian thought as she took the dressing gown into her eager hands. Like a flame, roses embroidered all over. A contrasting sash hung from two silk loops stitched into the side seams, a strange sort of green. Lillian touched the sash with her finger. She could only imagine the kind of world in which she owned a dressing gown such as this, or had cause to wear one. But she had tried it on once, never forgotten the feel of silk on bare skin.

That evening, once high tea was finished, the washing-up done, Lillian and Miss Macdougall took a stroll along the front to take in the air, then a loop back via the High Street, before returning to the boarding house for supper. A constitutional, that was what Lillian called it, to mark the beginning of Miss Macdougall's break. Lillian always attempted to get Miss Macdougall to treat herself when she came to Portobello. A room with a view of the beach.

An evening at the dances. Tuppence for a tram into Edinburgh to visit the castle or shop at Jenners. But Miss Macdougall was content with the narrow single bed, a walk along the promenade, or an evening in the parlour sipping sherry and listening to Lillian play the piano for the other guests. The only indulgence she insisted on was the willow-pattern china.

'It makes me feel at home.'

Portobello of an evening was a riot of lights and noise. Crowds walked along the promenade arm in arm. The roller coaster at Fun Palace hitched up and up and up, before rattling down. The dance band at the town hall practised for later, the honk of the brass competing with the records blaring from the amusement arcade on the other side of the road. Lillian felt the thrill of it as she walked arm-in-arm with Miss Macdougall. As though she was a girl again, like her daughter, all of life in front.

'Why don't we go in for the early feature?' she said as they approached the County cinema on Bath Street. 'Isabella's doing the breakfasts, so I could lie a little longer in the morning to make up.'

'Now that's an idea,' said Miss Macdougall. 'What's playing?'

The two women hurried towards the picture house to take a look at the billing. But the queue was long, snaking down the wide marble steps and along the pavement far beyond where the two women were walking. Lillian was disappointed. She couldn't remember the last time she had been to the pictures. Used to go a lot with Ted, sneak out to the Central on the High Street without his mother knowing, fresh handkerchief in her pocket, hands smelling of lilies of the valley where she'd borrowed a smear of cream from Miss Macdougall's pot after doing that evening's washing-up. One plate after another. One saucer after another. One cup. One knife.

She remembered skipping out the backyard while Old Mrs Dawson entertained the guests at the front, running through the streets with her skirts held high so as not to trip and miss the opening feature. Then jiggling from foot to foot as the queue moved slowly towards the ticket booth, until at last she got to the front, sliding the money beneath the glass, skipping up the stairs. A chummy seat, that was what she was after, right on the back row. Ted would come in separately once he'd cleaned up from his shift, Lillian's heart pounding beneath her best frock as she settled herself on the red plush, waited for him to arrive.

They'd first kissed at the Central, as the lights went down, Lillian and Old Mrs Dawson's son. Lillian couldn't even remember the film they'd seen, just the taste of his tongue. She had dreamed of it after, on the cot in the bedroom, licking cherry soda from his lips, him pressing in. When she woke she had been befuddled, her head muzzy, Old Mrs Dawson scolding her for being late with the breakfasts. But that hadn't stopped Lillian wanting to do it again.

Now, she tightened her hand on Miss Macdougall's arm. 'It shouldn't take too long for the queue to move. We can wait.'

But Miss Macdougall had slowed, hesitated as they came towards the front of the queue, drawing Lillian away from the crowd at the entrance.

'Oh, I don't know, it's not one of my favourites. Perhaps

we could have a nice evening at home, just the two of us. Cards, or the piano. I'd like that. Do say yes.'

As Muriel walked her further from the cinema, away from the rattle and noise of the High Street towards the sun setting over the sea, Lillian could not resist glancing back, as though searching for her younger self in the queue. Best frock. Hair up. Holding the arm of a lad she couldn't get enough of. It was then that she saw what their guest had seen. Not a ghost from the past, but Isabella. Best frock. Hair worn up. Holding on to the arm of a boy Lillian had never seen before, laughing as he tossed money in for their tickets. Lillian saw the way her daughter looked at the lad as they disappeared inside. She knew that Miss Macdougall had seen as well. But she never said a thing. Not then, not after. By which time it was all too late.

A week later, after countless breakfasts and suppers, a never-ending rotation of eggs and tea, Lillian took a break. She changed from her work overall into a dress and went for a walk along the promenade before returning to lie in her room. Downstairs, in the warm lull of the afternoon sun, Miss Macdougall played the piano, Isabella alongside. Lillian could hear their laughter drifting up the stairs as she lay on her bed. She listened to her friend playing a duet with her daughter, felt so tired suddenly, limbs too heavy to lift them from the eiderdown, her head from the pillow. She gazed towards the ceiling, thought about what Muriel had said. About Isabella's plans, how they were all getting older now. What does it mean to be tied to a place? Lillian wondered. With a cord that can never be severed. A place that will keep you alive, but might eat you whole, too.

Lillian woke to find the bedroom in darkness, the sun long gone, shadows stretching across the carpet to touch the wardrobe. The boarding house was still, nothing but the subtle shifts and sighs of people sleeping in the other rooms. Lillian heard the soft chime of the clock on the parlour mantle, the half-hour. It was already past eleven o'clock, perhaps even midnight. Lillian had missed the whole evening. Serving the drinks. Bringing in the sandwiches for supper. Washing the cups and making the preparations for breakfast. She must get up and do some of it now, she thought, before it was too late. Lay out the china and fill the urn. Put the pans on the stove. She lifted her feet from the bed, placed them on the carpet. She was still fully clothed, her tea dress with the yellow roses creased, stockings askew at the ankles. She slid her feet into her slippers, pulled on a cardigan, headed for the door.

As she stepped onto the landing she encountered Mrs Cantwell coming out of Room One to use the bathroom. Mrs Cantwell was muttering as usual, a low conversation with herself as she headed to the toilet, disappeared inside. Lillian waited for the flush of the pan, the running of the taps, until Mrs Cantwell appeared again, head wrapped in a scarf to protect her curlers, went back to bed. There was silence on the landing as Lillian set out past the other rooms – Mr and Mrs Oldham in Room Two, Mr and Mrs Duthie in Three, Mr Innes in Five – towards the dog at the top of the stairs. Nobody was stirring. But as she stepped across the dark carpet with its Turkish pattern, she heard it. Laughter drifting from the back corridor, the access to Room Four.

Lillian crept up the narrow staircase to the second floor in her stockinged feet, knowing that she ought not. What was it Muriel had said to her only the other day?

'Let her have her freedom.'

Lillian complaining again about Isabella being late for the chores.

'She's got plenty of freedom,' Lillian had replied, sweeping crumbs from the dining-room table. 'And tips from the guests which she keeps for herself.'

Neither of them had mentioned the queue to the cinema, the light in Isabella's eyes as she gripped hold of the boy's arm, how he had gripped on to her, too. But Lillian knew that this was what both of them were thinking of. The glow on her daughter's cheeks.

Muriel placed the silver candlesticks on the mantelpiece. 'She's just experimenting, isn't she? Seeing what it means to make something of yourself.'

'Plenty of opportunity to make something of herself here, if that's what she wants. No need to go anywhere else.'

'But what if she wants something else, Lillian? A different life.'

Ham rolls. A cupboard full of china. Also money for the taking and a winter to relax. Lillian surprised herself with the hostile edge to her reply.

'What, like your life, Muriel? Like the freedom you had before you came here?'

Now, as she reached the small landing on the second floor, saw the line of light falling from Room Four, Lillian knew she should make up with Miss Macdougall. Say something before Muriel told Isabella all her secrets. And those belonging to the boarding house, too. It was only tiredness on her part, Lillian thought, the way she had spoken. Normal behaviour on Isabella's for a girl of her age. Boys would come and go, and guests would come and go, and seasons would come and go, and they would get through it, the boarding house continuing the way it always had done, with its secrets and its treasures intact, the Dawson family in charge. Lillian would raise her hand to knock softly at the door, slide into the room with its pattern of strawberries across the wall, join her best friend and her daughter on the narrow bed. Then Lillian glanced through the door, into the room, let her hand fall.

Lillian had never seen Miss Macdougall wear the kimono dressing gown, not once in all the times she had visited, even though she brought it with her every year. But now Lillian stood riveted, as through the crack in the door she watched Miss Macdougall turn in the lamplight, a ripple of orange silk floating about her naked flesh. It was as though her friend had barely aged since the last time Lillian saw her without any clothes on. Still long-limbed and slender, skin as pale as the best bone china in the buffet. So unlike Lillian, with her solid hips and broad arms, hands red from washing dishes. Lillian felt her body hot beneath her crumpled dress as Miss Macdougall turned towards the door, slid the flame of the dressing gown from her shoulders like an animal shedding its skin, said, 'Would you like to try?'

At once Lillian felt it again, the subtle slither of cold silk on hot skin, the deep pool of it at her toes, the sweep of the sleeves embroidered all over with roses and leaves as she held her arms out. She put her hand to the door, fingers and palm pressed to the familiar grain, ready to push it open, step inside, let her own dress fall to the floor like she was an animal, too. Only for her daughter to say it instead:

Yes. Yes, please.

Lillian watched from behind the door of Room Four as her daughter slid one arm after the other into the dressing gown's long sleeves, turned before the mirror. The dressing gown rippled over Isabella's pale Scottish thighs, her breasts. Lillian saw how her daughter's flesh burst from her girdle like a plum smashed on the grass, the gleam of her skin. Also the perfect curve of her stomach, protruding from the dressing gown's soft folds where it ought to have been flat. Then Lillian looked towards the mirror at the far end of the room, found Miss Macdougall lying naked on the bed, gazing back at her.

They argued in the kitchen the next day. Breakfast had been served, dishes piled in the sink, the room filled with the stink of burnt toast and steam dripping from the tea urn. All the guests had gone out. To lie on the beach. To ride a donkey along the sand. Isabella had been sent out, too, to get in the messages in preparation for dinner. Meat pie and potatoes, apple Charlotte for afters.

'Things are different now, Lillian,' Miss Macdougall was saying, standing by the dresser with its row of orange teacups. 'We can get her a place at a mother-and-baby hospital when the time comes, bring them home after.'

'No.' Lillian stood at the sink, hands in rubber gloves deep in dirty froth. 'Not in my house.'

'I can pay, if it's about money.'

Lillian stared through the window into the side return, the dark, mossy passage. 'I don't need your money, Muriel, if that's what you're thinking. We've got the house. That's enough.'

And a reputation, that's what Lillian was thinking. Reputation was everything. Once you lost that, you lost it all, wasn't that what Old Mrs Dawson used to say? If you want to keep the money flowing in.

Lillian had kept the money flowing in, that was what she knew. All those years when she was young, skivvying in Old Mrs Dawson's shadow, doing what she was told. All those years when she had been on her own, Ted gone to the war, never returned, nothing for Lillian but a young child running under her feet and a thousand guests to cater to. She had done it her way, changing with the times as the world changed, re-making the boarding house in her own image to make sure the clock kept time. Fresh lino and a shiny tea urn. The best meals on the promenade. Visitors who came back year after year. A clean house, that was what Lillian had built, not somewhere that needed to take guests in the winter, hidden away from the neighbours and anyone else who might want to gossip, bringing shame on them all. Now here was her own daughter who'd brought dirt right in the door, would take the rest of them out with it, if Miss Macdougall got her way.

Lillian stared into the washing-up, the smears of egg on the plates. Behind her Muriel shifted by the dresser.

'What about the boy? Does he know?'

Lillian made a dismissive sound, clattered a dish onto the draining board. 'What about him?'

'Maybe he'll stick by her.'

Lillian turned from the sink, gloves dripping. 'You of all people should know better than that.'

There was silence between them then, Miss Macdougall sliding her eyes from Lillian, touching a finger to one of the teacups, setting it swinging. My cups, Lillian thought. Not yours. Lillian pulled off her Marigolds, left them lying by the half-finished dishes, fussed with the kettle on the stove. She could feel the boarding house pressing on her as she attempted to light the gas, outside the interminable hordes on the beach. One match. Then another. Three times before she got the gas to take, clattered the kettle onto the burner. As the small blue flames popped and hissed Lillian leaned back against the counter, folded her arms.

'We'll deal with it the way we always have,' she said, refusing to look in Miss Macdougall's direction. 'Keep it in the family. No need to involve anybody else.'

'Lillian . . .'

The kettle started with its boil, a slow whistle. Neither of the women moved. The whistle grew to a squeal. When Miss Macdougall spoke next, her voice was so low Lillian thought for a moment she had imagined it.

'I could take it.'

The squeal from the kettle was shrill now, a high pierce, vibrating in every one of Lillian's bones. She turned, grabbed the kettle from the stove, an abrupt silence. Then Lillian said it.

'I keep a clean house, Muriel. Always have done. And I know how to keep it that way.'

Miss Macdougall left early that year, still had ten days left when she laid her suitcase on the bed in Room Four, packed it with her skirts, her blouses, her hairbrush, pressed the little metal clasps shut, *click clack*, carried it down to the hall. Outside the sun shone and people crowded on the sand, children running in and out of the shallows. Everything smelled of motor oil and sticky ice cream, dung from the donkey rides drifting on the breeze.

'You don't have to leave, Muriel,' Lillian said as they stood together in the hall of the boarding house. 'You've paid for three weeks, you should stay for three weeks.'

Miss Macdougall laughed at that, not a happy sound. 'I think it's best if I go now, Lillian, don't you? You and Isabella have a lot to talk about. I don't wish to interfere.'

'It wouldn't be interfering.'

'Wouldn't it?'

Miss Macdougall looked at Lillian then with a steady gaze that never wavered, waited for her reply. Lillian looked away, smoothed the apron she had forgotten to remove. Muriel seemed so different from when she had arrived. As though she was the one who had joined the new era, left Lillian floundering in the old. Lillian glanced towards the back of the hall where Isabella stood in the gloom, arms folded across her stomach. It wasn't obvious yet, she thought. Unless you knew. But everyone would know soon enough, unless Lillian got her way.

She thought of a baby then, curled and swimming inside her daughter, as once her daughter had curled and swum inside her. Then of a child lying in a cot in the big room at the front, crying and crying as it waited for her mother to come, guests clattering to and fro, calling for their supper. No clean sheets for the bed. The bathroom needing a scrub. A problem with the boiler. Then the whispers of Mrs Wren and her like, spreading the news across Portobello and beyond. A house with two women and a baby, no men to be seen. Then she thought of a newborn in a pan of water, bubble at its lip.

Ted's mother would have known exactly what to do, that was what Lillian thought. Protect the reputation of the business. Otherwise what are you left with? She looked towards the grand staircase with its carpet and its china dog, the bedrooms above, beyond that the attic, dark skeleton holding up the roof. Also fresh wallpaper in the bedrooms, the television set in the parlour, the new tea urn large enough for twenty cups or more at a time, guests arriving year in year out. Lillian had a house to keep, that was what it amounted to. And that was where the future lay, for her and Isabella. Take care of the house and everything in it, that was what she had learned from Old Mrs Dawson. And the house will take care of you.

'I have a present for you.'

Miss Macdougall had her hat on now, suitcase waiting by the open front door. She came to stand beside Lillian, but she was holding the gift towards Isabella. The package was a slim thing, wrapped in tissue smelling faintly of cloves. Lillian knew at once what it was. A dressing gown made of silk the colour of a Portobello sunset. Isabella knew it, too.

She shook her head, cheeks colouring. 'I can't take it.'

'I want you to have it,' said Miss Macdougall.

Isabella glanced towards her mother as though seeking help.

'What are you looking at me for?' said Lillian. 'It's you she's offering it to.'

Miss Macdougall stepped forwards, pressed the package into Isabella's hands. 'It's yours now, dear. Do what you want with it. I'm sure it will be useful, for when the time comes.'

She put her fingers over Isabella's for a moment, a quick squeeze, before withdrawing to lift her suitcase from the blue and terracotta tiles, step through the open front door. Mother and daughter watched as Miss Macdougall wound back through the garden the way she had come. Past the roses and the potato patch, the raspberry canes, treading the path to the gate. Their guest didn't turn when she reached the door in the wall, just opened it and stepped through onto the promenade. Then they watched as Miss Macdougall walked into the crowd, her distinctive hat keeping her visible until the throng was too much, and she disappeared.

It took Lillian a couple of days to realize that Muriel had left behind her Mackintosh. Found it hanging on the hat stand by the grand mahogany front door. Lillian fussed with it for a bit, before deciding to leave the coat where it was. But she couldn't help herself smoothing the folds, dipping her hand into each pocket. Just to check. In one she found a piece of paper, a note written on it in Miss Macdougall's neat hand. There was an address and a phone number. Also a message:

You know where I am, Lillian, in case you change your mind.

Five

Portobello, Edinburgh's seaside, 1925.

The resort was thriving, a playground for the wealthy and the poor alike, attracting all comers to its beach and its amusements, donkey rides on the sand. Boys in caps and girls in petticoats, picnic rugs and soda in glass bottles, a paddle in the sea. Portobello was a honey pot. A place where anyone could have a good time. A place that could make a person rich.

The new girl was fifteen when Mrs Dawson first hired her to work at the boarding house on the promenade. A large property with three floors and a garden, it had been owned by the Dawson family for more than forty years. Mrs Dawson intended to keep it that way for at least another forty, double if she could.

She gave the girl the job straight out of school, liked to get them fresh, if she could, mould them to her routines. Lillian was already well trained, had grown up in a family where the daughters put in the work. But Mrs Dawson knew that her new recruit would learn what hard work really was once she started. Days filled with a whirlwind of frying bacon and cleaning out the closets, cooking lunches and polishing the furniture, cutting sandwiches for tea and turning down the beds. Also providing endless cups of the Dawson's pale brew, the speciality of the house, teapots filled from the huge urn kept in the back kitchen, then ferried to the dining room with its table and its china. She'd had the girl begin at once, the season already upon them. It was a good job, Mrs Dawson knew that. Plenty to see and do, sometimes even tips from the residents. Then there was Ted, of course.

Mrs Dawson's son had just got a job working on the new power station they'd built near Westfield. Solid prospects and excellent wages. Now Mrs Dawson wanted a reason to keep him in the house. Lillian was perfect, a respectable girl, a hard worker, but someone who liked to have fun, too. The two of them had already been to the pictures together at the Central on the High Street, Mrs Dawson waving them off with an extra penny for an ice cream in case they fancied lingering after. She knew that Lillian's mother did not approve. But that was not because of Ted. That was because of the boarding house.

Mrs Dawson knew that it wasn't the summer season work which gave Lillian's mother second thoughts. But what went on the rest of the year once the tourists were gone – storms blowing in from the sea, girls alongside. The other element of the Dawson business, necessary to keep a big property earning through every month of the year. *A laying-in house.* That was what some people called it. A refuge, that was what Mrs Dawson saw. For girls who had got themselves into trouble, needed someone to dig them out of it again. As long as they were prepared to pay, of course. Mrs Dawson knew that she could have taken in travelling salesmen, or young professionals just starting out. But she liked to think of the winter season as another kind of service, beyond high tea and scrubbing out the toilet pan. Something that ran through the Dawson family's veins like letters through a stick of Portobello rock.

The season went with a whirl. One of the best, sunshine all the way, rooms booked right through to September. The girl proved herself an asset to the boarding house, working hard all summer, didn't take advantage. She thrived on the cut and thrust, the never-ending calls for attention, good with the guests, couldn't do enough.

When it came to an end, Mrs Dawson offered Lillian a room, rent free, in return for her staying on. The girl accepted at once. Mrs Dawson overheard Lillian telling her mother that she was practically one of the family now. She and Ted were planning to get engaged when she turned sixteen in a few months' time. Mrs Dawson was pleased. Things were going to plan. Lillian was the new broom that the boarding house needed, that was what Mrs Dawson believed. Could make a future for them all here, if she could be persuaded to stay.

The season had closed completely by the time their newest guest appeared, the weather on the turn. Not even twenty yet and trailing lilies of the valley as she arrived in the hall with two suitcases and a Mackintosh draped over her arm. She came from the south, on the recommendation of a mutual acquaintance who had holidayed in Portobello once, out of season, too. Personal recommendation, the way the news spread around about what the Dawson residence had to offer. Reputation was everything, that was what Mrs Dawson knew.

She sent Lillian to answer the ring on the bell. Might

as well get her acquainted with this side of the business right from the start.

'Gosh,' their new guest exclaimed as Lillian hauled open the huge mahogany front door. 'You're young, aren't you?'

But it was Miss Macdougall who was the young one, that was what Mrs Dawson thought as she ushered her in, stood by as Lillian took the lady's coat, her hat, her case.

'She's come for a rest.' That was what Mrs Dawson had told Lillian as they made up the bed for their latest arrival, fresh sheets and a purple satin eiderdown professionally laundered. 'A paying guest.'

'What's she need to rest for?' Lillian asked as she smoothed down the blanket, placed the eiderdown on top.

'Her laying in.'

'What's a laying in?'

Mrs Dawson gave a strange smile. 'You'll see. If you want to stay.'

Miss Macdougall was staying in Room Four until her confinement. Room Four was a narrow space on the second floor, looking over the side return. It had a new rug on the floor, had been furnished with the prettiest chest of drawers borrowed from one of the better rooms at the front, a neat wardrobe and a washbowl on a stand. There was no view, which was a shame, but the other rooms were getting their autumn makeover, so this was the best for now. The bed was a single with a metal frame and a new mattress. Mrs Dawson had caught Lillian lying down on it only that morning, before she spread the sheet. It wasn't the nicest room in the house, but it was best for the circumstances. Not every girl wanted the world to know that they had been caught out without a ring on their finger. They preferred having a floor to themselves, their own bathroom so they could check themselves in the mirror. And Mrs Dawson preferred it that way, too.

After Miss Macdougall had been shown to her room, Mrs Dawson instructed Lillian to fetch the willow-pattern china from the buffet in the dining room, to get their guest a tray of tea.

'Might as well make it look nice.'

A side plate. A cup. A saucer. A knife with an ivory handle. She watched as Lillian studied the blue-and-white set, with its pavilion and its tiny boat, the miniature figures on the bridge. The hired-in girls always wanted to eat off the willow pattern, but she and Ted and the rest of the family only ever used the white earthenware.

Now, Mrs Dawson led Lillian up the narrow stairs, knocked once and waited on the landing to be admitted. When they entered, they found the new guest sitting on the bed, laid back on the pillow, the huge bloom of her stomach displayed for all to see.

'Oh,' said Lillian. 'I didn't realize . . .'

'Mrs Dawson didn't mention it?'

Miss Macdougall seemed anxious. She glanced towards Mrs Dawson, who watched her new girl's face. But Lillian covered well.

'No, it's just – I wasn't expecting you to be this far along.'

The china on the tea tray rattled as the girl gripped it tight on each side. Mrs Dawson could see that her new help was wondering what it must be like to have something so huge inside you it stretched your stomach until it must burst.

Where does a baby come out?

That was what she heard Lillian asking Ted later.

Between the legs, silly.

Ted had seen it all, and then some, growing up in the boarding house. Nothing was a shock to him. But looking at this new arrival, as she lounged back on the pillows with a dress that barely came below the knee, Mrs Dawson could quite imagine that Lillian would never believe that a lady's legs could open wide enough for anything like that.

'Put it there.'

Mrs Dawson gestured to the top of the pretty chest of drawers for Lillian to lay the tray down. There was cake to go with the willow pattern, a Dundee made specially, inside the cherries, two circles of almonds on top. Normally, tea and cake were taken in the parlour. But the season was over, a new one begun, so the normal rules did not apply. Besides, a girl in Muriel Macdougall's condition needed spoiling. That was what Mrs Dawson had learned.

Lillian put down the tray and stood waiting, eyes averted from their guest.

'Thank you, Lillian. You can go now.'

Mrs Dawson didn't want her new arrival tired before she'd barely got her feet through the door, would need her strength for what was coming. But Miss Macdougall sat up a little.

'Oh, can't she stay? I could use the company.' She gestured to the end of the bed.

Mrs Dawson noticed that the purple satin eiderdown was already rumpled, resisted the urge to tweak it. Instead she smiled.

'Of course. Be good for you to have someone nearer

your own age to talk to. I'll go get a jug of water for the bowl once we've opened your case.'

It wasn't a bad thing for Lillian to get to know the laying-in guests, that was what Mrs Dawson thought. It would help when the time came, keep everything straight as they'd agreed. Miss Macdougall smiled, patted the bed covers. Lillian sidled over, perched on the edge with a pink spot on each cheek as Mrs Dawson opened the suitcase with a *click clack*. There weren't any sandwiches to make, no ham rolls or slices of tomato to lay on serving plates. Even the urn was cold. So what harm would it do?

'How old are you?' Miss Macdougall asked by way of introduction.

'Nearly sixteen,' said Lillian.

'I'm nearly twenty,' said Miss Macdougall. 'Practically an old maid.'

Though how their guest could be an old maid and almost nine months pregnant was a riddle Mrs Dawson left Lillian to work out for herself. Instead, she concentrated on lifting out the various items of clothing Miss Macdougall had brought with her. The clothes were good, in the modern style. Quite different from Mrs Dawson's house dresses and wool stockings. She laid a few things on the narrow bed, let Miss Macdougall indicate where they should go. She saw that Lillian could not resist putting a finger out to touch the hem of a skirt, the cuff on a blouse. Lillian wasn't dressed in the height of fashion either. They were not the right sort for that.

Mrs Dawson left the girls to it, headed downstairs to the kitchen. She filled the large china jug with water, let it run over for a moment to give the girls some time.

Outside, in the side return, a clump of willowherb danced in the breeze. The willowherb was almost over now, autumn coming and with it the change. Mrs Dawson thought of the fresh bloom on their new guests' cheeks, how it would inevitably change, too. Perhaps it was time to begin again, that was what she thought as water ran cold over her hand. Bury the secrets of the past and build the boarding house anew. Muriel Macdougall could be the last, Mrs Dawson thought. After that a fresh broom.

Upstairs, the girls had reached the underwear. They lifted it from the bottom of the case, a world of satin and silk. Mrs Dawson watched through the door as each item was revealed. Nightgowns in white lawn. Bloomers and matching cami tops. Also a corselet. Miss Macdougall was laughing as Lillian held the corselet against her kitchen apron, let the thing unfurl. Pale green satin, lace trim and suspenders hanging down. Beneath her own dress, Mrs Dawson felt the creak of her stays, the bones stitched in. This was Miss Macdougall's trousseau, that was what she knew. Purchased for a wedding that never happened.

Then there was the dressing gown.

The dressing gown was a gorgeous thing, a flutter of dark orange silk covered all over in hand-stitched embroidery, roses and leaves in contrasting colours, sash to match in a strange sort of green. It lay across the end of the bed, waiting to be hung in the wardrobe. Mrs Dawson had never seen such a fine thing before, and certainly not in her house.

'I'm keeping it for after,' said Miss Macdougall, reaching a hand to stroke the fabric.

'After what?' said Lillian.

'The baby, of course.' Mrs Dawson saw the flush on

Lillian's cheeks as Miss Macdougall laughed. 'Try it on, if you like. But you'll have to take your clothes off first.'

Then she stepped into the room, put the jug of cold water down.

It was only later, after supper, both girls playing the piano in the parlour, when Mrs Dawson discovered the rest. Small knitted cardigans, two nightgowns and a pair of booties, a cap with ribbons falling from the ends. A layette for a laying in, folded between tissue paper scented with cloves. All the things the ladies brought with them sometimes, just in case they changed their minds.

Despite the glory of her underwear, Miss Macdougall turned out to be an easy guest to look after. She took her tea in bed every morning with a slice of toast, then appeared in the hall promptly at ten a.m. for her daily perambulation on the promenade. Normally Mrs Dawson would have gone with her, liked to guard her charges against intrusion, as though she was their mother hen. But this time she encouraged Lillian to accompany their new guest. The two of them set out, arm in arm, walked one way, then the next, before returning at eleven, after which Miss Macdougall would entertain herself playing the piano in the parlour until lunch. In the afternoons she walked on her own in the garden, or dealt some cards, took high tea at five, not much more than an egg and some bread. She never asked for anything unusual, seemed happy with the simple things.

'Probably can't afford anything more,' said Mrs Dawson when Lillian mentioned Miss Macdougall's frugal tastes. 'No one else to provide.'

Despite the trousseau, despite wearing a thin band on

her left hand, Mrs Dawson understood that Miss Macdougall was alone in the world.

In the fourth week of her stay, when Miss Macdougall was getting near her time, Mrs Dawson took her for a walk on the promenade.

'You stay in today, Lillian,' she said. 'Get on with the laundry.'

Miss Macdougall might have frugal ways, but she had plenty of clothes needing washing. Lillian was already up to her elbows in Lysol by the time they set off.

'We'll be back in an hour,' Mrs Dawson said. 'Have the tea ready for us, will you.'

The weather was cold, an autumn day, September spilling into October. Mrs Dawson had made sure that Miss Macdougall was wrapped up warm with a muffler and gloves. They walked for half an hour along the promenade towards Joppa. Even with the baby large inside her now, Miss Macdougall's walk was graceful, while Mrs Dawson's was stolid, as though she was a prison officer escorting her charge. When they reached the bandstand, Mrs Dawson suggested that they sit for a while. Miss Macdougall seemed more tired than when she'd first arrived, reality bearing down, no doubt.

Together they watched the sailboats tack back and forth on the Firth, small white triangles against the choppy surf. She must get some new paper for the passage, thought Mrs Dawson, with sailboats just like these ones. Miss Macdougall's fee would pay for it, the passage needed a refresh. Next to her, Miss Macdougall fiddled with her gloves. Mrs Dawson left her for a moment, before laying her hand in its black woollen mitten over Miss Macdougall's.

'You remember what we talked about,' she said. 'About when the time comes, what will happen after.'

'Yes.' Miss Macdougall didn't look at Mrs Dawson, continued to stare out at the water. But her hand stilled.

'And you're still happy with that? What we agreed.'

Miss Macdougall didn't speak for a moment. When she replied her voice had a quiver to it. Fear, that was what Mrs Dawson knew. And not surprising.

'I don't want any trace.'

That was what her guest said, still hoping to start over. Mrs Dawson felt it then, a little well of sadness at what would be lost.

'Right, then,' she said, took her hand from Miss Macdougall's. 'That's settled. We'll go back now, have some tea to warm us.'

But Miss Macdougall did not rise to walk with Mrs Dawson back to the boarding house.

'Leave me here for a bit, will you,' she said. 'So I can sit and watch the sea.'

Mrs Dawson returned to the boarding house on her own, came in via the side gate rather than the front, unlaced her walking shoes and left them in the back passage to dry. Then she went into the kitchen to help Lillian with the tea. But the kitchen was empty. Lillian had not done the tray. There were no cups and saucers waiting on the table. No willow pattern or slices of Dundee cake. The kettle had not been boiled. Mrs Dawson frowned, went along the passage to the hall, stood for a moment listening to the house as it listened to her. Then she headed upstairs. And up again. To the little landing outside Room Four, watched through the door.

Lillian stood in Miss Macdougall's bedroom in front of the long mirror, shoes slipped from her feet. She had rolled her thick stockings to her ankles, peeled them off, too. Her house dress lay over the end of the metal bedframe. She had removed her slip and her bloomers. Now she stood in front of the open wardrobe, compact body firm and muscled from all the work Mrs Dawson had her do, reached for Miss Macdougall's dressing gown.

Mrs Dawson stood gazing at her help as Lillian slid first one arm, then the next, into the beautiful orange sleeves. She could only imagine the lightness of the fabric against Lillian's naked body, what it must be like. The silk would be so cool on her skin, slippery on her collarbone, a sort of marvel after workaday cotton and wool. Mrs Dawson stayed silent as Lillian stood in front of the tall mirror admiring herself, turning to see how the embroidery glinted in the light from the window. The dressing gown was the perfect length for the girl, falling about Lillian's limbs to brush at her toes. The long slash at the front fell open to reveal a glimpse of the girl's flesh, the soft mound of her pubic hair. Mrs Dawson could hear Lillian's breathing, fast and shallow, saw the flush at the base of her throat. She knew what the girl was thinking. What must it be like to wear such a thing every day? To have the kind of life Miss Macdougall must have, somewhere far from here.

Mrs Dawson watched Lillian, as Lillian watched herself. Then the clock downstairs chimed the half, there was the sound of the front door opening, a faraway clatter in the hall as Miss Macdougall returned. Lillian turned then, clasped the dressing gown about her in fear of being caught.

Found Mrs Dawson staring back. The two women looked at each other for a moment, Mrs Dawson's eyes like two stones, Lillian's like a creature caught outside its burrow. Then Mrs Dawson said:

'Take it off. I run a clean house here.'

The cries woke them in the night, dark outside and Miss Macdougall spreadeagled in the top-floor bathroom, blood all over her thighs. Lillian stood helpless in the doorway, Ted behind her, as Mrs Dawson squatted by the pan next to their guest, tried to haul her up. It was only a few days since they had walked on the promenade and stopped to watch the boats. But everything was different now. The baby was coming, no time to waste.

'Ted, you light the boiler,' Mrs Dawson instructed. 'Lillian, help me get her back to the room. Then bring towels. I'm relying on you now. Can you do it?'

Lillian hesitated, then nodded, flit to her side.

Miss Macdougall gave a gasp, cried out again, her leg slithering on the cold bathroom lino. Lillian put her hand to Miss Macdougall's arm, steadied her friend as Mrs Dawson waited for the pain to subside.

'Lift her now,' she said when Miss Macdougall had wilted again. 'On three.'

And together they helped their guest to her feet, soiled nightgown falling to her knees, on the floor a puddle of liquid, the briny smell of the sea. As they crossed the landing to Room Four, Miss Macdougall shuddered, reached a hand to her crotch as though to hold the thing in. Mrs Dawson gripped her guest's arms.

'Lillian, you get the towels. Now!'

By the time Lillian returned, Miss Macdougall was sprawled on the narrow single bed, hands fixed to the frame. Lillian handed Mrs Dawson the most worn set of towels from the press, an old sheet, too.

'Good girl. We'll make a decent helper of you yet.' Then Mrs Dawson sent her to fetch a pail of hot water from Ted in the kitchen. 'And have him make some tea while you're at it. We might be some time.'

Miss Macdougall laboured all night, calling and crying, sweaty hands grasping onto Mrs Dawson as though she might crush her. At Lillian, too. Scrabbling at the eiderdown and the sheets. Mrs Dawson saw how Lillian sweated, damp patches blooming beneath her arms, hair stuck to her forehead, until her dress was limp, her apron crushed, as though she was the one birthing the baby rather than Miss Macdougall. The girl would understand now how a lady might open her legs wide enough.

Mrs Dawson sat at the end of the bed, checking periodically beneath the towel she had draped across Miss Macdougall's thighs. She was unperturbed by her guest's cries, by the guttural moans. There was a reason they were in Room Four, far away from anyone else who might come knocking. Besides, she had seen this many times.

At four a.m. Miss Macdougall fell against the pillows, began to cry, tears mingling with the sweat on her face and her neck.

'I can't do this,' she wailed. 'I can't.'

Weeping like the baby she was trying to birth.

'Should we not call the doctor?' Lillian whispered.

Miss Macdougall lay as limp as the girl's apron, head wedged against the metal frame. Blood stained the bed sheets, amongst other things. Mrs Dawson could see that Lillian was afraid. But her reply was sharp, a warning.

'No need for doctors here,' she said. 'I've done this a thousand times. Besides, I've got you to help.'

Lillian didn't realize how lucky she was to have come to help during this modern era, when Mrs Dawson treated her winter girls like proper guests, rather than something to be hidden, then thrown away after. She reached forwards, touched a hand to Miss Macdougall's ankle. The girl was clammy. Not a good sign.

'Come on now, Muriel,' Mrs Dawson said. 'One more try and it will all be over.'

But it wasn't until dawn had spread along the Portobello shoreline, light creeping into the sky, that the baby finally came. Miss Macdougall was delirious by then, lying exhausted on the pillows, limbs an awkward sprawl. Lillian was exhausted, too, her face drained of colour, slumped on the floor by the bed, breath harsh in her throat. As the baby slid out, Mrs Dawson heard the birds outside beginning with their call. It was a new day, she thought. Another era begun. She fumbled beneath the towel, lifted the slippery child clear, didn't hold it up for Miss Macdougall to see. Instead she spoke to Lillian in a low voice.

'Get me the water.'

The second bucket Ted had left at the door.

The water was cold now, slopping in the pan as Lillian carried it in. Mrs Dawson had her hand around Miss Macdougall's ankle once again.

'Are you sure, girl?'

Miss Macdougall turned cow eyes towards her.

'Don't let me see it,' she whispered. 'I can't see it.'

Mrs Dawson nodded, let go of Miss Macdougall's ankle. 'As you wish.'

'But what if it's cold?' Miss Macdougall attempted to rise from the pillows, voice a high pitch. 'I don't want it to be cold.'

'Now now, dear,' said Old Mrs Dawson, dragging the bucket of water towards her. 'Don't be silly. We'll wrap her up warm.'

There was no sound of mewling. No sudden cries as Mrs Dawson dipped the baby in, washed blood from its temples and its feet. Lillian turned away for a moment to grab a muslin cloth to wrap the child in once it was clean, and Old Mrs Dawson took her chance. When the girl turned back, the baby was submerged in the bucket, small bubble clinging to its mouth, lying in the pan like a doll, skin as smooth and translucent as the best of Mrs Dawson's china. What remained of the cord was wrapped about its neck, like a miniature noose. Like the hanged man on the tarot cards dealt out at the fair. Mrs Dawson saw Lillian looking, the dark hollow of her eyes. She reached a hand to Lillian's wrist this time, gripped tight enough to bruise.

'We do it the old way in this house,' Mrs Dawson said. 'The way my mother taught. It's what the girls want.'

It was Lillian who looked away first.

'Good girl.'

Mrs Dawson smiled, then loosened her grip. She fumbled around the far side of the bed for a moment, slid a barrel-shaped biscuit tin towards her across the floor. The tin was large, catering size. There was an image of a family on the lid. A mother. A father. A girl. A boy.

'Get me something from the drawer, Lillian, won't you,' Mrs Dawson instructed. 'To clothe her.'

Watched as Lillian rummaged amongst Miss Macdougall's trousseau, pulled out the nearest thing that came to hand. A corselet. By the time the girl turned back, the newborn had been folded into the tin. Its blank eyes. Its soft heels. As though it never existed. Mrs Dawson took the corselet from Lillian's cold hands, laid it on top. Then she fitted the lid, slid the tin across the floor towards Lillian, took a key from her pocket, presented the girl with that, too.

'You take her up,' she said, indicating the door in the corner of the room. 'I'm getting too old to be crawling about in the attic now.'

PART FOUR

Essie and Emily

One

Isabella Dawson's funeral is a strange affair. A small huddle of strangers gathered at the crematorium in Seafield. Not far from where Granny Pound is buried. Not far from Portobello where the old lady breathed her last. Despite the cool weather and exposure to a crowd, I feel quite at home.

I stand with Daphne and the rest of the crew at the back of the gathering. We are here to pay our respects to the woman who has kept us in business for the last two weeks. It was Daphne who ordered it.

Might be the only ones.

But as it turns out, Isabella Dawson had more friends than any of us realized. Or at least plenty of rubberneckers. Sometimes in Edinburgh, that amounts to the same thing.

I count the crowd as we wait for Isabella Dawson to arrive in her coffin. There is Margaret Penny from the Office for Lost People still wearing her fox. Pastor Macdonald who's been invited to do the eulogy. The bearers who will carry Isabella Dawson in and lay her down. Also the members of the indigent funeral rota whose names were top of the list when the call came. I list them in my head, based on Dr Anju's descriptions. Margaret Penny's mother, Barbara, with her grey NHS stick and turquoise funeral suit. Her friend, Mrs Maclure. There is the Heir Hunter's aunt who is wearing some sort of

Chinese robe and an enamelled clasp spearing her steel-grey hair. Also a nun hovering nearby. Another sister, that is what I'm thinking. But not one I want to get to know just yet.

The women of the indigent rota have their heads together, whispering amongst themselves. But I am close enough to hear. They are watching the Heir Hunter, Solomon Farthing, next to him a man neither I, nor they, have ever seen before. The main attraction of the day.

The man they are interested in is tall. He is dressed in a suit. Elegant, that is what I'm thinking. Dark tie. Shined shoes. Sprinkle of silver in his hair. He is the object of keen attention from the members of the indigent funeral rota as they speculate at the luck that is coming his way.

'Worth a fortune.'

That is what they are saying. Because of the house, that is what they mean. A grand property on the promenade at Portobello. Once a private dwelling. Then a hotel. After that a boarding house, all sorts washing in and washing out. All gone now, of course, Isabella Dawson's life's work distributed north, south, east and west. I find myself smiling at the idea that somewhere in Edinburgh somebody is loading up one of her cake stands. Or setting out her gravy boats to make their dinner table complete. I have my own selection, of course. Two side plates, willow-pattern, tiny figure standing on a bridge. I slipped them from the stack when everybody else had their backs turned, smuggled them out in my caddy. Sasha and I use them for cake at the weekends. The pink and yellow of a Battenberg looks good against the white and blue.

'A million,' Barbara Penny says now, stamping her grey NHS stick on the gravel as though laying down a bet.

'At least,' replies Mrs Maclure. She is clutching a bunch of ox-eye daisies that I know she must have plucked from the roadside on her way in.

'Needs a lot of work.'

Solomon Farthing's aunt has an imperious manner, as though whatever she says must be correct. But I know she hasn't been inside Isabella Dawson's boarding house for years. Or maybe ever. And certainly not since we cleaned it. Attic to porch. Porch to attic. Or some of that, at least.

'Maybe he'll keep it. *Memento Mori*.'

The other members of the rota look annoyed at this intervention. As though the owner of this opinion does not belong to them. I know better. Sr Josephine belongs everywhere in Edinburgh where succour is required.

'You could introduce us to him, Barbara,' Mrs Maclure says. 'You knew her, didn't you?'

I am as surprised as the rest of them at this piece of news. I didn't know that Isabella Dawson ever met Margaret Penny's mother. Then again, this is Edinburgh. A city where everybody knows everybody else.

'A brief acquaintance.'

Barbara Penny doesn't look any of them in the eye as she says this. But they don't need to worry. The man is coming over to introduce himself.

His name is Mr Macdougall. Mr Edward Macdougall.

'But everyone calls me, Ted.'

That is what he says as he shakes each of their hands, gives a slight bow. His silver hair glints in the autumn light. The women of the indigent rota simper. Even Barbara Penny, and she must be getting on for ninety if what Dr Anju tells me is correct.

Ted Macdougall comes from the south.

'Home counties.'

Has never visited Edinburgh before. A shame, that is what I'm thinking as he talks about the delight of seeing the castle on its hill. Edinburgh has some very nice cemeteries. Seafield is not one of the best.

Sixty-six years old. A former solicitor, newly retired.

'Born in 1953,' he says. 'Nine months on from the coronation.'

All those parties in the street. I watch as the women of the indigent funeral rota do their sums. It doesn't take a lot to work out that something untoward went on.

'A shock.' That is how Ted Macdougall describes the call he received from Solomon Farthing. 'Mother never said I might have Scottish ancestry.'

'What was your mother's name?' Mrs Maclure says. 'If you don't mind me asking.'

'Muriel. Muriel Macdougall. I don't suppose you knew her?'

The members of the indigent funeral rota give a collective shake of their heads. Muriel Macdougall had no connection with Portobello whatsoever as far as they are concerned. And if her son is to be believed. But I know better.

Will see you on the 12th. Save the room.

That is what I'm thinking. Not to mention pen marks hidden inside a wardrobe:

Miss M stinks

Ted Macdougall delivers a eulogy then, for Muriel Macdougall, even though he's already told us she's been dead for a good few years.

'The best mother I could possibly have. Bar none. A wonderful woman.'

But really, he is Isabella Dawson's long-lost son.

Solomon Farthing has dug Ted Macdougall from the archives, so that he might claim the boarding house as his own. I watch as the women of the indigent funeral rota screw their mouths into tiny puckered buds at his paean to Muriel Macdougall. They might not have liked Isabella Dawson. Or even known her. But the members of the rota will always put the reputation of an Edinburgh citizen above any interloper from outside.

'I was adopted,' Ted says now. 'At birth. Never even heard of an Isabella Dawson until Mr Farthing's call.'

But she never forgot him, that is what I'm thinking. Because, even inadvertently, Isabella Dawson has left him a very particular gift.

HOUSE OF HORRORS

That was the headline in the *Edinburgh Evening News*. But I know there is much more to Isabella Dawson's boarding house than that.

Next to me, Monika frowns, pokes me with her elbow. A sharp jab. She is warning me to pay proper attention to where it is required, rather than somewhere it is not. She nods towards a couple of people several steps in front of us, conversing with Margaret Penny from the Office for Lost People. McDermid and Sharp, also come to pay their respects. Two women who know everything there is to know about this city. Then some more.

McDermid and Sharp are here on business, like the rest of us. Never know what new clients might be acquired when standing around a grave.

Part of the job.

That was what Daphne said when she gave us the order to attend. We are here as a team. No masks. No shoe covers. No coverall suits. Just respectable clothing and appropriate shoes. It is the first time I have been out in public without a coverall suit for months, standing here as though I might as well be naked, everything I am revealed. But for the first time in a long time, being stripped bare in public feels good.

Sasha is attending too, of course, standing a little way in front with her hands clasped behind her back. She is here on business as well, professional all the way. She has tied back her hair, a single black cascade. Her silver knuckles are glinting in the afternoon sun. But she has removed the skulls from her ears.

Not appropriate.

That was what she said as we stood in front of the bathroom mirror this morning, me lifting aside the great rope of her hair so she could twist off the butterfly backs. Sasha's neck was soft, scented with pomegranate. I bent to bite it. She dropped the skulls into the sink.

Next to Sasha is someone I should have known would be here, but did not expect. Dr Anju, her silver hair tamed somewhat, but still wearing her fleece with those floury handprints on the front. Dr Anju is the only person at the farewell who actually knew the deceased, as far as I am aware, other than Barbara Penny, of course. Or perhaps she has simply come to honour a fellow hoarder, before returning to her own apocalypse. Either way, Dr Anju's nut-brown face is aglow in the cold September weather. Being outdoors obviously agrees with her. She should try it more often. Dr Anju looks over her shoulder and winks at me as she shuffles back to make herself at home within the ranks of the indigent funeral rota, all religious denominations and none. Her grin is even wider as she discovers herself standing next to the nun. Therein lie fireworks, that is what I know. The nun is wearing sandals. But her feet are bare, like Isabella Dawson's feet were bare when they carried her out. I think of a pair of brown lace-ups, abandoned by a bed. Dr Anju is carrying a large bunch of willowherb, somewhat wilted now.

Life is strange. That is what I am thinking as I stand ready to say goodbye to a woman I didn't know other than through her rubbish. A Mackintosh. An anorak. A doll with a bud for a mouth. It plays tricks, first one thing, then the other. Leaves us uncertain of what is up and what is down. A woman lies dead in her bed for two years before anyone even bothers to check, and then there's a crowd for her farewell. I think of all the things Isabella Dawson once owned and what is left of her now. A ladies' bureau rescued from amongst the orphans. Two willow-pattern plates. A painted dog with a chip on his nose. Also, nestled in the dip at the base of my throat, a tiny knucklebone.

Dr Anju sidles across to stand by me. She is like a squirrel. Beside her I am a fattened calf.

'Did you do as I suggested, Essie?' she says as we wait for Isabella Dawson to arrive.

Attend to my dreams, she means. Attend to my dreams.

'I did,' I say as Daphne frowns in my direction.

'And what happened?'

They came true, of course.

She is standing on the other side of the chapel forecourt, at the back, just like me. She is wearing her stab vest with all its defensive paraphernalia. But even that can't disguise how skinny she is, nothing but angle and bone. I gaze at her and she stares back:

An eye for an eye

She looks exactly like the photograph, red swimsuit and a pair of jelly sandals, hair in rats' tails. But all grown now. Not a ghost covered in plaster dust. But a girl calling to me as we run on the beach:

Essie!

Bare feet and salt on our skin, wind whipping my hair as I call back to her:

Em!

She never waited for me then, but she is waiting for me now. Wearing the costume of a police officer. Though I know what she has secreted underneath. Not a red swimsuit with a white, pleated skirt, collarbone like a blade. But a different photograph, faded with all the years that have passed. She carries it with her everywhere, that is what she said. An image of a girl squinting into the camera, hair tangled about her head like a miniature typhoon. This girl is wearing a bikini. Pink and blue, legs covered in sand. She has a small pot for a belly, flesh on her arms and thighs. Along one side of the photograph is a cut edge that fits with another cut edge, like two boys lying in a bed, curled side by side. She held it up for me to see as I crouched in the attic of the boarding house, Isabella Dawson's graveyard scattered about my feet. At first I didn't recognize myself. Then she held up the other one, too. After that it was like a cloth had been wiped across the dirty glass of my memory. My brothers and my sister, making their way into the light.

My sister is like a toothpick. All scrawn, no meat on her bones. She needs to learn how to eat, that is what I'm thinking. Which is one thing I could show her, to make up for everything she could show me. She has the morning off, that is what she told me. But only till the button is pushed, Isabella Dawson committed to the flames. After that she must return. To a boarding house on the Portobello promenade. A kitchen. A parlour. A water closet and a bedroom with a view. A garden full of weeds. Also a doll's house and an attic. Not to mention everything else. She is on guard duty. Like the china dog, I said. That made her laugh. Isabella Dawson's boarding house turned into a proper crime scene now.

'Bloody hell, Essie,' said Sasha when she heard the news. 'What did you do?'

'Nothing!' I protested, pink and yellow crumbs stuck about my mouth from the Battenberg I had just shoved in. I was celebrating. Despite all the bones that fell through the ceiling, it wasn't me who turned out to be the murderess in our family. That is what I've learned.

'A bloody graveyard in the attic,' Sasha said, pulling out a chair and sitting down without even taking off her coat. 'Hundreds of them. Too many to count.'

I shrugged, felt the little notch at my throat rise and fall as I swallowed. I knew what Sasha's news meant.

Finders Keepers.

Wasn't that what Granny Pound said when she let me sort the washing? Which means the knucklebone I found in Isabella Dawson's boarding house belongs to me now.

Daphne was phlegmatic when she heard the news.

'There's always something.'

As though discovering the remains of a hundred dead infants is nothing more than an inconvenience to be lifted and sifted and sorted away. So that the attic can be swept and bleached, along with everything else in Isabella Dawson's boarding house. Job complete. I can see Daphne now speaking in a low voice to McDermid and Sharp. And McDermid and Sharp are speaking in not-so-low voices to Margaret Penny. Who is nodding, her fox nodding alongside, black eye gleaming in the misty autumn light. I know what they are doing. Lining up The Company for another cleaning job. The careful removal of children and all their fragments from the attic of a boarding house in Portobello, not to mention a thousand dead flies, too. The Edinburgh Way, that is what's in operation as I watch from my place at the edge of it all. A word here, another there, until the right ear is reached. A funeral is a good place to network, that is what I know. Get every sort of job done while the deceased goes to her repose.

I think of the men and women in white suits crouching in Isabella Dawson's attic now. Not cleaners for The Company, or anyone else. But a different type of specialist. Crime-scene investigators, there to gather evidence, find out what has gone on. Sifting through Isabella Dawson's secrets with lilac-coloured gloves. I have seen them before, of course, at previous cleaning jobs. And when I was hiding in a cupboard, eye pressed to keyhole, imprint on my skin.

They were cleaning, that was what I thought. Getting things back to normal for when Emily would get home. Emily liked the house clean. But Mummy didn't care. She turned over our cereal bowls and didn't even bother to pick them up till she caught me licking Shreddies from the floor.

I watched the cleaners from my hiding place in the cupboard, coming and going in their white suits and their masks until their work was finished, only one of them left. She turned off the big light that was shining on the kitchen floor and it was dark again, the house quiet, so at last I could *Breathe, Essie. Breathe.* I closed my eyes, thought about sleeping. About curling on the floor of the cupboard like I was a baby again. Like my brothers liked to curl, sleeping front pressed to back in Jonno's bed after Mummy had given them a bath. But when I opened my eyes again, the cleaner hadn't left. She was standing right in front of the cupboard as though she knew that I was there. I tried to hold my breath. Stay small, Essie. Don't make any noise. But the cleaner was looking at me through the keyhole. An eye for an eye. She put a finger towards the door, as though to push it open.

Who's there? she said.

And I couldn't help myself.

It's me, I said. *It's me.*

Two

Rescuing, that was what Emily Noble called it. Her sole purpose in life. Cats and dogs. Elderly relatives who had a tendency to wander. Lost children, of course. Or perhaps there was another name for it:

Repatriation.

Putting together two things that had been severed, tying back the cord.

She arrived at the very end of the day, around about shift change, everybody else going out as she went in. She had checked, of course, didn't want to leave anything to chance. Be prepared, that was what DCI Franklin had taught her. Just not for this, perhaps.

The entrance to the mortuary facility in Dundee was the same as it had been the first time she came – unremarkable – an atrium blocked by security gates that required a pass for entry. Emily approached the reception desk, tried to maintain a neutral expression, flashed her badge.

'I've come to see Anwar.'

The anatomy technician, her new best friend. The receptionist smiled, lifted the phone, waited for the answer that Emily knew would never come. Anwar and his colleagues were knee deep in the attic of a boarding house in Edinburgh. A new case to take up all their available time.

'He's not answering, I'm afraid,' said the receptionist. 'Can I try someone else?'

'Oh, that's annoying.' Emily frowned, a little wrinkle in her forehead. 'We've been working on a case together. He has something for me. I've come to collect.'

There was the sudden flash of another call coming through on the switchboard. The receptionist answered, eyes sliding from Emily for a moment.

'Yes, yes. I can sort it . . .'

Then the to and fro of the security personnel, the changing of the guard. As one signed in, another signed out, the receptionist trying to hand over the sheets, phone still cradled in the crook of her neck. Emily mouthed at her:

'I know the way.'

Smiled her thanks as the receptionist pressed the switch that allowed Emily access to the Centre for Anatomy and Human Identification. Or not, as it had turned out in this case.

Everything in the mortuary was as clean and gleaming as it had been three days before, no nasty little secrets scattered over the tables for everyone to see. All the usual exhibits had been stored away, slid back into the fridges in their body bags until their final reports had been signed and delivered. But Emily knew that her bag of bones had already gone beyond that stage, been consigned to history, for being too old. Or too young. Either way, a case that had gone cold.

She'd checked in advance, of course, discovered that the thing she sought had been removed from the mortuary, didn't even make it to the fridge, even by way of a halfway house. Instead, it had been claimed by another wing of human identification – was waiting to be signed off by the

Fiscal to an archive that specialized in infant remains. She headed past the dissection room and the teaching suite and along a different corridor, searching for the office where the archive was stored. When she found it in the basement, she discovered it was floor-to-ceiling with Perspex boxes stacked about the walls. It was rather like Isabella Dawson's boarding house, but cleaner, more neatly filed.

The boxes were similar to those into which babies were deposited in a hospital when their parents tried to catch up on their sleep, newborns waiting to be tagged and numbered like the cadavers in the mortuary fridges, before being sent home to live. There were so many similarities, that was what Emily thought as she stepped into the office, closed the door behind her, turned the lock. Birth. Then death. She pulled up her sleeve, checked the note scribbled on her arm:

URN: EC119 X375

Everybody was reduced to a number in the end. It was the rest of it that was complicated, messed with your mind.

Emily surveyed the scene she had found herself in, a sort of makeshift morgue. Each one of the Perspex boxes in this office contained an infant, that was what Emily had been told. A teaching resource. An archive of babies that never got to live. Some of them were old. Others older still. All of them reduced to nothing more than their skeletons; sometimes not even that. She could see some of the babies through the sides of the containers. A rib cage here. A spine there. Occasionally a skull. Her breath echoed loud in her head as she lifted one child after another, till she got to the prize.

The box, when she came to it, was unremarkable. Nothing to indicate the trouble it had caused. She placed it on a desk in the centre of the room, lifted the lid. She expected to find a bag inside, transparent, the word *Evidence* marked on the top. Also, the date of discovery. Place of discovery. Name of the forensic anthropologist who had completed the work – Professor Watt, the angel with a bright halo of hair. Also date of dissection. Though, of course, the contents had already been dissected long before they ever arrived here. By age and time. By whatever internal chemicals make a human dissolve. But when the lid came off, Emily discovered that there was none of this, just a small collection of bones with no identifying features other than the number on the outside of the box. There was no sign of a black bin liner or a sheet of newspaper to keep the bones warm. Not even the remains of an orange dressing gown.

The bones were a sad affair, reduced now by their new circumstances, no longer a person reconstructed on a dissection bench. Emily could see them all, jumbled together on the floor of the box. A tibia. A fibula. Some bits that must be toes. Also a skull, its empty gaze welcoming Emily as she peered into its non-existent brain:

An eye for an eye

That was what her sister would have said.

Emily reached into the Perspex box and touched one of the bones, as one might touch a newborn, watch its hand twitch. Here they were, the massacre on the shoreline recovered from the beach at Portobello, no nearer to identification than they had been when Emily rescued them from a dog with one white eye. The tiny remains of a girl, perhaps. Or a boy. Or someone in between. A child who could have grown up to play on a beach with his brother. To run figure-of-eights on the sand.

A small shard shifted, the slender curve of a rib, and Emily withdrew her hand, touched her own rib where it rose and fell beneath her stab vest. This child died long ago, that was what Emily knew. Thirty years. Fifty. Probably more than seventy, if the remains discovered in the boarding house were anything to go by. But of course, there was no proven link between those bones and the ones in front of her now. Either way, it was too many years for anyone to count. Too many years for anyone to care. But Emily Noble knew that the child had been alive once, even for a moment, waiting for the warmth of sun to fall upon its skin.

She dug into her pocket, pulled out a plastic bag. Then she began to decant. One bone after another, all the nubs, the little hollow flutes. When she was finished she got out something she had stashed beneath her stab vest on the way in. Another bag of bones, similar in size and dimension. Not a dog. Or a cat, But a chicken carcass, boiled and bleached. It was her sister who had suggested it. Camouflage of a sort.

Her sister was a giantess. That was the truth of it. She had grown to twice Emily's size, would not fit into any of her hiding places anymore. When she came down from Isabella Dawson's attic after the bones fell, Emily discovered a moon of a face. Thick limbs. Flesh gone soft. Emily would not have recognized her sister if they'd passed each other in the street. But the hair was the same, untidy, just like it always had been, a sort of tornado about her sister's head. Despite all the years that had passed, it looked just like it did in the photograph that Emily carried with her always, slipped into whatever she was wearing so that it might reside near her heart.

Essie.

That was what Emily said in her head as she watched her sister now from across the chapel forecourt at Seafield, all about them the bones of the dead.

Essie.

Calling to her as she ran across the Portobello sand.

Her sister turned to look then, as though she must have heard. She was no longer wearing her coverall suit. Her mask. Her shoe covers. Her gloves. Had unveiled herself to say goodbye to a woman she hadn't even met. It made Emily smile inside at the thought of what her sister had been doing – digging in the dirt to earn a living, as Emily dug into the dirt to earn a living, too. Just like when they were young, her sister had learned how to keep everything hidden under a pile of someone else's rubbish. But just like then, when somebody called to her, she could not resist revealing herself. Along with the secrets tucked away in Isabella Dawson's attic, of course. Brought them both forward, into the light.

Emily watched her sister and her sister watched her as they waited for Isabella Dawson to arrive. Emily was wearing her official paraphernalia, was going on to Portobello to do guard duty for DCI Franklin, standing at the back gate of a boarding house denying entry to all but the people in coverall suits. Amber Ogilvie would be there, that was what Emily knew. And the other vultures, too. It would make her very happy, Emily thought, to stand at the cordon and refuse to let them in.

She gazed at her sister and wondered what it must have been like to crouch in the attic amongst so many bones. Then again, she knew what her sister was wearing beneath her respectable clothes. Not a photograph, a girl in a red swimsuit, cut from her other half. But a notch of something tiny and knobbled, nestled at the base of her sister's throat. The minute Emily saw it she knew where it belonged. Not with the other bones, scattered amongst the joists of a boarding house attic, intermingled with the dust. But with a skeleton laid out on a dissecting table in Dundee. Leg bone. Ankle bone. Toes and teeth. Rescuing, that was what Emily had called it. But there was another word:

Reunification.

That would do, too.

Emily Noble exited the room that contained an infant bone archive, with a plastic bag in her hand, inside that the partial remains of a skeleton washed up on a Portobello beach. She left behind a chicken carcass, just because she could. She made her way back along the corridor towards the mortuary room, would have passed that, too, if only she hadn't glanced through the open door. Walk away, that was what she said to herself. Leave no trace. But the moment she saw them, Emily knew she would not be able to resist.

They were sitting in the equivalent of an out-tray, waiting to be incinerated, thrown into the flames. A black plastic rubbish sack, ravaged by the tide. Some dried-out sheets of newspaper from 1996. Through the glass Emily could see a girl watching, V-neck jumper, hair in bunches, eyes following as she made her getaway. Emily faltered only for a second before diverting, entered the room and folded the newspaper once, twice, tucked it beneath her stab vest. This child was still out there somewhere, waiting to be found.

Then she recovered all that was left of a kimono-style dressing gown, torn and faded, missing its sash, but still covered in a beautiful scatter of embroidery, roses and leaves stitched by hand almost one hundred years before. Emily stuffed the dressing gown inside the plastic bag containing the bones, wrote *Evidence* with a black marker on the outside just in case anyone asked. The dressing gown was old now, a shadow of its former self, but as Emily prepared to leave again she couldn't help wondering. What must it have been like to own such a thing? To wear it down to breakfast, the cool slither of real silk on bare skin.

There was the sudden sound of lights blinking *on on on* in a nearby corridor as somebody approached. A technician appeared, holding another Perspex box with a sample inside. She started in surprise at seeing Emily standing in the entrance to the mortuary room.

'Gosh, sorry. Didn't see you there. Can I help?'

'No thanks. Just leaving.'

Emily held up the treasure in its evidence bag as though to reassure the technician that she knew what she was doing. Which, of course, she did. She was already down two flights of stairs before the technician even thought to ask what exactly she had taken with her.

'Goodbye,' Emily said as she exited.

This time the receptionist didn't even raise her eyes to check.

In the car, driving back to the Athens of the North with the bones of a newborn on the passenger seat, Emily wondered how many there were in Isabella Dawson's attic. Ten lost infants? Twenty? Maybe even a hundred, if Solomon Farthing's guess was correct.

A laying-in house.

That was what he'd called it when the bones came tumbling down. A boarding house that had stayed in the same hands for several generations, holidaymakers in the summer season, something else in between.

'What's that when it's at home?' Emily had asked.

'A place to have your baby,' Solomon Farthing replied. 'And leave it behind. To avoid your disgrace.'

The mortuary in Dundee would be kept busy for weeks, that was what Emily knew, maybe months. All of Isabella Dawson's secrets laid out beneath their bright lights. A teaching opportunity, that was what Professor Watt had declared. But as she drove home, a rescued carcass on her passenger seat, another name for it was circling inside Emily's brain.

Annihilation.

Something Emily Noble knew all about. The destruction of the soul.

Three

I wake up and my sister is here. She has not disappeared in the night, or the early morning. She has not abandoned me to live a half-life waiting to understand. What happened then? What happens now? What might happen in the future? Instead she is sitting at her table in the window bay nibbling the chocolate off a Bounty Bar. I raise myself from her sofa where I have been resting.

'Did you get it?' I ask.

My sister's flat is kind of like the one I share with Sasha. But different, of course. Third floor, a view of all the neighbours. But not a dirty tenement with a door to the street left on the snib. It is more yellow brick and balconies too small to stand on, patches of mown grass on the verge. My sister's home is nice, but I prefer mine with Sasha. There is life in the place where I stay, whereas here the walls are empty. There is nothing to eat in the kitchen cupboards but breakfast bars and a packet of Ritz crackers, not even any cheese. Before I lay down on my sister's sofa, I ate my way through the box of Ritz crackers, watched a girl across the street dancing in her bedroom. I could dance too, I thought, if I wanted. So I did.

Now my sister lays it before me on her table. We are both thieves, that is what I realize. It makes me smile inside. The plastic bag has writing on the outside. *Evidence.* But still I can see it, all the little nubs and flutes.

'They do look quite like a cat,' I say. 'Or a dog.'

'Or a chicken, perhaps,' my sister replies.

I told my sister about the carcass burned to the bottom of a stockpot. About a red anorak abandoned in a water closet. About a doll dug from a grave of rubbish, hair in disarray. Also about treasure discovered inside a biscuit tin abandoned in a kitchen. Not a lady's ring, a row of opals winking at me like cats' eyes. But a tiny notch of bone.

Now, I unhook the cheap chain from about my neck, slide the bone onto the table next to the skeleton inside the plastic bag.

Theft.

That was what my sister's plan was called. Or worse.

Tampering with evidence.

Rather like I have done myself. But not everyone wants to see the evidence, even if it is right in front of their eyes. That is what both of us know. My sister picks the bone from the table, rolls it in her palm.

'Probably won't even notice that it's missing,' she says. 'Left behind in a biscuit tin to toss into a skip.'

What would it be like to be left behind in a tin? I think. Like a missing button, or an old safety pin. Then again, I know all about what it means to be left behind. It's just the rest of it I don't remember. What happened before. What happened after. What might happen next.

Emily, my sister, the police officer, has a file in her kitchen drawer. I found it when she was out, on her rescue mission. It is a brown folder, like the folders in the social worker's office in town. The moment I saw the file I felt it, the tourniquet in my chest turning, the dark pressing down. But this time I didn't open it on my own. I waited for her to come back.

Now the file sits on the table between us, alongside a bag of bones and an orange dressing gown. We both know what is in it – a way to join the dots. But sometimes connecting the dots only leads to a picture that is more complicated; a fractured, splintered thing.

My sister looks at the file. Then she looks at me. I don't shrink under her gaze. Instead, I rise. Sunlight filters through the living-room window and I see that her eyes are gleaming. She digs into her pocket and lays them on the table. Four tiny dolls fashioned from scraps and wire. Two boys. Two girls. I look at my sister and my sister looks at me:

An eye for an eye

Then I say it, 'Tell me.'

So she does.

1996

Portobello, Edinburgh's seaside, 1996.

It was a hot day. August. The school holidays winding towards their end. Locals walked their dogs along the promenade. Children dug holes on the beach. A few day-trippers ran into and out of the surf. At the last remaining amusement arcade on the front the machines flashed and played their tunes, lads competing with each other to win the highest score. Younger kids gathered about the door, fiddling with the broken bubble-gum machine, begging for a go inside. On the concrete sea wall, teenagers huddled together to eat chips and play on their Nokias. Portobello was quiet, a downbeat sort of place. At the play park, a girl wearing a summer frock and a green ribbon in her hair clambered onto the swings. A man stood watching, scratching at his arm.

Emily woke to sunshine filtering through the curtains, the whole room aglow, no condensation on the wrong side of the glass this morning, pooling on the sill. Across the room Essie's bed was already empty, clothes tossed all about. Emily slid from the polyester sheets with a prickle of static, pulled on her red swimsuit with the white buttons and pleated skirt, took a pair of shorts from the tumble of clothes piled on top of the chest with the broken drawers. Then she folded her nightie and laid it beneath her pillow. Emily's parents didn't mind mess, were happy to live in chaos. But Emily preferred to keep everything neat if she could.

In the bathroom Emily squeezed toothpaste onto her finger, rubbed it on her gums. She could hear the wail of the baby rising from the kitchen. The baby was always crying. Never seemed to stop. Emily spat into the sink, rinsed it around with her hand. Then she went down the stairs. The carpet burned on the soles of her bare feet as she skidded over the treads. The walls were marked with crayon. The whole house was a dump, that was what their father said. A stinking place to live.

At the foot of the stairs, Emily saw her favourite jelly sandals abandoned by the front door. Essie had tried to run away with them the day before, even though they didn't fit her. Essie always tried to borrow Emily's things, though she was only five and Emily was nine. Essie was a thief, that was what their mother said, used to smack her on the head if she thought Essie had taken something that belonged to her. Emily stood in the hall smoothing her hair with her fingers, ran one along her collarbone where it stood out from her skin. Essie was chubby, a fat little thing. *Piggy*. That was what their father called her. But Emily was skinny, all bones and angles. He preferred it that way.

In the kitchen, her father slouched on the far side of the room, by the kettle. He was hungover as usual. Emily could smell the sour stink of Tennent's from where she stood by the door. Essie was sitting at the table shovelling Shreddies into her mouth, Jonno next to her doing the same. Essie had cereal stuck to her cheek, milk puddled next to her bowl. Their father was trying to spoon Nescafé into his mug with a shaky hand. Next to him was a plastic milk bottle, barely a dribble at the bottom.

'Who used the last of the milk?' he was saying. 'There's never any fucking milk.'

Across the room Emily's mother lounged against the kitchen cabinets, smoking a B & H. Her fingers were stained. Her T-shirt was dirty. She wasn't wearing a bra. Emily noticed two damp patches blooming across the fabric of her mother's top. The only milk in the house. In the high chair the baby cried, eyes blurry with tears, cheeks raw. Nobody moved to comfort him. Emily could tell from the slow droop of her mother's eyelids that she had taken her pills again this morning, the ones that were meant to help her sleep but made her twitchy, wired like a dog. The air in the kitchen was stuffy, not enough for all of them to breathe.

Emily's mother stubbed out her cigarette on a plate smeared with peanut butter, hauled the baby from the high chair, held him over one arm. With the other she scuffed Essie on the head for licking milk from the surface of the table, took away Jonno's bowl though he hadn't finished eating.

'Drink it black,' she said to their father, turning on the tap to splash water into the sink.

He didn't answer, reached for a slice of white bread, stuffed it into his mouth. Emily's mother reached, too, for the dirty mugs congregating by the kettle. Their hands clashed and the almost-empty pint bottle got knocked onto its side, the last of the milk dripping onto the kitchen floor. The next thing any of them knew their father had his hand about their mother's throat, thumb and fingers pressing in.

'I told you to get more milk, you bitch.'

And she was spitting in his face, screaming louder than the baby.

'Get the fucking milk yourself.'

Emily slammed the front door, ran down the path towards the street. In her pocket she had several coins. Behind her she could see Essie staring through the letterbox. Two eyes following.

'Let me come too, Em.'

That was what Essie had said as Emily buckled on her jelly sandals. Emily had pushed Essie back with her arm.

'No. Stay here.'

Forced her little sister inside, shut the door. From the kitchen she had heard the familiar sound of their parents arguing, the smash of yet another plate.

Outside, it was warm, sunlight glancing off Emily's hair. She ran to the end of the road, then slowed to a walk. Mrs Wren's shop was three streets over, on the corner of the High Street. Emily dawdled, rattled the coins in her pocket. The coins were hot, her hand sticky. But it didn't take her long. The bell rang as she entered and Emily heard Mrs Wren calling from the back room.

'Be with you in a minute.'

She stood at the counter looking at the sweeties lined by the till. Fruit Salads and liquorice laces. Mrs Wren appeared from the back wiping her hands on her overall.

'What can I get for you today, young lady?'

Mrs Wren knew all the children in Portobello, especially the thieves. Emily reached a hand towards the display. But Mrs Wren got in first, a sharp slap.

'No need to touch.'

Emily withdrew. 'Fruit Salads, please. Four liquorice laces.'

'Anything else now?'

Emily slid her fingers into her pocket for the coins, heard again her mother's shouted instruction: *Fetch the milk, Emily.*

Shook her head at Mrs Wren.

'No thanks.'

The tide was out that morning. Emily sat on the sand and sucked at a liquorice lace, made it last as long as possible. The sun was hot on her face. She took off her jelly sandals, dug her toes in. Emily loved the beach. And the promenade. The amusement arcade and the swing park. She watched a couple of kids playing at the edge of the sea, thought of Jonno and the baby crouching over their orange bucket, picking out shells while she ran in a figure-of-eight around their sandcastle, behind her Essie trying to keep up:

Em!

Always following where Emily did not want her to go.

She stood up now, walked towards the sea where it lapped the beach in tiny waves. Emily would not be going home any time soon, that was what she had decided. She would stay out, play on the swings, walk on the prom, feel the tarmac warm beneath her feet, try and get into the arcade.

Inside the house, Essie watched her sister disappear down the street until she couldn't see her anymore. Then she let the flap of the letterbox go and it sprung onto her fingers, trapping them for a moment. But she didn't cry out. She had been told before. By Em. By Mummy.

Keep quiet, Essie. Don't make any noise.

She lingered in the hall while in the kitchen Mummy and Daddy shouted and the baby wailed. She could hear Jonno sobbing.

Essie. Essie.

Put her hands to her ears so she could shut him out. But all she could hear then was the sea roaring in her head, like it roared inside a shell. She let her hands drop, sidled to the kitchen door, shouted as loud as she could:

'Shut up! Shut up!'

But nobody was listening. Jonno's face was scared where he crouched beneath the table. The baby was in its high chair, arching his back as though he might tip out, bang his head on the dirty floor. Essie went to stand by the chair, just in case, held the baby's ankle. On the far side of the table Mummy scratched and scrabbled at Daddy's face.

'I'll fucking kill you.'

Daddy grabbed at Mummy's T-shirt, her neck, slipping on the dribble of milk.

'Not if I do it first, you bitch.'

Daddy's Nescafé was scattered on the floor. A plate was smashed. Mummy bit at Daddy's arm. He let go. She retreated to the sink, panting, hair all about her face. Daddy was in the corner by the kettle. He stood staring at the wall. They all watched him. Except Mummy, who was reaching for her cigarettes, the green plastic lighter. Mummy's hands shook so much she couldn't get it working, flicking at the lighter with her thumb.

'Fuck's sake.'

Then Daddy turned, something in his hand.

'Run, Essie! Run.'

That was what Mummy was shouting, as she held up her arms.

Essie ran into the hall, skidding on the nylon carpet, falling and skinning her knee. She battered the front door from the inside, tried to turn the handle, lift the flap. But the front door was locked and, anyway, Em had told her to stay. From the kitchen Essie could hear her mother's screams:

'Get off!'

Daddy shouting. Then the sudden smash of something hard, a thump, somebody hitting the floor. After that, nothing but the baby crying on and on and on.

Essie pressed herself into the cupboard under the stairs. It was quiet in the cupboard. A good place to hide. The only light was a needlepoint filtering through the keyhole. Essie crouched, pressed herself as far into the corner as she could get, making herself small. Across the hall, in the kitchen, she could hear the sound of Mummy talking to the baby in a sort of monotone.

'Shut up. Shut up. Shut up.'

Jonno was whimpering. Mummy barked at him.

'Shut the fuck up, Jonno.'

From inside the cupboard beneath the stairs Essie heard the sound of her mother cursing, someone scrabbling on the floor as though they were trying to drag something. The two boys were wailing now, wouldn't stop. Then Mummy was wailing, too.

The next thing Essie knew, Mummy's voice was close, calling to her in a sort of whisper:

'Essie? Where are you? We have to go upstairs.'

Essie didn't reply, held her breath instead. She had been told to keep quiet. After a moment, she inched towards the cupboard door, its tiny keyhole, pressed her eye to see. Mummy was standing in the hall, the baby struggling in her arms. Jonno clung to Mummy's leg the way she hated, Mummy gripping him by his arm, so tight her brother's skin was pinched.

'Shut up, Jonno. I'll wash it.'

Jonno's pyjama trousers were covered in something dark, a smear in his hair. Also on Mummy, all over her T-shirt, her arms, her feet.

'Essie,' she was calling. 'Essie, love? Time for a bath.'

From the back of the cupboard Essie heard the water running into the tub upstairs, the closing of the bathroom door. The boys' crying was muffled now, Jonno's sobs. There was the sound of Mummy speaking to them, over and over, the thump of feet on tiles. The door opened, was banged shut again, Mummy swearing.

'I told you, stay here.'

Jonno shouting, a faint, 'No!'

After that, the quiet.

Essie waited – for hours, it seemed – before opening the door. In the kitchen Daddy was lying on the floor as though he was sleeping. Essie touched his shoulder. 'Wake up, Daddy.' But he wouldn't. All around him a dark pool spread across the tiles, got into Essie's toes. Essie backed away, across the kitchen, across the hall, slid into the dark of the cupboard again, curled onto the floor. She would sleep, too, that was what she was thinking. Make no noise.

*

Essie woke to darkness pressing in. Outside the house was silent, waiting. She lay, listening, wondered where she was, what had roused her. Not the baby crying, but something else. Someone calling her name.

'Essie?'

Her mummy standing in the hall, right outside the cupboard. She was clean now, hair wet. But her eyes looked funny, as though she couldn't open them. She was calling to Essie, her voice slurry:

'Essie? Where are you? Come and kiss the boys.'

Essie put her hand to the catch that opened the cupboard door, a soft click and she could be there, nestling into her mummy's lap, hand stroking her hair. They could clean up together, get everything nice for when Daddy woke. Em would be back by then with the milk and they could start again. Breakfast bowls and Shreddies. Nescafé stirred into a mug. Essie put her fingers to the inside of the door, felt the wood grain rough on the tips, took one more look. Mummy had disappeared.

Next time Essie woke, it was to the sound of the front door opening, the brush of it across the mat. She froze in the dark of the cupboard, held her breath as footsteps entered the house, soft, like a creature. They stopped for a moment before starting up the stairs. Essie tried to close her mouth like she'd been taught, pinch her lips together like the little gold kiss on top of Mummy's purse. She held in her breath and counted – *one, two, three, four* – listened to footsteps overhead crossing the landing. Into the bedroom. Into the bathroom. Into the boys. Then the hurried scurry as they came down the stairs again.

This time the breathing was loud, right there, by Essie's

ear, so quick it was like a creature panting, as though they had been running, or playing hopscotch on the beach. There was a pain in Essie's chest, tight behind her ribs. The breathing was so loud Essie thought she might burst. She closed her eyes, pressed her small hands to her face, heart racing . . . Then the breathing stopped, and the only sound was her.

Essie stepped forwards then, one small foot in front of the other, pressed her eye to the keyhole, felt its imprint on her skin. Outside in the hall, everything was grey. A figure was standing in the doorway to the kitchen. Essie blinked, looked again, caught the sudden glitter. Em. Her sister. Still wearing her swimsuit and her jelly sandals, holding a knife in her hand.

Emily came back because it got too cold on the beach. The afternoon was spooling towards its end by then, light beginning with its fall. She had spent all day playing outdoors, dancing on the sand and hanging around by the amusements. She hadn't thought to bring a top when she left the house, running and running to get away. Also, she was hungry, nothing to eat all day but Fruit Salads and liquorice laces. It was time to go home.

She slipped through the door as though she had never been away. Keep quiet, Em, don't make any noise. But Emily had never liked being told what to do. Inside, the house was silent, a strange kind of stillness. She stood on the mat for a moment, waiting, caught a shiver. Then she crept up the stairs, to get her sweatshirt. Her arms had goosebumps all over now that the sun was almost gone.

On the landing, she hovered for a moment, not sure

what to do. She pushed open the door to her parents' room, found it the same as always. Clothes on the floor, the stink of B & H. Her and Essie's bedroom was just as Emily had left it that morning, the neat fold of her nightie beneath her pillow, her sister's usual mess. But there was no sign of Essie's pyjamas. No sign that her sister had got dressed that day at all.

In the bathroom there were damp towels on the floor. She stepped across them, looked into a bath half full of water, the tap a constant drip. One of the baby's plastic boats floated in circles on the surface. Her mother must have put the boys to bed early, Emily thought. She went out onto the landing to their room, stood by the door. There was no sound from inside. Emily put her hand to wood, felt her feet suddenly frozen, hesitated as though something might be wrong. Then she pushed the door open, saw them sleeping together in Jonno's bed, skin still damp from the bath.

It was only as Emily came over to the bed, leaned across to kiss the baby, that she realized something was not right. The baby was too cold, lilac fringing his lips. Emily hesitated, saw the crust of something white on the corner of his mouth. Then she peeled the cover back, discovered Jonno dressed in clean pyjamas. But he was cold, too.

Downstairs Emily stood outside the cupboard in the hall. She could hear the *thud thud* of her heart. White noise in her ears. Her breath was coming fast and shallow, like it might run out of her before she could catch up. Blood pulsed in her wrist, in her neck. She blinked as she stepped towards the kitchen, the black mouth of its door. Everything was in shadow, but still she could see it. The smashed plate. The breakfast bowls awry on the table. Shreddies scattered on the dirty floor.

Nobody had cleaned up, that was what Emily was thinking. She stepped into the room, something tacky on the soles of her jelly sandals. Her foot kicked at an object, sent it spinning. A knife. The solid black of its handle warm in her hand.

On the floor at the far end of the room was Daddy. A dark shape huddled on the vinyl. Emily approached. She could smell it. The stink of cheap lager. Those hands which squeezed at her mother's throat. She thought of Jonno in his bed, his arm around the baby, the tiny crust of white. Then she raised the knife over the dark shape, caught the glitter as the blade came down . . .

The blade was dull by the time Emily heard it. Her mother, propped against the kitchen cabinets, whispering, staring at her eldest daughter, blood on Emily's arms, the soles of her jelly sandals, the red swimsuit with the white buttons. They gazed at each other in the grey light, her mother's hair damp, Emily's in disarray. Then her mother said it:

'You should have brought the milk.'

Emily ran, for the second time that day. Out the door. Down the street. Along the promenade. Forgot all about her little sister hidden in the cupboard, what she might have seen, too.

EPILOGUE

Portobello, Edinburgh's seaside, 2019.

They did it together, like a little ritual, away from the main bit of the beach. They carried their bundle from the busy section, to the far end, where none of the tourists bothered to walk. The sand was fine here, white and soft in the hand, a thousand tiny grains running and trickling one into the other as though through an hourglass, time marching as it must.

They did it when the tide was up, but on the turn, knowing that whatever they put in would be carried to a new adventure, surfing the waves in the Firth as it drew them towards the open sea.

'We should say something,' Emily said as seawater lapped at their ankles, sand wet beneath their soles.

Ashes to Ashes

That was what she was thinking of. But it didn't seem right, somehow, with froth tickling at their toes and salt on the breeze. Those words belonged to dark skies and the heavy thump of a clod hitting the coffin, hair slick with rain. Whereas here it was light dancing on the water and the warmth of September sun on their skin. Edinburgh was experiencing an Indian summer, the perfect way to end.

'I think we should wade a bit.' It was Essie who said it. 'Just to make sure.'

The bones must go out on the tide, that was what they had agreed. Didn't want them to wash up again with the seaweed, just in case. Not a boy. Or a girl. So together they hitched up their clothes to reveal their flesh. They waded quite far, giggling at the soft lap of the water on their legs before Essie said it.

'Here. This will do.'

They loosed them into the water as though releasing a goldfish into a bowl, held the remains of the dressing gown on the surface till it began to sink and the bones began to float. They watched as the faded orange silk ballooned beneath the water, before being borne away by an under-current, like a jellyfish heading for a new adventure further along the coast. All about them small bones drifted on the surface. A tibia. A fibula. A tiny spike of rib. The bones circled for a moment like the remains of a shipwreck, before they began to separate, some moving further towards the horizon, others slipping in the eddies to land somewhere at the two girls' feet. Emily and Essie watched as the bones were covered by the shifting sands, as though they were nothing more than empty shells. Then they looked again at the surface of the water, discovered that the rest had vanished, too.

Afterwards, they had an ice cream for a wake. Two 99s, with raspberry sauce. Sitting together on the sea wall below Isabella Dawson's boarding house, inside men and women in white suits crouching in the attic, still counting everything that remained. It was a calm day, the sea a gentle sway. Out in the Forth a container ship lurked on the horizon. Boats with white sails tacked east and west. They ate their cones down to the nub, licking out the ice cream until there was nothing left but the hollow point. Essie ate slowly, with a concentrated focus. Emily nibbled hers as though she was a mouse. When she was almost done, Emily stared at the tip of cone left in her hand, before turning to her sister squinting in the sun.

Essie was alive with sunlight, her hair glinting, little strands lifting here and there in the breeze. Her pale skin glowed as she brushed wafer from her top onto the sand below. Her eyes were gleaming. Also her smile. Life, Emily knew, was not black and white, but grey. Like the sea in normal times, a never-ending churn. Except for days like today, when the sun shone unexpectedly and suddenly the world became the colour of the Mediterranean, all glitter and warmth. Then everything that had seemed impossible became possible, a great opening of the soul.

She looked at the last nub of her cone pinched between her fingers like a tiny bone, lifted it to her mouth, swallowed it whole. Then she placed a hand over Essie's hand, held on tight.

Afterwards they ran into the sea together, two sisters, one bony, one a giantess. They came out cleansed. Their hair soaked. Their lips chilled. Their skin tasting of salt. They came out holding hands, to autumn sun shining on their limbs, all the dirt washed away.

Acknowledgements

Thank you: Clare Alexander and all at Aitken Alexander Associates; Maria Rejt and Alice Gray at Mantle; Rosie Wilson, Ellie Bailey, Ami Smithson, Alexandra Payne, Gillian Mackay, Samantha Fletcher and all at Pan Macmillan; my fellow Edinburgh writers, Theresa Muñoz and Pippa Goldschmidt; PC Emily Noble of Police Scotland for lending me her name and rank (again); Professor Niamh Nic Daeid for showing me around the Leverhulme Research Centre for Forensic Science at the University of Dundee; Professor Lucina Hackman for fielding questions about the work of the Centre for Anatomy and Human Identification (CAHID) in Dundee; Professor Sue Black, Baroness Black of Strome for assistance with questions of place, procedure, age identification of infant skeletons and other forensic anthropology delights; Jack and Doreen Duthie for their memories of that boarding house in Portobello; Vince Bell for the original story of the bones in the ceiling; and Val McDermid and Jo Sharp for allowing me to baptize The Company in their names – I trust I have not taken too many liberties with their capacities (or not) for cleaning, extreme or otherwise.

It goes without saying that my characters are entirely fictional and any similarity to persons live, dead or somewhere in between is entirely accidental. Just as all mistakes (and inventions) are my own.

I read several books and articles about the practice of extreme cleaning for this novel. They were all instructive, but I'd like to note the particular influence of *The Trauma Cleaner* by Sarah Krasnostein – an insightful and inspiring investigation of one woman's life in death, decay and disaster.

Thank you to my family for their continued love and support. As befits a book about brothers and sisters, this novel is dedicated to my own resolute tribe. Thank you Catherine, Christopher and Peter for years of excellent book chat and always having my back.

Much of this novel was written during the Covid-19 lockdown and I'm not sure I would have got through either quite so well if it hadn't been for my wonderful partner, Audrey Grant, who has once again been a tower of creative strength.

Loved *Emily Noble's Disgrace*?
Discover Mary Paulson-Ellis's first novel,
The Other Mrs Walker . . .

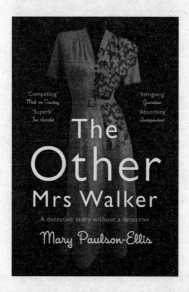

An old lady dies alone and unheeded in a cold Edinburgh flat on a snowy Christmas night. A faded emerald dress hangs in her wardrobe; a spilt glass of whisky pools on the floor.

A few days later a middle-aged woman arrives back in the city she thought she'd left behind, her future uncertain, her past in tatters.

She soon finds herself a job at the Office for Lost People, tracking down the families of those who have died neglected and alone.

But what Margaret Penny cannot yet know is just how entangled her own life will become in the death of one lonely stranger . . .

Waterstones Scottish Book of the Year

'One of the strongest debuts of the year' *Herald*

'Full of twists and turns' *Independent*

'A wonderful, inventive debut' Fanny Blake, *Daily Mail*

Discover Mary Paulson-Ellis's second stunning historical mystery, *The Inheritance of Solomon Farthing*

An old soldier dies alone in his Edinburgh nursing home. No known relatives, and no will to enact. Just a pawn ticket found amongst his belongings, and fifty thousand pounds in used notes sewn into the lining of his burial suit . . .

Heir Hunter Solomon Farthing – down on his luck, until, perhaps, now – is tipped off on this unexplained fortune. Armed with only the deceased's name and the crumpled pawn ticket, he must find the dead man's closest living relative if he is to get a cut of this much-needed cash.

But in trawling through the deceased's family tree, Solomon uncovers a mystery that goes back to 1918 and a group of eleven soldiers abandoned in a farmhouse billet in France in the weeks leading up to the armistice.

Set between contemporary Edinburgh and the final brutal days of the First World War, *The Inheritance of Solomon Farthing* shows us how the debts of the present can never be settled unless those of the past have been paid first . . .

'A richly rewarding, gripping page-turner' Val McDermid

'Paulson-Ellis writes with verve and vividness' *The Scotsman*

'The characterization is great and the atmosphere powerful' *Daily Mail*